DIVISION BELLE

Vanessa Hannam

HEADLINE

First published in 1997 by
HEADLINE BOOK PUBLISHING

10 9 8 7 6 5 4 3 2 1

British Library Cataloguing in Publication Data

Hannam, Vanessa
Division Belle
1. Politicians' spouses – Great Britain – Fiction
2. Great Britain – Politics and government – 1979
   – Fiction
3. Political fiction
I. Title
823.9'14[F]

ISBN 0 7472 1952 4

Typeset by Avon Dataset Ltd, Bidford-on-Avon, Warks

Printed and bound in Great Britain by
Mackays of Chatham PLC, Chatham, Kent

HEADLINE BOOK PUBLISHING
A division of Hodder Headline PLC
338 Euston Road
London NW1 3BH

With special thanks to
Margaret Hanbury, Georgina Perry
and Marion Donaldson.

Let us roll our strength and all
Our sweetness up into one ball,
And tear our pleasures with rough strife
Through the iron gates of life:
Thus, though we cannot make our sun
Stand still, yet we will make him run.

Andrew Marvell
From *To His Coy Mistress*

To John and my wonderful family with love

Chapter 1

Helena responded quickly to the discreet tap on the thick mahogany bedroom door. Behind her, seated in the bay window overlooking the park, James was working on his red dispatch boxes. It was already dark and Helena wanted to pull the thick satin curtains, but her path was blocked. Finding no more appropriate surface, James had scooped all Helena's things off the dressing table and dumped them on the embroidered silk bedcover of the giant four-poster. Now he worked at his improvised desk, his large frame balanced on the dainty dressing-table stool.

As Helena opened the door James lifted his head to see her reflection in the mirror. Fortesque, the Duke of Hampton's aged butler, stood respectfully on the threshold. He held a small silver tray on which lay a black silk bow tie.

'His Grace has asked me to give you this,' he said quietly.

James rose swiftly and crossed the room, almost pushing Helena aside. He took the tie and before closing the door thanked the butler enthusiastically, apologising for the inconvenience. Fortesque looked gravely at his polished black shoes, and, shaking his head slowly, replied, 'The only thing, Mr Askew, is for you to sack your man.'

James closed the door with a sniff of irritation, throwing the tie to join the heap of Helena's make-up on the bed, then slumped back on to the dressing-table stool.

'Careful, darling, it's not meant for big men like you. You'll break it,' Helena said cautiously, for she was anxious not to stir up yet another row. The commotion over the forgotten tie had been bad enough.

'What did the old fool mean, "sack my man"?' James asked.

Helena replied to the reflection in the mirror, thinking how good James looked with his new white evening shirt open at the neck. His hair had been recently and expensively cut in preparation for this weekend at Markham Court, an indulgence of which she felt mildly resentful.

'I expect he can't believe a cabinet minister doesn't have a man who packs for him,' Helena said. 'I suppose most of the other guests do. Haven't you noticed how grand they all are?'

'So you're on a week's notice then.' James spoke without raising his head, his gold fountain pen flying over the pages on the dressing table as he worked. Helena longed for him not to divide his attention in this way. To be like he'd been when they first married. He'd been so enthusiastic then. They had made all sorts of plans for family holidays and outings. He had done things with the children from Helena's previous marriage. At first they'd all quite liked going to the constituency in Sussex, and James had been to a local estate agent and found details of a lovely big farmhouse to replace his small bachelor cottage.

But then had come the offer of the job in the Cabinet. He had accepted without discussing it with Helena. She had not really understood the ramifications. The reduction in income was the first thing. James had to give up all his work outside Parliament, and money – or rather the lack of it – soon became a constant theme in their dialogue. Plans for a permanent move in Sussex were abandoned. Talk of holidays ceased. James became preoccupied with an almost fanatical economy drive. Rosaria, Helena's Italian cleaner, must be sacked, he said. They couldn't afford a cleaner.

'But, James darling,' Helena had said, 'if I spent my time doing what she does I couldn't paint, and I earn five times what I pay her so what would be the point?'

Helena had won that round, but it was just the first of many assaults on the life she had struggled to create for herself and the children in London. James became increasingly absent at family meals. He returned late in the evenings and worked on his ministerial boxes. The children often felt they were unwelcome in their own home, having to keep quiet so as not to disturb James. They began to resent him and the feeling was mutual.

Helena soon realised the demands of the job were stopping James sleeping. He would get up several times in his short night. She would hear the click of the lock on the red boxes in his study on the half-landing. She had tried to keep the children out of his way when he was at home, but in the rough and tumble of the small house it was impossible. Someone suggested that if they had a child of their own James would find it easier to cope with Helena's children. She had tried. Then James had started to sleep in his dressing room. 'You need your sleep and I know I disturb you . . . It's just for a bit,' he'd explained. But that had been several months ago and, as the arrangement had continued, a coolness had developed between them.

Helena's days now began with the dull thud of unhappiness when she thought of the state of her marriage. If only James would look at her, be with her . . . make her feel valued.

'Well, if you had a butler I don't suppose he'd be expected to do all the things I have to do,' Helena said now. 'I'm really sorry, James, I didn't forget to pack your tie on purpose.' She bit her lip, she couldn't stop herself. She felt so demoralised. Before they'd set off, she had been trying to finish a portrait she was commissioned to paint of the opera singer Maria Reiner, and then she had had to see to arrangements for her two daughters, Kirsty and Harriet, and her dog, Clovis, who were staying on at the house in Richmond Terrace, Pimlico, with Maria, the au pair, in charge. After which she had to sort through her clothes to find something suitable for all the different occasions that might arise this weekend at the Duke and Duchess of Hampton's stately home. Worst of all had been finding something to ride in: the best she'd been able to come up with had been a rather old-fashioned hard hat and jodhpurs that had seen better days, along with her old green velvet riding jacket. A good woollen skirt and various pullovers (central heating was often feeble in these big old houses) and then something really smart for the evenings made up the rest of her wardrobe.

Helena walked quickly towards the bed and picked up her evening bag. She noticed some of her face powder had been spilt on the antique bedspread and, worse, on her bag, and she quietly set about trying to brush it off with a corner of her clean white handkerchief. She looked towards her husband's back view.

'It's bad enough having to pack for myself for a grand weekend like this, especially when the few posh clothes I have are down in Sussex ready for constituency things. I should have brought some clothes back to London, but last weekend was so hectic with all those wine and cheeses I forgot.'

James looked up, hearing the crack in her voice. He could tell from her body language that she was about to cry. He didn't want her upset tonight of all nights, when he planned to impress Caroline, their hostess. A weeping wife would do his image no good at all when there was important business to be done.

He had been a bit impatient recently he had to admit, but Helena's behaviour was rather strange at the moment. She never used to complain and he had secretly admired the way she coped with so much. Now she seemed to have changed. James had been brought up to believe that flattery and appreciation discouraged effort, and he seldom veered from his belief. He had kept Helena on her toes and he was sure she must even have surprised herself at times with her ability to rise to the occasion. He had a vague impression that she had been rather odd since the pregnancy business – thank God it had been a false alarm. With a son and two daughters by her former marriage, he felt they had well and truly enough to cope with already. Why add yet another child? He had reacted vehemently, in fact he rather regretted just how articulate he had been on the subject. 'Not part of my plan,' he had said and Helena had exploded: 'So I'm just part of a plan! What sort of plan? Do let me in on the details, or is it a Parliamentary secret?' Still, he thought she was surely over all that. It would have been such a mistake – and with this up-turn in his career an irrelevance. And now with all his work piled on him like the labours of Sisyphus, he just couldn't feel any urge to make love to her. The way Helena saw married life, with all its intimacy, had become too intrusive. He had to put his career first – surely she realised he didn't have time to indulge in sentimentality now? Still, she would have to be humoured. He rose from the dressing-table stool and put both arms about her shoulders. She didn't look up and her body stiffened. She went on rubbing the bag, refusing to look at him. James held her a little away and appraised her. 'You're beautiful tonight, darling. Is that the thing you wore the night we first met? It suits you so well. I shall never forget how lovely you looked and you haven't changed. Please don't be upset. You must enjoy yourself, you deserve a rest.'

Helena was indeed wearing the cream silk Armani trouser suit she had worn the night they met four years ago. She'd bought it second-hand and there had been a tiny blob of nail polish under the left sleeve. She recalled how she had not wanted to go to the dinner party and had told her mother so when she had rung her from Devon.

'Don't be silly, Helena, you must go!' Cornelia had exclaimed. 'You're becoming a recluse. You're in your prime, darling. I know you've had one or two bad knocks with the men you've met recently, but that doesn't mean there are no nice men out there. Go and get yourself something fabulous from that designer dress agency in Knightsbridge. I'll treat you to it.'

Helena remembered how she'd noticed James right away. He'd stood out from the other men: he'd exuded power and confidence, his rather dry sense of humour, dark looks and intense gaze all compounding the attraction. He had been the answer to her prayers. The hostess had asked Helena to play the piano and so she had, a piano version of Schumann's life and loves of a woman. She hadn't performed perfectly – she'd been a little flustered – but she'd entered into the spirit of the music, and the scent of peonies in the room had heightened the emotional tension. It was then, so he told her later, that James Askew's controlled, ambitious heart had involuntarily missed a beat, and he had decided there and then to marry her. It had only gradually dawned on her since that, as far as he had been concerned, her credentials were perfect, especially since she had a ready-made family.

Helena smiled. She couldn't keep up a sulk for long, especially when James decided to be charming. She leant towards him and briefly enjoyed the comfort of feeling his chest against hers.

'I'm sorry, darling. I'm exhausted. It was the trip to Sussex yesterday afternoon. It was silly of me, I know, but I felt I had to pop down to see Ray's wife in hospital. I took the girls, you know. I picked them up early from school.'

James looked down at her, and his mouth tightened almost imperceptibly. 'Well, it was good of you, Helena, but quite beyond the call of duty. If one of the Association wives gets ill like that, you can send flowers. You don't have to get in a car and take the entire family down.'

'I didn't go because Ray is one of your important constituents. I went because they're both friends.'

'Helena, how many times must I tell you? You can't have friends in the constituency, it just doesn't work. Just as you shouldn't get pally with people who work for you – you're far too pally with

Rosaria and Maria. You've done it here, too – all that chatting to that ridiculous old butler.'

'Why shouldn't I talk to him? He's a dear and he's very worried about his wife. Apparently she usually unpacks for the women guests but she's in constant pain, waiting for a hip replacement.'

A shadow crossed James's face. He could see what was coming next: Helena would be trying to get in touch with the health authority. He had to admit she sometimes pulled off some amazing things once she got going. But this was neither the time nor the place for Helena to pull off one of her Mary Poppins stunts. His eyes glazed and he gave her a warning look. 'Quite,' he said crossly. 'Well anyway, I have a little work still to do. Why don't you go and join the others for drinks? Can you explain I'll be down in a few minutes?'

As Helena walked towards the door she said nothing, but her thin hunched shoulders betrayed her dejection.

James had a memory flash. Sixteen years ago he had been an ambitious young barrister, married only six months, when Myra faced up to him on just such an evening as this. They had been staying with friends when she had told him their marriage was over. He remembered the exact words. 'Even if it was a lie at least if you had told me I was the most important thing in your life, it could have worked. But you didn't, James. You didn't. Don't make the same mistake again if you ever marry some other poor bloody woman. All you think of is your own career. You're such a mean-spirited sod. Life is for living. I'm leaving.' He had thought she was joking – after all, they had hardly started their life together – but she wasn't. She'd moved out the very next day.

'Darling,' James called to his wife's back view. She didn't turn but she stood still. 'Whatever you may think,' he said quietly, in the grave voice he knew Helena found reassuring, 'you're the most important thing in my life.' For good measure, he added, 'Honestly, I don't think I could live without you.'

Helena turned around slowly and stared at him. What a Jekyll and Hyde character James had turned out to be.

'It's the truth,' he said, meeting her gaze without blinking. For a moment her anger held, then she broke into a wide smile and came swiftly to him, putting her arms about his neck and laying her head on his shoulder.

'Thank you for saying that,' she said tenderly. 'It makes all the difference.'

He'll never know how much difference, Helena thought to herself as she leant against the door and looked down the wide galleried corridor towards the top of the staircase. Things had been so bad between them recently she had almost come to the end of her tether. She had tried hard to do everything right but these days nothing she did seem to please James, and the endless unacknowledged compromises she had made at the expense of her own work as a professional portrait painter had begun to make her resent the whole Parliamentary system, which expected two for the price of one. Those few well-chosen words of James's had stopped her saying what was on the tip of her tongue.

As Helena approached the bottom of the wide staircase she nearly missed her footing. Across the flagged hall the door to what she assumed must be the Chinese drawing room, where guests were bidden to assemble for dinner, stood open and voices could be heard.

'Minister of the Environment . . . Second marriage for both . . .'

'But, Bertie, who is she then?' a female voice demanded imperiously.

Then Helena recognised her host, Bertie Hampton's gravelly voice. 'Her mother is Puffer Gladstone's girl.'

'Puffer Gladstone? He's been dead for years. He was slightly mad, wasn't he?' The female voice became louder.

'No, no, just eccentric. A lovely man . . . but did make a hash of things. Spent most of his life building a model railway that went right round the estate.'

There was the statutory, 'Really?' delivered by one of the party in the tone of flat boredom which generally received particularly startling information in the Hampton circle.

'Used to take smart house parties on it . . . wore a conductor's hat and blew a whistle,' Bertie rumbled on. 'That's why he was known as Puffer.'

Helena was torn between wanting to escape back upstairs and hanging around to find out what popular myths circulated in the chattering classes regarding her family background. She drew back into the shadow of the many-antlered heads peering haughtily through disdainful glass eyes from the vaulted walls and ceilings of the great hall.

'Dashed shame if you ask me,' Bertie's voice continued to what must now be a captive audience, since all background conversation had come to a halt. 'Estate went to rack and ruin, his daughter inherited, virtually went bankrupt. What old Puffer needed was a wife like Caroline. She would soon have sorted it out.'

Helena heard chortling.

'Well, good thing the granddaughter's done something sensible, married someone like Askew. Hear he's tipped for the next PM,' a male voice said.

'Better-looking than he appears on the television. Handsome pair. I'm all for a bit of mixed blood in the aristocracy,' said a bossy female voice.

'Have to hand it to him.' Bertie's voice again. 'His mother went out cleaning.'

'Oh? I thought she was a postwoman, or did she take in lodgers? Anyway, completely self-made, but this is new Britain. Good luck to them, I say.' The group seemed set to add more to his demographic summary of the class system, but Helena had had enough and aware that eavesdroppers seldom hear well of themselves, she strode purposefully towards the drawing-room door.

'Ah, there you are. Just wondering where you and James had got to. In fact, we were talking about your grandfather,' Bertie said, warmly taking Helena by the arm. 'Actually,' he continued, 'I was just about to tell everyone how my father used to say Puffer gave the finest speech he ever heard in the Lords – on the erosion of the Great Barrier Reef by starfish.'

Bertie Hampton had one of those benign English faces that are both pleasing and yet unremarkable. He was, Helena guessed, in his mid-fifties. He had perfect manners, which were a testament to years of good breeding. It was widely accepted that his wife, Caroline, at least twenty years his junior and a former actress, had not married him for love, but the union worked well enough. She ran the Hampton estate with icy brilliance and was a good mother to their two children, whom Bertie adored with unquestioning indulgence. Of his wife, however, no one was ever quite sure if he loved or hated her. It was notable that Caroline had not made any effort to make

Helena Askew feel at home. She usually behaved this way to other attractive women, but Bertie knew the consequent lack of close female friends was the least of his wife's concerns, for she had plenty of male friends. She was deeply engrossed in conversation with one of them, as he called across the room to her.

'Darling, Helena Askew is here. Do come and welcome her.'

Caroline had been enjoying a long siesta when the Askews arrived. Now the Duchess of Hampton responded reluctantly to her husband's summons, excusing herself from her conversation. She swept across the room, wearing an extraordinary orange and black dress with bat-wing sleeves, which trailed on the floor behind her, her blonde hair dramatically sleeked back.

Helena, who had a keen sense of the ridiculous, almost became victim to unsuppressed laughter. She thought Caroline looked like an outsize wasp as the bat-wings extended to maximum effect and Caroline graciously extended a hand in such a way that Helena half wondered if she were expected to curtsy.

Caroline did a quick summing-up as she approached and she did not like what she saw: a woman who was naturally beautiful with only the barest of make-up, an amused expression on her face that gave her a demeanour of serenity and confidence, and, she could readily see, the sort of woman men found very attractive. Her mind worked swiftly.

'My dear, I'm so sorry I wasn't here to greet you. Of course I've heard so much about you from James.' She said 'James' with maximum use of the pause and a husky inflection that denoted a certain intimacy. 'How could one fail to recognise you?' she added in a vaguely menacing tone. She hesitated as the man to whom she had been talking joined her, leaning a little over her shoulder. She had no choice but to effect an introduction, making a note to alter the seating at dinner. She was not, after all, going to sit Helena Askew next to Michael Elliot.

James's firm step announced his arrival. He loomed behind Helena and, putting a strong arm about her shoulder, he spoke theatrically for the benefit of the eight pairs of eyes now watching them.

'I'm so sorry, darling. I hope you explained I had to catch up on the dreaded boxes.'

'Boxes? What boxes?' hissed Bertie to Helena.

'Oh, his red cases of ministerial work. The civil servants adore filling them up before the weekend. James is never without them; he guards them with his life. They even have a special seat when he flies.'

James looked down at the top of her head, at the beautifully coiled chignon of smooth black hair, then raising his eyes, he addressed the waiting room. 'I have a wonderful wife, you know – beautiful and patient. Was ever a man so blessed?'

Helena turned a little and caught his eye, for an instant faintly embarrassed by such fulsome praise, which was so out of character. But all the same she decided she was not exactly averse to it, but Caroline certainly was.

'Come, James,' she said. 'People are longing to meet you. Can you spare him for a moment?' she added gushingly to Helena, and then as if as an afterthought: 'By the way, I love the Armani. I had exactly the same suit years ago, but of course these things never date.'

'You don't seem to have a drink. Shall I catch Fortesque's eye? Would you like champagne?'

Helena looked up, and Caroline's companion, a tall man with greying hair and intense, deep blue eyes, returned her look with an unnerving sort of boldness.

'I hear you're a painter,' he continued.

The fact that she had the distinct impression he had given Caroline's behind the slightest of nudges as she set off with James in tow intrigued Helena. She glanced quickly at Bertie Hampton, wondering if the Hamptons had the sort of open marriage which seemed to be fashionable in the circles in which they mixed. Certainly Michael Elliot, a business tycoon, made enough appearances in the gossip columns to suggest that he would not be averse to such behaviour.

'Yes indeed,' Helena replied with a bright smile. 'It is what I would like to be full time, but at present it's a struggle. And I don't think people ever take painters and writers seriously when they live with them. I was in the middle of a very tense piece of work the other day, the client was in a hurry – it was a golden wedding surprise for her husband – and someone not too far from here told me I should hoover the inside of the grand piano.'

Michael Elliot let out a bellow of laughter and shot a glance in

James's direction. The attentive guest he now saw holding the rest of the room's attention with his accounts of the latest twists in the Parliamentary scene seemed a far cry from the nit-picking husband worried about the interior of the piano.

'Well, it's quite clear you need to take a grip on yourself if you have a dirty grand piano,' he said. 'And don't tell me you're a pianist as well?'

'I do play a bit. My mother is what she calls a failed singer and she made me learn the piano in order to have a resident accompanist, but I was never very good at that. I'm a hopeless sight-reader. Do you play?' Helena asked, sneaking a closer look at Michael. She found him compellingly attractive.

'No, sadly not, but I have a nephew, of whom I am very proud. I think he'll make a career out of the violin one day—' Michael was interrupted by the appearance of Fortesque at the door. 'Dinner is served,' the butler announced.

Helena noticed James had now moved with Caroline away from the rest of the guests. She saw Caroline take his arm and together they swept past her into the hall. James did not even catch her eye.

After the rather dank atmosphere of the vast house, the morning air was chill and crisp. The riders had left Markham Court behind them, bathed in a soft yellow light, its huge front portico standing like a sentinel overlooking the gentle green and winter brown of the park, and the old Elizabethan stables where they had saddled up. The early frost had melted, and now Helena glanced through the intricate tracery of bare branches of oak and ash, sycamore and beech, to where the sky glittered bright blue. With a cackle of alarm, a cock pheasant whirred magnificently out of the dead bracken and flew off between the massive tree trunks. And all along the banks the dark green moss was studded with tiny yellow stars – celandines, the first heartening sign of spring.

Bertie was in high spirits, cantering up ahead on his fine black hunter, Balthasar, while Helena and Sara, his cousin – a delightful grey-haired grandmother, her cheeks ruddy from the chill air – followed on the bays, Nimrod and Ailsa's Pleasure. No one else had been up for the ride after the previous late night. The women caught up with Bertie.

'Let's slow down a minute, then head over there,' he said, pointing along a track. At the bottom of the gently sloping valley between the trees they glimpsed the white flash of a river. In fact they could hear its roar even now. 'Henry the Eighth hunted in these woods, you know,' the Duke went on. 'Estate continues over the other side of the valley for another four miles or so, but when we get to the bottom we'll turn right and follow the river. That'll bring us out at the village. It's almost twelve – we can have a drink at the Hampton Arms.'

'How nice to have a pub named after you,' Helena laughed.

'And a village too,' Sara joined in.

'Well, not me personally,' Bertie said modestly. 'Some very ancient fifteenth-century twerp, I expect.'

Helena thought Bertie was charming – the sort of man you could gently tease and who could tell a good story against himself.

'How many farms did you say there were on the estate?'

'Only ten now,' Bertie said. 'We're down to just five thousand acres, along with this forest, of course, and the huge wood on the other side of the valley. Used to be much more, of course, but death duties and all that . . .'

'So where have they found gravel?' Sara asked.

'Almost at the bottom of this wood, and it continues on round to one of the tenant farms at the back of the village – which will have to go, unfortunately – the farm, I mean.'

'But this beautiful wood!' Helena exclaimed. 'These oaks must be hundreds and hundreds of years old. Just look at the size of their trunks.'

'Yes. Damn shame. But needs must. Markham Court's on its uppers, I'm afraid. If it wasn't for dear Caroline, I'd probably be in queer street by now.' Bertie gave a sardonic laugh. 'Caroline's got a shrewd head on her shoulders, and she and this chap Elliot are working out some deal to quarry the gravel. Then we're creating this huge waterpark as part of the infill – that's where James comes in,' he explained to Sara. 'Been a spot of bother with the planning wallahs. James and Caroline and Elliot have been working out the best possible solution – it's got to be "ecologically sound" and all that.'

The horses had slowed to walking pace, but even so, Nimrod started to slither a bit on the wet ground. The river came into view,

12

its rough waters throwing up fans of wild froth, drenching its banks.

'It's beautiful,' Helena said, looking with an artist's eye. 'I'm so glad we came. I don't get any chance to ride in London. There's nothing so invigorating, is there?'

'James ride?' Bertie asked.

'Alas, no.' Helena's voice held a faint tinge of regret. 'And he's too busy to learn now, with those endless boxes to sort through, meetings, conferences and constituency gatherings. My mother still keeps an old pony for my children in Devon, but I haven't been there much lately, and the pony's a bit on the small side for me anyway.'

Sara smiled at Helena. 'I suppose it must be quite lonely, being a cabinet minister's wife? I've always imagined you'd have a wild social life, endless parties, that sort of thing.'

'Well, we do get invited out quite a lot, James and me, but it's James they're interested in. They usually frogmarch him off and lionise him, while I'm left twiddling my thumbs and being polite to strangers. Or very often they don't invite me at all! Then there are visits to old people's homes, opening jumble sales and fêtes, hospital visits.' Helen laughed. 'That's why this weekend is a real treat. I'm having such a good time and it's wonderful to get out into the fresh air.'

She fell silent. Mentioning the pony had reminded her of the awful row she had had with her mother and their long war of attrition. They had always been so close – till Helena had married James, that is. For some reason her mother didn't like James – it was a gut feeling, she had said. Then it turned out James couldn't stand her either. They seemed to grate on each other's nerves, and both were very proprietorial about Helena, which hadn't made her life easy; it was as though they were fighting over a bone. Helena wished she hadn't turned her thoughts to the lot of the Parliamentary wife either. Almost every weekend James expected her to go down to the constituency and to his damp cottage a mile or so from Sugden, an old market town that had tripled in size since the war turning it into an ugly new town surviving mostly on its electronics factory. Coffee mornings, wine and cheese parties and rubbing shoulders with bossy women were the delights on offer there. Helena shuddered. For the last three years she had loyally done as James had asked, neglecting her former life and her mother. But this weekend had made her think

13

a lot about Cornelia. She missed her and her house, Maryzion, where Helena had been brought up.

The riders could see light at the end of the track now, and shortly afterwards it became a tarmacked road. Up there ahead was a bridge and beyond it a picturesque half-timbered pub.

Suddenly Helena resolved that when she got back to London, she was going to make it up with her mother. Things simply could not go on as they were.

Chapter 2

Helena remembered that house party at Markham Court as she and Maria prepared the vegetables for her own dinner party at Richmond Terrace.

The weekend had all been wonderful except that the Duchess had continued to be very offhand with her, and had tried to ensure that no direct conversations had taken place between Helena and Michael Elliot, of whom she seemed quite proprietorial. However, while Caroline was ensconced with James on Sunday afternoon, discussing the proposed waterpark, Helena, Bertie and Michael had gone for a lovely walk in the grounds, and she had continued to find Michael extremely attractive. At supper on Sunday evening there had been a certain amount of eye-contact between them. With her husband at the same table Helena felt this light-hearted flirting could never be taken seriously. Afterwards she'd persuaded James it would be a good idea to invite Michael to their dinner party this evening.

James seemed to have made a special effort that weekend to be as pleasant as he'd been when they were first married. He'd been very attentive to her – in public at least – though he had reverted to his usual peevishness as they drove back to London. Still, it was a long time since she had had such fun.

'Mrs Helena, you want me to collect the girls?' Maria broke into her reverie.

'Oh yes, please.'

'Then give them early meal. What time guests come?'

'Seven thirty for eight. God, I haven't even done the flowers yet!'

'Mrs Helena, you not to worry. Everything will be fine. You see.'

Helena thanked heaven for Maria. She had become a true ally when Helena felt she was getting so little support from anyone else.

'Wives don't have memorial services.' The Chancellor of the

15

Exchequer, Reggie Goodall, placed his glass on the damask cloth and stared at the bowl of white roses in the centre of the table. Helena was certain that he must be joking, then saw that he wasn't.

'That is the most sexist remark I have ever heard,' she said. 'I am sure you wouldn't want to be quoted on that, especially as you're rather proud of your stand on equal pay for women.'

From the other end of the dinner table James flashed her a clear message: you've said enough.

'And surely – ' Helena decided to press further – 'Nancy was a wonderful person . . . all that charity work . . . so energetic,' and then, 'Would Alexander still have his seat if it hadn't been for her?'

Cutlery scraped in an awkward silence. The Chancellor placed a meltingly delicious helping of smoked salmon mousse in his mouth, but a frown formed on his brow. Helena most clearly had overstepped the mark.

'The least said about the whole affair the better,' he said. 'We all feel very let down; especially after all the trouble Hilda took with her. But of course, it's devastating when a Party wife takes her own life.'

So that, apparently, was that. Helena fussed nervously with the collar of her brown chiffon shirt.

This dinner was Reggie Goodall's first opportunity to meet Helena on her home ground. She was certainly a very attractive and accomplished woman, he thought, but a loose cannon, rumours said. Mrs Askew was the sort of wife the Party did not need: a woman who spoke her mind. But Hilda could surely give her a few tips, coach her in the behaviour required of a cabinet minister's wife.

'What a charming room this is. I do admire your taste.' The French Ambassador's wife turned to James. She was impeccably groomed, in a plain black dress – probably Guy Laroche, Helena thought – and wearing a double row of the most exquisite baroque pearls as big as plover's eggs. 'And those paintings of children in the drawing room too – who is the artist? They're so . . . how shall I say . . . perceptive and vibrant.' She gave Helena a vivacious smile.

Reggie Goodall took the change in conversation as an opportunity to remove a small leather diary from the breast pocket of his ill-fitting off-the-peg suit, and make a note to have a word about Helena Askew with Mark Raymond, the Chief Whip. Reggie loathed the chap personally, but Raymond was powerful, efficient and ruthless – a man to get things done, and also a man to keep on your side.

'They're mine. I paint portraits. I trained at art college and took a few commissions but I let it lapse until I was on my own again. Then I started doing pastels of friends' children and now I do adults too . . .'

Helena's voice trailed off. It had been on the tip of her tongue to tell Reggie about her commission to paint the Leader of the Opposition's children but then she remembered she had not told James yet. In any case Reggie Goodall had stopped listening. Helena got the clear impression that to him her painting was a little hobby to fill in the time while her husband was doing far more important things.

'Helena, darling.' James was trying to attract her attention. 'Helena,' he repeated, 'you must get together with Mrs Goodall. Hilda is wonderfully helpful, a guiding light for all our Party wives, isn't that so?' he said – somewhat unctuously, Helena thought – to Reggie.

Further down the table Hilda Goodall, in an electric-blue outfit, leant across the French Ambassador and took over the conversation.

'It's all about team work. Reggie and I pull together, it's the only way. He takes a great interest in the activities I lay on for the wives. Such a pity you haven't yet managed to come on one of our outings, Helena dear. Mary has, haven't you?' She turned to the Minister of Agriculture's wife, who was looking exceedingly bored and had hardly said a word all evening.

Her husband, Bernard, who was seated next to Helena, took up the conversation. 'Lovely dog you've got. Great dog person myself.'

'Oh, what's yours?'

'Nothing to beat Labradors. Jason, Petronella, and Humphrey.' Helena thought: how appropriate – he looks just like one, with his long pale face and wide jowls, and his soulful brown eyes.

Even Mary looked temporarily animated at the mention of the dogs' names. 'We've always had Labradors, haven't we, Bernard?'

The conversation was flagging. Helena smiled graciously.

'May I offer you a little more bread and butter?' she asked Hilda, noting that, even by candlelight, the woman was hideous. Hilda, who was hugely fat, had already demolished at least half the thin slices of brown bread that accompanied the mousse. A crumb had settled on the hairs that sprang from a large protuberant mole on her upper lip, and the tablecloth around her plate was strewn with more crumbs.

Helena turned once more to the French Ambassador's wife, hoping to resume their conversation.

'We Tory wives are jolly self-sufficient,' Hilda boomed to the Ambassador. Monsieur Ponson could not prevent himself from recoiling a little as she leant towards him, but recovered sufficiently to respond to her with his usual charm.

'Oh yes?' His face assumed an expression of interest. 'And how so?'

Helena looked up from her plate and found Michael Elliot watching her with rapt attention. Out of devilment, because of the way Caroline Hampton had so obviously tried to keep them apart, Helena had intended seating Michael next to herself, but at the last moment had funked it. Instead, she had the Minister of Agriculture on one side and the French Ambassador, a definite Lothario, on the other.

'Well, I always say to the younger wives – ' Hilda was still booming on – 'when they complain about loneliness or the things they have to do for the Party, is it appreciation you want? If so, you shouldn't have married a politician.'

Helena stole another look at Michael. As she had half predicted to herself he was now appraising Jenny, James's rather plain researcher, who had been invited to make up the numbers.

'We like to present a united front . . .' Hilda was still at it. 'My outings are very helpful. Next week we have a demonstration on rugmaking and a nice coach trip to a stately home.'

Jenny was now chatting to the Minister of Agriculture about the ongoing topic of mad cow disease. It seemed, too, there was some chemistry there, as she suddenly blushed deeply. Helena chanced another look at Michael, and found his eyes fixed admiringly on her again.

Madame Ponson took up their conversation once more. 'Are they your children by any chance, those portraits?'

'Yes, indeed. By my first husband, Anthony. He died five years ago – a heart attack. It was very sudden. I did those portraits just before . . . Do you have children?'

'Oh yes, but they have, how you say, flown the coop. Is that not so, Philippe?'

The Ambassador was watching the last piece of bread and butter disappearing into Hilda's mouth.

'I think you would find the Prayer Group particularly helpful, Helena,' she was saying simultaneously with her eating. 'After all, we need guidance when we work in our constituencies. But then, I hear you don't go down there all that often. Poor James, he really must find it difficult.'

Helena caught the Ambassador's eye, and as his face crinkled in amusement, her anger was dispelled. She smiled at Hilda. 'Well, I used to almost every weekend, and I would now if I had time. I hear you're absolutely marvellous. Is it true the cleaning allowance at Number Eleven is only a few pounds a week? I hear you have to sweep up the cheese footballs after official parties yourself.'

'How very droll. What do you mean? Is this cheese football a new Parliamentary sport?' the Ambassador asked, thinking this was definitely game, set and match to his hostess.

Hilda could barely conceal her disapproval and Helena could almost feel her eyes boring through the flimsy chiffon blouse she was wearing. 'Yes, well, we all have our hands full, no doubt. James tells me you have a little hobby – painting, isn't it? But I always say one's husband's career comes first.'

James, Michael and the Minister of Agriculture now switched their conversation from nostalgic reminiscences of the Major era, when the Party had started his term in office with a bigger majority than their present cliffhanging one, to slurry disposal, then to Greece's position on the European currency. This inspired a long pontification on Reggie's part before they moved on to the Prime Minister's cabal in the Cabinet: his cronies, Mark Raymond, the Chief Whip, and Henry Smythe, the Foreign Secretary, along with a few others. Helena allowed her mind to wander briefly from the dinner guests – all of whom had been invited in order to massage the progress of James further up the Parliamentary ladder.

Petals had dropped from the roses and as she thought of water lilies softly resting on a blossom-coloured lake, she was a million miles away. Her mother called this 'wool-gathering', and James tended to find it an irritating habit.

Maria came in to take away the plates, then returned with the main course. The Ambassador looked on appreciatively as noisettes of lamb were served, along with tiny parcels of green and orange vegetables.

'Lovely wine, darling,' Helena said as she held up her glass to her husband, only half expecting him to respond with some complimentary remark about the food, which had taken her the best part of the day to prepare.

'Yes, a brilliant year, '82,' he said, and there was a murmur of agreement from the other guests. But, not in the mood for interruptions, he quickly reverted to the conversation, which had now turned to the recent weekend at Markham Court.

James's face had become flushed. His enthusiasm at being taken up by the Hamptons was more than obvious, Helena noted. Doubtless the feisty Duchess Caroline had much to do with it, even though Helena had sussed that the whole weekend was quite unashamedly a ploy to involve James even further in the waterpark venture, their hosts' latest venture to fend off bankruptcy.

Madame Ponson listened attentively. 'Quite a dark horse,' she commented on the Duchess. 'Not many people know about all the wonderful work you say she does for charity, unless you mean that charity begins at home. I hear she will do almost anything to prop up the family fortunes.'

Madame Ponson now had everyone's attention; few London dinner parties proceeded without mention of Caroline, Duchess of Hampton. 'Have you seen that commercial for washing-up liquid she was in?'

'Yes, well, but some of the proceeds are going to good causes, and that's where I may be able to help. They've thought up this marvellous scheme for a waterpark to conserve rare birds,' James said.

'How interesting,' Madame Ponson went on. 'Philippe knows the bankers where the husband works—'

'Grunfeld's,' Michael interjected.

Madame Ponson looked displeased at being interrupted. 'He has no aptitude at all,' she went on. 'She has all the energy. In fact, she is one of those women who should have been a man.'

'She would certainly need a change of shape for that,' Michael chipped in, with eyebrows raised.

20

'Well, it's obvious,' the Ambassador commented, 'the Duke should go back to running the family estate and let her do the banking side.'

'Quite right,' Madame Ponson agreed, 'but such a thing would not work in France. It is a fundamental difference between the French and English. Take the Englishman from his estates and he withers and dies; put the Frenchman on his and he would rather die.' Madame Ponson spread out the immaculate fingers of her right hand as if to invite communal admiration of her manicurist's skills.

Maria brought in the next course – poires Belle Hélène. Helena hadn't intended the pun, but the Ambassador turned to her with a smile and raised his glass. 'To la belle Hélène,' he said. Everyone smiled except James, Hilda and Madame Ponson.

'Where does this Caroline come from?' Madame Ponson continued.

'Come from?' asked James. Helena could sense James's dislike of the turn of this conversation. He had been a grammar school boy, from a humble background, and had experienced much of this sort of thing himself on his way up through the system – questions about where he went to school, and was he related to the Wiltshire Askews? It was partly because such a highly successful politician as James should have this vulnerability that Helena had initially been attracted to him. She could see his mouth tightening now.

'I'm not interested in where Caroline came from, only where she is at the moment,' James said.

'Well, you're quite right, of course,' Madame Ponson said, but could not resist adding as her final word, 'She has a most amusing dress sense. There was an article about her in *Paris Match* recently. I said to Philippe that I thought it was most unkind.'

Helena noticed that James had pursed his lips again; he hated gossip. Trying it with him was like hitting a tennis ball into a mattress. She was about to turn the conversation when Maria came in to tell her that the police officer from behind the Speaker's Chair had telephoned to say there would be a division in fifteen minutes. A fleet of limousines could be heard revving their engines in the street outside. James got up abruptly, apologised to his guests and left the room, followed by the Chancellor and the Minister of Agriculture.

James had walked straight past Helena's chair without a word. She looked down at the tablecloth to conceal her disappointment.

When she looked up again Michael Elliot was watching her with a concerned expression.

'Madame Askew,' the Ambassador was saying to her, 'would you consider it very rude if I took advantage of this pause to make a telephone call?'

While she led him into James's study, she heard a flurry of chatter as the ladies scattered in different directions to powder their noses. When she returned to the dining room, she found herself alone with Michael.

He sauntered over and stood beside her. 'That was a sumptuous meal, Helena. You are a consummate and beautiful hostess.'

He was standing very close, although she thought the sensation was definitely not unpleasant. She could feel his light breath on her cheek.

'So, I never quite found out how you fit in with the Hamptons,' she said in an attempt to be formal.

'Oh, I've known Bertie since I was in my teens. We met at St Moritz. And, as you must have gathered, I'm sort of helping them in their business venture. But let's not talk about that now. You're far more interesting.'

Helena felt a little wary.

'Your husband's in a crotchety mood tonight,' he said boldly. 'I'm wondering whether he deserves someone as lovely as you.'

She felt herself blush. Michael was a wolf in wolf's clothing, but his charm was irresistible.

The ladies were returning, and Michael moved casually away to a respectable distance.

Helena ushered them all into the drawing room, where they waited for the others to return after the vote. The Ponsons were talking to Hilda Goodall and Mary, the wife of the Minister of Agriculture, had suddenly become animated and was complaining bitterly to the divorced researcher Jenny about the inconvenience of security measures at her Putney home.

While Helena offered her guests drinks and put more logs on the fire, Michael wandered around the room. The walls were so densely covered in pictures that the yellow striped paper was hardly visible. It was easy to see that the pastels were of Helena's children. Their identity was obvious: two little girls with Helena's oval face, and pale ivory skin, and dark thick, tangled hair. They both had her deep violet eyes. The little boy was not dark like the girls but had tawny curls and blue eyes. His expression was both hesitant and innocent, as if he knew that the adult world might let him down. Helena came to stand fairly close to Michael, and he could smell her perfume and feel the silk of her flowing skirt as it brushed against his hand.

'That's Rollo, my youngest,' she said, looking sad. She was remembering that Rollo had been only three when Anthony died.

'How old is he?' Michael asked.

'Eight.'

'And those beautiful girls, so like their mother, even the deep violet eyes.'

'Kirsty is thirteen – nearly fourteen – and Harriet's eleven.'

'The little boy isn't like his sisters. Was his father fair?'

'No, not really. In fact he looked a little like you. No, Rollo's the image of my mother. James finds him difficult, and that's probably why.'

'Well, I suppose the stepfather thing can be tricky. I never had a resident father; my parents never married. I was brought up by my mother. I expect that's why I like women so much.'

Helena smiled. 'Were you an only child, then?'

'Not at all. I have a sister – and a half-brother, Simon, my father's legal son. We don't see all that much of each other now, although at one time we were very close.'

'Did you go away to school?'

'No. We lived in Switzerland and my sister and I had a governess most of the time.' Michael changed the subject. 'And there's the famous piano! Well vacuumed, I hope.'

The Bechstein took up most of the garden end of the long room, and a Schumann score, well marked in what he supposed was Helena's writing, was open on the stand. The piano was covered with photographs in silver frames. One in sepia was of a handsome couple in sixties wedding outfits. The woman with the light-coloured hair was her mother, Helena explained.

It occurred to Michael there was almost nothing in the house that gave a clue to the occupancy of Helena's husband: no trace of his personality. This was clearly Helena's domain.

'I remember you telling me at Markham Court about your music.

What a lovely old piano. How do you find the time to play?' Michael asked.

'I do try to play a little each day. One of my daughters is quite good so we do duets together, but not when James is at home. It's a small house and it disturbs him.' Helena turned her wedding ring.

They sat with their coffee cups on a dark green velvet sofa and talked about houses. Michael's was in Cheyne Walk. Helena told him about the old rectory she and Anthony had had in Suffolk, then the Victorian house she had lived in in Wandsworth after she was widowed and before she moved to Pimlico after her marriage to James. It was then that Michael saw her face begin to look distinctly sad.

When his hand brushed over hers, it was hard to tell whether the move was deliberate or not. She fiddled momentarily with her coffee spoon, but did not take her hand away. Michael's touch had felt so strong, protective and Helena's stomach contracted and she knew that she was blushing again.

'Would you have lunch with me tomorrow? I can get my driver to pick you up.'

She gave a little start. The invitation was a bit sudden.

'I'm quite harmless, promise. James worked for me before he became an MP, as you probably know. He was that most invaluable of friends, an unofficial adviser. He helped me set up my companies in the early days. But he would never get tied down. I suppose he knew he was destined for greater things than business, and I must confess he made the right decision. He did terribly well at the Bar and would have made pots of money if he hadn't gone into Parliament. I sometimes wonder if he regrets his decision.'

Michael could see Helena wanted to know more about her husband's life before she met him. He knew James must be feeling the pinch without his large fees but then he remembered how odd James was about money. 'He would never accept proper payment for the work he did for me, just a few shares, which he eventually cashed in, and the occasional case of very good claret.' There had always been something a little daunting and prissy about James, as if he were above the sordid business of making money.

'He can vouch for me.'

Helena laughed. 'He might, but the gossip columns won't. They

24

say you're an infamous seducer and that you're having affairs with at least two married women.'

The more she looked at him, though, the more attractive he became; and it felt wonderful to be noticed. Parliamentary circles had a knack of defeminising Members' wives: all part of maintaining the status quo, while the husbands indulged in their peccadilloes within the security of Westminster's close circle.

She could hear the cars returning from the vote. As she rose from the sofa, she was aware of Michael's admiring glance, and wondered for a moment if she should feel guilty. She had been enjoying his attentions, even encouraging them. James had been so cold and distant for the last months, why shouldn't she respond to Michael Elliot's interest in her? It was perfectly harmless.

After the guests had gone, and James had retired to bed without even a 'good night' or 'well done' or, the best of all, 'I love you', Helena stacked the dishwasher and thought about Michael. She had eventually agreed to phone him in the morning. There was something about him that reminded her of her first husband, Anthony; he had that same way of enveloping the people around him. And he had made her feel special. His colouring was similar too; she supposed that, had he lived, Anthony's dark hair would also have turned a distinguished shade of grey. He had had thick hair too. She wondered if James had noticed Michael's advances. She guessed not. She laid out the children's breakfast, then went upstairs, past her bedroom, to the top floor to check on her daughters.

When she returned James was fast asleep in his dressing room. There was no welcoming gesture in their bedroom, the covers were still firmly tucked. She slipped quietly into the bed and lay waiting for sleep. The light from the street slanted through a chink in the curtains on to the wall above her dressing table. She could see the faint outline of a picture, one she had painted a long time ago. It was faded now. It was a delicate watercolour, a white Georgian country house painted in full summer. Roses and clematis clad the walls and fell about the windows in careless disarray. The blue front door was slightly open to convey a sense of what lay within.

Helena's thoughts strayed back to that house by the sea where she had borne her three children, loved her husband, tended her wild garden, fed her chickens, and walked the Suffolk marshes with her paints, her children and her picnics. How smug I must have been then, she thought. Everything was so secure; nothing bad ever happened. She remembered the chickens crooning as they scratched behind the hedge on long, hot summer afternoons. Harriet and Kirsty would come home from school and collect the warm brown eggs from the henhouse, and they'd have them for tea with Helena's homemade bread.

'How long till Daddy gets home?' they'd say. 'Tell us, Mummy, in minutes.'

'Seventy-four and a half minutes.'

'Can we stay up for supper tonight? Oh, Mum, you did promise.'

And they would wait in their dressing gowns, looking down the drive to the white gate in the soft evening light, pellucid from the reflection of the sea.

'Mummy, he's here! It's seventy-six minutes, he's two minutes late.' And there he would be, in the middle of a tangle of quilted dressing gowns, the little girls' fragrance of baby powder and freshly bathed skin combining with that unmistakable commuter train smell.

Anthony would enfold them and tickle them, giving them his full attention. Helena always knew that her turn would come – their moment, the moment each longed for throughout the hours apart. She would be standing halfway down the stairs, Rollo in her arms. Anthony would look up and at the precise moment that his eyes met those of his wife, the little girls would release their father and stand back quietly observing the arch of love under which they stood as their mother and father held each other.

Helena had frozen all these images in her mind. She could not have imagined her future.

She was cutting sweet peas in the garden when the phone call came. She remembered the church clock had struck eleven. The daily called her from the kitchen window. Helena put down the trug on the gravel path and ran into the house. Anthony had been away on a business trip and he was now on his way home. She thought that would be him on the phone to say when his train would arrive. She ran into the house expecting Anthony, but instead it was a stranger.

'Are you sitting down?' the stranger said. And then came the news that exploded Helena's world into a million tiny agonising fragments.

Anthony had had a heart attack, at the age of forty. He was dead.

A future of loneliness stretched before her. The village people were silent when she went to the shop, embarrassed, almost frightened to be with her in case they caught some of her grief. 'How could such a thing happen?' they said to each other. The vicar prayed for the little family in their tragic loss. The silence was absolute. And so Helena moved to London, and the real nightmare had begun.

She had felt so lost, made so many mistakes. She simply hadn't known how to gauge other men. Some of Anthony's male friends had seemed so concerned, but when it came down to it all they wanted was sex. For them she was just an attractive and available woman. And their wives had shown such suspicion. Because Helena was now on her own, couples she had been friendly with for years had stopped inviting her to dinner parties.

James was like a refuge when she had met him: someone from a completely different world. He had been mature, ten years older than she was – upright, decent, attractive-looking, if a little dour . . . but an honourable man.

But the closeness Helena envisaged would be part of their marriage had not developed, and all these years later Helena still felt alone. She lay crying quietly as she often did. Tonight, however, she decided she would change things. She would accept Michael Elliot's invitation. Something different, something comforting had entered her life, and even the danger it represented was better than the aloneness.

Chapter 3

James emerged from the bathroom in a cloud of steam. He could hear the sparrows cheeping in the garden. Helena was barely awake, lying with arms outstretched, a confusion of blue-black hair on the lacy pillow, a creamy breast peeping from her nightdress. James felt slightly shocked by her abandoned appearance, which failed to summon any desire in him. He walked over to the window and muttered, 'Bloody things,' as he yanked open the curtains, ignoring the elegant tiebacks. He felt suffocated by Helena's femininity, festoons of fabric and lace everywhere, and the way she always followed his clumsy trail and fussily rearranged things.

He stood by the chest of drawers and silently put on his socks, shaking them out one by one as he did so. Helena lay with her eyes closed, but he could tell that the very act of his dressing irritated her.

They had been married almost three years now, he thought – six times longer than his marriage to Myra. That had been an un-mitigated disaster, he remembered with shame. She had run off with Tony, one of his junior colleagues in chambers, and eventually they had emigrated to Australia. They'd lost touch after the divorce. He looked over again at Helena, who had fallen asleep once more.

Since becoming a minister he'd been working so hard and it was easy to find the work could become his whole life. He was in his element in politics, knew he was respected, and there were murmurs even now that he could make Party leader. He knew too that he had put family life to one side, but the children were Helena's anyway, and he thought he could rely on her to knuckle down alone. Then about four months ago Helena had told him she wanted another baby. She had just slipped it into the conversation one evening. He had been appalled.

'Surely you want a child to hand things down to?' she had said, by way of explanation, and then she had suggested it would help him to accept her children and the whole domesticity thing, which he seemed to find so difficult.

James had put her right. He had no desire to reproduce, he didn't believe in inherited wealth and, besides, there were too many people in the world already.

But then Helena had got very emotional and had told him how unhappy she was, how she saw so little of him since he'd become a minister. She even suggested he should resign and try to save their marriage. She couldn't bear the loneliness. She had cried and cried. James had never seen her like that before. He could not tell her the truth: that besides the fact that they could barely make ends meet, the whole earth mother thing, the need to go on reproducing, the very act of giving birth, (she'd even suggested she'd want him there when it happened) was one big turnoff.

He went back into the bathroom and quickly re-emerged. 'I'm out of deodorant,' he said, and threw the empty can on the bed.

He felt more and more like a lodger, yet knew much of the blame lay with himself. He had too much on his mind. When they had married he thought her everything he needed. She was beautiful, intelligent, talented, upper class. And she came with a ready-made family. Those first years had been good but then the feeling grew that he was always being compared with her first husband – the all-too-perfect Anthony, who since he was dead had become un-impeachable. And then the children hadn't really taken to him, even though he had tried at first. He found he was getting bored by the endless prattle about schools and music lessons and ballet classes, and their hair and what they should wear, and their friends and their homework. He was being smothered in domestic detail. Perhaps he'd spent too much time on his own before he met Helena. He'd begun to feel that he rated only fifth best, after the children and her mother, perhaps sixth best even – after the damned dog. And she was tactless – like last night, holding forth to Reggie, questioning his judgement. Raymond, the Chief Whip, would be on to him about it. 'Can't have meddlesome wives in the Party, Askew,' James could almost hear him saying it.

Still today would be busy, which would keep his mind off domestic problems. He had an early meeting with some specialists from the European Union about slurry pollution. At eleven he had a meeting with South West Water and it was beginning to look as though the Hampton development wasn't quite what he had been led to believe. The gravel quarrying was far more extensive than Caroline had indicated.

Yesterday he'd received a petition forwarded from the local MP, an old Tory duffer called Arthur Hall, the protest signed by ninety local people. Apparently the excavations would destroy one of the tenant farms. The farmer had been given notice to quit and offered only minimal compensation. His family had been tenants for over a hundred years.

The letter also contained a complaint that the quarrying was far too close to the village. It would spoil the beautiful landscape. Hedges and a substantial part of a very ancient wood were going to be ripped up. There would be endless noise and dust. Well, they'd been through all this at the inquiry already. The County had passed the plans. The scheme had already been called in for review and he'd now had the report on it.

The planner, it seemed, didn't look too kindly on it. His conclusions were similar to the local people's. He said that if they infilled with a wildlife waterpark, it would have to cover a much larger area than originally envisaged. He was suggesting twenty acres. He wanted thousands of tons of topsoil for the surrounding areas, planted with deciduous woods of the usual mix, but to include some more mature trees (another expense for the Hamptons). He'd recommended free public access at all times, which meant safety precautions, staff, fire paths, ramps, buildings, quite apart from stocking the lake when it was finished.

James imagined Caroline would not be very pleased when he told her, but he had a plan that might help. And he was having a word with the National Heritage Secretary later that afternoon.

In his study he began putting his papers for the day together and checking his mail. In a file for Helena he placed the invitations, letters, a copy of the Whip for the week, the telephone bill, which he regarded as far too high considering he himself wasn't in to make calls a good deal of the time, and an offer of a free cervical smear for Parliamentary wives – which he'd opened in error. It was to take place in a Portakabin outside the Admiralty. 'Bring a dressing gown' as there was to be a long wait, he read. He wrote 'Good idea' on it, and then went on to annotate the other items. 'Yes' to drinks with Martin Matthews, the Home Secretary. The whole telephone business was ridiculous. The children should not use the phone at all. It was establishing a bad habit. On the bill he underlined all calls over three minutes and made a mental note to work out what the VAT would be on them – Helena should pay her whack. He scribbled a memo to her to this effect. Thrift was something his mother had instilled in him from an early age. After that he wrote Helena a reminder about the constituency fundraiser on the following Friday when Marcher was guest speaker.

He placed the file on Helena's desk, then went downstairs, pausing outside the kitchen door. It was half ajar. Somehow he couldn't go in.

Harriet and Kirsty were eating their cereal. There was no sign of the au pair. Helena was standing beside them in jeans and a white shirt. 'Where's Maria?' James heard her ask.

'Doing something in her room, Mum,' Kirsty replied, inclining her cheek for the ritual morning kiss.

'What about me?' Harriet said. The two sisters were as different in character as they were identical in appearance; were it not for the variation in height, they would have been mistaken for twins. Harriet felt her younger sister label keenly and needed constant reassurance from Helena.

'Darling Harriet, your hair looks lovely like that.'

Harriet had tied her hair back from her face in a tight ponytail in contrast to her sister's chaotic tangle. Harriet's life was conducted in a nervous obsession with neatness and order. Helena had said to James that, of all her children, Harriet still grieved most silently and terribly for her father, and that the neatness was, in a sense, an attempt to reclaim order in her shattered world.

The children were sitting at a round table at the end of the kitchen. Through the french doors was the garden, where crocuses, almost over, peeped through the cracks in the paving, a trough of narcissi stood under an almond tree laden with blossom. Clovis, Helena's pug, sat on the quarry-tiled floor, looking up at the table hoping for a plate of half-finished cereal.

'Mum, you look happy this morning. I know why,' Kirsty said in her strong carrying voice.

'Do you now?' Helena said.

'Rollo's breaking up for Easter before long and you're counting the days until we'll be a family again,' Kirsty said.

Still James hesitated to go in, the feeling of exclusion holding him back.

'Mum, do we have to go down to James's smelly old cottage this Easter? Can't we go to Granny's?' Harriet asked.

'Yes, Mum, James hates Easter,' Kirsty said. She tittered. 'Do you remember when Clovis cocked his leg on the disgusting bright red sofa last time?'

James Askew had a knack of entering a room at precisely the wrong moment, and he entered now, swathed in a dark cloud of umbrage. It gave him, momentarily, a position on the high moral ground.

The girls rolled their eyes to heaven, then, hoping to restore things right, chorused, 'Good morning, James!'

James ignored them.

'Morning, James,' said Helena. 'Sleep well?'

'Yes, thank you, darling,' James replied.

Helena always felt that James's 'darling' was strangely anonymous. Or was it that he could not say 'Helena'?

She put her hand gently on his arm to get his attention. 'What are your plans today?'

There was no answer; he was engrossed in removing a fingermark from the kitchen door with a corner of his handkerchief. Then he sat down and buttered some toast.

'Come on, girls, you'll be late. Kirsty, find Clovis's lead, will you? I must take him for a walk when you've gone.'

James looked up from his toast. 'Talking of Clovis, I think he's lifted his leg in the hall again.' On hearing his name the pug looked up and wagged his tail at James. 'Dirty brute,' James said, looking down at Clovis with an expression of loathing.

'You'd better tell me where, and I'll see to it now.' Helena gritted her teeth.

'To the lefthand side of the front door. You can't miss it.'

Helena took some Jif, a bowl and cloth and ran up the stairs.

How bloody typical of him to be so negative. He had got her on the run. He'd still not said a word about last night's dinner. All the effort that had gone into it – she doubted if he had a clue how much work was involved – and not a word of thanks. She scrubbed at the wall, fuming inwardly. He loathes my dog, he loathes my children, he sits there pontificating behind his papers, expecting me to run round in circles for him, and it's my house! She wondered how he would have managed last night but for her. And he couldn't even be bothered to say thank you, she thought. Just went to bed without a word. What sort of marriage is it?

She hurried back down the stairs to the kitchen. 'Undoubtedly caused by the strong smell of Labrador on Bernard Keatley's trousers!' she said. 'Poor Clovis must have thought the house was being invaded by the Labradorian hordes.' She had to make a joke of it, although she was smouldering.

James did not even bother to look up from *The Times* – instead, she saw his hand emerging from the side holding out his coffee cup, waiting for his Helena to fill it.

'James, can we talk?' Helena asked after the children had gone to school. James could sense trouble, and slipped into an evasive action mode. Helena was spoiling for a fight, which usually happened after an occasion such as last night's dinner party.

'Perhaps tonight, Helena. I'm sure it can wait. You know the car got here at eight thirty.' James did not move *The Times* from his line of vision as he spoke; only the use of Helena's name was unusual.

Helena snatched the paper from him, hurling it to the floor. 'Tell the car to wait. No, on second thoughts, I will.'

James could hear her feet pounding up the stairs, the front door opening, her voice talking to the driver.

He felt panic overtaking him. He knew exactly how the dialogue with Helena would run. In a curious way the situation reminded him of the rows his parents used to have in the steamy back parlour behind the sub-post office. The situation was the same: the aggrieved woman looking for recognition and praise – though his mother had been right to protest, she had worked her fingers to the bone. He looked quickly in his diary and was relieved to see that he had no meetings until ten. He thought he would just try to leave anyway and hope Helena would have calmed down by evening, but she came clumping down the stairs and stood in the doorway.

'James, you could at least have said "good night" or "thank you" last night. You wouldn't dream of behaving like you did to me to one of your constituents.'

James stood up to look more threatening and hoped Helena would shut up and get out of the way. 'Helena, I can't deal with this now. I have a meeting this morning. If you've some problem leave me a note on my desk. You're overwrought – perhaps that's why you were so rude to the Chancellor last night. You know Reggie's my greatest supporter. You belittle everything I stand for, you've no respect for the Party, for any of the things I value. As for those pampered brats of yours—'

'Fuck the Party, James, fuck all of it. I didn't marry the sodding Party. I thought I married a man, not a machine.' Helena stood defiant, on the verge of tears.

As he approached the doorway, he thought for a second that she might try to hit him. 'Don't use foul language, it's unbecoming. Perhaps you should go and lie down. I'll be back for some supper tonight – there's a tiny window between votes. Now, may I get past?'

The reasonable tone merely served to inflame her. She lunged at him, gripping his arms. 'No, James. I've had enough, you don't sleep with me, you don't talk to me. You behave like a lodger. If you go on like this you can get out. I'll fend for myself if I have to. For God's sake, all I want is some love and appreciation. Is it too much to ask?'

It was the word 'lodger'. He had thought the very same thing himself. He hated the associations. Lodgers had haunted his child-hood; grey, smelly commercial travellers hovering in the dark recesses of the small house, with the Askews' post office in the front room. They were always in the bathroom, taking the last of the warm water. There was never any privacy. Helena was spoilt. She didn't know what hardship was; even the death of her husband had been romanticised. People admired her courage and beauty but, if they could see her now, shrieking like a fishwife, they would view things differently.

All women were the same, selfish and unreliable, except his mother, that is. James had imagined Helena was different: a goddess, calm, cool, fulfilled, in control. How wrong he had been.

He felt ill. He had to get out. 'Helena, I have to go.'

James made as if to push past, but Helena stood firm. 'Can't you even say just one kind thing?'

'Such as what? Just look at yourself!'

She began to cry.

'Helena, look,' he said more gently. 'Life isn't just romance. I have to make tough decisions every day. I need someone strong and supportive to stand by me, as much as you do.' Then he added, 'If I can't give you what you want, then perhaps you'd better take a lover.'

He regretted what he'd said instantly, especially as she hit him hard with her open hand. She had never hit anyone in her whole life, not even the children. There was a moment's stunned silence. James raised his hand as if to hit her back, but hesitated.

Helena moved from the doorway. He walked past her and up the stairs. She heard the door close, and he was gone. She looked up through the basement window and watched. He stood on the steps outside, watching for his ministerial car.

James Askew, Cabinet Minister, looked immaculate, his thinning dark hair in perfect order, his navy pinstripe, his dark blue overcoat with velvet collar adding to his stature. He looked confident and smiling, with his perfect set of teeth, his skin shining and healthy, the eyes blue-green and cold as the sea. Helen sank into a chair.

The slurry meeting was a ponderous affair. Eventually James could not resist looking at his watch and was quite relieved he had to call a halt so that he could get to his next meeting on time.

After the meeting with South West Water and before he met the Chief Whip, who wanted a chat, James thought he had better patch it up with Helena. He got his PPS, Charles Swinton, to organise some flowers to be sent round and make up some suitable message. Charles wasn't sure how James addressed his wife, or what he liked her to call him, but he did his best. 'To darling Helena. I'm sorry. From your loving husband.'

When the flowers arrived, it was Maria, the au pair, who took them in. Helena, ten minutes before, had climbed into Michael Elliot's chauffeur-driven silver Lexus and was speeding towards lunch, though not before she'd consigned the memo about the telephone bill, and the smear test letter, to the dustbin.

Chapter 4

'Mr Elliot, Mrs Gruner is on the phone from Basle.'

Michael had told his secretary, Joanna, that his sister was going to phone him and he'd like to speak to her when she did. The two bankers from Zurich seated opposite Michael leant forward at the most unwelcome interruption. They were negotiating on behalf of a large German corporation for a major holding in one of the companies that was a part of Elliot Enterprises, which had interests in aggregates, waste management and defence equipment. Labour was so much cheaper in England – there were no long-term contracts or protracted legal suits about unfair dismissal and pension rights. Michael knew the Germans thought they were on to a good thing. The fact that they would be paying double the figure Michael had paid to acquire the company the previous year seemed to have escaped them. Adèle's telephone call was perfectly timed. He would leave the two men to stew for a few minutes, giving the impression that he was not in a hurry to accept their terms.

Michael was in total control, aware that his image was enhanced by the perfect setup: a house full of beautiful antiques and paintings, staffed by immaculate servants, and Joanna, his secretary, who inspired confidence, her English good looks accentuated by a crisp high-necked blue and white blouse. Michael's manner was always charismatic. He had that way of making anyone feel that he or she was very special; he believed that the road to successful business was always to make the people you were dealing with like you at the time. This, coupled with his very astute business acumen, had helped make him extremely rich. Money brought you power, not only to control your own life, but to control others' too. Michael enjoyed that feeling.

Michael had always operated close, but never too close, to the edge. It was here that there were rich pickings. He had evolved his own system of morality when it came to business. Some of the companies that were part of Elliot Enterprises bordered on the dubious, but Michael could justify their existence. As far as his employees were concerned he was generous and fair. Loyalty was bought not just with money, but with kindness and understanding.

'Excuse me, I shan't be long.'

He turned with a smile to the Swiss. 'It's a family matter. Please make yourselves at home. Joanna, could you ask Carla to bring in some more coffee?'

Michael was wearing a new suit, a pale Prince de Galles check made by Brioni in Milan. He looked more than usually elegant. Joanna had noted from the diary that Michael had a lunch guest and the staff, as they sometimes were on these occasions, had been given the afternoon off. Michael had suggested that Joanna take her mother to tea at the Ritz on his account.

Having bounded up two flights of stairs to the first-floor drawing room, Michael sank on to one of the deep brocade sofas near the fireplace and lifted the receiver.

'Adèle?'

'He got it! He got it! There were fifty contestants and he got it. Darling Michael, he wouldn't have done it without that wonderful violin. He played like an angel. We can't ever thank you enough.'

'Well, tell the boy that I couldn't be more proud of him. You know, he probably would have done it anyway. I think he's inherited Mother's talent. I can't talk for long now as I'm in the middle of a meeting but I'll ring you tonight. By the way, I've tickets for Covent Garden when you're in London. I hope you can come. I'll let you have the details later.'

When he had replaced the receiver Michael didn't hurry back to the ground floor. He paused for a moment, looking out of the long windows through the tangle of budding grey-green wisteria to the river. The windows were closed, excluding the noise of traffic on the Embankment, and the room was silent. Boats were moving up and down the Thames, and he thought for a moment of his mother. He wished she were alive to hear the news that her grandson had won the coveted Basle Music Prize. It seemed such a short time since he'd sat doing his school work in the window of his mother's house in Basle, watching the barges move silently up the Rhine – such a slow journey against the flow of the river, but so fast when they sped down on their long journey to the sea. He was very pleased that he had helped the boy.

There was a strong scent of lilies as Joanna had bought two huge basketfuls that morning. It was something Helena had said the previous night that had made Michael want to fill the room with their cool erotic elegance. Joanna had done well, as usual.

At twelve thirty-five Michael brought the meeting to a close. He would keep the Swiss in suspense for one more day.

'Would you like to come up and see my latest acquisition? I know you expressed an interest in the early Impressionists. I've something on approval.' Michael spoke to them as a pair, for they had conducted all their dialogue in that way, nodding or shaking their heads in unison. He did not register them as individuals anyway, they were cogs in a wheel, with him setting its pace. They accepted the invitation with a slight bow and followed Michael up the thickly carpeted stairs. They passed the dining room on the ground floor where lunch was conspicuously laid for two. Carla could be heard in the kitchen and there was an appetising smell of garlic and basil.

The silver Lexus drew up outside the house in Cheyne Walk at exactly twelve forty-five.

Michael's drive, Luigi, helped Helena out of the car and before she could take in the details of the house, Luigi's wife, Carla, opened the door. Smiling broadly she took Helena's black cashmere shawl and showed her up to the drawing room.

The Swiss were taking their leave. Michael attempted a hurried introduction and he noticed how admiringly they looked at his luncheon guest. Today Helena's hair hung loose, caught at the back by two combs, and tendrils clung to the pale skin of her forehead. She wore very little make-up and in the daylight her skin was clear with a slight sheen. She wore a white silk blouse and a black skirt which clung tightly to her waist and hips and then flared around her knees. She had the look of a Spanish dancer, and again Michael thought her impossibly young-looking to be the mother of three children, one already in her teens.

Helena hardly registered that each of the Swiss took her hand and held it somewhere short of his lips, before making a little bow, so great was her pleasure at seeing Michael again.

She was surprised at how powerful his presence was. He took her silk-clad arm gently and kissed her on both cheeks. When he took his hand away, she still felt its imprint, and he saw that she laid her own where his had been as if to retain the warmth of his touch.

'You look lovely. I was going to ask you to wear your hair like that, but thought I was perhaps being too forward. Come and sit down. I've been looking forward to seeing you in this room. It suits you perfectly.'

'Such flattery, Michael. But do go on. By the way, I like your tie; I gave my godson one like that for Christmas.'

Michael lifted the flap of silk to look at it. 'Well, you see, we have the same taste. I realised that when I came to your house. What a wonderful evening! What a battle-axe that Goodall woman is.'

'The Ponsons had the worst of her! James admires her, though – she's an exemplary Parliamentary wife.'

'Which, according to her, you are not. Though it sounds as if you spend a good deal of your life working on James's behalf. It would be a waste if you spent it all that way and never enjoyed yourself! No, I've decided to be your knight in shining armour, who'll wake the beautiful Helena from her long sojourn with the Hilda Goodalls of this world.'

'Oh, it's not quite so bad as that,' Helena laughed. She went to admire the lilies, as Carla appeared with two crystal glasses on a silver tray.

'Chablis. Hope you like it,' said Michael as he handed Helena a glass and held his to it. Helena was different from the usual type of woman he romanced. He sensed she could easily take fright if he were too hasty. He decided to tease her a little.

'To us,' he said, raising his glass. 'What are your plans for this afternoon?'

Helena did not reply but bent over the lilies and inhaled their wonderful scent. When she raised her head she had a smudge of pollen on her cheek.

She looked touchingly vulnerable. Before she could move out of reach, he took a clean white handkerchief from his trouser pocket and wiped the pollen away.

'What I meant was, there's a wonderful exhibition at the Tate, Hindu Art. Can I take you to see it?'

Helena smiled. She had half expected him to suggest an afternoon in bed and had prepared her reply – inventing an appointment with one of the girls' teachers. She hoped her pleasure at being able to spend the afternoon with Michael was not too obvious.

'Oh, what a lovely idea. I get so tied up in knots with my own painting, it's always refreshing to look at something completely different.'

Michael had hoped to bed Helena that afternoon, but now he thought there would be much enjoyment in the chase too. And perhaps she was not going to be so easy to seduce after all! When he did make love to her, it would be like sampling a long-awaited ripening peach. Their eyes met and held in the round Georgian pier glass above the fireplace. Their gaze held for a second.

Helena looked away. She remembered James's words about getting a lover, and flushed.

Michael saw her expression change and a frown appear on her brow. He suspected she would be experiencing the pangs of guilt after the first minuet in the game of adultery. Michael himself did not believe in guilt. James Askew was clever and probably a good minister, but he had known him a long while and was well aware what a cold fish he was. His departure from the dining room the previous night had spoken volumes about him. No, Helena needed rescuing.

They went downstairs to the dining room and Carla's superb cooking. Smoked salmon in fresh dill sauce, small veal escalopes sautéed in white wine, garlic and tomato purée, coated with grilled mozzarella and fresh basil grown on the kitchen window sill. They had the lightest of zabaglione for pudding. While Helena ate with pleasure, Michael talked of his life and Helena heard about his mother.

'Not *the* Josephine Elliot?' Helena exclaimed. 'My father collected her records. He said she was one of the finest *Lieder* singers he'd ever heard.'

'Yes,' replied Michael, 'but her real love was opera. She sang with the Basle Opera for years, but her voice was never big enough for the great houses. That's why she did so much *Lieder*.'

'So where did you and your sister live when you were children?' asked Helena.

'In a wonderful old house in Basle, right on the Rhine. It was

41

rented from the City, but my father bought it for my mother later on and my sister lives in it now with her husband and two children.'

'I'm an only child myself. It must be nice to have a sister.'

'Well, yes . . . Adèle's a pretty normal, happily married woman. Her husband's a rather eccentric professor who's compiling an immense study on birds. They're a happy, really close family. I adore them. As a matter of fact, the eldest son, Peta, has won a major music prize. I heard today just before you arrived.'

'That's wonderful. But what about you? What were you like as a child?'

'Well, my father was always away, so I had to be the man of the family from an early age. I suppose it's made me rather opinionated, difficult to live with.'

'Is that what your wife said? I hear you're divorced,' Helena ventured, cupping her chin in her hand and absent-mindedly removing a bright red rose from a silver bowl on the table and twiddling it.

'We are but that wasn't the reason. She's an independent soul. She knows exactly what she wants or, more to the point, doesn't want. For example, she didn't want children, neither of us did. I have a string of godchildren . . . and I like to help Adèle's family. I didn't think about it to start with – perhaps I was too busy worrying about Adèle and *her* children – but there comes a time when you want to have children of your own. So we parted. I envy you your children.'

Helena looked intently into Michael's face as he spoke and his expression softened. His mouth was firm and generous. Suddenly she felt shy and glanced down at her plate as she replied.

'I've had to learn to compromise. My children are everything to me. In a sense they keep me in touch with my life before their father died. I don't suppose I shall find happiness of that kind again.' She lowered her voice as she continued, ' – I'm not normally so open about myself.' She added, a little doubtfully, 'I expect you're wondering why I accepted your invitation, the wife of a cabinet minister . . . Well, at first I tried really hard to be a politician's wife but the truth is I find the political life absolutely contrary to the message it tries to convey – I mean, family values and all that. James really wants our children away at boarding school so that I can be there for him at the drop of a hat. If I listened to him, I'd be even lonelier than I am now. As it is I hardly ever see him. He's out every night and then every weekend he wants me to go down to the constituency and pull raffle tickets out of biscuit tins.'

'The thing I don't understand,' Michael said pensively, 'is how a woman like you married him in the first place. I wouldn't have thought he was ever your type.'

'Well.' Helena was on the point of telling him how she'd made such a mess of everything, how after Anthony had died, she had just gone to pieces, totally lost, just drifted, but she paused. Michael had such a beguiling way of extracting information. And she wasn't sure she wanted to confide in him yet. He gave her a dazzling smile, and she relented. 'I didn't realise that all marriages weren't as good as my own parents', and I'd been wonderfully lucky with Anthony. And James has his good qualities too. But he's so preoccupied with his ministerial duties, I'm just low on his list of priorities.'

Michael refilled her glass. 'You know, of course, that I've known James a very long time,' he said. 'He acted for me a number of times in some tricky situations. Brilliant man. He won a state scholarship to Cambridge, I'm told. He was certainly a very competent, inspired lawyer, and a brilliant orator. I met his first wife, you know. Not as beautiful as you. Didn't last long. I think James is really a bit of a loner.'

'Yes, he did warn me when I first met him.' She felt perhaps the conversation had gone far enough in this direction.

'Does your sister ever visit London?' she asked.

'Well,' Michael replied, 'she may well be coming over soon. You ought to meet her, you'd like her. I'll try to arrange something.'

'Tell me more about you as a child,' she asked for a second time when they were seated, drinking their coffee, in the drawing room.

'Oh . . . I had a hard time as a boy, in Basle. My parents weren't married so we were more or less ostracised. That's why Adèle and I had a governess instead of going to school. It's one of the reasons why I don't want to live in Switzerland. But I've kept in touch with my half-brother, Simon, my father's legal son. He is about three years older than me.'

'Quite different, very introspective, brooding type. My father arranged for us to meet, without my mother or his wife knowing. We liked each other a lot and we've always stayed in touch.'

'So why did you decide to live in England? My father always used to say the English middle classes did the crossword and the upper classes fiddled their tax returns. I can't see you falling into either of those categories.' Helena laughed as she said this.

'You're right,' said Michael. 'I have my money abroad, though, nicely tucked away in Liechtenstein among other places. It all started with my father to make sure my mother was provided for when he died. Technically in Switzerland you can't leave your mistress anything, but one thing I'll say for the Swiss: they'll co-operate with any authority except the tax officials.'

'What did you say your father did?' Helena asked, knowing he hadn't.

'He was a very clever banker called Steiner. My mother's real name was Epstein – a lot of Jews change their name from Epstein to Elliot. He would never leave his wife and Simon. They lived in Zurich but he spent every weekend with us in Basle. Adèle and I hated him when we were young. After all they do say that "the children of lovers are orphans". My mother adored him, though, she must have had to, to have lived that life for so many years.

'Apart from providing for my mother, my father left us very little. I've made my own way, and it hasn't been that easy. I feel I have to warn you, I've a fairly jaded opinion of the human race.' Helena was taken aback at his cynicism. She remembered how proprietorial Caroline Hampton had been. Caroline too was a tough character. Just what had the two of them got going between them? Suddenly James's presence, enjoying the Hamptons' lavish hospitality, did not seem innocent any longer.

'Why are you helping the Hamptons – Caroline I mean?' she asked. 'You introduced her to James, knowing she has big plans for her waterpark and that James could help if there are environmental issues. Is she on the level? I . . . I . . . I didn't mean to get on to this, but I'm worried. James isn't going to be offered any backhanders, is he?' Helena felt foolish the moment she had blurted this out.

An uneasy silence descended on the room. Michael looked mildly irritated. Helena realised she had gone too far, and she bit her lip nervously.

'James will come to no harm. You underestimate him – he's much cleverer than you think. But, as the saying goes, there's no such thing as a free lunch.'

Chapter 5

Kiri Te Kanawa was singing Strauss's *Four Last Songs*, while Helena gently teased the skins off some baby new potatoes. The room smelt of mint. On the kitchen table were two steaks on a board, a sauce Béarnaise sat waiting in a bain-marie and fresh mangetouts were prepared for a look at some boiling water. There were two smoked salmon mousse left over from the previous night's dinner party. Next to the cooker was a treacle tart from Marks and Spencer.

As James rarely came home for dinner, Helena had made a special effort. She was even wearing her hair in the way James liked it. She did not want another scene. The girls had promised to make themselves scarce so that she could smooth James and restore some harmony into their life. She needed to collect her scattered emotions – her upset about this morning, her determination to meet James more than halfway now, and her resolve that, although her lunch with Michael had been perfectly innocent, she would keep it a secret.

She had lit a fire in the drawing room and put James's yellow roses in pride of place on the piano. They were beautiful, but she wasn't sure what message James was trying to convey through their colour.

Knowing she had a little time to spare, Helena picked up the telephone and dialled her mother's number in Devon. The housekeeper, Mrs Finch, answered.

'Miss Helena, what a lovely surprise. When are we going to see you? I hope you're coming soon?'

'That's why I'm ringing. Is my mother there?'

'She just popped outside to shut up the bantams. Hold on, I'll get her.'

While Helena waited she thought about the coolness that had developed between her and her mother in the last months. The situation had made her very unhappy, she knew that it was not her mother's fault, and she was well aware of the effect it must have had on her. Cornelia had more or less kept the family sane after Anthony died. Her three grandchildren had come to think of Maryzion as home after Helena had moved to London. What must her mother feel now that she hardly saw the children and lived alone in the big house that had once been so full of life? Helena felt terribly guilty.

In trying to make her marriage work she had thought that Maryzion must be distanced, she knew how James hated to hear them all talking about it. He had never liked going there. He said her mother behaved like a 'grand dame' and he found her friends patronising. He thought that they were spoilt and pampered. Helena had tried to explain how it wasn't really like that, that everyone was trying to keep up appearances. She explained how hard they had worked to make ends meet after her father died and how, even now, the whole place might have to be sold. Helena kept stressing her mother's role in this, but she knew the contrast in their backgrounds riled James. He felt like an outsider and he was, she knew, terribly jealous.

But the weekend at Markham Court, and now talking to Michael this afternoon, had altered her perspective. She had seen how Caroline and Michael had the courage to take what they wanted. It made her realise just how much Maryzion meant to her and to her children. It was a house where they all found reassurance. Helena missed her mother, and she had decided to take the situation in hand before it went too far.

'Hello, darling.'

'Mummy,' she blurted out, 'I'm so sorry about everything. It's nothing to do with you, it's just that I've been trying to work things out . . . but we all miss you so much. Can we come for Easter?'

'Of course, it would be wonderful.'

'James won't be with us, he's got a lot to do in the constituency. He's going to be livid when I tell him I'm coming down. He thinks the children will come to you on their own and that I'll go to Sussex and do my bit at the Easter fundraising event. But I do so want us all to be together – like old times. And I've hardly seen my son since he was packed off to boarding school.'

'Darling, surely James realises Rollo must be counting the days until term finishes?'

'I can't talk to James about Rollo. Look, don't let's discuss it now.'

Helena went on to mention their visit to Markham Court, as she knew her mother was both fascinated and appalled by the new style of aristocrat epitomised by Caroline Hampton.

Soon they were back on their old relaxed footing, enjoying the gossip, when suddenly Helena heard the front door slam.

'Mummy, I'll have to go. James is back. Talk to you soon . . .'

Then there was silence. Kiri's voice had stopped in mid-flight. Helena heard James on the staircase, which in itself was unusual. He rarely came downstairs to greet her on his homecoming. She always went to find him and there he would be, watching the television in his study on the half-landing. Now, as he came into the kitchen he looked worried; his face was abnormally pale.

James stood just inside the room. He wasn't going to risk being trapped by Helena until he had sorted a few things out. Ideally, he would give anything to eat his dinner in front of the television and not have to discuss Helena's latest escapade. But at the moment things were far from ideal. He took a deep breath.

'Is it true what I heard today? That you've accepted a commission to paint David Banks's children?' James moved to the opposite end of the kitchen table where he faced his wife challengingly.

'I was going to tell you, James. How did you hear?' Helena asked, her heart pounding.

'If you can imagine anything more humiliating, I learnt it from the Chief Whip, Mark Raymond. Don't you realise what implications this has for me as a cabinet minister?'

'What implications? My God, that Whips' Office is like the KGB.' Helena placed both hands on the table and leant towards her husband.

He noticed her knuckles turn white and he backed away and straightened his tie.

'The wife of a cabinet minister painting a portrait of the Leader of the Opposition's children,' James replied incredulously.

'I don't know what all the fuss is about. It can't affect your position,' said Helena. 'It's nothing to do with politics.'

'If you believe that, you'll believe anything.'

'Well, David Banks evidently doesn't think so.'

James gave his tie another angry tug. His voice had lost its steadiness. That was one of the irritating things about Helena, she made him lose his cool. He could hold his own on the floor of the House of Commons when the Opposition were baying for blood but when Helena put on that don't-give-a-damn act he lost control.

'I can't allow you to do it.'

'But I'm a painter. I was at school with Violet Banks. She's a friend of mine.'

James glared at her. Neither of them spoke, then Helena's normal pale complexion began to flush and two angry red spots appeared on her cheeks.

She tried to keep her voice level as she continued, 'Surely you can see this is a great chance for me?'

James's mouth tightened and he made as if to leave the room but then turned back. 'If you do this, you'll be making fools of all of us. I'm not asking you, Helena, I'm telling you. Indeed, I'm giving you the chance to withdraw gracefully and repair the damage already done.'

Helena couldn't believe her ears. 'You must be joking!' she spat.

'Helena, I forbid it.' James thumped the table and the smoked salmon mousse danced on their beds of rocket salad.

'*Forbid it?*' Helena repeated the words slowly in disbelief. 'I don't think you're in a position to forbid it. We need the money.'

James made quickly for the kitchen door, his voice menacingly quiet. 'I have given my view and I mean what I say.' He left the room to prevent further discussion.

Helena heard his steps on the drawing room floor above. After a few moments she followed him upstairs, intending to get him a drink.

He was standing by the piano angrily scooping up all Helena's music, and he did not turn to look at her as he spoke. 'This place is a mess, and I meant to say to you last night, will you please move your son's bicycle from the hall?'

This was too much for Helena, the gloves were off. 'For God's sake, James, pianos are supposed to be played and bicycles are supposed to be ridden – and life, in case it hadn't occurred to you, life is supposed to be lived. Rollo will be back from boarding school soon, and he expects to find his things waiting for him. You're such a misery all the time, James. Please, please, couldn't we have a nice evening, just for once?'

'I get no thanks for anything I do around here,' James continued.

'Least of all paying out thousands a year to support your children.'

James tweaked angrily at a loose button on his suit. It flew off with a clatter on to the parquet floor. He tapped his foot in irritation. 'And I can't even get my buttons sewn on.'

Helena straightened her shoulders and called on all her resolve. She really couldn't face any more rowing. She walked over to the table by the window where there was a tray of drinks and poured James a gin and tonic. Turning towards him, she held up the glass. 'Oh, come on, James. I've made you a lovely dinner. Have a drink and sit by the fire with me before we go down.'

James looked at his wife. As he did so, the last dart of evening sun slanted through the window from a gap between the roofs on the other side of the street and caught her head and shoulders. It picked out the shine of her wonderful hair and the amber flecks in the tiger tulips which bent gracefully towards her from two horn-shaped vases on the mantelpiece. Her mascara had run a little and her eyes looked bigger than ever. She appeared theatrical, majestic and somehow beyond him as if she had slipped away and he couldn't follow. She stood very tall in front of the flames, bathed in golden light: even the brass fender glittered at her feet. He felt the power of her beauty and just for a brief moment he wished he could tell her how lovely she was, how much he admired her for the way she coped with everything but the words froze in his mouth.

He took the drink and gave Helena a weak smile. 'Come on, we're both tired. Let's have dinner. I have to write a speech afterwards and if you don't mind I'd like to watch *Morse* at nine-thirty. This is the first night I've not had to be in the House for weeks. I need to switch off.'

Helena had a brief pang of guilt that she'd allowed the row to escalate. James didn't see things the way she did. He looked exhausted. He seemed to have aged even in the last few minutes. His face had furrowed into dark lines, even his eyes drooped slightly at the corners and there were shadows beneath.

A strand of his hair had found a will of its own and stuck out like an antenna. She couldn't resist the temptation to smooth it back for him as they left the room.

James fell on the steak with relish, and it restored his good humour and made him more generous. 'Helena, you're a marvellous cook,' he said, 'and the food you cooked last night was superb.'

Too late, Helena thought. He should have said something last night or this morning when she was so upset. Well, she would use the opportunity of his good mood.

'James, I must talk to you about the children's Easter holiday.'

'Yes, we'll be going to the cottage as usual. There are a lot of constituency engagements. You're doing the raffle at four coffee mornings, and we are both expected at the Association Ladies' Night and, of course, there is the Rotary Dinner—'

'Actually I'm going to Devon. Mummy is longing to see the children and I've said we will go to Maryzion for Easter. Will you come, James darling, for part of it? You need a break, it would be good for you. We could go for a long walk on Dartmoor.'

'Well, that's bloody marvellous, isn't it?' James exploded. 'I don't ask much, just a bit of support. Send *them* to your mother's.' He paused, then continued, 'You know I think you've gone slightly mad, Helena.'

A piece of steak flew out of his mouth and landed on Helena's sleeve. She picked it off and threw it to Clovis.

'It occurs to me, Helena,' said James, getting up from the table, 'that bloody little stinker of a dog gets far more care than I do. I'm going upstairs to watch *Morse*. I can't think of a single thing to say to you.'

Helena remained seated, from where she addressed the disappearing figure of her husband. 'I can think of something to say to you, James. Perhaps in the future you would consult me before you accept a whole weekend's engagements on my behalf? I just might have a few commitments of my own. And what are the children supposed to do while I'm out in the constituency?'

'That's just it, Helena. When I married you I naturally assumed that I would come first. A happy man makes a happy home. I'm not a happy man.'

A few moments later Helena heard the noise of the television. She made a conscious effort to calm down and get her mind on to something pleasant. She had been elated about the Bankses' painting commission, which she'd hoped would mean she could buy a new car and pay off her overdraft. But the main thing was feeling good about herself again. She decided to drop her mother a line about

Easter. It would be more discreet than telephoning her grievances, as the phones were tapped. Despite what James had said, she was definitely going to Devon, not Sussex, and she knew her mother would be relieved that James would not be coming. The prospect of a few days at Maryzion and restoring contact . . .

As she cleared the plates and tidied the kitchen Helena could not know that James's face no longer betrayed any discontent. He had been thinking: Easter on my own, what a relief! But Helena must not know. And there would be no more rows for a bit. All he wanted was some peace and quiet, but the thought of Helena at large and independent made him strangely nervous. He hadn't really meant it when he had told her to take a lover. He could hardly believe he had said such a thing. Helena was a young and beautiful woman and she probably did get bored at home every night on her own. Still, she was fairly level-headed, and when push came to shove he could always get her back into line. Easter on his own was not such a bad idea.

Chapter 6

'So nice to sit down together at last, Hilda.' Reggie eased his large pin-striped behind into the wooden chair and drew it up to the pine table in Number Eleven's pine-decked kitchen. 'Pity I had that working breakfast with the Bank of England yesterday.'

'The price of responsibility, Reggie.'

'Scrambled eggs and buck's fizz. Eggs were half cold by the time they got to me. They weren't as good as you do them, dear.'

'How d'you like the new egg cosies? I was given them by the Westminster Sewing Circle. So thoughtful of them. They know I can't sew, but one can't be good at everything and I always give the ladies a pot of marmalade each at Christmas.'

'But you don't make marmalade,' snapped Reggie.

'No, but they don't know that. I just take the labels off and put new covers on. As long as they're happy, Reggie dear,' replied Hilda. Reggie glanced out of the window, his mind wandering. 'Looks foggy.'

'No, it's just that the window-cleaner hasn't been.' She nodded towards Number Ten, already on to a new subject. Only her husband could match her random thoughts. 'Meeting in Paris today, I believe. Going with Bernard.'

'Not another outbreak of mad cow, I hope?'

'Some special meeting at the OECD.'

Reggie removed his egg cosy, and synchronised with Hilda as they both neatly sliced off the tops of their eggs and simultaneously gave little laughs.

'Well, the Askew woman: what did you make of her?' Hilda had been dying to know Reggie's opinion. She had formulated her own views early on.

'A jolly good cook.'

'But the bread wasn't wholemeal.'

'And very decorative – until she opens her mouth.'

Hilda retorted, 'I thought you were going to say, "until she opened her blouse." There was no need for her to do that. You could see right through it.'

'Far too independent. Not a political animal really. Arty type. And I haven't had time to tell you the latest. She'd only decided to paint David Banks's children!'

'Outrageous!' Hilda's leathery lip trembled. 'I certainly hope James has nipped that in the bud. We don't want those sorts of goings-on in the Party.'

'You'll have to take her in hand, Hilda. James is too important to us. At least the Cabinet think so.'

Reggie paused for a moment. When he thought about Mark Raymond, the Chief Whip, he could feel his blood pressure rising. The man thought he and the Prime Minister could 'bounce' the Cabinet. Why, only yesterday they had done it again. In they had swept to the emergency meeting about Euorpe, and they had made the decision. The only one who stood up to them, apart from himself, was James Askew. Askew was clever and the other members of the Cabinet were beginning to see that if they wanted to be heard there would have to be a change of leadership to someone who believed in listening to other people's views. And James was completely straight. But that Mark Raymond . . . Of course everyone knew how clever he was at pulling in Party funds. Invitations to dine at Number Ten, vague mentions of knighthoods, and a lot of useful introductions were the usual bait, and no doubt for many it was a shrewd investment. But in Reggie's view the Party paid the price. James Askew would be a new broom and under his leadership they could get rid of all the festering conspiracies.

'A lot of people would like to see someone like James Askew in Number Ten and they're just beginning to stand up to be counted. Nothing would give me greater pleasure than to see that arrogant snob Raymond knocked off his perch. At least James Askew would run a tight ship, with no secret meetings behind the scenes.'

'It's all to do with vocation, isn't it, dear?' said Hilda, looking fondly at her husband. 'The marvellous thing about you, Reggie, is that you, an officer and a gentleman, can see the virtue of someone like James Askew.'

'My dear,' said Reggie, 'we live in a changing world. We have to look to young men like Askew. They are the meritocracy. People like Raymond are the plutocrats we must get rid of.'

Hilda could see Reggie's colour begin to rise. She changed the subject. 'Would you like some special thick-cut lemon?'

'Oh, that looks nice.'

'What was James's father? A subpostmaster, wasn't he? From Cardiff? He's got no accent now, has he? You could never tell, could you?'

'James has really had to work to get where he is. He told me his mother used to go out cleaning sometimes, *and* do a post round in all weathers just to help him stay on in the sixth form – pay for his uniform and the school trip to the Austrian Tyrol . . . Unlike Jenkins, son of Jenkins & Co, brewing family. Pots of money.'

Reggie Goodall had never been entirely convinced the Prime Minister had achieved his office through merit.

Hilda took a deep breath, and stroked the pleats straight in her navy-blue skirt. 'So you didn't notice?'

'Notice?'

'The way Helena Askew was looking at the French Ambassador.'

'Oh, I think you've got it wrong there, Hilda.'

'No, I swear she put him next to her deliberately.'

'Well, correct me if I'm wrong, Hilda, but he was sitting next to you as well.'

'And so he should have been . . . So what did you think of that man Elliot. What a smoothie! You should have seen the way he was chatting up James's assistant.'

'Elliot's a good chap. Gives us about fifty grand a year.'

'You mean Party funds?'

'Indeed I do. Couldn't do without chaps like him. Of course you can bet your boots there's some Elliot financial enhancement in it too somewhere, but this latest scheme, with the Hamptons, seems sound. Bit of local opposition, I believe, but nothing that can't be overcome.'

'What's his company?'

'Ah, that's the sixty-four-thousand-dollar question. He's always creating new ones and dissolving old ones. Can't keep up with him. But his Western Environmental Services group is the one involved in the Hampton deal – quarrying, mining, civil engineering, you name it. Now there's waste disposal, I hear.'

'Oh, here's little Pinky.' Hilda had lost interest. 'Where's Perky?' She addressed the monstrously fat ginger tom who'd just lumbered in through the door and was now rubbing hairs on her pristine skirt.

'Shrewd fellow. Bit devious, I suppose. The sort of fellow who follows you in through a revolving door and comes out in front.'

'I thought that was a Romanian.'

'Well, not far off. Bloody Swiss.'

They both laughed.

'At least they're not in the European Union. Here Pinky!'

'Have the top of my egg.' Reggie addressed the gross heap of fur on the lino. 'No,' he turned back to Hilda. 'There were rumours some years ago now. He was caught arranging some deal to export five million high-density fire bricks to Iran. Claimed they were for hospital incinerators. Some of us thought otherwise. But nothing could be proved and the case was stopped. I believe it was James who defended him at the time – before he became an MP. Elliot's always got an eye for the main chance. Keeps most of his money abroad. Liechtenstein, I heard.'

'Oh here comes Perky. Here, Perky.'

The doorbell rang.

'Damn. There's my car.'

'Don't forget to bring back some chocolates from Brussels.'

When he had gone, Hilda made a note in her diary to ring Helena Askew.

Chapter 7

'I've been in touch with the Duchess's office. She'll be arriving in the Central Lobby at twelve forty-five, James.' Charles Swinton, James's PPS, uttered the word 'Duchess' in hushed tones. Caroline Hampton was a very feisty woman and one heck of a celebrity. James saw that he had gone up in Charles's estimation.

James was one of the few ministers who knew all the tricks of the trade in so far as his conniving civil servants were concerned: little things like allowing the odd document to be slipped to the bottom of the pile, or inserted into something else, in the hope the Minister would not see it. But nothing ever got past James. 'The civil servants run the country, but not my Ministry,' he had told Charles recently. It was this sort of remark that singled James out from the rest. He could read a brief in seconds and commit it to memory. As a result, his debating powers were awesome. He sliced the Opposition with reams of statistics, all from his head and always right. He was a master of the single turn of phrase which became a banner headline in the following day's press.

But he was not a clubbable man, and was rarely to be seen in the bars and the tea rooms. However, he had influential supporters and a number of powerful business contacts. His name was being mentioned in the relevant circles now that the PM's standing in the polls was so low.

Today James was wearing a very well-cut double-breasted suit in navy and white stripe (off-the-peg from Huntsman). Although James always looked immaculate he rarely looked dashing as he did today.

Pity about the timing of lunch, James thought. He had tricky questions in the House that afternoon. The trouble was Environment simply hadn't had a policy. What it did have, however, was a budget deficit. James had a policy now, though, and he intended to brief the Cabinet.

Charles handed James the file on the afternoon's Question Time. James sat down and went through the details with complete concentration. The chimes of Big Ben struck nine forty-five. He closed the file.

'Right, Charles, I must away. I don't want to keep the Cabinet waiting. I'll be back here before lunch to sign some letters – and don't worry about this afternoon, everything's under control.'

The Cabinet meeting began as a gloomy affair, and had a distinctly unpleasant atmosphere. Robert Jenkins was in his late fifties, but his stately, somewhat pompous demeanour made him appear much older. Tall, slim, with thin greying hair and a supercilious manner, he had been chosen as leader as an antidote to Major. He was very much of the old school and recruited a number of his long-standing chums to the Cabinet. There were no women, for Jenkins felt more at ease without them – you always had to make allowances with women around. He was thick with Mark Raymond, the Chief Whip – they had been at Eton and Oxford together – and James always had the feeling that neither of them particularly liked him. Nonetheless it paid to keep on the right side. There was an unofficial split between the Jenkins chums, which included the Foreign Secretary, and James's allies: Reggie Goodall, Bernard Keatley, Martin Matthews – the Home Secretary – and Peter Cardew, Heritage Secretary, among them.

This morning's meeting was rather critical. James had to quell the unrest about the shortfall in the Environment budget and at the same time come up with a plan to reassure the public that waste disposal, the big issue, together with environmental 'enhancement' – the new buzz word – were being dealt with properly. When it came to his turn, he proposed that a substantial sum from the National Lottery should be made available as subsidies to councils and private concerns, if need be, for these purposes.

The PM looked sombre. 'And you think the public will swallow it? Give us an example.'

James launched into the Hamptons' wildlife waterpark scheme, how it would enhance the local amenities, attract tourists to the area, dwelling as little as necessary on the gravel extraction that would take place beforehand. He had expected opposition from

Jenkins, but the Prime Minister was beaming.

'Bertie Hampton,' he said. 'Fine chap . . . he was my fag at Eton. Excellent. Excellent.'

Having seen the direction in which the wind was blowing, Jenkins's cronies murmured approval, and James had already primed the Heritage Secretary, so there was no problem there.

After this, the meeting brightened up. The PM had fulsome praise for James's handling of the tricky question of water pollution on *Newsnight* the evening before.

They then went on to discuss the alarming reports in the *Daily Mail* that day about the flood of illegal immigrants coming into Britain now that Hong Kong had seceded. People from mainland China were claiming the same rights as those who had been resident in Hong Kong before secession. The talk went round and round in circles, and it was suggested that visas might have to be withdrawn from those who already had the right to come.

Just as this discussion was drawing to an unresolved close, the PM's PPS interrupted with bad news. The elderly Member for Nunstead had collapsed and died of a stroke that morning as he got out of his bath.

Nunstead, James thought, his heart thumping. That was the Hamptons' constituency. He was aghast. That meant there would have to be a by-election. It had been a safe Tory seat, but could it be said there were *any* safe Tory seats now?

The Cabinet meeting had finished late. Reggie sidled up to James in the hall of Number Ten, to arrange a quiet drink with him at his club – the Garrick – later, and muttered the usual platitudes about trouncing Labour at the by-election, and the usual veiled references to the power of Mark Raymond, all taken on board by James.

He was irritated by Reggie's obsession with Raymond. James made it a policy never to quarrel with anyone, it merely created hostages to fortune. But the thought of the Nunstead by-election had sent alarm bells ringing in his head. As he walked to his ministerial car, he remembered the situation at home where the subject of Easter had, by mutual agreement, being dropped, and resolved to extend his maxim of not quarrelling with anyone to his future relations with Helena, whatever the provocation.

Still thinking about Nunstead, James rushed past the statue of

Winston Churchill, and into the Central Lobby. There were a lot of people about. He stood for a moment by the desk where a uniformed usher with a microphone paged visitors.

A number of Members had just been showing constituents around the Lords and Commons. It was difficult to get a line of vision to where his guest would be arriving. His eye was drawn to a party of schoolchildren standing under the great chandelier. It had once fallen to the ground, narrowly missing several visitors and leaving a mark on the ornately paved floor. The group involuntarily moved back as a Member of Parliament recounted the story and, through the gap, James saw Caroline Hampton arriving. He felt an involuntary thrill when he saw her. She looked magnificent. She was, in every sense of the word, a big woman. Everything about her was a statement.

She wore a navy suit, the flared jacket heavily braided in thick gold, a skirt that stopped just above the knee, navy tights and very high-heeled shoes with gilt buckles. Her thick gold hair was tied back in a large black velvet bow. In contrast to Helena's more casual approach to dress this woman exuded power, and power was what James coveted and admired. He felt excited, stimulated, and for a moment he imagined her without clothes . . . then he took control of himself.

A ripple of interest ran through the crowd as James crossed the floor to greet her. This was all very gratifying since politicians, like actors, want to be recognised. The theatre of the moment did not escape Caroline. She rose to the occasion beautifully. The crowd watched the ritual greeting with hushed admiration. Two celebrities in one go was something to remember.

'James, my dear,' Caroline enthused, as she offered him each cheek in turn for a pristine kiss. She extended both hands and held his momentarily. She was wearing cream kid gloves and the feel of the leather was smooth against his bare palms. He led her through the lobby and past the historical murals on the way to the Strangers' Dining Room. They passed the entrance to the Lords, and Caroline graciously acknowledged greetings from a couple of peers.

'Do you want to have a drink in the Pugin Room before we go into lunch?' James asked.

'No. Why don't we go in? I'm absolutely exhausted,' she said, placing a languid hand on her chest.

Caroline *was* tired but not for the reason she would wish James to suppose. He must get the impression of a woman dedicated to her family and charitable works, concerned with keeping the bailiffs from Markham Court for the good of the nation. The reality had not, in fact, been at all unpleasant. She had woken at nine, had a long bath, been to the hairdresser's and then on to open a jewellery exhibition at Chelsea Town Hall. She had been offered a choice of gifts from a velvet tray by way of a thank you. She had not chosen the least valuable as was customary – her eye had been irresistibly drawn to the token gems, particularly a pair of superb diamond earrings. She was wearing them now, and they caught the light as the head waiter, George, showed her and James to their table by the window with a view of the Thames.

'What an amusing menu,' Caroline exclaimed. 'I've never eaten boiled beef and dumplings, and what on earth is spotted dick?'

The head waiter had been listening attentively and came swiftly to the rescue. 'Allow me to suggest that your Grace chooses something from the other menu.'

He pointed to the calorie-controlled page and, before Caroline could comment, James interjected, 'Not that calories need worry you, of course, but may I suggest smoked salmon and then perhaps a steak Diane, and maybe a glass of champagne? I won't be drinking, as I never do at lunchtime. I have to answer questions this afternoon.'

'Excellent,' crooned Caroline. 'That will do perfectly.' She started fussing with her bag, a large black Hermès model that Michael had given her. It had cost over two thousand pounds, and the waiting list for this particular item was now a good six months. She couldn't resist showing it off, although the display was lost on James, which she knew was just as well. James disapproved of the widening gap between the rich and the impoverished underclass. That was why he was going along with Caroline's plan. A wildlife scheme for the preservation of waterfowl and which also provided good walking space for the public was an entirely laudable vision.

Caroline gave James her full attention, while he spoke of her waterpark scheme. She put both elbows on the table and joined her fingers under her chin, flashing an armoury of rings. She looked encouragingly at him, her large mouth thickly painted pale pink. The effect was very lavish.

James did a thing that was totally out of character, and surprised even himself as he suddenly said, 'You do look marvellous. That outfit suits you to perfection.'

'Thank you,' Caroline replied. 'I bought it in Florence. It's made by Liola, and there are two shops in London, but I never have time to go shopping. If you want the address I can always give it to you; after all, you might like to get a little something for that lovely wife of yours.'

James acknowledged this information with a perfunctory nod and changed the subject. He had no interest in women's clothes and couldn't quite think why he had started on the subject.

Caroline found James extremely attractive and different from the sort of men she usually mixed with. He did not have the artificial finesse of the upper classes, so that when he spoke she felt he really meant it. She liked conversing on an equal footing without the subtle undertone of sexual patronisation. Caroline was bored with the upper-class men she now met through her marriage to Bertie. James was taciturn to a degree and had a disconcerting habit of not responding to remarks batted in his direction. His obvious intelligence was to her an aphrodisiac. He regarded everything with a frightening perception she now realised from the way he had discussed her plans for the estate; like a computer he took it all in and stored it for future reference. She guessed this was part of his legal training. She knew he had made quite a name for himself at the Bar. She remembered Michael saying James was far too bright for politics, he should have stayed at the Bar and become an international lawyer.

But looking about the room, Caroline sensed the headiness of power that must inevitably attract a man like James Askew to the House.

'You know, it's wonderful of you to give us such support with our scheme. I simply don't know what I would have done if you hadn't come along,' Caroline gushed.

'Please understand,' James said, 'delightful as you undoubtedly are, I think the scheme will stand up on its own, although some more modifications are still required, I'm afraid.

'Regarding the waterpark,' James went on, 'my inspector has come up with his proposal that the waterpark will have to be much bigger than you originally intended. Furthermore,' he went on rather pompously, 'he's recommended replanting the large deciduous wood. There will have to be public access at all times – which, of course, will mean a lot of safety and fire precautions, people on hand and a hefty insurance premium, public facilities, lavatories, a picnic area, car parking, a covered place for when it's raining, et cetera . . .'

'My God, what's all this going to cost? Where's our profit?' Caroline stopped short of saying they were only in it for the money.

'I'm not sure yet but I think I may be able to swing a grant your way. I'm hoping that there will be some funds available in the near future. But keep this under your hat for the moment, metaphorically speaking.' He looked at her sleek blonde hair and her eyes glittering with pleasure.

'Oh, James, that would be marvellous. A subsidy would be an enormous help towards costs. Can I tell Bertie?'

'No, don't mention it to anyone just now. Let's keep it a secret for the moment. Nothing has been ratified as yet.'

'You're an angel, James.' She gave him an enormous, ravishing smile. 'There is just one other little thing I ought to perhaps mention.'

'What would that be?'

'Well, Michael has come up with a plan for infill. Apparently one of his companies deals in waste materials. He says he could use some of the area for infill – it's just building rubble, that sort of thing, I think. It would help pay for all these other embellishments you've just mentioned.'

'I suppose there's no objection. If it is anything other than rubble, of course, I could not give the Department's go ahead. But I'll get my people to look into the exact ruling. I'm sure there won't be a problem,' James replied.

'Oh good,' Caroline said, uncrossing her legs as she spoke. James heard a faint swish of silk and felt a distinct stirring in the lower regions.

'We did so enjoy having you both for that weekend.' Caroline swiftly changed the subject before he could think too deeply about the 'rubbish' she had mentioned. 'It was especially nice to meet your wife.'

James received the remark with a nod.

Caroline continued, 'She has such natural good looks. I suppose, living such a marvellous artistic life, she doesn't have to bother even going near a hairdresser or that sort of thing.'

James wasn't sure if Caroline were being altogether complimentary. He felt a little defensive, especially as he felt guilty about Helena. He had been very hard on her the other evening and said some things he regretted. In his heart he knew that she was trying her best, and when the chips were down she could knock spots off the Hamptons of this world. And it *was* Helena's natural beauty and confidence in her place in the scheme of things that had most attracted him. He wasn't going to have Caroline Hampton invading his private territory in this way.

'Thank you,' James said. 'Helena *is* very beautiful, isn't she, and she's also a good painter. What a shame her grandfather, the old Earl, never ran his estate as you do yours. When her mother took it on it had gone to rack and ruin.'

Caroline had been very put out that first evening of the weekend to discover Helena was so grand. She had never had the benefit of a silver spoon. Marrying the Duke had opened up a new world for her, but even that was a constant challenge where she had to have her wits about her if the family were to survive. Networking was part of her life and most of her contacts were men. It usually helped if they were unhappily married or not married at all. She was feeling her way with James. She could usually spot holes in other people's marriages and she didn't scruple to exploit them. She didn't like sex much but used it as a means to an end. The main thing was to let the man think you liked it. Her actress training and her years of touring had taught her a lot about human nature. She never did get the big classical or leading stage roles she'd always hankered after, but she had found them in real life and she was good. James's obvious attraction to her was not entirely to do with sex: it was linked to his enjoyment of her aura of power. She went everywhere and knew everyone. She was one of that dying breed, a salonnière. Invitations to Markham Court were coveted by the great and the good, and James knew that getting on in life was, regrettably, at least as much about who you knew as what you knew.

'I suppose you won't have heard about old Arthur Hall. He died of a stroke. So you're going to have a by-election.'

'Well, it won't affect us,' Caroline said. 'We don't have a vote!'

James looked sanguine. 'It may well affect you. The place will be buzzing with the media. Let's hope some of your tenant farmers and villagers don't decide to make trouble. Life could be made very difficult for you . . . and for us . . . our Party, I mean.'

'I'm always frightfully nice to the villagers. Once the park's in place, it'll attract visitors, and they'll get more money for their grubby little pub and so on,' Caroline said. She gave James another ravishing smile.

He felt his insides crumbling.

'By the way,' Caroline said, 'did you get the slippers with the portcullis on them?'

'Oh, I'm so sorry. I kept meaning to thank you. How on earth did you get them made so quickly?'

James still had the slippers in his office – he hadn't dared to take them home.

'I didn't, you can buy them in a shop in St James's Street. All the old peers get them, and they have others with ducal or earls' coronets. I hope your wife didn't mind. It's really a thank you in advance from Bertie and me for all your help – especially now . . .'

James was relieved at the mention of Caroline's husband; that put the gift on a slightly more respectable level. He thanked her profusely and while so doing saw the Chief Whip approaching the table.

Mark Raymond crossed the room with more of a glide than a step. He was of medium height, rather portly, his protruding stomach covered by a waistcoat and decorated with the thick gold chain of his fob watch. He was one of the few people who still sported pin-striped trousers and a black coat. His hair had long ago receded and he wore his baldness in much the same way as his figure, with the air of a man of power and importance. His appearance was both elegant and sombre, and when he spoke his voice, though quiet – a trick he had perfected to make people listen – had a somewhat menacing tone.

'I didn't give you my personal congratulations this morning, James. I thought you did very well on *Newsnight*,' said Mark, looking down at Caroline as he spoke.

James didn't really want to have Mark hogging his time with his guest. He did not get up, but made a hasty introduction, hoping Mark would say a swift hello and then depart.

But Mark did no such thing. 'May I?' he said, pulling out a chair and sitting down before James could reply. He turned to Caroline. 'It's very good to meet you. Your husband works with some relatives of mine – at Grunfeld's. They're very pleased with him. I hear good reports. My mother's family started the bank.'

James listened to him egregiously flattering Caroline, and remembered what Madame Ponson had said at the dinner party about the Duke's ineptitude for banking. Mark was a slippery customer. He didn't like him and, more to the point, he didn't trust him.

Mark didn't like James either. He thought he was a dangerous breed of politician, a man with principles but no feelings. He did not qualify for the inner circle, those who knew they must toe the line, dine at the right tables in the Members' Dining Room, keep close to the Whips, keep tabs on fellow MPs who might be stirring up trouble, and accept that decisions were made outside the Cabinet, unlike James Askew and the like who felt it their duty to listen to their constituents. The inner circle knew best, and many a decision was made in the drawing rooms of their houses in the quiet expensive streets around Westminster. But James was clever and it had been decided that it was dangerous to have him in the rebellious ranks of the backbenchers.

Nor did Mark Raymond like the friendship that had developed between Reggie Goodall and Askew. Reggie had, of course, been one of the inner circle but he seemed strangely absent from their meetings these days. Raymond resolved to keep the situation firmly monitored. Word had it that Reggie was talking of James standing against the Prime Minister if the leadership question came up. Mark wanted to hedge his bets so he would keep on the right side of Askew for the time being, but he was formulating a plan. He was aware of James's potential; at this point he could still be a force to be reckoned with.

The two men fell into discussion about the by-election at Nunstead, and then the latest scandal to hit the Party, a Member fighting off bankruptcy after losses at Lloyds and a disastrous business venture.

'It's all right, old boy, we have the situation under control. One of our benefactors has come in with a package to bail him out. We can't have another bankruptcy forcing yet another by-election,' said Mark, putting his thumbs in his waistcoat pockets.

'My word, do you mean that a Party supporter will pay off the debts to avoid his losing his seat?' Caroline asked.

'That's partly what the Whips' Office is for, to prevent these things. We had one chap who killed himself. Very nasty business, and caused us all kinds of inconvenience. Had he come clean we would have bailed him out. I may not look it, my dear, but I'm really a sort of agony aunt,' Mark said with a wry laugh.

Caroline noticed, when he laughed, his face moved but his eyes remained unsmiling and beady.

'I never knew things like that went on. Do tell me more,' she said giving one of her ravishing smiles.

'Now what exactly can I tell you? Oh, James, I expect you know the story of Lance Dingle. When he came to confess to me that he had decided to reveal to his constituency he was having a raging affair I told him that I had long ago stopped believing in God, but I didn't feel it necessary to tell my constituents.'

Mark watched James carefully as he told the story. Caroline laughed heartily but James did not. Then Mark signalled to his luncheon companion who had been chatting by the door and, with an elaborate farewell to Caroline and a nod to James, left the room.

James looked at his watch; it was two twenty.

'Sorry, I'll have to go. Would you like to watch the Speaker's Procession on its way into prayers?'

Caroline declined the offer, but as she stood up, she gently placed her hand over his on the table, and looking him directly in the eye, said she had some further plans for the waterpark to show him at her flat in Westminster Chambers, if he'd care to drop in later on.

James hesitated for just one moment, then said he'd definitely try to make it after Question Time. The unexpected openness of the invitation had stunned him; he felt a reckless desire to put her to the test.

He saw her to Westminster Hall and watched her hurrying into a taxi, her navy jacket pulled tightly around her, shoulders hunched a little. It was always cold in there, even in midsummer, as if harbouring the chilling conclusions of the many dramas in its long history.

Chapter 8

Michael turned on the steps of his club. He'd decided a meeting on neutral territory would be best. Caroline had threatened to descend on Cheyne Walk, and he didn't want Simon meeting her. He liked to keep his life in neat, separate compartments, especially the women in it.

It was chilly and about to rain. The wind rattled an empty crisp packet along the pavement. Cars were revving up in the traffic jam. He looked down Pall Mall towards Waterloo Place, and saw the slim figure of his half-brother hurrying towards him, black umbrella waving. He glimpsed his face. Simon still had his amazing good looks. As he came nearer, though, Michael could see that he was agitated. How long had it been since he'd seen him? A good five, or even six months. It was when Simon had just got back from Africa where he'd been lecturing. He was ashamed he'd left it so long, but life had constantly intervened.

'Still the fat cat,' Simon said, observing Michael's immaculately sleek appearance and laughing as they shook hands.

'It's so good to see you, Simon. Let's have a drink at the bar, then we'll find a quiet spot. But you can start telling me all about it now.'

'Excuse me, sir,' the doorman interrupted politely, addressing Michael, 'but would your guest care to wear one of these?' He held out an array of sober-looking ties.

'Oh God,' Simon said, and grudgingly took one, hurriedly knotting it.

Simon had phoned in a bit of a state the night before – he said he had a problem he'd like Michael's advice on. Michael's first reaction had been to wonder about hepatitis or AIDS, but looking at Simon he thought he seemed well enough, quite healthy despite his perennially thin figure. It wouldn't be the first time, though, by any means, that Michael had been called upon to get Simon out of a jam. Simon courted disaster.

'We've got lots to catch up on,' Michael said.

'We certainly have.'

They went through to a room with dark wainscoting and shiny green leather chairs, shaded with heavy brocade curtains. It was not really Simon's sort of place, but Michael liked its Englishness. Usually it was empty at this time of day, although now a few old buffers were seated with their drinks, scanning the *Telegraph* sports pages, and pipe-tapping.

'What will you have?' Michael asked.

'A G & T would be good, a double,' Simon said.

When they were seated, Michael began the interrogation. Simon was obviously hesitant to start.

'So how's the faculty?'

'The faculty is great. I couldn't have a nicer set of colleagues. We all got on tremendously well. Very friendly lot.'

There was a pause while Simon looked everywhere but at his half-brother. He opened his mouth, hesitated, then: 'Michael . . . I'm married.'

'Married? You?' Michael looked stunned. 'You're certainly full of surprises. This must have been very sudden. When did it take place? Why didn't you tell me? I feel a bit . . . well, greatly, hurt.'

'Oh, it's not like that. It's not a marriage in the normal sense of the word. I did it to help someone . . . though I'm very fond of her. I admire her. But you know me, Michael, well . . . you know I'm not exactly a straight guy.'

A fair-haired man in a green suit looked up sharply from his racing page with Biro poised.

'You mean you've got yourself into a pickle?'

'You could say that. You see. Well,' and then it came pouring out. Michael listened transfixed. How could Simon have got himself into a mess like this in so short a time?

'I had a research student in my department. Very bright. She's Iranian – Sarida. Came over here on a three-year student visa and loves it. Well, Sarida fell in love with an American guy – before my time of course, a couple of years ago. She got pregnant, then he scarpered. Didn't want to know about the baby – he just went back to the States and vanished. She went ahead and had the baby. Oh, everyone was very supportive. She's just the sort of student we could do with more of.

70

'Anyway, she had a baby daughter. Sweet little thing. Then her visa ran out. Well, by then she thought she didn't want to go back to Iran. She's become very Westernised, sophisticated, liberated. And also there was a complication. Her father, who had been a friend of the Shah, didn't think it would be a good idea. So she thought she'd better get legal advice.'

'Who did she go to?'

'Marten & Sayed, I think she said. They're supposed to specialise in her sort of case.'

'Well, you want to be careful. There are some dubious companies around who're in it just for the money. There are rich pickings to be made.'

'So she discovered. It's all a bit late now. Apparently they didn't give her good advice. This Sayed chap told her she ought to apply for political asylum, when he should have told her to get an extension on her student visa.'

Michael's attention strayed briefly from Simon. Mark Raymond had been seated behind a newspaper at the far end of the room – Michael hadn't seen him – and now he was getting up to leave and was coming over on his way out.

As he passed them he gave Michael's shoulder a squeeze and mouthed unctuously, 'Good to see you, Elliot. Must get together soon,' while his probing eyes raked over Simon's casual clothes and cropped hair, a quizzical eyebrow raised, the trace of a supercilious smile. His curiosity about Simon had been roused, just as it was about the acquaintance of anyone he knew. A face, a snippet of conversation, a gesture, body language – all would be stored away in that vast memory of his, to be brought out again and used, if required, at a future date.

For some reason, Michael thought, maybe because they were both Jewish, Raymond seemed to think they should be friends. Michael didn't particularly like Raymond, but he had had his uses in the past, and would undoubtedly have them again.

'Who was that creepy man?' Simon asked.

'An acquaintance,' Michael said.

'Anyway, where was I? Did I tell you they turned her down for political asylum?'

'Yes, you'd just said that when we were interrupted.'

71

'Well, we all got together and had a meeting about her. We thought the best thing for her to do would be to apply for the extension, as she should have done in the first place. But they turned down her application again. Obviously they thought she was trying it on this time, whereas it was really totally legitimate. The Dean even wrote a supporting letter, but they still turned it down.'

'So you married her?'

'In February. It seemed the only solution. We're all so fond of her. I'd got to know her quite well, she's got such a sweet little baby, and I was single and unattached. I thought maybe it would work out – no sex, of course – that she could move in with me and we could find a *modus vivendi*. So we had a registry office wedding in Manchester. The prof was best man, and two of my students agreed to be witnesses. Sarida moved in, plus the little girl – Soraya. But I only have a small flat, and it was quite obvious after only a week it wasn't going to work out. We tried. She was very considerate, but even so . . . I need space. The baby was upset all the time. She cried and cried. Sarida was always on the phone or in the bathroom when I wanted to be. The bathroom was festooned with clothes drying. Anyway we held out for three weeks. She said she hadn't given up her other flat – she'd let a friend stay in it. So she asked the friend to move out, she moved back and I had my peace again.'

'So?'

'So, what we didn't know was that the immigration authorities had been watching my flat and Sarida's. Now she's been hauled in for questioning. I'm due to be questioned soon. I don't know what the hell to do.'

Michael thought. 'Well, if you're serious, the very first thing Sarida must do is move back with you. Can't you get a bigger flat? Surely your mother would come up with the money?'

Simon looked doubtful, and underneath all his left-wing posturing, Michael glimpsed a spoilt boy, who had always had everything his own way even though everything he'd ever done had been a reaction to his parents' opulent lifestyle.

'I have a few useful contacts,' Michael said warily. Then his mind suddenly clicked. 'In fact, I have a very useful one. The Chief Whip, Mark Raymond, the man who just came over, he can pull strings and get you out of this mess.'

'That awful man?' Simon looked confused. 'What can he do? No, I was going to ask you . . . I have someone else in mind, a proper cabinet minister, James Askew. If you remember, it was I who first introduced him to you.'

'Askew? He's Environment. Why do you want to ask him? Raymond, I assure you, would be far more useful. He pulls all the strings, makes all the Ministers jump to his tune. Besides, he owes me a very big favour. I'll ask him and he'll get the Home Secretary on to it right away. No problem.'

'But, James—' Simon still looked confused.

'I really don't think James Askew could help all that much. He's not a very senior minister, and immigration isn't his province. Anyway, since you were friends at Cambridge, if you're that keen on him being involved, you could surely ask him direct?'

'Well no.' Simon was looking down at his drink, distinctly ill at ease.

'You were *just* good friends, I presume?' Michael asked in a sudden intuitive flash.

Simon looked up, his expression so vulnerable, so serious. 'Um. Not exactly, no.'

Michael's heart gave a leap. My God, he thought, surely not? And yet in a way it all fitted together. 'You mean you were lovers?'

'We were passionately in love,' Simon said in a hoarse whisper. 'But he was terrified our affair would become public. He always took extreme measures to keep it secret. In the end, he finished it because he couldn't stand the strain of it all. I thought I wanted to die when he ended it. That's really why I went abroad: I had to get away from everything that reminded me of him. We never kept in touch afterwards. He insisted the break must be total.'

'I see,' Michael said, and thought James must be even more terrified of the cat being let out of the bag now. What a stupendous piece of news! The holier-than-thou James Askew had a secret past. Here was treasure indeed. However, Michael's face, as it turned to Simon's, showed nothing of the turmoil of excitement within him, only compassion.

'Well,' he said, 'I still think the best outcome would be for me to see Raymond and discuss it with him. For the moment, let's leave Askew out of it. Believe me, the Chief Whip has far more clout. I'll

73

have him round for a drink. You'll see. We'll soon get things moving.'

For the moment, indeed, Michael had other favours to ask of James Askew.

Chapter 9

James hurried out of the Chamber and made his way along the central lobby as Big Ben was striking six. At St Stephen's Entrance he noticed the Lobby correspondent of the *Guardian* bearing down.

'James . . . Mr Askew . . . may I have a word?'

'Sorry, Peter, I really have to dash. Late for a meeting. Can we make it tomorrow?'

'Not really. I'd like a comment from you on Arthur Hall.'

'Ah yes.' Damn, he thought. 'Fine chap. We'll miss him. He'll be a great loss.'

'And what do you think about the Tories' prospects in a by-election?'

Oh God, James cursed inwardly, I'll be here for ever at this rate. 'Excellent,' he lied. 'No problem. We'll romp through. Must dash.'

Without making further eye contact or waiting for a reply, he walked smartly across the road and round the corner into Marsham Street where he hailed a taxi. He could have walked the whole way: it was no distance to the mansion block where the Hamptons had their London flat, but he didn't want any more hitches, nor did he want further encounters with journalists, and he most of all did not want to be seen. He was in a turmoil: already riven with guilt, but in a state of high excitement; it was as though he were being driven to Caroline's against his will. Her invitation was impossible to resist, yet he knew he was taking a risk.

He now realised why he had found it so easy to get a cab: there was a traffic jam round Parliament Square, backing up in all the surrounding streets. Car horns were hooting and idling buses were belching out clouds of fumes. James was feeling more tense than usual, strung out, almost as though he were in a race. Come on, come on, he thought, willing the traffic to move. At last – in fact seven minutes later – the cab was drawing up outside the imposing entrance to the mansion block. With his heart thumping wildly, he paid the cabbie, tipping him generously rather than waiting for change.

Inside, thank God, the porter was in a servile conversation with a middle-aged woman – 'Yes, madam. Certainly, madam' – and James hurried past, straight to the lifts at the back. One came almost immediately, and he stepped inside. As he did so he heard the rapid tap-tap of the woman's high heels. He pressed the button to close the doors, but it was one of those lifts that wait before moving off. The woman was breathless as she entered.

'Thank you so much for holding it. You're too kind,' she said, giving him a look as though she half recognised him – the price of appearing on *Newsnight* and *Question Time*. Normally he felt flattered by such recognition but now he was distinctly alarmed. Hoping she would get out before the fourth floor, he stared straight ahead in a thoughtful manner. She however continued to look at him with curiosity.

The lift jolted and stopped on Caroline's floor. The woman was getting out too. James fumbled at the clasp of his briefcase as though he were preparing for a business meeting. His playing for time paid off. There was no sign of her as he headed along the thickly carpeted corridor for number forty-five, the fire doors making a sensuous sucking noise as they closed behind him. He paused before a big gilt mirror to smooth his hair and compose himself.

At the large mahogany door he rang the bell, and assumed an expression of calm, as he imagined Caroline looking at him through the spy hole.

The door opened, and Caroline stood aside to let him in. Then she closed the door and leant back against it, her hands behind her back – the message needed no interpretation.

James kissed her lightly on the mouth, but the response was so passionate and yielding that he felt immediately aroused.

He drew back briefly. 'You look wonderful,' he said. 'There's something different about you.' He looked into her face, and they both felt the same urgent message.

'Just my hair,' she whispered, tossing her head a little. 'You've never seen me with it loose.'

It made her look sensual and irresistible. She was wearing a silk shift which had fallen open provocatively as if waiting for him to make the next move.

'God, you turn me on,' he said, pulling her towards him, his hands sliding down her thighs and feeling the tops of her stockings and her suspenders. He pressed her to him roughly, exploring under the parted silk shift, his excitement mounting as his hands wandered over her buttocks and he realised she was wearing nothing but the suspender belt. She sighed and moaned as his hands found their way.

'Let's go to bed,' she whispered hoarsely, leading him through the cool white drawing room. He could smell some sort of aromatic essence as she took him into the bedroom.

Caroline was in her element. It was very little to do with sex and much to do with the power she would feel when she added James Askew to her list of conquests. She liked men. She liked the way their minds worked. Once she had slept with a man she knew so much more about him. She knew James had not had sex for some time, she could tell by the eager way he had picked up the bait. She looked forward to meeting that perfect wife of his again, making small talk with her, the wife not knowing how much she, Caroline, knew of their most private life.

Caroline was lying back on the bed with her shift rucked up, abandoning herself to his frank gaze as he undressed. Suddenly it was as though all the tension that James had experienced over the last months was becoming unbearable. He felt a mixture of anger and elation. He lay down, seized her and flipped her over, like a doll. Nothing could stop him now. He drove inside her.

Caroline, who had been expecting an onslaught from the missionary position, was surprised by the lack of ceremony, but she found herself complying with the indignity of the situation. James scraped at a pillow and stuffed it under her hips. She felt the sweat from his hair, as he laboured above her, the tension unbearable until the joyous moment of release. He let out a muffled groan, as he heard Caroline gasp.

'Please could you get off me,' she asked politely a little later, as he lay limp and exhausted on top of her.

He rolled on to his back, putting his hand to his sweaty brow and said, 'I'm sorry. Did I hurt you? I really didn't mean to.'

Caroline, who was no stranger to bedroom encounters of this nature, mustered her composure. She had felt herself becoming aroused by James's violent lovemaking – something she generally avoided when she went to bed with a man from whom she wanted something. She liked to be in control and she was clever at simulating. But James had taken her by surprise and she had not had time to go through the normal ritual of feigned orgasmic appreciation. Now though, she decided it was her turn to take him by surprise, make sure this was an encounter he wouldn't forget . . .

James did not know how much time had passed but in the hot room, he was almost yielding to sleep. He felt blissfully relaxed, and empty. He closed his eyes, felt himself drifting, then Caroline's hands were expertly touching him and he found himself responding. She pulled him on top of her and soon she was moving beneath him. Then she was crying out and tearing at his back with her nails. The noises she was making shocked him; they were so animal and unreal, and any desire he might have had disappeared.

To his relief she became still.

'Thank you. You were amazing,' she lied, but she noticed how cold his eyes were as he looked down at her. She really wanted him to leave now. 'I knew you would be a marvellous lover,' she crooned, as she slid from under him and began dressing.

James quickly got off the bed too and started putting on his underpants. He watched her as she walked towards the drawing-room door, put out a deft hand for a comb from the dressing table and secured her hair into an elegant knot at the base of her neck. Then she turned to him with a brilliant smile.

'You deserve a drink,' she said.

She looked untouched, as if she had just returned from a cocktail party, and it occurred to James that he had not even seen her breasts. He buttoned his shirt and fastened his tie. Suddenly he felt terribly tired.

He was upset to see there were marks on the bedcover and there was also a musky smell of sex. He wanted to wash, a cool drink of water, to obliterate the whole episode from his memory.

As if by telepathy Caroline called from the other room. 'The bathroom's through to the right.'

Standing by the wash basin and looking in the mirror he could see dark circles under his eyes. He splashed water on his face and reached for a crisp linen towel on which he saw there was a large ducal coronet. It made him feel better . . . the Cabinet Minister and the Duchess, he thought wryly. What a long way he had come. Passing through the bedroom again, he looked over once more to the bed and tweaked its cover free of telltale creases.

Caroline stood composed and beautiful in front of the fireplace. She held out a glass to him, smiling brightly. 'Chablis with a lump of ice, very refreshing . . . Let's drink to next time,' she said.

Then she saw his expression and knew there would not be a next time.

'Don't worry. I always stay friends with my lovers,' she said.

He looked at her. She had enjoyed it, that at least was a relief. He had begun to doubt his talents as a lover. He had done things with her he would never do with Helena. Helena was not that sort of a woman; with her sex was all above love. What he had done with Caroline was nothing to do with love, but it had been exciting. On balance, though, he regretted it and he would try to forget it had happened. But he liked Caroline, there was something rather brave about her and she was right, they would remain friends.

As James got into a taxi he remembered with horror that he had left his dinner jacket at home. He needed it later as he was guest speaker at a livery dinner. He had meant to send the car to get it but had forgotten. He told the taxi to go directly to Pimlico. He would have a quick bath, not such a bad idea in the circumstances.

He hoped Helena would be busy. He didn't want to have to talk to her. She'd probably have a feeling about him, she was very intuitive.

But as he paid off the taxi the front door flew open and Helena was on the step, all smiles.

'What are you doing back at this time? What a lovely surprise. Would you like a cup of tea?' she called.

She seemed genuinely pleased to see him. Suddenly he felt terribly guilty. Covered in confusion, as if to hide his feelings, he hurried up the steps, and abruptly told her he was in a terrific hurry. He would have a quick bath before rushing to a dinner. He asked her to arrange for his car to collect him in half a hour. He was glad when she went to do this and he no longer was compelled to avoid looking her in the eye.

Chapter 10

On Friday, as she had long promised herself, Helena had a telephone chat with her friend Beth, who had recently become Deputy Head of a large comprehensive school in Edinburgh. Helena confided in her how worried she was about Rollo, who hated his boarding school. Beth sympathised with her and told her to take a firmer line. She too thought boarding schools for eight-year-olds were barbaric. 'Take him away,' she said. 'Or find him something nearer home.'

How good it had been to talk to Beth, Helena thought afterwards, even though she didn't think life was as clear-cut as Beth saw it. It was rare that one had a straight choice to make between good and bad, right and wrong – everything seemed to overlap.

After she had finished a bit of work in the studio, James had rung to say that because of an emergency Cabinet meeting he was running late and he would not be home by five-thirty as he had promised. Just as she had put the phone down, it rang again. It was Michael. She felt a surge of pleasure.

Michael wanted to know if she had time for a quick drink and a walk by the river before James returned.

Since their first afternoon together, they had met a number of times – they'd gone for a long walk by the Thames, had dinner in a small Italian restaurant, even had lunch at Bray.

They had talked about her marriage. 'We were really happy the first year or so,' she'd told him, 'but since then things have just sort of deteriorated. I suppose I hadn't thought it through, what it means being an MP's wife, living in someone else's pocket.'

'You can't allow your instincts to be stifled by someone else's demands,' Michael had said. 'You're a good painter. Surely, you should just get on with your life. James doesn't have a right to every moment of your time. His expectations shouldn't diminish all your ambitions.'

'You're right. I'm beginning to see that.'

Helena thought: here I go, he's seduced me into saying far more than I intended, yet he never gives anything away.

One day she had boldly asked him if Caroline were his mistress. He had not responded well, but had been edgy, and silent for a moment. Then he looked Helena straight in the eye. He had to make a few things clear: that he swam in several different streams, each separate from the other. Helena would have to learn that when she was with him, she would have his complete attention but never quite all of him. No one woman ever had that. He had moved his head slightly to one side, giving his face a less approachable air, and he said the words slowly as if to emphasise them. 'Caroline is an old and dear friend. I admire her very much. I've a number of friends who mean a great deal to me, but you are quite unlike any of them.'

They had looked steadily at each other. She had thought she understood what he was saying, but she wasn't sure. Jealousy could have no place in her relationship with him.

Since that afternoon, he'd telephoned her every day. She was almost unable to think of anything else, in the grip of feelings beyond her control. Whenever she approached her work in the studio, his presence, his voice, his gentleness intruded. Over and over again she had gone through every scrap of their conversations, every gesture, every accidental and not so accidental brushing of hands, the light kisses as he left her, analysing for every nuance of meaning. At the same time, she saw herself reacting almost like a teenager. It was bewildering to be struck with this sort of heady obsession at the age of thirty-five. And yet her body was alert, just waiting, waiting for their next meeting.

'I'm afraid I can't,' she now told Michael, in answer to his invitation. 'We've got a fundraiser dinner in the constituency. James isn't back yet and I must ring them to tell them we're running late.'

'So I'd better get off the phone, in other words?' Michael said.

'Yes, I'm afraid so.'

'Till next week then.' The phone was abruptly put down and Helena sensed he was miffed.

She rang Cynthia, the agent, and explained they would be slightly late. Cynthia was not amused. Ministerial duties, as she frequently complained, should not come before constituency matters, especially fundraisers, and this one was very important. Lord Marcher, the guest speaker, had been a tremendous pull; they could have sold all the tickets twice over.

Just as Helena replaced the receiver the phone rang again. Helena suspected it might be Michael, but it was the Matron from Rollo's school. She felt disappointment, then immediately her mind focused in an intense anxiety. Rollo was in the sick bay; he had come down with abdominal pain and a slight temperature that morning. Helena looked blankly at the kitchen wall above the telephone. She didn't know what to do.

'Matron, can I ring you back when I've had time to think? . . . Yes . . . I'll talk to you in about half an hour. Goodbye.'

'Mum, what's wrong?'

Kirsty had come into the kitchen at the tail end of the conversation. Helena sat down in the wicker chair by the table and nervously bit the skin around the end of one of her fingernails. She glanced up at Kirsty and was astonished to see her sporting some long dangly fish-shaped earrings. She was also wearing eyeliner.

'Kirsty, where did you get those earrings?' Helena asked. 'They're extraordinary.'

Kirsty raised her hand to feel one of them and replied, 'Aren't they lovely? Granny sent them to me.'

'Kirsty, you've had your ears pierced! When on earth did you do that?' Helena was shocked. If she hadn't been so worried about Rollo she would have been very angry.

Kirsty saw her advantage. 'Mum, can we talk about it later? All the girls at school have it done and, by the way, don't blame Granny. She thinks you know all about it. Not that I lied or anything, I just didn't say you didn't know. That's not the same thing, is it?'

'No, Kirsty, but you shouldn't have gone behind my back. Couldn't we have talked about it?'

'Well, you've been ever so odd lately. Harriet and I are worried about you, Mum.' Kirsty sat down in the chair next to Helena.

'Oh, I'm sorry, darling. And now Rollo's in the sick bay – he's got awful stomach cramps and has been sick. I should go down now.'

Kirsty was dreading another weekend in Sussex. 'Wouldn't it be better if Harriet and I stayed here, and you went to Oxford to see

Rollo? You'll only be missing the dinner and some smelly coffee mornings.'

'You mustn't talk like that, Kirsty. They're very important.'

'Why shouldn't I talk like that? You do.'

'When?'

'I heard you the other night rowing with James. You said "ghastly weekends".'

'Oh did I? Well, I didn't mean it. I was angry. What else did you hear?'

'Everything. We both did. We always do. You think we sit in our rooms not caring, but it's awful. We want to come down and join in but Granny says we mustn't. She says you and James have to sort it out.'

'So you talk to Granny a lot about us?'

'Well, yes. I heard James shouting about the phone bill. Well, he shouldn't worry because Granny always rings us back so she pays for most of the calls.'

'Oh I know, darling, I know. Let me give you a hug. I've been a rotten mother recently.'

'No you haven't, you're never a rotten mother. Anyway you stood up to James about Easter. We're going to Granny's and I wanted to come down and tell James I remember him promising to keep Easter clear, and then he tells you he's fixed up all those things for you to do.'

'I know, darling, but it's all sorted out now,' said Helena.

'It's not sorted out. It will just go on and on. What are we supposed to do in Sussex? I hate going there, and I miss Daddy.'

Kirsty put both her arms around Helena and cried. Helena held her close.

Neither of them had heard the door open and close. James was standing in the kitchen doorway, still wearing his coat. He was in a very bad mood. After the Cabinet meeting, he'd had to go back to his office and had been on the point of leaving when the phone had rung. It had been Michael Elliot, asking him to push through the Hampton business. More like turning a blind eye to certain irregularities.

This was the part of politics James intensely disliked. People were always asking for favours. The Hampton development was turning into a mess. He'd given Michael a polite brush-off. He had heard the anger in Elliot's voice, but he'd cut him short. Too bad.

'Helena. Are you ready?'

'I am, James, but there's a problem.'

'Well, tell me about it in the car. We're late.'

'I can't. I have to talk about it now. Rollo's in the sick bay at school – he's got awful stomach pains.'

'Is he in danger?'

'No, I don't think so. But it might be appendicitis.'

'Did they say that?'

'Well, no, but . . . the doctor's seeing him again later.'

'Come along, Helena. There's nothing you can do. The boy's in good hands. Have you left all your numbers with the school?'

'Not yet. I said I'd ring back. I don't think I should come down with you, James. I think I should drive to Oxford.'

James had had a hard day. An emergency Cabinet meeting had come fast on the heels of two ministerial visits. Then he'd been delayed at his office. The drive down to Sussex loomed ahead. He had let the ministerial car go as, strictly speaking, it should not be used for constituency functions. Helena was a good driver and he had planned a catnap and to write his speech for tonight.

He spoke with exaggerated patience. 'Helena, the boy's in good hands. We can be contacted at any time. If necessary, you can go to Oxford tomorrow.'

He looked worn out. She felt torn. If only this hadn't come in the middle of all the other rows, she might have been able to act more resolutely. 'Oh, all right. Let's go. I'll ring Matron from the car,' she said, picking up her bag. When she saw Kirsty's face she knew she had made the wrong decision.

At seven-twenty they phoned Cynthia, the agent, from the car to say they were fifteen minutes away. 'We've been stalling,' she replied briskly. 'I'm afraid the photo call will have to be very quick; everyone wants their dinner.'

Cynthia awaited them on the hotel steps. She wore a black trouser suit and her short dark hair was shaved at the back. Her only concession to femininity was a choker pearl necklace. The effect was incongruous, the more so as the other female guests were attired in their best cocktail dresses, Crimplene and easy care in primary colours and all finishing just below the knee. It had been rumoured that Cynthia was not her proper name and she had assumed it to promote a falsely superior background. Helena had often tried to get pally with her but Cynthia had long ago decided that wives were to be kept at arm's length and firmly in their place. Let them step out of line or worse, into the wrong line, and they were trouble. She knew she had a special relationship with James.

As Helena and James walked into the lobby of the uncomfortably named The Horse's Arms Cynthia greeted them both: Helena with little more than a perfunctory nod and James with a kiss firmly on the mouth. James waited until her back was turned before wiping his mouth with his handkerchief.

James knew the importance of letting his agent feel she was the only one who really understood him, and that it was necessary to let a little sexuality creep into the body language. In fact he found Cynthia physically anodyne, but the necessity of flirting with the ladies on the executive, the marvellous band of unsung heroines who addressed envelopes and arranged coffee mornings, was something most Members accepted. They were the backbone of the Party . . . and Cynthia established the pecking order when she kissed James. He loathed this aspect of his constituency life, but he had learnt to do it. His work at the Bar had been no less theatrical. And so he went along with it and as a result Cynthia was a marvellous agent, one of the best.

'This way. Lord Marcher's in the Granada Suite and the photographer's waiting,' said Cynthia. Helena had often thought her affected way of speaking made her sound excitingly central European but there, as far as Helena was concerned, the favourable comparisons ended. Cynthia's past was a complete mystery.

She turned to Helena again. 'You can wait here. I expect you'd like to freshen up after the drive and we only want James, our guest of honour, myself and the Chairman for the photo.' She turned her back before Helena could respond and she and James disappeared through the swing doors.

Helena found her way to the bar where she had been told some of the guests were having a pre-dinner drink.

'Oh Helena dear, we wondered what on earth had happened to you. Dinner's been put back to eight fifteen so we're all getting tipsy.' One of James's Ladies' Committee members took Helena by the hand

and led her to a table where several of the women were seated. Helena declined the offer of a gin and tonic and reluctantly sat down next to the Associate Chairman's wife, Beryl, a sprightly woman in her sixties.

'So how long did it take you to get here?' was Beryl's first enquiry, followed by another and another. How long did it take James to get to Westminster? How long did it take them to get to the cottage from the station? She leant forward listening intently to Helena's replies, clasping her snakeskin handbag to her chest while she spoke. This gave her the appearance of expecting imminent departure, but that would have made things far too easy. The questions continued swiftly, focusing now on Helena's domestic arrangements, the cottage and where they lived in London. Helena was evasive. Beryl had been through this on countless previous occasions and James had warned Helena to be careful when talking about their life in London. On no account must the constituents think their life was easy, it might create envy and resentment. Helena knew that Beryl and her husband Frank were worth millions, having sold their family farm for development, but she also knew James was right. Beryl would be the first to complain if she thought their Member of Parliament was living high, wide and handsome.

Beryl eased herself forward in the slippery plastic armchair. Traces of lipstick had run down the fine lines around her mouth. She tightened her lips before delivering her parting comments. Helena was transfixed by the mouth, and as it compressed itself she was reminded of a small lethal sea creature.

'Well, I don't know. Two homes and all that domestic help. I do think MPs have the most marvellous life and it must be lovely for you, going to all those dinners and not having to do any cooking.' Beryl rose to her feet. 'It's been very pleasant talking to you. I do hope we'll see you at our coffee morning, one on Easter Sunday and two the following week. They'll help to fill your time during your holiday.' Beryl lingered over the word 'holiday' and was gratified to see that the entire group was now listening. She continued, 'Robert's wife always gets to events and she has a job running the Oxfam shop and, of course, their constituency is much further from London. I believe she even does secretarial work in her husband's office. She's such a lovely person and such a help to her husband.'

'She sounds a treasure,' replied Helena. 'Of course, I'd be delighted to help in the office here, but I have to earn enough to support my three children, and unfortunately the Association can't afford it.' Beryl flounced to the powder room.

'Come on, girls, let's get Helena a gin and tonic. I think she deserves it,' the pretty young woman on Helena's right said.

'Do you know, I think I will after all,' Helena replied.

On the way into dinner Ray bounced up to Helena. 'Saw you talking to her ladyship Beryl. She's all bum and varicose veins. Don't listen to her. You've a great following here. My wife and I'll never forget the way you came to see her in hospital, bringing those lovely kiddies of yours and all those flowers. You're a breath of fresh air round here. You've livened the place up no end.'

'Oh thank you, Ray. You've really cheered me.'

'Well, I mean it. Before you came the place was moribund, a few old ladies like her ladyship. If they'd broken wind on a duck pond they wouldn't have moved a mallard. By the way, how are the little ones?'

Helena told him about Rollo.

'You oughtn't to be here if your boy's ill. Where did you say he was, in Oxford?' Ray put his hand on Helena's arm. 'Look, Helena, if you need running to the train or anything, just give me the wink. If the school rings, well, I'll be watching to see if I can help.'

Helena smiled. 'Thank you, Ray, I know you mean it.'

They took a quick look at the seating plan set up on an easel just inside the dining-room door. 'Oh lucky you, next to Lord Marcher and Frank. Well, you won't get a word in edgeways with Lord Marcher if he's got Beryl on his other side,' Ray said, rolling his eyes to heaven and giving Helena a wink.

Helena sat miserably at the table. She thought about Rollo. Was his illness her punishment for being happy for the first time in ages? She wished she were a long way away from the Florida cocktail, a mixture of tinned grapefruit and hard glazed cherries, followed by overdone roast beef curling at the edges and floating on a syrup of glutinous gravy.

A pretty waitress came round with the vegetables. She leant over Frank's shoulder. He didn't notice her plump bosom as it brushed his ear, he was too busy piling food on to his plate.

'Potatoes, sir?' she asked. 'New, roast, boiled or sauté? . . . Carrots, cauliflower, sprouts? . . . Yorkshire pudding?' Frank took everything and piled it on his plate until it spilled over the edge. The waitress smiled happily when she saw her contribution to the early demise of the obese Conservative Chairman. (Her father was a Labour candidate.) 'Enjoy your meal,' she chimed, as she moved towards Helena, who took a spoonful of carrots.

Frank did not turn to Helena as he said, 'They do lay on a lovely spread here. We don't have another meal this weekend, just a light supper tomorrow. In any case, we usually have our meal at six and watch the news on the tele. James has been on a lot recently.'

Helena had a gloomy picture of Frank and Beryl's front room complete with his and hers TV tables, and wondered if they ever considered life might hold more than constituency functions and tele. She tried desperately to make conversation with Frank's profile. Lord Marcher, as predicted, was monopolised by Beryl. Helena had to admire him for doing his stuff.

Frank, on the other hand, did not think it was part of his remit to talk while he was eating. He wished Helena would get on with her dinner and leave him in peace.

Helena found the silence oppressive and embarrassing. Finally she heard herself saying to Frank, 'Have you ever been in love?' Frank was busy separating a large piece of beef from what looked like a rubber band.

He turned to Helena and his mouth opened, revealing the amassed contents, like a cement mixer. 'Mind your own business.' His face went very red and he gave an immense swallow and continued inspecting the rubber band.

'Excuse me, madam. You're wanted on the phone,' the hotel manager interrupted. Helena felt sick as she picked up the receiver in the lobby.

'Now don't worry, he's in very good hands,' the Matron said soothingly. 'We've just moved him to the Radcliffe to keep him under observation. They think it might be appendicitis. The symptoms are about right. He's still in quite a lot of pain and he's been sick again . . . No, the consultant says he doesn't plan to do anything at the moment . . .'

'I'll come up right away.'

'Well yes, Mrs Askew, if I were in your place I'd try to get here tonight.'

When Helena put down the receiver she felt terribly alone.

'How is he?' The voice came from Ray. He stood very firm and solid by Helena's side. 'I can run you to the station now if you like. Then you'll be home by half-past ten, you can pick up your car and be in Oxford just after midnight.'

It struck Helena at that moment how strange it was that it never occurred to her or Ray that James should be at her side, but that is how it was with political families. She knew that now.

James did not look round as she approached. He was deep in conversation with Cynthia. She tapped him on the shoulder.

'Rollo's in hospital. They may have to operate.'

There was no reaction from James but Cynthia turned round. 'Oh dear. James told me your son was ill. I must say, as I said to James, I'm very impressed. You made the right decision coming here tonight in the circumstances. You're beginning to be a good political wife, Helena – very loyal.'

James saw Helena's face and hissed under his breath. 'Don't say it, Helena. Just for once. She didn't mean it like that.' He quickly took her arm and steered her away from the table.

She looked at James and angry tears welled in her eyes. 'James, if you know anything at all, you know how wrong it was of me to come here tonight, and I'll never do such a thing again. The children must come first. I'm going now. I'm getting the train and leaving you the car so that you won't be stranded.'

'But you'll miss the speeches. I really think you're over-reacting. There's nothing you can do. You should go up tomorrow morning. You always over-dramatise things, Helena. Have a brandy and calm down.'

'I've brought the car round to the front.' It was Ray. Helena turned to him; he took her arm and they left.

Nobody else noticed her go. James went back to the table and the hotel manager came over to him. 'Your wife seemed very upset. Is anything the matter?'

'A minor domestic problem,' James replied.

Chapter 11

It was Sunday, not yet nine o'clock in the morning. Rollo was safely in bed at Richmond Terrace. It had not been his appendix after all, but a twisted gut, and Helena had brought him back from Oxford yesterday morning. She had left him momentarily in the care of Maria and Rosaria, who were fussing over him like broody hens.

Battersea Park was wonderful at this hour, with few people about. Helena was walking with Michael under the great plane trees, the sun and drifting clouds making their shadows dance on the grass. The air had that earthy smell of spring, and a feeling of expectation, almost at the end of that long period of waiting before the fresh soft green leaves burst forth.

'So you're going to your mother's over Easter – on Good Friday you say. You've squared it with James?'

'Well, almost.'

'Is he going too?'

'No, he'll be in the constituency.'

'How on earth will you do the trip in that tiny car of yours?'

'With difficulty.'

'It so happens that I have to go down to the Plymouth headquarters on Good Friday. I could give you a lift if you like.'

'That would be wonderful. But there will be quite a lot of baggage to go as well as me and the three children, and Clovis.'

'I'd be delighted. No problem. I can even bring you back as I'll be in Plymouth quite a bit at that time.'

'You could see Maryzion . . .'

'Yes. I'd love to see it. You've told me so much about it, I feel I almost know it already.'

'It's a really important place for me. And I'm sure you'll love my mother.'

'Yes, I'd like to meet her. She sounds fun . . . and wise. Won't she think it rather odd though? Me coming with you, I mean.'

'Well, not if you're giving me a lift.'

'If you think it's all right . . . ?'

'Where do you stay when you go to Plymouth?'

Michael looked edgy. 'I have places.' His answer did not invite further questioning.

'It's just that . . . you could stay at Maryzion for a night . . . if you liked.'

Michael squeezed her hand. 'A lovely idea, but not on, really.'

'My mother's very broad-minded. She wouldn't breathe a word to James,' Helena said, remembering her mother's tolerance in the dreadful period after she was widowed, when she'd been trying to find her feet and had made some awful mistakes with men.

'I'll think about it,' Michael said. The whole idea had taken him by surprise, but it was a very pleasing surprise.

An hour later, coming downstairs with Rollo's breakfast tray Helena heard the telephone ringing. It was her mother.

'So how is he?' Cornelia's voice sounded anxious. 'Kirsty rang me yesterday. Why didn't you tell me? I would have come up to London straight away to be with the girls.'

'Mummy, I'm sorry I didn't ring you myself, but I was so rushed and I knew Kirsty would call you. The news is fine. He's just had some scrambled eggs in bed. I brought him back to London yesterday morning.' Helena explained about the twisted gut. 'They've given him some wonder drug which relaxes the insides. It's supposed to right itself after a while.'

'Will you still be able to make it down for Easter?'

'We're coming on Good Friday at tea time. James did promise to keep Easter free but then he fixed up millions of constituency things. I might have to leave the children with you after Easter and make a dash to Sussex. I suppose I should. It's a ten-day recess.'

'Surely, darling, you should see how Rollo is, then decide? You sound tired.'

'I am rather. I've been trying to catch up on work.'

'Kirsty told me you're going to do a portrait of David Banks's children. I would have thought Labour and Tory wives wouldn't mix.'

'Well, David Banks's wife is Violet Campbell. Remember? She

was at school with me. I'm not going to give up my friends, and I really can't let James's politics interfere with my professional life. I need the money, apart from anything else. And it'll be lovely seeing Violet regularly again.'

'It will raise a few eyebrows, though.'

'Dead right. The Whips have probably got out their little black book already and added this to my list of transgressions. Our phone's tapped, so I hope they're enjoying this conversation.'

There was a pause at the other end of the line. Cornelia had forgotten that the phone was tapped and she thought, with amusement, of the endless hours of domestic trivia she discussed with Kirsty.

'Well, I hope whoever listens has a selective ear. We must be terribly boring,' Cornelia said.

Helena realised she must be more careful about what she said on the telephone. She hoped her mother would pick up her code.

'By the way, Mummy, we're getting a lift down. A friend has to make a trip to Plymouth. James has put every possible obstacle between him and a family Easter. He just doesn't want to come to Maryzion. I was talking to this friend recently – she said it wouldn't be any problem, as it's on her way and she has a big car. She'll drop us with you, then go on.'

'Oh, yes.' There was a silent acknowledgement at the other end of the phone.

'You don't mind, do you, Mummy?'

'Of course not, dear.'

Cornelia felt slightly taken aback, but she wasn't going to sound it. She had heard the slight change of pitch in Helena's voice and her almost breathless excitement.

'It will be nice to meet your friend. Will she be staying?'

'Um . . . I don't know. I'm not sure . . . Anyway, she's longing to meet you.'

'I'll make up an extra bed, just in case,' Cornelia said.

Cornelia went on to explain how, to relieve the sense of isolation and help with the bills, she had let out some rooms in the house – 'to a charming American who's doing a PhD in music at Exeter University. And guess what? He likes accompanying singers on the piano. Hugh Faulkner found him for me and, by the way, Hugh and

Dorothy are coming to dinner on Saturday night.'

'Oh, Hugh's such fun. How's his book going? When I last saw him he was writing about medieval music. How's the dreaded Dorothy?'

'Hugh's book comes out soon and then he's thinking of taking a year's sabbatical. Dorothy wants to move to London. She's become a big number with her magistrate's thing, Chairman of the Parole Board or something.'

'Golly, it shows how out of touch I am. I won't let this happen again. You'll see more of us and we're going to have a lovely Easter. I must go, I can hear Rollo calling.'

' 'Bye, darling.'

Helena went upstairs to Rollo. He lay surrounded by gadgets and his Game Boy. The television blared from his desk. Clovis was stretched out on Rollo's pillow chewing a rubber lookalike of Mrs Thatcher, which squeaked gratingly on every bite.

'Darling, that's naughty. You shouldn't let Clovis do that,' Helena said, rescuing the piece of sodden, mangled rubber, but she couldn't pretend to be cross for long. Thank goodness Rollo was home, and that she'd stuck to her guns over Easter.

Chapter 12

The sun shone strongly as Lady Cornelia Douglas drifted off to sleep with the spaniels on her lap. She lay in the gazebo at the southern corner of the garden, protected from the chilly April wind, which ruffled the apple trees and the flowering cherries. Every now and then there was a gentle rustle and a snowstorm of blossom came tumbling to the ground. When she woke, the lawns were a pale shade of pink; they reminded her of confetti. She dozed off again thinking of her wedding day. She remembered every second of it, as if it had just happened.

Her husband, Gerald, had been dead for eight years now. It had been Midsummer's Day, the roses in full bloom. He had discovered the lump the previous month, and the life simply trickled out of him, slowly at first, and then with a ferocious urgency, as if he had another engagement elsewhere and had to be going. When he finally left her for his private journey, the first he had made without her for thirty years, he did not say goodbye. He slipped away quietly, like an honoured guest who does not want to spoil the party by announcing his departure.

The nurse who looked after Gerald in the last few weeks thought Lady Cornelia slightly unhinged. She had never seen grief like it. She told the GP that Lady Cornelia might die of a broken heart. But then her daughter came for a month; she held her mother, stroked her. They cried quietly together, and sat in the gazebo where Cornelia now rested.

Very slowly, Cornelia started to arrange the flowers in the house again, talk to the gardener, and at last to sort out Gerald's things. She went to the hairdresser in Exeter and in a cathartic gesture, cut off some of her long tawny-coloured hair. She felt better for this, more in control, and as if to compensate for the loss of the hair which Gerald had so adored, she bought six bantams with long plumed trousers. They were her consolation while she viewed the puzzle of her future. With the help of Mrs Finch, who lived in the lodge cottage and was Cornelia's friend and right hand, she prepared part of the house for a tenant so that she would not be alone during the long winter.

Eventually Helena had returned to Suffolk to her family. She was heavily pregnant. The baby came early and Cornelia went to help her daughter. When she returned to Maryzion she was, as Mrs Finch said, 'her old self again.'

When Gerald died, Cornelia was forty-eight, and her son-in-law Anthony commented to Helena, 'Your mother won't be alone for long, you can take it from me. She's a very attractive woman.'

Events proved him correct. But today Cornelia was alone for the moment, through choice rather than necessity.

She awoke feeling calm and happy. For an instant she could not remember why, until she brought her mind back to the April after-noon and remembered the reason for the reassuring feeling of contentment. Helena and the grandchildren should be arriving to stay for Easter soon. She continued resting in a happy state, somewhere between sleeping and waking, and then applied her mind to the plans for the weekend.

Helena was getting a lift down with a friend, who just happened to be going to Plymouth. Cornelia was not going to jump to any conclusions, although she had caught that note of giddy excitement in Helena's voice, and guessed that the 'she' was really a 'he'. I hope Helena's not going to do anything stupid, she thought.

Cornelia adored all her grandchildren, but she had a very special relationship with Kirsty, possibly because she could have been Cornelia's own daughter, the late baby that she and Gerald had still prayed for, even after years of trying to provide a brother or sister for Helena. Cornelia believed in miracles but this was not to be. Instead, fate gave her Helena's three children, her grandchildren, and then deprived them of their father. Cornelia and Helena, two women, mother and daughter, were bound together by their grief, and their love for these three precious children.

That was until James Askew appeared on the scene, but Cornelia decided not to let the thought of the ill match with James spoil the afternoon.

Kirsty had warned her that the boarding school where poor Rollo had been sent had insisted his thatch of red-gold hair be cut into short back and sides. 'You'll get quite a shock, Granny. He looks awful. His hair sticks up like a lavatory brush and he's terribly thin,' she said over the phone.

Cornelia knew the children ached for their trips to Maryzion, where their rooms, containing most of their possessions from the house in Suffolk, cried out for them, and the pony Cornelia looked after for them had grown fat from lack of exercise. Rollo would one day inherit the house, and she had always hoped Helena and Anthony would take it over until Rollo came of age.

James seemed set on breaking the dynasty: he had told Cornelia that he disapproved of inherited wealth.

'Then why are you serving in a Conservative Government?' she had asked him.

He avoided a full answer, lecturing her on the meritocracy and his own rise to power without the advantage of a silver spoon.

Cornelia looked at the house, basking in the spring sunshine, awaiting the arrival of the family. She was convinced that houses had souls. But Maryzion had been so empty in the last two years. She sensed its moods and tried to reassure it. Today it was able to open its doors and windows, welcome the light and air into the shuttered silent rooms. It waited eagerly for the children's voices, the banging of doors, the running of taps in the claw-footed cast-iron baths. The nursery staircase would creak and sigh as the feet pounded up and down the worn cord carpet. And all the familiar noises of Cornelia's childhood would echo through the house with rejoicing.

Cornelia heard Mrs Finch's voice calling down the garden. 'Lady C., I'm just off now. I'll be back tomorrow at nine. Don't do the vegetables for lunch, I'll do them. The dinner's all ready, just heat up the fish pie. Have a lovely evening.'

Cornelia felt a sudden chill, as the mound of Cavalier spaniels that lay on her lap leapt up in unison, barking hysterically. They raced down the gravel path in the direction of Mrs Finch's voice. No one arrived or departed from Maryzion without the canine chorus.

She looked for the shorthand notepad from which she was seldom separated. It had fallen to the floor while she'd slept. When she retrieved it, she noticed the gazebo floor was covered in petals, and leaves from the previous autumn's gales. She made a mental note that she and Kirsty could clean it out tomorrow. It would be a good chance to talk to her; Cornelia suspected there would be a lot of talking this weekend. She looked at her list, a long one even by her standards. She noticed with satisfaction that most of the items were ticked: sheets, towels, lay fires, flowers, plant urns on terrace, Easter eggs, rabbit – Cornelia and Helena planned to give the children a rabbit for Easter and it was now in the stable block, master of a brand-new hutch which would be transported to Richmond Terrace. Under all this were the menus for the weekend. Cornelia felt a thrill of anticipation.

Chapter 13

Michael had just come from an intriguing, and ultimately satisfying, meeting with Mark Raymond. In the end he had agreed to a drink at Number Twelve Downing Street, the Chief Whip's official residence. Michael had been there only once before, and enjoyed Raymond's sumptuous surroundings. Here, he felt, was the seat of power, with Number Ten but a step away. And Raymond was a welcoming host.

After the standard amount of pleasantries, Michael had mentioned almost casually that he had a bit of a problem on which he would value Raymond's help. He had seen the instant flicker of suspicion or was it fear in Raymond's eyes.

Of course, Michael guessed, Raymond was obviously worrying about Michael's generous contribution each year to Conservative Party funds, and would be anxious not to put it in jeopardy.

Michael had told him about Simon and Sarida, suitably edited, and had asked if he would put in a good word for them with the Home Secretary. He could see instantly that it went against the grain. Raymond did not like to be cornered. It was his accustomed role to do the cornering. However, with Michael he had met his equal in that field. But Raymond agreed, albeit somewhat truculently. Raymond then moved on quite blatantly to discussing the financial health of Elliot Enterprises, and enquiring whether the Party could continue to rely on the benefit of its substantial support.

Michael had given him a weak smile, and told him that much would depend on how well the development of Western Environmental Services and his landfill projects went over the next few months.

Raymond had grasped the implications immediately and deftly changed tack.

'Heard all about the Hamptons' development. Sounds exciting. Sorted out all the problems with Askew, I take it?'

'I'm sure Askew will come round to my way of thinking,' Michael said. Raymond had understood instantly that Michael had some new card up his sleeve.

'Bit of a maverick is Askew, very bright, totally straight. Unbelievably ambitious. Inclined to rock the boat for everyone else. Always felt he was a menace on the back benches; that's why he was given Environment. But of course he won't stop there. There's a rumour he might challenge the leadership, and he does have a growing following.'

Michael had nodded encouragingly.

Raymond had flowed on: 'A number of us would like to stop him in his tracks, shunt him off somewhere to some graveyard like the Home Office. He'd be out of the way there – and he'd have plenty to keep him occupied with the great flood of immigrants we're getting from Hong Kong and elsewhere, and the prisons overflowing – this new move to release lifers would scupper him.'

Michael had listened in amazement to the torrent of spite. He hadn't realised James had so many enemies. 'Love to know what makes him tick,' Raymond had added.

Raymond was being remarkably indiscreet. Was he coaxing Michael to come up with some dirt on James? If so, he would be disappointed. Michael had no intention of showing his trump card. He was still ruminating on the best way to make use of Simon's startling revelation. And at the moment his centre of interest was James's wife.

Michael had known Helena for three weeks but had not seduced her; for him such restraint was a record. Helena was different from his current mistresses, who were beginning to bore him. She was a challenge. In some ways she was quite bold, but she had a curious vulnerability as well, especially where her marriage was concerned. He saw she was still bound up in the powerful memory of her first husband, Anthony, and had thought that by marrying James – and he knew of old that James's aloof impenetrability could be magnetically appealing to women – she could somehow relive an ideal marriage. But her honeymoon with James was well and truly over; he could see that James continually undervalued her and she was locked in a pattern of capitulation.

Having sought to replace her first husband, Helena had been

dazzled by James's rather glamorous image and had failed to see how very different James and Anthony were. Michael believed that James would always let her down, because he had fought hard to get where he was; he could not afford the luxury of being there for Helena's family and indeed for her own feminine needs. He had long ago learned the habit of being entirely focused on his own life and ambitions. And from what Michael gathered he lacked the capacity for tenderness, probably because he had never experienced it as a child . . . and underlying this was the fact that he had no passion for women and though Helena did not show it openly, he was sure that beneath that serene, rather sad face, lay a great reserve of emotion waiting to be tapped. Still, Michael would not rock the boat.

Michael sensed he was falling in love with Helena. The trip to Helena's family home at Easter, in theory, offered possibilities. What he would really like to do would be to sweep her off on her own somewhere, but that wasn't going to be possible just yet. She was very close to her mother and he knew she was anxious to mend the rift between them. But he also sensed she wanted to win her mother's approval of him. Her devotion as a daughter, as well as a mother, was one of her attractions. Helena had told him of the bond between her daughter Kirsty and her grandmother too, and that made another reason why Michael wanted to meet them all. The occasion presented the perfect opportunity to infiltrate Helena's family – in a casual sort of way – it all sounded rather beguiling.

Where they lived was only thirty miles or so from Plymouth, where Western Environmental Services had its headquarters. He had arranged a special meeting with two of his colleagues there, to finalise details on a new project.

The phone rang – it was Caroline to say that she'd just heard from James that the grant was going through. 'Half a mill – not bad! That should cover a few trees and fish!'

'Fantastic! By the way, I'll get back to you soon on that other matter. I'm off to Devonport to tie up some details.'

'Will you be able to call in on your way?'

Michael caught the anxiety in her voice.

'Bertie's going up to Scotland for some fly-fishing. I'll be home all on my ownsome.'

'I'm afraid I've a horribly tight schedule,' Michael said. 'But talk to you soon. And well done. It's great news. James told me he had passed the revised plans. I believe the JCBs have already moved in on the farm?'

'Yes, the lorries are rolling.'

'Sorry about my schedule.'

He could sense the disappointment in her voice as she said goodbye.

Well, James might not understand women, but he had come up with the goods – and quickly too. Michael congratulated himself. James had been a difficult fish to play but as bait Caroline never failed. The weekend at Markham Court had been set up with this in mind, but flirting with James's wife had turned out to be an un- expected bonus and not at all what he had planned.

As a result he had not seen his other two mistresses for some time. The one who worked in the American Embassy in Berne didn't mind much. She had another lover anyway and there had often been long gaps in their affair. But he had noticed recently that her American Express bill, which he paid, had been getting very large. He would see her about that when he went to Geneva.

Anna Van Cutsum was a different matter. He had to confess he had behaved very badly, even for him. She was in love with him, he knew that, and he had even thought he was in love with her. A year ago she had got pregnant. He had not asked her to marry him and she had had an abortion. Two months later Anna married an Italian banker. She had only been married for six months when she and Michael had started their affair again. She had rung him several times last week and he had not rung back.

He thought of Helena and wondered if she might be the woman who could really hold his interest.

His mind reverted to Caroline's scheme, and what it would mean for him. He would have to talk to James again about his reward. Michael had already suggested a future directorship in Western Environmental Services, and share options in the group. James, being the straight soul that he was, had demurred. Had it been any other politician Michael might have thought he was angling for more, but he suspected James did not want his pristine political image tarnished in any way, if the rumours were true that he was in line for the leadership. Michael had then suggested that the share options

102

could be in his wife's name, but James had rejected that too. Thinking about it now, though, Michael had a better plan, especially as James would be out of the way down in his constituency and he would have the field free in Devon.

From what Helena had told him in her amazingly frank way, James and Cornelia couldn't stand the sight of one another. It had obviously suited James to alienate Helena from her mother as he would have more control over her that way. Michael thought the grandmother had every right to speak her mind, particularly on the subject of Rollo. Cornelia had opposed James's plan to send the boy away to school. Michael was quite frank with Helena when she raised the subject: to him the ubiquitous suppressed middle-class Englishman owed much of his condition to the public school system. He looked forward to meeting Helena's family. He already had a picture of them in his mind – the children as he had seen them in Helena's paintings in Richmond Terrace and their grandmother, a little on the plump side with grey hair, twinset and pearls.

Michael intended to make a play for Helena in Devon. After all, he might lure her off to a hotel – say on the Saturday night – after he had finished his business meeting. It was time she became the woman that he imagined she had once been.

Meanwhile he had to make a quick call to Simon to tell him what Mark Raymond had said and to try to stop him panicking.

Michael drove the short distance from Cheyne Walk in record time. He had rung Helena before he left and she had told him she had been quite frank with James about Michael giving her a lift down to the country. He had been uneasy but was in no position to protest as he had persistently refused to help her to buy a new car to replace her clapped out Renault. Now James was well and truly out of the way.

As Michael rounded the corner into Richmond Terrace he saw that the front door was open. There was a commotion on the pavement, and piles of luggage, carrier bags full of Easter eggs, tennis rackets, a dog basket and a canvas holdall, struggling to contain bundles of brushes and paints and an old easel. Helena's pug dog, Clovis, was tied to the railings.

Michael drew to a halt and was confronted by the children he knew to be Kirsty, Harriet and Rollo. The girls stood still on the pavement and stared at him, the little boy standing between them stepped forward and held out his hand in greeting. He had thick red-gold hair that stood straight up from his head, freckles all over his nose and a chipped front tooth.

'I'm Rollo Johnson. These are my sisters,' and he nattered on, introducing them.

Helena appeared at the door wearing a long brown and white checked skirt, a flowery knitted sweater and ropes of amber beads. 'Oh Rollo, do shut up. I'm sorry, Michael. Just tell him to be quiet – we all have to. Now, have you met Kirsty and Harriet?' The girls stepped forward and solemnly shook Michael's hand.

'Is this all to go?' Michael asked.

'Yes, and there's going to be more on the way back.'

Michael opened the boot, looking doubtfully at the available space.

'Michael, come inside and have a cup of coffee while the children load the car. They're brilliant at it, I promise. It's years of practice.'

Helena preceded Michael into the house. She smelt of Rose Geranium, he thought as he followed her down the hall. When they got to the turn in the stairs to go down to the basement kitchen, he was assailed by a rich smell of coffee and an urgent desire to hold her in his arm and kiss her. He wanted to taste her mouth before he clouded his taste buds with the coffee. The animal feeling between them was so powerful that words were superfluous. He didn't know how he would be able to sit in the car with her for four hours if he didn't kiss her now. The moment was sharpened to a searing intensity by the game of abstinence they had played so deliciously with each other for the last three weeks. He had spoken often in an idiom which suggested the nature of his desires, his mouth so close that they had shared each other's breath, his hand had brushed hers, he had undressed her with his eyes a thousand times while she sat still, revelling in every second as if her body were being massaged with sensual aromatic oils; and now the need to consummate was compelling.

They came to each other on the curve of the stairs, slowly and sweetly, his mouth gentle, tender. Helena allowed him to push her back against the jumbled pile of coats that hung on the wall. She surrendered and Michael tasted her mouth; it was, as he had imagined, like honey.

With one hand he held the back of her neck, while the other sought her breasts and her nipples. Their bodies moulded together, their lips parted and Helena's head fell back against the wall. Eventually he drew away. He looked down into her open face.

'My darling, beautiful Helena. I knew you would taste like that. You are the most exotic, wonderful creature I have ever known. I want to show you what it is to be loved. I want to wake up that sleeping passion of yours.'

'I know,' said Helena. 'But we must wait.'

Michael knew that he was falling in love with her, at least by his own idea of being in love with a woman, which had happened many times before. Such was his enthusiasm for women that with each one he thought it was different, a new challenge. Women were to him all-absorbing in the first stages of an affair. He swept them off their feet, and they would find themselves carried along on a great tidal wave of excitement. Michael, the lover, would look at them and see the undiscovered woman within; he would create a confidence and energy which they had so far failed to harness. He could see so much in Helena, so much talent and dormant sexuality. He wanted to be the one who took her by the hand and showed her what she could achieve, how she could consummate a truly passionate affair. He wanted to love her, and he wanted his own child out there helping to load the car. But further than that he did not look. He did not want to see the dark side of women, the tears and tantrums, the dreary mechanics of domesticity – he saw the goddess in every woman. The big imponderable was how a goddess could become a wife. When his sister Adèle asked him how he would ever be able to settle down, he would laugh and say he was a romantic, and that romance died behind the bathroom door. 'Well, Michael, you will always be able to have separate bathrooms,' she had teased.

He looked at Helena's son Rollo and dismissed the many un-answered questions he would have to address if he were to commit himself to the thing he had never seen as a child – a conventional married home. His own parents' relationship had remained fresh and urgent without the shackles of marriage . . . and as a result, although his father had been a distant figure, he never remembered him as anything other than a hero.

'We've done it! We've done it!' Rollo shouted. 'Why's mummy

leaning against the wall? Isn't she very well?'

'Oh shut up, Rollo. You don't know anything!' It was Kirsty who spoke. As she did so Michael caught her eye, her solemn expression changing into a slight smile. Michael felt he was going to like Helena's children.

So, would it be better to travel than to arrive? Michael asked himself as he listened to the children on the way down in the car. It would be difficult for anything to live up to their descriptions of the house and the place, or indeed their grandmother.

He was finding out a lot about the children. They were very uninhibited but then he didn't know many children well. These children never mentioned their stepfather and Michael came to the conclusion that this was not because they disliked James, more that he had chosen to be a negative force.

As they turned off the motorway the children timed the remainder of the journey and fifteen minutes later they arrived at the gates of Maryzion.

A thin wisp of smoke came from the chimney of the lodge cottage, a reminder that a sharp frost could still seal the bright April afternoon. The net curtains moved as the car swept past and up the long curved drive under an avenue of limes, vivid green tendrils showing the first buds of spring, filtering the sunlight as it fell on the daffodils edging the pale grey gravel. The house nestled in the fold of a hill, sitting foursquare, the land rising gently behind it. Originally Jacobean with some later additions, it was built of light sandstone, host to clusters of rusty-green lichen. Leaded mullioned windows reflected the late afternoon sun as it dipped behind the tops of the trees in the opposite valley. An impressive oak front door stood behind a portico supported by substantial stone columns and over it all presided the family coat of arms, a shield of four quarters, two griffins supporting the family motto, *Nil Desperandum*.

A woman appeared in the doorway, tall and slim with tawny hair tied back in a coloured scarf. She wore brown velvet jodhpurs and a white lace blouse frilled at the neck, a bright paisley shawl draped over her shoulders.

Shrieks of 'Granny' confirmed the woman's identity.

The car had hardly come to a halt before the doors opened and the woman was entwined in an octopus of arms and legs. Cornelia hugged the three children to her.

Helena kissed her mother and then introduced Michael. Cornelia gave him a look of frank appraisal. She had already taken in the vignette of her daughter side by side with him and thought immediately that they looked a pair; it was his likeness to Helena's first husband, Anthony, which instantly struck her. The general bigness of the man – he had the same sort of movements – almost as if he were about to wrap himself around you.

'Mummy, Michael isn't staying tonight. But may he come back and stay tomorrow? Will that be all right?'

Michael was about to open his mouth in surprise. This had not been on his agenda, but he had not had the opportunity to talk to Helena in private in the car.

'Darling, of course it's all right. Now let me have a proper look at my grandchildren,' Cornelia replied.

Helena stood back, waiting for the children to finish greeting their grandmother, and Michael watched the pecking order: first Rollo, who quickly disentangled to cuddle three Cavalier spaniels who sat primly in a row while Clovis tore around them, barking, in frenzied circles. 'Look, Granny, Clovis thinks he's a sheep-dog!' Rollo shrieked.

Then came Harriet, who solemnly produced a small package out of her anorak pocket which Cornelia realised must be opened there and then. Harriet watched intently as her grandmother examined the contents, a small piece of cross-stitch tapestry neatly embroidered with a black and tan spaniel and the words 'For a Special Grandmother'.

'It's a surprise, Granny. No one saw me do it, not even Kirsty. I kept it in an old bit of pillow case on top of my cupboard.'

Cornelia's delight was obvious. She bent down until her face was on a level with Harriet's and said quietly, 'This is the most beautiful thing I've ever been given.'

Finally there was Kirsty, nearly the same height as her grand-mother. Cornelia put her hands on Kirsty's shoulders and held her a little away in order to look carefully at her. 'Darling, you're so wonderfully tall, just like your father, and you're wearing my earrings. Did you tell Mummy Grandpa gave them to me? I wanted you to have them as we're both Pisceans.'

Michael missed nothing. He saw at once a transformation, as if they were a bunch of parched flowers that had been placed in a deep restorative vase of water. He decided it would be a lovely idea to come back on Saturday and stay here.

'Come on in, it's getting cold. There's going to be a frost tonight; there often is after these beautiful spring days,' Cornelia said.

They clattered into the flagged hall. A log fire hissed in the stone fireplace, there was a smell of wood burning and potpourri. Ancestors peered down on them from portraits lining the hall and a dark oak staircase. Michael now wished he were staying here tonight, and not having the meeting in Plymouth.

'Now you must stay and have a drink, or would you like some tea?' Cornelia asked.

Michael liked the idea of tea. And he wanted to see more of the house before he left. The children all disappeared, and Michael heard their voices echoing on some distant landing. Even Clovis knew exactly what he was doing: he shot down a passage towards what Michael guessed was the kitchen.

'What a relief!' said Helena. 'Not a child to be seen. I expect they've all gone to their rooms to check everything out. How's the pony, Mummy?'

Michael realised that in a delicious way Helena was teasing him, not giving him the opportunity to put up any alternative plan.

'Oh, he's fine. I expect they'll want to go and see him after tea . . . Darling, do you want to tell them it's all laid out on the kitchen table? Mrs Finch has made them their favourite chocolate cake. It's lovely and warm in there. I've had a wood-burning stove installed since you were last here. The Aga was getting very decrepit and smoky, and I spend a lot of time in there now with my work.'

'Work, Mummy?'

'Typical reaction. I'm not senile, darling and I have a lot to tell you. But come on through, we won't bore Michael with that now. There's plenty of time.'

As Helena went to tell the children about tea, Cornelia led the way into the drawing room and Michael noticed her fine figure. The jodhpurs were very revealing.

The drawing room was bright and full of light. Its walls were covered in yellow silk now bleached with age: two worn gold brocade sofas were just visible through mounds of soft tapestry cushions and plaid rugs; chintz curtains, their colours muted with age, fell to the wooden floor and on to the Aubusson rugs. Everything had a faded look. There were two large windows with deep window seats, and an arched door led out on to a terrace. A gate-legged table stood in the window with tea for the grown-ups set out on a white lace cloth.

'Do sit down,' Cornelia said, and went to put a log on the fire. Michael hurried to help her, and as the fire flared he stood for a moment in front of it, enjoying the warmth. 'What a wonderful smell, wood burning, beeswax furniture polish and flowers. Exactly how an English country house should be.'

'Yes, the wood is apple. Isn't it lovely? No other timber smells like that. Sadly we lost some trees in the autumn gales. Can you smell the jasmine? I'm so pleased with it. I brought it in from the greenhouse two days ago.'

'What a beautiful room this is!' exclaimed Michael, looking about him. 'So gloriously light. Isn't it unusual for a house of this period to have its major windows facing south?'

'How clever of you! Yes, it's true most houses of this period were built facing north. The plague was believed to have come from the south. My ancestor who built it married a Spanish naval officer's daughter. She missed the sun terribly and so he built the house in this way. Her picture's on the staircase, and Helena bears a striking resemblance to her.'

'She does have an exotic look about her – rather like you.'

'Would you like some tea?'

Michael's appreciation of Maryzion's beauty was not lost on Cornelia, nor was his masculine elegance. He wore well-cut Ralph Lauren jeans and a yellow cashmere sweater under a soft vicuna flecked jacket. He looked at home in the room.

When Helena returned from the kitchen, she helped herself to a cup of tea in a delicate Crown Derby cup and saucer, and took a crumpet. Then she sat on a fender stool in front of the fire, watching Michael and her mother talking. It seemed the most natural thing in the world for Michael to be sitting there in the drawing room at Maryzion, like an old friend. He sat in the dark red velvet wing-backed armchair that Anthony had always chosen, his long legs stretched out in front of him, crossed at the ankles. Helena felt a wave of intense happiness.

*   *   *

As they shut the heavy oak door, they could hear Michael's car turning on to the drive. Cornelia hurried back into the drawing room from the cold of the hall. She looked over her shoulder. Helena was standing still, deep in thought, unaware that her mother was watching her. Being at Maryzion again, a place not imprinted with James's 'no jam' attitude, and seeing Michael so relaxed in the place she loved, made her happy. During her marriage to James, and particularly since he'd been a minister, she had become less and less in touch with the things she loved. Michael had opened her eyes to the state of her marriage, perhaps he had even stopped her sinking further into depression. She had made a decision: life was too short. She would not become one of those down-trodden Parliamentary wives, who ran to their husbands' bidding only to be swopped for younger models when they had lost their chance to make decent futures. If Michael Elliot was to be the catalyst so be it.

Cornelia saw that she was smiling, a dreamy smile that needed no explanation.

'Is it all right if I leave the terrace door open?' Cornelia asked. 'I love to hear the children playing in the garden.'

'Of course. I so love it here. It's as though all the happy times we've had here are still going on.'

'It's up to us, darling, to see that they keep happening, the happy things, I mean. Anyway,' Cornelia continued, 'I'm longing to talk about that gorgeous man. And, surprisingly, a nice, quirky, different sort of man. It just shows you should never believe what you read in the papers. Hold on, let's have a drink while you tell me about him.' Cornelia poured Helena a gin and tonic and one for herself and sat on the window seat beside Helena's chair.

'Oh, just before we settle down, I want to hear the weather fore-cast. I think there might be going to be a frost.' She switched on the television set.

It was still the regional news. '. . . a Good Friday vigil in protest at the destruction of beautiful woodland and fertile farmland,' the reporter was saying. The picture showed swarms of young people flooding into a picturesque village, with a pub called the Hampton Arms in the background.

'Good Lord! Look, Mummy, it's Markham Court,' Helena said.

110

The mob looked really angry. One of the protesters was explaining how terrible the plans were, and the cameras showed the very wood Helena had ridden through with Bertie, part of which was to be destroyed.

'Whoever is behind this is totally insensitive; it shows a complete disregard for country people and our heritage. People like this should not be allowed to ride roughshod over ordinary people's feelings,' a woman was saying.

Who did they mean, Helena wondered, the Hamptons, James . . . Michael?

The reporter went on: 'This controversy is unlikely to die down quickly. Markham Court lies within the constituency of Nunstead where a by-election, because of the death of Arthur Hall, MP for Nunstead for the last twenty years, will be taking place, and it can almost be guaranteed that this is only the beginning.'

'Bugger the Tories!' came a voice from the background as the picture faded.

After the weather forecast, Cornelia switched the television off. Helena was very quiet, a bewildered look on her face. Cornelia wasn't sure if Michael and Helena were lovers and she had decided not to ask, since the chemistry between them was so palpable that the outcome was inevitable. Her main concern was where was her daughter's marriage in all this, and, although she didn't like James much, she was worried for Helena, who was behaving in a rather foolhardy way. She was so vulnerable. Michael had seemed to her so charismatic, so confident, women must surely be throwing themselves at his feet. If he made love to Helena, could she resist falling in love with him? Sex was one thing, love another. Would he sweep into Helena's life, give her moments of joy and then leave her like a butterfly without wings? If that was his intention, though, why would he have come here? Cornelia began to worry about the effect on the children, but from the little she had seen of him, Michael was a very human sort of person. He obviously liked Helena's children, which James did not. It was time Helena had a man about who could inject some fun into all their lives. Cornelia concluded she just wasn't ready to make up her mind about Michael Elliot yet.

'Mummy, you're giving me a funny look,' Helena said as they settled by the fire. 'I know what you're thinking. I remember you looking at me like that when I told you I wanted to be a ballet dancer – and I was the tallest girl in the class.'

'I'm wondering . . . if this man will lead you a dance. He obviously finds you very attractive.'

'I've decided that, just for a while, it's time I had someone around me who made me feel good instead of in a constant state of apology. I can't paint properly when I am miserable and one never knows, one day I may be dependent on that. I'm fed up with a life that seems to belong to other people. If I wasn't so happy every second I'm with Michael, I'd be seriously worried about myself. I mean, I honestly began to think I wasn't capable of being happy any more.'

'It can't be all James's fault, darling. He isn't a bad man; he just isn't in touch with his feelings,' Cornelia said.

'Of course it's not *all* his fault. It's his job. It's like living in a ménage à trois. Him, me and the red boxes. I'm sure he'd rather be in Westminster than at home. It doesn't bother him. I think it's because he doesn't allow himself to have those sorts of feelings – having fun and . . . just living.' Helena held her glass up to the window and twirled it as it caught the light.

'Well, if a man has no feelings, how can he ever experience love?'

'I suppose it's partly my fault. I thought I'd grow to really love him, and I thought he loved me. But perhaps I was a trophy. He got me and a ready-made family, like choosing something from a mail-order catalogue. I shouldn't have married him. I was still in love with Anthony, still am. That's why I haven't been to bed with Michael yet. I know you understand what I'm talking about. That's why you've stayed true to Daddy's memory all these years. Nobody can ever take his place for you.'

The terrace door flew open and Clovis came panting in, carrying something in his mouth, followed by Rollo.

'Granny, he's got half of the chocolate cake. We took it outside to make a hoard for our camp and Clovis spoilt it, as usual.'

Helena and Cornelia knew they still had a lot to talk about but they were both grateful for the interruption.

Michael didn't head immediately for Devonport, but came off the motorway and took the narrower road to the airport where he had arranged to meet two of his Leichtenstein colleagues coming in on the Dash-7 from Gatwick. He hardly thought about Helena, his mind was totally focused on his business ventures. The men were already waiting for him when he arrived, stamping their feet to keep warm. There was Jakob Wasserman, who had been his trusty chief accountant for many years, tall and portly, wearing a vicuna overcoat with its astrakhan collar turned up; and the shorter, bespectacled Gunter Strauss in a green loden coat and trilby. He was a research chemist now in his fifties, a man Michael had personally recruited from a leading chemical company in Frankfurt.

The weak sun had gone down and there was a chill east wind. It was a bare four miles into Plymouth, and the silver Lexus was fast. As they neared the old Devonport dock area, the streets became deserted and dim with only intermittent lights. Seated alone in the back Wasserman was leaning over the seat and holding forth to Strauss in German about the Waterfront Regeneration scheme now underway, and pointing out the landmarks, while Michael interrupted occasionally with a few pleasantries, asking about their families and what they would be doing over Easter and Passover. He turned in through the old dockyard entrance. The moon was now up, and coldly reflecting the beautiful classical proportions of the old buildings in the one high-rise of steel and mirrored glass, newly erected on the site. This was the British headquarters of Western Environmental Services. Except for a light coming from the reception area, the building was in darkness.

Michael parked the car and they walked towards the entrance, the cold giving the noise of their footsteps a sharpness. They could hear the distant hoot of a ferry, perhaps the Roscoff or Santander, coming into Millbay Docks. As the electronically controlled doors rolled open, Michael just caught sight of the security guard at the reception desk hastily pushing some lager cans out of sight, and with studied nonchalance glancing at the sports section of the *Daily Mirror*.

Above the reception area was a silver plaque listing the names of the sixteen companies under the umbrella of Western Environmental Services.

The guard greeted the men in a suitably deferential manner. Michael showed his colleagues along the carpeted corridor to a lift and they rose silently to the fifth floor. Here he unlocked the door to a suite of offices. They entered a spacious carpeted area, furnished with a huge antique partner's desk and leather chairs, one wall being completely glass and offering a magnificent view across the glistening white estuary to the twinkling lights of Saltash.

'Scotch, everyone?' Michael politely stuck to German to make them feel at home. He went over to a bookcase of dummy leather-backed volumes, which folded down into a bar, with crystal decanters and an engraved Victorian mirrored back. He poured their drinks and handed them around.

'To Gaia Impex,' he said.

'Gaia Impex,' they repeated and raised their glasses.

Early on Saturday they would get down to real business and finalise the last details of this company, whose headquarters would remain in Liechtenstein, although Gunter Strauss would be running the Plymouth base. There were profits to be made in a relatively new but rapidly growing field: toxic waste. It was well known that there were quite a number of low-profile, small speciality chemical manufacturers – all over Europe and elsewhere – who were prepared to pay extremely well for losing unwanted waste with no questions asked. Finalising these last details of Gaia Impex meant they would be up and ready to go. And Michael already had some sites in mind. He was a 'hands-on' sort of business man and many of his employees respected him for that.

Tonight, however, was a social occasion. Joanna had reserved them a table at a small exclusive restaurant on the Barbican, only a five-minute drive away at this hour. And Good Friday notwithstanding, the restaurant had agreed to remain open – Michael being a highly valued customer. So they dined on grilled lobster with sauce cardinal, served with an excellent Sancerre. After which Michael drove them to a discreet hotel Joanna had also booked, where extra services were provided. Michael then returned to the Devonport building, and took the same lift, this time to the top floor. Here he had a spartan flat with a plain living room, a bedroom simply furnished with a single bed and a few cupboards, a shower room and a small kitchen. Had any of his business colleagues or his many friends glimpsed this flat they would have found it strangely out of keeping with the Michael Elliot they thought they knew.

Chapter 14

'I hope you don't mind, we always dress for dinner. It's a legacy from my darling husband,' Cornelia told Michael when he returned to Maryzion on Saturday evening.

As he came down the oak staircase in his Devonport dinner jacket at precisely eight o'clock, he heard the soft murmur of voices coming from the drawing room. He paused at the threshold and saw Helena standing by the fire between Kirsty and Harriet; she was talking to a large grey-haired woman. His eye was drawn to Cornelia, who stood by the window, in black trousers and an ivory-coloured crepe tunic, her hair coiled up and exposing a splendid pearl and diamond choker necklace.

Michael liked the company of women and considered himself an authority on female behaviour. Cornelia had about her a sexual confidence which might attract a man of any age yet she seemed to live alone. Michael began to think he understood when he saw she was talking to a tall cadaverous-looking man, in ancient dark blue smoking jacket, old-fashioned in style with twirls of braiding around the cuffs. He leant forward a little as if to minimise the height differential between Cornelia and himself. He was handsome, the sort who is attractive at any age, with greying hair and kindly eyes. He frequently laughed as he spoke, a rather sardonic laugh as if he might be indulging in the endearing English habit of the self-deprecatory story. This was a man, Michael decided, who took others seriously but never himself. Cornelia was engrossed and did not notice Michael. She laughed at something the man said and then touched his wrist with the lightness of a moth. Then Cornelia turned and saw Michael in the doorway.

'Oh, Michael, there you are. I hope you didn't have too much of a rush. Come, let me introduce you to our dear friend and neighbour Hugh Faulkner. His wife is talking to Helena and Kirsty.'

Hugh gave Michael an interested, though quizzical smile and shook his hand firmly. 'Cornelia has been telling me about you. I expect you've joined the long list of admirers of the Douglas dynasty. What a family! Just look at Kirsty.' He glanced towards the fireplace where Kirsty was politely making conversation with Hugh's wife, Dorothy. 'She's grown into a beautiful young lady. She must be as tall as you, Cornelia. And as for Harriet, in her quiet way she'll be the charmer.'

Michael felt a nudge and, looking down, saw Rollo holding a plate of canapés, twirls of savoury-filled pastry. 'Have one of these. I don't like them, they're full of a sort of fish jam. I gave one to Clovis 'cos I thought it was a cape gooseberry, which are his favourite, but Clovis wouldn't eat it so I put it back on the dish and someone not far from here has just eaten it.' Rollo smiled angelically.

'Rollo, come here a moment,' Cornelia said. She took him to the window seat and words were exchanged. Rollo looked solemn and it was obvious Cornelia was finding it difficult to keep a straight face. The two of them returned to Michael and Hugh.

'Sorry about that,' Cornelia said.

'Why do I have to go to bed, Granny?'

'Rollo,' Hugh said. 'Have you had one of my special drinks yet? Only chaps with strong heads are allowed those. Come with me.'

Rollo followed Hugh to the grand piano where Hugh was clearly in charge of the drinks and then returned with a glass of champagne for Michael.

'The house is beautiful,' Michael said to Cornelia. 'The *pièce de résistance* must be the open fire in my bedroom, a real luxury.'

'You're sleeping in my father's old dressing room and he always insisted on a fire, even in April. It's a tradition.'

'I don't know how you manage to keep this place going with so little help. It must have had at least six live-in staff in your grandparents' time,' Michael said.

'Oh, more than that,' replied Cornelia. 'But times change and we have to adapt. I feel I must try to keep the whole thing going for the family. I never feel it's mine, you see, just that I am a trustee.' Cornelia removed something from her drink. 'Oh heavens, a dog's hair.'

'I suppose the house isn't big enough to open to the public?' Michael asked.

'No, there are stacks of wonderful houses much bigger and grander than this around here, and half this house is empty and shut up anyway. My parents closed off some of it a long time ago. And I've made a flat at the end of the house for a lodger, which is quite a help.'

'You've never thought of running some sort of business here? Like shooting? My group of companies has a roving shooting syndicate. We go all over the place, at twenty thousand a day,' Michael said.

'You've obviously read my mind,' said Cornelia. 'I've a plan up my sleeve but I have to talk to Helena about it. Anyway, you must come and meet Dorothy.'

Cornelia led the way and en route introduced Michael to the other guests: a young couple described as 'new neighbours', a small birdlike woman who was an architect, and a middle-aged man, Rodney, wearing small metal glasses. 'My wife's away singing with a choir in a Mozart festival at Aix-en-Provence. Cornelia looks after her friends, and so here I am as spare man for Jane, the lovely lady over there. She's Cornelia's best friend and devoted dog-sitter.'

Jane's husband, it turned out, was a writer, currently engaged on a biography of Ataturk. Much to Cornelia's surprise Michael seemed to know a great deal on the subject, and she wondered if he was making it all up.

Eventually Michael found himself with Helena, Dorothy and Kirsty. He took Dorothy's hand and drew it towards him with a slight bow, his customary continental greeting. Dorothy looked like a Roman column. She wore a long grey ribbed knitted dress. Her chin receding into her neck and her hair cut in a round grey bob completed the effect. She took her hand away from Michael, surreptitiously wiping it down the side of her dress. 'You are not English then?' she said, growing taller as she spoke.

'How did you guess?'

'It's obvious. We don't meet many foreigners down here. Where do you come from?' she demanded.

Michael caught Helena's eye and saw Kirsty give her mother a nudge. Harriet buried her face in her glass and Michael noticed her shoulders heaving with suppressed giggles.

Michael furnished Dorothy with heavily censored answers to all her enquiries. He couldn't think that Dorothy and Hugh Faulkner had ever had much in common, although she'd probably been pretty once. She was one of those women who revel in middle age, and the position it gives them in their perceived pecking order.

Dorothy held the definitive view on every subject, affirming her authority with an awesome list of 'close acquaintances' with intimate knowledge of the matter in question.

Helena saw her chance of escape, when Rodney approached and greeted Dorothy with a kiss, his heels leaving the ground as he did so.

'Come with me, Michael. Our final guest has just arrived. Mummy's admirer – he's a widower, the Lord Lieutenant Sir Francis Stanhope,' Helena whispered.

'Miss Helena, Mr Askew's on the telephone. I told him you're just about to go into dinner but he said it wouldn't take a minute.' Mrs Finch stood by the drawing-room door, her dark blue nylon overall rustling against the wood. She touched Helena's shoulder protectively as she left the room. 'Don't worry, Miss Helena, dinner can wait a few minutes.'

James wanted Helena to come back after the weekend and join him in Sussex. He was getting a lot of flack. 'There's trouble brewing and I need you here.'

Helena told him she had seen the item about Markham Court on television.

'It's important for us to present a united front,' James said.

Helena sighed. 'OK. I'll come down later in the week.'

'Good night, both of you. Please don't wait for me, I'm used to locking up for the night,' Cornelia said when the last guests had left and the dirty glasses and coffee cups had been stacked in the kitchen.

'It was a lovely evening, Cornelia,' Michael said, 'and I look forward to a tour of the garden tomorrow.'

'I hope the weather stays fine,' Helena said. 'We have all sorts of things planned: an easter egg hunt in the garden; and Rollo might just find a real rabbit. Isn't that right, Mummy?'

'Yes, darling, and don't forget we're going to show Michael the sea tomorrow. A family walk after lunch, I think.'

Helena kissed Cornelia good night and Michael followed her up the stairs. He saw that Cornelia was watching them, smiling, but with a slight look of apprehension. Michael caught her eye and knew what she was thinking.

Michael had explored the rooms upstairs before he came down to dinner. It was, after all, important to know the terrain. Helena could easily slip away from him if he went about this important stage in a clumsy way. He had decided to invite her to his bedroom and not to invade the sensitive territory of hers, which he had been amused to find could not have changed much since her childhood. He expected all sorts of hurdles. He now understood more about Helena and her feeling towards her mother; and also that there was a lot about her mother she did not know.

As they reached the landing at the top of the stairs Michael took Helena in his arms. She leant her head back and gave him her mouth with no sign of restraint.

'Darling, will you come to my room when the house is quiet? There's a decanter of whisky in there. We could have a drink by the fire and talk. I—'

Helena silenced him with a finger on his mouth, which he kissed, fearful that they might wake the children by talking on the landing.

'I'll come when Mummy's gone to bed,' she whispered, and walked along the landing with a seductive swing to her step. She knew he was watching her.

Michael went to change out of his formal attire into the white towelling bathrobe which lay invitingly on a basket chair. The cracked lino in the bathroom was still wet from his bath. His earlier ablutions had been watched by numerous infant and animal faces peering from the many pictures on the walls: Victorian watercolours and pastels, children on ponies, children holding little dogs in pony traps and in a dogcart. Then he flopped on to the bed, stretched out and helped himself to a chocolate Bath Oliver biscuit from a tin on the bedside table. He closed his eyes and thought about the last twenty-four hours.

He'd seen an article in *The Times* on the Markham Court demonstration. It was a nuisance, particularly as this was only the beginning. It wasn't of course the first time he'd been given a rough ride by the local community when he'd started exploiting a site and he was pretty hardened to that. But he could have done without the by-election at the same time. It meant that, given the Tories' precarious position, Markham Court was going to be a focus of attention for the whole of the British media till the damn election happened. James, he noted, had come in for a bollocking. There were already rumblings about the Environment subsidy. Michael hadn't realised that it was the very first one offered under a new scheme. What would James think if he knew what he and Caroline had in mind for the site? He'd phoned her that morning and told her not to say anything to the press. More importantly now, though, was the need to keep James in his pocket. It was a pity the man was so prim about accepting gifts. But he smiled when he thought of what Simon had disclosed – and Caroline had surely done her bit. They knew each other so well he did not ever have to ask her.

And there was Helena. At the right moment he would offer her the share options and tell her not to tell James – it could be their little secret. That way, Helena would feel more independent from James and at the same time the shares would be a safety precaution for keeping James in line, if ever that proved necessary.

With that sorted out, Michael relaxed. He thought about Helena's family. They were full of innocent charm, light years away from the cut-throat world of business. Being here was like sinking into a delicious warm bath. He liked the children, Helena's mother was delightful, and the house was civilised. Its faded glory gave it such an aura of gentleness. It was not as big as he had imagined, though it was comfortable, if a little shabby.

There were things Helena obviously didn't know about her mother and it was this perhaps that held the key to the barrier he still felt when he got close to making love to her. James had unwittingly played an important role in both women's lives. It must have been the withdrawal of the grandchildren which forced Cornelia to look about her and find consolation elsewhere.

Helena thought her mother still led a life of lonely grief, excluding the possibility of accepting another chance of happiness, but in reality Cornelia had found her way. Helena must be told her mother had arrived somewhere else and maybe she herself would follow.

He was beginning to wonder if Helena had decided to stay away when the door opened. She came into the room wearing a Chinese peignoir. She held it together with both arms clutched about her waist, her hair caught on top of her head with a tortoiseshell clip.

'I'm sorry about the get-up,' she said. 'It's so long since we have been down here that I forgot I didn't have a decent dressing gown.'

'Come here,' said Michael, opening his arms to her. She climbed on to the bed and snuggled beside him, her head on his chest.

'You smell wonderful . . . Did you enjoy tonight? Do you like Mummy?'

'I think your mother has tremendous style.' He thought of all the effort she'd put in to make the evening a success. 'It's very important to keep the little things going if the big things are falling apart,' Michael said, gently stroking Helena's brow.

'What'd you mean by that?' Helena asked.

'What I mean, Helena, is that your mother has a gift for getting her priorities right.'

'I'm glad you approve.'

'I'm not the only one to approve of your mother. I suspect Hugh has quite a lot to say about her daily life, not to mention her night life.'

'Don't be daft. Mummy doesn't have a night life. She hardly goes out at all.'

'Maybe. But has it ever occurred to you that she stays in and has fun, and not on her own?'

'If you mean Francis, yes I know they go to the theatre sometimes in Plymouth. He's devoted to Mummy and I've always hoped they'd get married, just for companionship.'

Michael made a move to get up from the bed. 'You stay there. I'm just going to get us a little whisky and put some more coal on the fire.'

When he returned, Helena sat cross-legged against the pillows. She took the whisky and Michael perched on the side of the bed.

'Helena, surely you realise your mother and Hugh are madly in love? They've clearly been having an affair for quite some time.'

Helena gulped. She stared at Michael and her face darkened. She got off the bed, pulling her dressing gown around her and headed for the door. The clip had fallen from her hair and it hung wildly about her shoulders.

'How dare you?' she said. 'You come here to my family home, you sleep in my grandfather's bed, and you say things like that about my mother. My mother will never love anyone else but my father in the way you mean. Besides, Hugh's married. How could you? How could you? I doubted that I could get into your bed and be made love to by you. Now I know I never will.'

Helena left the room silently. There was just the disturbance of air as she went.

Michael was stunned. He remained sitting on the side of the bed for a long time. Eventually he stood up and looked out of the window at the garden. The moon had risen to a bright glow. He felt sharply the loss of a shared viewing of its deep, dark rays. He felt alone and sad.

Cornelia was not quite asleep when the door opened. 'Mummy, it's me. Can we talk for a minute?'

'Yes, darling, of course. What time is it?' Cornelia propped herself up on an elbow amidst a mound of white lace pillows.

'It's about one.' Helena turned the light on beside her mother's bed.

'Darling, please turn the light off, just open the curtains. We'll soon see in the dark. Come here and put a pillow behind your head and lie on the bed.'

Cornelia could see Helena's face shining. She had been crying.

'What is it, darling? Has something happened?' she asked.

'Mummy, I'm going to come straight out with it. Are you having an affair with Hugh?'

'Darling, what a strange time to ask me such a thing. Surely you'd guessed? How could I survive down here all alone?'

'What do you mean, "survive"? And what about poor Dorothy?'

'Their marriage has been effectively over for years. Dorothy wants a divorce and she also wants to live in London. They had been waiting for the children to finish university.'

'But you can't possibly love him in that way. I mean . . . you know what I mean.'

Cornelia sat up and looked at her daughter. 'Helena darling, adultery is but one of the marital sins. But as you're in my bedroom instead of the bedroom I would have thought you would have been in, I'd better tell you what Hugh means to me.'

'Yes, tell me. But tell me first that you don't love Hugh more than Daddy.'

'Helena, there's room for more than one love in a life. If not, most of us wouldn't survive. I'll tell you about love, at least of my love for Hugh. He makes me feel beautiful, not like a middle-aged woman looking for safety. He does it because he's completely reassuringly kind and loving. He doesn't expect anything, he has no preconceptions, no straitjacket habits, his mind is fresh. When he sits opposite me I feel ageless, and when we talk, words simply flow. When I'm alone I long for him, and the comfort of his presence.'

'But what about your future? What will you do? Will he look after you?' Helena cried.

'He puts up clever umbrellas for the future. I never doubt him for a second. Darling Helena, your father and Hugh were best friends. I think Daddy would approve.'

Helena was still. The gilt clock by the bed softly ticked the minutes away in the silent room and then her mother continued.

'Helena, you should be happy for me. I shall regret the things I've not done, not the things I have.' Cornelia waited for Helena's reply.

'Oh, Mummy, I've been so stupid. I know I'll regret it if I turn Michael away. I've just had a row with him. It was something he said I didn't understand, but now I do and he was right. I said some awful things to him.'

Cornelia took Helena's hand. 'I can't tell you what to do, Helena,' she said. 'That you must decide for yourself.'

Helena stood up, and went to the door. 'Shall I close the curtains?' she asked.

'No, I'm happy as I am.'

'Yes, I see that now,' Helena said.

Michael had fallen into a deep, unhappy sleep. He did not hear the door open. He felt soft fingers on his face, but was not surprised. Somewhere between sleeping and waking he felt the warmth of the woman's body as she settled beside him in the bed. The shadow of her hair fell on the pillow as he turned to her. 'I opened the curtains. I thought the moon could be our lantern,' she whispered.

Chapter 15

Helena awoke while it was still dark, to the delicious sensation of Michael sleeping beside her, his gentle, regular breathing, his slightly animal smell, the exciting newness of his body.

Now she and Michael were lovers, she thought contentedly, it changed everything. It took away the unrelenting, constricting hurt that she had felt for so long. Suddenly the whole world was waiting to be savoured. James's overbearing peremptoriness suddenly became less significant. While she had been flirting with Michael she had felt no remorse; now that she had committed herself to him in the flesh guilt blossomed. But, after all, James had told her to take a lover. He may well have said it in anger but he had never apologised, nor made any attempt to retract the remark. But how would he feel when he discovered she had taken his advice? She made a vow to herself to be pleasanter to James. Perhaps she would even phone him today, it being Easter Day after all. And she would make the effort to go to the constituency for a couple of days, but then she would make it clear to him that there was a limit to how much of her life could be sacrificed to his. She knew now she must make an effort to have a life of her own.

Outside it was growing lighter. She could hear the sparrows and, yes, a blackbird singing its heart out.

The day stretched before her with an unfamiliar lack of tension: a happy morning doing the Easter egg hunt, family lunch and then a long walk by the sea.

It was mid afternoon when they had piled into two cars and made for the coast. The tide was on the way out and the beach deserted except for a young couple strapping a screaming child into a push-chair. Away to the left the azure-blue sky would yield to a bank of dark grey cloud, and with that the sun would finally say goodbye to the day. Helena was looking forward to an early supper and settling down to a leisurely evening with Michael, her mother and the children. What could be more marvellous, for Michael did not have to leave until the following morning?

'Don't hurry back,' Helena called as she and Michael set out for home in his car, and knowing that Kirsty was longing to have a chat with her grandmother on her own. 'We'll get the supper. We've got Harriet, Rollo and Clovis.'

'Come on, Granny. You can sit here.' Kirsty spread out her anorak on a piece of rock.

Cornelia was happily tired. It had been a wonderful day, once they had recovered from the family breakfast. Rollo naturally had managed to put his foot in it.

'Mum, what's an affair?' he had asked, his mouth much too full of cornflakes. And before Helena could stop him, and just as Mrs Finch came in with a tray full of bacon and eggs, he continued with an air of importance, 'Does it mean Michael is your lover, Mum, and do we have any sexual relations?'

'Rollo, that will do! You're always listening to things you shouldn't,' Harriet said sharply.

Cornelia looked across at Helena as she sent Rollo from the room muttering under his breath. Michael stood motionless at the sideboard and Helena blushed. It was this incident which assumed priority on Cornelia's list of things to discuss with Kirsty.

Cornelia sat down and looked across the empty sandscape to the horizon.

'Granny, are the dogs OK? Perhaps I'd better fetch them.'

'Good idea, take the leads. Let's get them in.' Kirsty set off at a run and Cornelia watched her granddaughter, like a gazelle, leap from rock to rock. Cornelia knew Kirsty to be troubled, but in spite of this, she was glad to see her glowing with health and vigour. She came puffing back with the dogs in tow, and sat on the anorak beside Cornelia.

'So, darling, tell me, how is everything?' Cornelia put a protective arm about Kirsty's shoulders. 'Truthfully now,' she added firmly.

Kirsty frowned, digging the heel of her Wellington boot into the sand.

'Not good, Granny, not good at all.'

'What's the worst thing?'

'Well, Rollo for a start, and that's all James's fault.' Kirsty kicked the sand again.

'How do you mean James's fault?'

'Rollo's completely out of hand. You saw how he carried on at breakfast.'

'But, darling, we mustn't be unfair on James. Being a cabinet minister is no easy job. He has so little spare time and, well, I suppose when he does have some he's not in the mood for inquisitive little boys.'

'But Rollo's miserable at boarding school. And when he shows off like this morning, it's his way of trying to be grown up and strong. He sounds as if he's being clever but when he gets back to school he gets bullied because he's a wimp. James made Mummy send him away, so it *is* all his fault. Rollo never used to be like this.'

'Does Mummy know how unhappy he is?' Cornelia asked gently.

'She does but she won't do anything about it. It's as though she's frightened of James. I've told her that if Rollo goes back to that school, Harriet and I are going on strike.'

'What?' Cornelia asked in alarm.

'We're going to refuse to get up.'

'I know it's not easy, darling, but I have talked to her about it, and so has Michael,' Cornelia said rather cautiously.

'Michael's great. I wish Mummy had married him instead of James. I hate James.' Kirsty pulled angrily at the finger of her glove.

'Darling, you mustn't talk like that. Besides, you don't hate James,' Cornelia said.

'I do. He doesn't love Mummy, not like Michael does. You can tell. Grown-ups think children don't know about love. Well, I do and so does Harriet. We talked about it last night in bed. When Mummy looks at Michael, her face is all soft and happy, and with James she's all tense. I loved Daddy so much, Granny. I wish we could have him back.'

Kirsty burst into convulsive tears. Cornelia opened her jacket and wrapped her granddaughter to her, cradling her, talking softly and soothingly into her tangled wind-blown hair. It tasted of salt from the sea.

'Look, I know what you feel about James, but he doesn't mean to be bad, darling. When he married your mother he was taking a huge step taking on you three. After all, he'd lived alone for so many years.

People get set in their ways. He must really have loved your mother then – to make such a huge commitment. He's just not used to children. I expect he still loves Mummy in his own way. And Mummy would do anything for you. Kirsty, you mustn't do anything silly. We'll talk to Mummy tomorrow when Michael has gone back to London.'

Michael, yes, Cornelia thought. A life-enhancing man, or rather, she could say, enhancing in the effect he was having on Helena, but there was something she couldn't quite put her finger on. What puzzled her was could he be as nice as he seemed? He wasn't, of course, anything like Anthony – except in looks. There was something very manipulative about him – the way he made you say things, see things his way, almost in spite of yourself. And of course it wasn't just his manner, but his whole personality that was so persuasive. But Helena had been heading for a depression – and the whole family seemed miserable – they couldn't have gone on as they were. If it took a Michael Elliot to snap Helena out of it, so be it. But she was shocked that she had colluded in their affair, especially when she didn't quite trust the man.

Chapter 16

Michael was well satisfied with how the Markham Court plan was progressing. The half-million subsidy to be paid to the Hamptons would be channelled through his company. Although he was paying the Hamptons for the privilege of extracting gravel from their land, another of his companies was contracted to do all the relandscaping, the making of the lake and constructing all the amenities, stocking the lake, replanting the wood. He had built in a very handsome commission, both for himself and the Hamptons.

There was, of course, the problem of the local protest groups at the site, who were currently camping out along the river. The project could have done without this adverse publicity, Michael reflected, but he had a shrewd idea that the story would soon leave the front pages. Funny how poor old Bertie was getting all the flak, while Caroline was keeping a very low profile, as he had advised her to do. The other thing, of course, was that Caroline and Bertie were having to pay a huge amount for infill, despite the lake. And it was here that Michael's company would kill two birds or even three with one stone, for he had a thriving business getting rid not only of building rubble but also industrial waste since his company, Wastaway, was paid both by the corporations getting rid of the waste and the people wanting the infill.

James, of course, would still have to be kept in line.

Michael wondered if James knew about himself and Helena. He doubted whether Cornelia, or Helena, would tell him. In a way he didn't care if they did although when dealing with people, it paid to have them at a disadvantage, just as in the arrangement with Bertie Hampton. But Bertie was a wimp, whereas James Askew was definitely a force to be reckoned with, and was in a position of considerable power.

The problem was that James was inscrutable – you could never really tell what was going on behind that calm expression and those cold blue eyes. He was trustworthy, too, so if Michael had to play any of his trump cards he thought James might well be able to bluff his way out of a tight corner. And his assurance was such that it did not seem to worry him when Helena vanished for hours at a time, or stayed away from him for days down in Devon. James was hard up, though, the price to be paid for being squeaky clean. All that fuss Helena had told him he had made over a phone bill. That was why Michael had just given her a mobile telephone, it would offer her more independence anyway.

The only thing that James seemed to expect of Helena was that she went with him and put up a good show at the constituency: something she was rebelling against with increasing frequency. Michael and Helena had spent several afternoons together since that pivotal weekend at Maryzion. And Michael had taken to telephoning Cornelia every so often for a friendly chat. It paid to have her on his side.

Michael emerged from his reveries, and glanced at the day's papers. Journalists were flocking to Markham Court like flies, their interest fuelled by the prospect of the forthcoming by-election. Michael could see that from James's point of view, the waterpark might become a disaster. The local Gloucestershire rag was headed: 'Who needs a waterpark?' Instead of it being a vote-catcher, a new amenity for the region, it might have the opposite effect. It was, Michael thought, time to consolidate his position with James. Better recruit Helena even further to his side and get her to sign the papers for the share options in Western Environmental Services. Squeaky clean James might be, but Michael felt he was still one step ahead of the MP. He would get everything ready, and choose his moment with care. There were a lot of possibilities here – not least the vicarious power he would have by his close relationship with Helena – and he stood to make a great deal of money from the Hampton venture.

Chapter 17

James ran from his official car through the driving rain and up the steps at Richmond Terrace, turning the key before a sudden squall blew his umbrella inside out and a lurking reporter shouted: 'Sir! Would you mind—'

Thankfully he closed the door. He felt miserable with the lingerings of a cold he'd caught down in the damp cottage, which suddenly seemed to have returned with a vengeance. He wanted sympathy but was surprised to find the place quiet and empty. It was four o'clock. He was rarely at home at this hour and had never really addressed the idea of Helena not always being on tap – not in London anyway. Of late she had become much pleasanter to him, though she had rarely visited the constituency with him again after that brief visit at Easter. Her feminine presence about the cottage had made it more homely, and she had even been polite to Cynthia.

He called out: 'Darling, Helena!' but his voice sounded hollow. He wandered into the kitchen. Everything was neat and tidied away, but there was no sign of Rosaria or Maria, nor the children – which was a relief. At present he couldn't cope with their demands.

He walked into the drawing room, poured himself a Scotch and water and sank into an armchair. His forehead felt sticky and hot, but the silence was a boon. Rather like the old days. How good it had been then, and his mind wandered back to his bachelor pad, but then also to the stark comfortless emptiness, the scratch meals, and – dare he admit it – the loneliness. There was a vast difference between being alone and being lonely.

The telephone rang, and he recognised Reggie's agitated voice.

'James. Tried to get you at the House. All hell's broken loose. Have you heard?'

'Heard what? What's happened? A riot at Nunstead?'

'No. Nothing like that. Henry Smythe.'

The Foreign Secretary.

'I thought he was off in Hong Kong, doing his goodwill bit.'

'Was. Had a heart attack on the plane coming back. Just landed him at Heathrow. Still all hush-hush. He may be out of commission for some time. Who knows, maybe for good.'

'Oh,' was all James could think of saying. He had no liking for Smythe – one of Jenkins's cronies, a snide, arrogant bastard who looked upon products of the State education system as way beneath his attention. Nevertheless, the news sent a frisson of fear through him. This was one of the hazards of reaching the top, the pressure, jet lag, rushing around, changes of temperature. Always having to put on a polite equable front even when faced with rudeness and unreasonable behaviour. But mingled with James's fear was also a sense of excitement.

'No skin off our noses, eh?' Reggie, well aware that both their phones were tapped, was nothing if not tactless. 'I'm just popping next door to see how the land lies. Just seen Raymond going in. Then I'll go on to the House. See you there.'

What now? James thought, and felt a sudden surge of adrenalin. All his cold symptoms had miraculously vanished. He was elated. What would this mean? A more precarious situation for the Party, perhaps. But depending on how bad Smythe was, there might be a reshuffle. Had to be. So there might be something in it for him? With Reggie's help . . . provided he could keep the lid on the Markham Court affair, which was teetering on the verge of becoming distinctly nasty. There was a whiff of something he couldn't quite fathom yet, something Elliot had hinted at on the phone when James had given him short shrift. He had a feeling he did not know the whole truth about Elliot's involvement. He would have to phone Caroline.

The straggle of journalists hanging about the street did not augur well either.

Who was the most likely candidate for Foreign Secretary, though? He doubted Reggie – diplomacy was hardly one of his strong points. Jenkins would want someone with a bit more sophistication. Matthews? A definite possible. Bigg-Hodgkisson – yes, well perhaps no; Carter a possibility; Parfitt, also a possibility. Himself? Just the thought of it sent a tremor through him. Of course, it was all speculation at this stage. And anyway Environment was too junior a Ministry from which to be promoted so far. He wasn't a Jenkins chum either. Come to think of it, though, there weren't many of those left!

Was a reshuffle really a possibility? he asked himself as once more he picked up his wet umbrella and headed for the front door.

It was half an hour later that Helena rounded the corner into Richmond Terrace. She parked her small Renault some way down the street. As she mounted the steps she saw something yellow on the doorstep. Carefully spread out was a banana skin. She picked it up and put it in the dustbin. A shiver went down her spine. The sudden deterioration of the weather and the offering on the step were ominous.

As she let herself into the house, she could hear that the children were back from school. She had faced up to James and removed Rollo from his boarding school. Getting him into the smart prep school around the corner had not been easy but Helena had pulled every string at her disposal. Not surprisingly, the school in Oxford was not so accommodating. James had refused to pay the fees demanded instead of a term's notice. 'Well, I don't blame James,' Cornelia had said. 'Really, Helena, you shouldn't even have mentioned it to him.' Soon afterwards she had sent Helena a cheque for three thousand pounds that she could ill afford.

'Nothing however could dampen Helena's new-found happiness, especially as that afternoon she had been to visit Violet Banks and made preliminary sketches of the children. The atmosphere had been bubbling with merriment, and she and Violet had had a wonderful time reminiscing about their schooldays. David was at the House, so they had not been under any pressure. And Helena had found that although each had gone her separate ways, with a husband on the opposing side, Violet was still the gentle, sympathetic person she had always been. It was just as though all the years had been but a moment. This was a friendship they promised each other, as they parted, they were not going to neglect, whatever their husbands thought. The three little girls were absolutely charming and full of fun and Helena had a self-confident feeling that she was going to do a good portrait. It was Michael who had encouraged her to defy

James, and how grateful she was. She sensed a new energy within herself for her work. She was going to paint Michael too, a commission that would cover her frequent visits to Cheyne Walk.

'A cup of tea, Mrs Helena?'

The children were watching *Neighbours* in the kitchen with Maria, whose voice came through a funnel of steam coming from a giant saucepan of pasta. The room smelt of Bolognese sauce.

'In a minute. Thanks. I'm just going to the studio.'

She was interrupted by the telephone and managed to get to it just before Kirsty. It was Michael.

'I'll take this in another room,' she said, hoping the children would not have noticed the excitement in her voice.

She ran upstairs and flopped on to her bed. The sound of Michael's voice thrilled her; she had not seen him for five days, since they had gone to see *Tosca* with Michael's sister.

'Come over later and have a spot of dinner. It'll do you good. Besides, we have some unfinished business.' Michael's soft, intimate voice made her entire body tingle as she pictured him. She inadvertently caressed her breast as she thought about him. James would be at the House until the small hours, and Maria had announced plans for an early night.

'I can't think of anything nicer,' she answered dreamily.

'I'll send a cab for you at seven forty-five. Don't dress up and . . . please wear your hair down,' Michael said.

As she replaced the receiver Helena reflected on the comforting simplicity Michael had introduced into their talk. There was an inevitability about it all which she found deeply reassuring.

Michael had already begun to help her make significant but subtle changes in her life, as if he had for a moment taken the pattern of her daily life and that of the people she loved and shown her a different picture, one within her grasp, a colourful canvas full of hope and expectation. She was learning to unknot the little 'packets' of pleasure she had kept tied up inside her for so long, fearing that exposure would turn them into a dull grey powder.

Tonight she felt an elation as only those who are in love feel.

On her way downstairs Helena popped into her studio. The house was quiet, the children had gone to their rooms to do their homework. Since her affair with Michael had started she had returned to her work with a great surge of energy. His enthusiasm had begun to colour her life and this was reflected in her painting.

Outside it was raining quite heavily and water pattered on to the glass roof. There was a small leak in the corner and some of the dark cotton sheeting Helena used to organise the difficult light in the conservatory had become wet. She took it down from the glass and draped it over the radiator to dry.

There was a heady smell of linseed oil, turps and damp moss. Helena picked up a brass jug and watered some of the jungle of plants standing in terracotta pots on the tiled floor. She noticed the fresh young shoots – a tender green, snaking sensuously to the light; outside a fat blackbird wavered broodily in the bushes in the little garden. The light was fading fast, but she could see the nest it had been building in the forsythia on the garden wall. She felt in harmony with all around her, and knew this feeling had influenced her work.

Helena and Michael were seated in the candlelit drawing room. Helena was wearing one of Michael's towelling bathrobes and a pair of his socks, and sipping champagne. They both knew they would soon be back upstairs.

Michael reached out and stroked her arm.

'You are so beautiful, Helena,' he murmured. 'No one else must see you like this, no one else must touch you.' He ran his hand tenderly over her breasts.

'Don't worry, Michael. I would never do anything so bourgeois as be unfaithful to my lover.'

They both laughed, and Michael got up, went to the sideboard and returned with a bowl of strawberries in one hand, some papers in the other.

He dipped one of the berries in some sugar and popped it into her mouth.

'What are those papers? Industrial secrets?' Helena asked flippantly.

'Not exactly,' Michael laughed. He leant forward and wiped away some strawberry juice from her chin. 'Look, Helena,' he said, 'this is rather a delicate matter. But I want to be serious just for a moment.'

Helena looked alarmed. He put his hand out to her again. 'Oh, it's nothing to worry about . . . It's just that, well, James has been so tremendously helpful over the Markham Court business – we could never have pulled it off without his help. But . . . well, you know what he's like. He can't unbend. And as usual he's being high-minded. I offered him some share options in Western Environmental – all very safe and quite legit, I assure you, all above board. Of course he's refused. But well, I know how with your children's education to think of, the expense must be a constant worry. I hope you'll accept these from me.'

'But I couldn't possibly. It wouldn't be right.'

'Listen, Helena. Trust me. You don't know what the future holds. Don't you want to be able to stand on your own two feet? Be someone in your own right? So that, well – if eventually the shit hits the fan you'll have the courage to do what you want to do, because you have something secure to bolster you?'

He dipped another strawberry into the sugar and popped it into her mouth.

Helena wavered. She remembered what his sister, Adèle, had told her at the opera only a few days ago – how generous he'd been to her son, helping him with his music studies. But that was his nephew – a blood relation.

'Well . . . I'll think about it, but not now.'

'Please . . . for me . . .'

Later Helena lay blissfully in Michael's arms again, and later still, when her front door had silently clicked behind her, she crept through the darkened house to her studio and switched on the light. She wanted a last look at her sketches before she went to sleep. She knew they were the best thing she had ever done. She also knew that if Michael walked carelessly out of her life, he would leave her a different person, secure in her confidence, in her family and in her talent.

Then, as she turned to switch off the light, a voice came out of the darkness: 'Where the hell have you been? I've been trying to get you all day.'

'Oh, I'm sorry . . . I had to see some clients and then I had a quiet supper with friends,' said Helena, trying to slip past James and get upstairs. She hadn't expected to find him waiting for her . She felt panicky. She had dressed in a hurry, her make-up must be smudged and she hadn't put her tights on; they were in her handbag. She suddenly felt cheap and she wanted to have a bath. Being confronted by her husband so fresh from her lover's bed was something she hadn't prepared herself for.

'What is the matter with you? You look odd,' said James. He didn't wait for an answer but continued briskly, 'Could we talk for a moment?'

Helena's heart began to pound. She thought desperately. What was she to say, admit her affair? 'Oh James, please not now . . . I—' she began.

'Yes, now. There have been some developments in the House today that I think you should know about.'

Helena took a deep breath. She hoped the relief in her voice would not be too obvious. 'Of course,' she replied hurriedly. 'But do you think I could have a quick bath and then come and make us both a cup of tea? I'm rather exhausted.'

'Well, if you must. But I'm knackered too and I have a stinking cold. In fact all this could not have come at a worse time. Will you be quick?'

Helena rushed upstairs. There was something very important brewing. It was so unlike James to want to talk this late. She bathed quickly and went downstairs. James had made a pot of tea and sat waiting for her at the kitchen table. The overhead bulb cast a down-light on to his face which made him look much older. Helena wrapped her dressing gown closely around her and drew her chair away from the table. She didn't want James to see her face too closely.

James started to tell her about Henry Smythe being taken ill. Helena interrupted breathlessly to ask if he were going to be all right. 'Don't interrupt,' James replied crossly.

When he had finished telling Helena of what this might mean in terms of his own promotion she was silent.

'Well,' said James, staring at her. 'Aren't you going to say anything?'

'I am really sorry, James,' said Helena as she assimilated what he had just told her, the implications for her children, her privacy, Michael, her work. She didn't know what to think.

'Well, I can see you're not pleased for me.' James's face had gone white.

'It's not that, James. It's the thought of what it will do to us,' said Helena.

'Let's talk tomorrow,' said James briskly. 'But there's one other thing to say, which is just as important.'

He paused to drain the teapot into his cup. 'I have a bad feeling about the Markham Court business. It could be my undoing if it escalates. I have to deadbat questions in the House next week and I'd like you to put on a show of support, be there in the gallery.' Helena was about to assure James she would be there when he continued, 'It's not much to ask. More important than tea with so-called clients and supper with God knows who.'

Helena got up swiftly. She didn't want James to see how angry she was. 'That's for me to decide,' she called from the kitchen doorway.

All the guilt she had felt evaporated. It was James's words 'so-called clients' that got to her. It was precisely this sort of attitude which had driven her into a lover's arms.

Later, as she slept she dreamt only of Michael. There was a lot of water in the dream and when she awoke she couldn't remember if the water was reassuring or threatening.

Chapter 18

Cornelia looked out of her bedroom window. The weather forecast had been right, the early morning mist looked promising. It was going to be hot, even for early June. It was seven o'clock. She had been awake for some time and had given up the idea of going back to sleep. She knew exactly why. It was worry, worry about Helena and the children.

Cornelia thought Helena's situation was unbearable. She was trapped in a marriage which simply did not work, was dead. And it was good for neither of them. It was also clear that Helena had become completely infatuated with Michael, who, it appeared, still had other mistresses. Cornelia found it difficult to reconcile the kind, charismatic Michael she knew with the facts as presented to her by Helena herself. Cornelia advised Helena to find out more about the women whoever they were, but Helena had replied, somewhat irritatingly, that it was something Michael had implied to her from the start, that she had for the moment accepted the situation, hoping it would change.

Curiously, though, the household in Richmond Terrace had assumed a kind of equanimity. Perhaps, Cornelia thought, her daughter had acquired the English habit of co-existing.

She decided to put Helena out of her mind. Today was Hugh's day. Mondays were special. The habit had started when Cornelia first used to miss the grandchildren after a lonely weekend. Something to look forward to, Hugh had said, but now things were subtly changing. Dorothy had informally relinquished her daily right to Hugh and he spent more and more time with Cornelia.

'You're not to do anything. Leave it all to me,' Hugh insisted, when, at one o'clock, he arrived carrying a bottle of white wine and a picnic hamper.

He led her through the lime walk to the gazebo, her favourite spot in the garden looking into the sun-filled refuge. Gone were her old deck chairs and the rickety card table. In their place were two capacious dark green basket chairs and a round table.

'I don't believe it. Where did you get them?' she cried delightedly.

'That's my secret. Do you like them?' asked Hugh anxiously.

'Darling, I adore them.'

'They're an early birthday present. I know it's at the weekend, but poor Mrs Finch has had them in her front room for a week already. It was she who helped me to get everything prepared for you today. Now let's have a drink to celebrate.'

'Hugh, you are the darlingest, dearest man in the entire world,' Cornelia said, giving him an enormous hug.

When they had settled down for a drink Hugh asked Cornelia for an update on her plans for the following week.

The subject of Michael and Helena soon came up.

'Do you want to go out with them on your birthday? Of course, if that's what you want, we will, but I don't think Helena can appear in public with him at the moment. It's not that I don't approve, darling, but I'm very worried,' Hugh continued tentatively. 'I'm worried that she's playing with fire, and I'm also worried about you.'

'What do you mean?' Cornelia asked defensively.

'I mean,' replied Hugh, 'it upsets me to see you writing out a cheque for Rollo's school fees. You can hardly afford to get that awful old car of yours fixed.'

'Well, I have news for you. I had a charming letter from Michael enclosing a cheque for three thousand pounds,' announced Cornelia.

'I don't understand,' said Hugh in a puzzled voice.

'To pay me back for the school fees. He said he had encouraged Helena to take Rollo out of the school and he could well afford it. He couldn't let Helena have the money, because James has access to her bank account. It could be extremely awkward at this stage. He adores my daughter, you know. I'll show you the letter he wrote. It brought tears to my eyes, Hugh.'

'If he adores her so much, why is he messing about with her? I don't think her life has got any easier since she met him. James may be difficult, but this will put his career in jeopardy. He must surely suspect something by now,' Hugh said.

'Well, I suppose so, but perhaps it suits him not to look too close. Anyway Helena is alive again. It's as though Michael has reawakened her. She's becoming strong again, and taking her work really seriously. She sent me a photograph of her latest sketches and they're wonderful. You don't produce stuff like that if you're miserable, I can tell you that for sure,' Cornelia said firmly.

Hugh thought it was time to change the subject. He thought Cornelia was much too indulgent. If she had a fault it was the way she always saw the good aspects of a person and the benefits of a situation. He loved Helena too, but when she married James, he had lost patience. He knew it would be a disaster. However clever James might be, the man was a prig, Hugh felt, but then perhaps he dared not be anything else. His credentials were precisely what he himself had achieved, and there were no safety nets for people like James. He could not afford to step out of the mould he had made, whereas Helena had no stereotyped concepts of how her life should be lived. She just wanted to be happy, for life to be a fairy story. That was how she had been brought up, this Hugh knew only too well. In fact, it was Cornelia's ability to create magic about her which was the thing he loved most. Dorothy had never had that gift. Cornelia had made Helena into her fairy princess and Hugh had seen Anthony play the role of Prince Charming; he knew James would never do this. But although Hugh disliked James he had a certain sympathy for him. It was obvious to him that the very qualities which had attracted Helena to him, his ambition and success and his apparent strength, born of a myopic obsession with his career, were the things which now stifled Helena. They were, quite simply, wrong for each other. The whole thing had made Cornelia very unhappy. Michael Elliot was charming, but, damn it, he was playing around with the wife of a cabinet minister. He was a renowned womaniser, and sailed pretty close to the wind as far as his business practices were concerned. Nor was Hugh at all keen on Cornelia accepting the man's money. Cornelia had her own life to lead and together they were making wonderful plans for their future. He had the details of two farmhouses in Tuscany in the car, and the plans already well advanced for turning the stables at Maryzion into holiday homes. Things were just beginning to take shape. He did not want this Michael Elliot wrecking Cornelia's peace of mind, or causing a scandal, with all the invasion of privacy that would mean for all of them.

Chapter 19

In the basement of Number Eleven Reggie and Hilda were having a hurried breakfast. The room, with its nicely fitted pine furniture, was looking a good deal brighter now that the windows had been cleaned.

Today the Goodalls were both in matching navy, though the seat of Reggie's pinstripe was distinctly shiny. Hilda was wearing a suit with big shoulder pads that emphasized her well-fortified chest, a baby-blue blouse and a skirt with knife-edge concertina pleats. Her stockings were a pale tea colour, accentuating the muscles of her calves, and her court shoes cut into her feet, causing the flesh to mound.

'You look very smart today, dear. Any particular reason?'

'The Chancellor of the Exchequer's wife must always look smart! And I think there might be a photo call today.'

'Doubt it. Doubt if the PM will make up his mind today; more likely he'll get someone to deputise as Foreign Secretary for the moment. Smythe's rallying, I'm told.' Reggie smiled as he stuck a soldier into his egg.

'Well, you never know . . . There was a lot of activity last night.' Hilda nodded towards the pavement where feet could be glimpsed passing. 'I saw Biggs-Hodgkisson going in at about nine thirty.'

'Where?'

'Number Twelve.'

'Ah, Raymond up to his tricks. I bet he's having a field day.' Having the Chief Whip as next-door neighbour was both a source of interest and irritation. Raymond and Jenkins were always popping into each other's establishments. Raymond had a house in Highgate where his wife and children kept to themselves but Raymond himself spent a good deal of time entertaining at Number Twelve.

'H'm. Well, if there is a reshuffle it might be a natural step to go from Defence to Foreign Secretary, but not if you've made a gaffe like he did.'

'I don't remember, dear. Can you pass me the Flora?'

'Surely you do—'

'And the marmalade if you don't mind.'

'That speech he made about "our Aryan heritage" to the Stockwell Tory Group?'

'What's wrong with that? We are Aryans, aren't we?'

Sometimes, Reggie thought, Hilda was a bit blinkered, though on the whole she was a good old stick.

Hilda munched loudly, and the crumbs gathered first at the corner of her mouth before they cascaded down her jacket.

'Sometimes I think they ought to have a woman as Foreign Secretary,' she ventured.

'A woman! As Foreign Secretary! Dear God. I would say Jenkins would be off his trolley if he asked a woman. What would our Arab friends say?'

'Well, years ago Maggie Thatcher was PM.'

'Yes, quite, but we've come to our senses since. The very idea. We've not a single woman in the Cabinet anyway, so the question doesn't arise. Foreign Secretary is too important a post for a woman.'

'What about Carter? I know his wife from the Westminster Wives. She's most supportive and he's supposed to be very up and coming.'

'Too junior – and not suitable for a Foreign Secretary,' Reggie said smugly. 'Turns out the only time he's been to the States was on a package tour to Florida to see Disneyland.'

'Then there's Roger Parfitt.'

'Unmarried.'

Hilda looked up quizzically from the fifth piece of wholemeal Nimble she'd been spreading.

'Bloody poofter,' was Reggie's dismissive reply. 'Anyway, you didn't see what I saw last night – very late it was. Must have been about twelve. You were fast asleep. Snoring away,' he added affectionately.

'Oh?' Hilda's eyes were glued to his, so that she didn't even acknowledge the arrival of Pinky, tail up, whiskers twitching. 'Who then?'

'Saw Matthews drawing up.'

'Matthews. But he's Home Secretary.'

'Not an impossible move, you know.'

'I would have thought James Askew might have been in line.'

'Well, no. Too junior, I would think. I get the impression that, always supposing there is a reshuffle, Jenkins wants one of his chums. Smythe, after all, is his closest ally. Probably what he's doing is just making a few plans for the future, testing the water you might say, just in case Smythe pops off or has another attack.'

'Matthews? I thought Martin Matthews was in James's camp?'

Reggie shifted uncomfortably. 'Well, he is, and then again . . . he keeps his options open. Only sensible. I don't think at the moment he'd come out openly for James – not with Jenkins firmly entrenched. But give him a bit of time . . . This is new, dear. Very nice. Where did you get it?'

'It' was a cruet set in the form of a boat, the pepper and salt being the owl and the pussycat.

'Surely you remember. Auntie Mabel gave it to us for our wedding. I found it when I was sorting out some jumble for the Westminster Wives' Summer Fayre. I do like something to brighten up our breakfast table. After all, it's about the only time we see each other these days.'

'By the way, have you had your talk with Mrs Askew yet?' Reggie asked.

'No. It's odd you should say that. Every time I've telephoned, she's not been there.'

'Busy woman, I expect.'

'Tosh! Mary said her sister saw her at Covent Garden with that man, Michael Elliot and his wife – well, she assumed it was his wife, but you never know with a man like that, do you?'

'I'm beginning to think James has got in a little too thick with Elliot. It may be that whole Markham Court business will blow up in his face. Lot of antagonism down there. And with the by-election only a few weeks away . . . In fact Raymond told me he's really worried about it. The press are on to something, he thinks.'

Reggie glanced at the *Daily Telegraph* lying face down beside his plate and turned it over to read the headlines.

' "Labour hopes at By-Election",' he read scathingly. 'Fat chance.'

The kitchen door was eased silently open.

'Yes, I saw it on *News at Ten* last night – Rentamob, sitting out in the woods at Markham Court. The poor Duke!'

145

Pinky, unacknowledged, made a disgruntled but dignified exit.

'What you don't see, Hilda, is that always supposing there is a reshuffle, if Matthews becomes Foreign Secretary, that leaves the Home Office open. I'm going to have another word in Jenkins's ear.'

Chapter 20

Michael, sitting in the dark in his drawing room, close to midnight, was not a happy man. He should have had a really good day. It had started well. In the morning he had flown to Dublin and finalised a big deal for Gaia with a new German chemical company based in Southern Ireland. On the plane he'd seen a reference to himself in an article in the *Guardian*. The journalist had been digging, had discovered that James had once been employed by him, and was now making a possible link between this fact and the grant for the Markham Court project. Small beer, he'd thought. But when he'd landed at Heathrow in the afternoon, there were several hacks waiting for him, chivvying him with questions. He'd fobbed them off. After all, it was all a long time ago and he himself certainly had nothing to worry about. He'd learnt that a question about Markham Court was to be raised in Parliament the following afternoon. Joanna would make sure he got all the details.

That afternoon he had had a meeting with Dr Ernesto Avida-Bals which had concluded brilliantly. Avida-Bals had offered him a deal for passing sums of money through a number of subsidiary banks in Lima and Santiago, which was very advantageous. It all sounded pretty solid. At six he had telephoned Helena but her mobile had been switched off. That meant there would be no dinner *à deux* that evening. Perhaps it was an ominous sign.

At seven Caroline had telephoned. She sounded peeved. Journalists were hiding in the grounds with telephoto lenses, and she had even caught one trying to climb in through a bathroom window on the first floor, having shinned up the wisteria.

One thing she was certain of, she told him: with all the journalists and protestors milling around, she couldn't take any more. Bertie was quite useless in these matters. He'd left home two days ago and gone to the Westminster flat. She too had decided to come up to

London tomorrow. Was Michael free for dinner tomorrow night – 'somewhere quiet?' she qualified the invitation immediately to show that it was definitely not a dinner *à trois* she had in mind.

'Oh darling, I can't make it,' Michael said immediately. 'I have a business meeting tomorrow that will go on till all hours.'

Caroline instantly caught the vibes. 'Well, like it or not, we have to meet soon to discuss the mess we're in. I want a few explanations from you. I hear you've been entertaining Mrs Askew at the opera. Not just once, but twice!'

So that was the real reason she was phoning.

'Along with several others,' he said, 'including my sister.'

'You've never introduced me to your sister.'

'She doesn't come to England very often and I can hardly introduce you as my mistress, can I?'

'And the second time?'

The second occasion was far more difficult to explain. He decided to say nothing. 'Let's meet later next week,' he said, and, finally appeased, she had rung off.

No, none of these things was the problem. The problem was Helena. She had the share options but had decided not to sign them. Pity. It would have meant, of course, that James could have been called to heel. But a disturbing element had entered Michael's life. Of course Helena was desirable, but now he found that he was actually in love with her – and badly, in a way he could not remember experiencing before. Of course he had offered her the share options for his own reasons but now he realised that he genuinely wanted to help her. This intense feeling wasn't something he could shut out of his life, or compartmentalise as he usually could. It seemed to penetrate every waking moment and filled him with anguish, as though every moment apart from her was a torment.

When he looked at her he envied James, envied the family she had given him and the idea had come to him – when they were watching *The Magic Flute* during the second opera trip, holding hands – of having a family of his own, of being faithful to one woman, sharing their lives and growing old together. But would he have the courage to adapt to such a life? Somehow he doubted it. And he gave a bitter inward laugh. He had left the decision for too long, played the field, shirked that sort of responsibility. He wondered if it were all a bit of a fantasy. His phone rang. Simon was on the line.

'Michael, have you had any luck with your contact in the Cabinet yet?'

'Yes, Simon, it's looking hopeful. I think the Home Secretary will do as I ask. Party funds are always an attractive priority. 'But it's late, Simon. Can we talk tomorrow perhaps? I was just about to go to bed.'

'Lucky you. I can't sleep any more.'

'I've told you before not to worry. We'll talk soon. Good night.'

Michael felt a little guilty. He had not given Simon's problem his full attention and had allowed too long to pass without following up his original approach to Mark Raymond. No wonder Simon couldn't sleep. Michael poured himself a large Scotch and was making his way upstairs to bed when the thought struck him that if there were to be a reshuffle James might be moved and that would leave him, Michael, in a sticky mess. Still, the first half of the grant money had already been paid over. He switched off his phone, and continued on his weary way.

So it was not until the next morning that he received the news that the Plymouth headquarters of Western Environmental Services had been broken into and ransacked.

Chapter 21

James was in a taxi, on his way to Number Ten, for the second time that horrendous day.

It had begun with Mark Raymond phoning him. He'd sent over a copy of the new *Private Eye* cover to James's office, with a picture of James and Michael Elliot shaking hands (James could not recall when this picture had been taken), and a caption which read 'Cash for Crap'. Closer inspection revealed that Elliot's head had been stuck on to someone else's body, but it made no difference to the message. Raymond had also sent over the cutting from yesterday's *Guardian* which James had already read. Raymond sounded almost gleeful when he rang, and James could not help feeling that the Chief Whip was deliberately stirring up trouble, in view of a probable and imminent reshuffle and the fact that James was not in his camp. It didn't really matter whether or not the allegations were true. Everyone knew that mud sticks, especially in politics.

James, however, was confident. He had nothing to hide. Westminster, with its pagan undertones, demanded the occasional sacrificial hero – the backbenches were littered with the embittered victims of enforced resignations – but James had made up his mind that he was not going to be one of them.

The next to telephone was Caroline.

'James, the Duchess is on the line. May I put her through?' Charles asked.

'Yes,' James replied briskly, 'and, Charles, while I think of it, Cynthia has been on the blower. The officers in the Association want the usual pound of flesh. Can you say I have an urgent committee meeting all morning?' The last thing James wanted was Cynthia or Beryl delivering a lengthy speech on the evils of the gutter press.

'Hello, James.' Caroline's voice sounded as if she were in an indoor swimming pool. 'I'm sorry about the quality of the sound, but this is my new phone. It can't be tapped, as I imagine yours is,' she said.

'Caroline, tell me, what the hell's been going on?' James's voice rose in a crescendo.

'I tried to telephone you yesterday evening,' Caroline protested, 'but your line was permanently engaged.'

'Yes, yes, I know. The press were on the phone all night. They even tried to talk to the au pair this morning. Our house is now surrounded. Helena could hardly get through the cameras to take the children to school. In the end we took the phone off the hook. Please explain exactly what all this is about.' James's voice had become decidedly angry.

'I'm just as upset and bewildered as you are,' Caroline said defensively. 'The whole thing's a complete nightmare. There's something very funny going on. Apparently someone rang the local press. They didn't leave a name, but they gave all sorts of detailed information about the fact that you'd done work for several of Michael Elliot's companies when you were a barrister, then all sorts of stuff about Western Environmental.' There was a pause.

'But what's all this to do with the project at Markham Court? This whole thing about the waste, too, seems totally out of proportion. What sort of waste are they talking about, for God's sake? I thought we had well and truly covered all this. I wrote to you making clear there was to be no waste in the infill, remember?'

'I thought Michael would have told you,' Caroline covered herself. 'I'm not sure he has told me everything. I have a feeling there's more to this. Whoever it was who rang implied you were expecting back-handers for easing the project through.' Caroline hesitated, she had not meant to put it quite like that. Well, you know,' she blustered. 'I mean . . . something of the sort, you know how they twist things . . .' She added, as an afterthought, 'They were not exactly specific.'

'I think we call it disinformation,' James said, with a touch of sarcasm.

'Well, whatever,' Caroline continued, wishing to make her point, 'I think you have an enemy somewhere who has it in for you or why would anyone do such a thing?' Caroline's voice trailed away; something had just struck her.

Charles put his head round the door. 'James, sorry to interrupt but the Whips' Office is on the line.' James could tell by Charles's face the news was bad.

'I have to go. Get on to your lawyer, Caroline, and I'll line Elliot up for a meeting. I'll get back to you.'

Five minutes later James put his head in his hands. For the first time in his Parliamentary career he felt fear. Of course the Opposition were on to it; he knew it was only a matter of time. Stan Pike – the scourge of the Establishment, anti-Monarchist, anti-anything remotely connected with the upper classes – had put down a Private Member's Question for this very afternoon. 'The Minister of State for the Environment to make a statement about his involvement in a waste disposal project at the Duke and Duchess of Hampton's Estate, Markham Court.' Mark Raymond's voice was at its smoothest as he gave James the unwelcome information. James agreed to go to Number Ten at once.

'Anything I can do, James?' Charles asked.

'Yes. Call the driver. I'll be back by lunchtime. Send out for sandwiches and lager and get the Department civil servant who deals with land use here. Also my lawyer and the Parliamentary Under-Secretary. I need to be well briefed by two fifteen.' James took a deep breath and told Charles about Stan Pike's PMQ.

The sun shone on the black bonnet of James's car as it swept up to the security gates of Downing Street. The uniformed officers had seen its approach. They made a gesture of recognition and waved it through. Unlike most ministers, James always sat in front. It was one of his foibles. Reporters were bunched on the pavement opposite the front door of Number Ten. As he got out of the car he looked up at the benign blue of the sky and felt like a condemned man on his way to execution.

The door opened and James was greeted in the hall by the Prime Minister's Private Secretary. He followed him up to the Cabinet Room, where the Prime Minister and Mark Raymond were seated at the long table opposite each other. The room smelt a little fusty. The heavily netted windows were tightly shut and the sun struggled through them as to the bottom of a contaminated pond. The Prime Minister rose to greet him. There was something threatening about his presence. James had a sense of foreboding.

'Good of you to come so quickly. Do take a seat,' the Prime Minister said coolly, indicating a chair three down from Mark, who remained still, like a waxwork.

'I'm sorry about all this, Prime Minister. I'm as shocked as you are about these ridiculous reports,' James blurted out.

'Well, ridiculous or not, it looks as if the Speaker is going to accept Stan Pike's PMQ for this afternoon,' Raymond said smugly.

The Prime Minister and Mark were enjoying his discomfort.

'I can deal with it. I have absolutely nothing to hide,' James asserted.

'I hear what you say,' Jenkins said quietly, 'but I think we need to talk it through.' He looked down at the short brief which had been given to him earlier. James recognised the handwriting: it was Raymond's. His suspicions were aroused. There was more to this: not concern for the environment or the possibility of ministerial ineptitude; no, this was internal politics.

The Prime Minister led James carefully through the various reports that had appeared over the last few days in the press, and James reassured him.

'These reports are utterly without foundation. I believe they are the usual media lies and I am perfectly sure the murky area is disinformation.' James looked directly at Raymond as he spoke.

'But I have it in front of me, James,' the Prime Minister said steadily, glancing down at the brief he held in his hand. 'On a number of occasions you advised Elliot on what look to me like some very dubious deals.'

The Prime Minister let his half-glasses fall to the end of his nose and observed James with a challenging lift of his head.

'Prime Minister,' James answered. 'I severed all links with Elliot's companies some time ago, long before it became obligatory owing to my ministerial office. Besides, Western Environmental Services did not exist as such, at the time when I was involved with the Elliot Corporation.'

Raymond looked displeased.

'Well, we appear to have sorted that one out,' the Prime Minister conceded. 'The problem is, Askew, that the grant that's been given to my old friend Bertie Hampton and indirectly of course to Michael Elliot, for the environment enhancement programme, now appears, according to the press, to be a subsidy for burying rubbish on a former beauty spot. They're wondering if you did it for a backhander. Have I got it right?' The Prime Minister replaced his glasses and referred again to the brief. 'And you do see all the stories knit together nicely? When certain people add two and two together and make five, there are those who believe you would not have gone to such lengths were it not that you stood to receive some sort of personal gain.'

'With respect, Prime Minister,' James said confidently, 'this is all a storm in a teacup. It is quite monstrous to imply that I have gained personally from this in any way whatsoever.'

'Yes,' the Prime Minister said, looking pensively at the brief, making notes with a gold Mont Blanc fountain pen, and trying not to look at Mark. 'I feel I can accept your assurance there . . .' he paused, then went on. 'Now what is this question of infill? I don't recall you mentioning that before.'

'I have to admit,' James continued breezily, 'the Duchess did voice her concern that the company who were handling the project had floated the idea of a limited amount of infill with waste, but I warned her, in the strongest possible terms, this would be unacceptable. In fact, I have a copy of the letter I wrote to her at the time reiterating this.' James produced a letter from the file he had brought with him and laid it on the table between the Prime Minister and Mark Raymond. 'I hope this clears the matter up and puts your mind at rest, Prime Minister.'

Three minutes later the Prime Minister indicated he was reassured and James left the room.

James arrived in the Chamber of the House of Commons at five past three. He had spent an hour going through the possible lines of questioning with Charles and the civil servant from the section of the Department dealing with land use.

He sat on the front bench five places along from the Dispatch Box. Questions to Bernard Keatley, the Agricultural Minister, drew to a close and a rustle of anticipation could be heard as the Leader of the Opposition entered the Chamber to a cheer from the Labour benches. He was swiftly followed by the Prime Minister and a counter-cheer from his own Members.

After fifteen minutes Prime Minister's Questions drew to a close and the Prime Minister swept past James, who was already sliding down the bench towards the Dispatch Box. As he passed he gave him an unexpected pat on the shoulder. This surprised James and caused him to look upwards and, in so doing, he was pleased to see Helena sitting in the public gallery in the row reserved for spouses and special guests. Seeing her anxious face he gave her a brief smile. Her presence did not go unnoticed, it was a boost to his image, the loving wife seeing her husband vindicate himself on the floor of the House. James was genuinely grateful to her for supporting him.

The Speaker rose to announce a Private Notice Question from the Labour environment spokesman, Mr Stanley Pike.

Stan Pike asked the Minister to make a statement about waste disposal at Markham Court, the estate of the Duke and Duchess of Hampton.

As James rose to reply a hush descended on the Chamber.

James explained the background to the gravel extraction and the proposals for a wildlife waterpark and denounced the scurrilous misrepresentations in the media as yet another example of the Opposition's dirty tricks campaign. This roused his own back-benchers to shouts of 'Hear! Hear!'

Stan Pike leapt to his feet with a look of anticipation on his face.

'Is it true the Right Honourable Member has connections with the owner of Western Environmental Services, Mr Michael Elliot, who has other plans for the site, namely waste disposal, which would be far more profitable and disgustingly unacceptable in such a renowned beauty spot and,' Stan Pike added for good measure, 'another example of Tory Government preaching one thing and doing another?' There were cheers from the Opposition benches. 'And will the Right Honourable gentleman deny that he was financially involved with the owner of the company and had a personal relationship with the owners of the Estate, another example of Tory sleaze?' Stan Pike banged the Dispatch Box with his fist and the Labour benches bayed bloodthirstily.

James rose imperiously to his feet. The house was silent. He leaned directly across the Dispatch Box towards Stan Pike, and his voice was sepulchral.

'I utterly refute these baseless allegations and challenge the honourable gentleman to repeat them outside the House. I have not, and never have had, a connection with Western Environmental Services. And with respect to my connections with the Duke and Duchess, I have here a letter which I am quite prepared to place in the library in which I make it clear I share the honourable gentleman's views and reiterate the Government's policies about the environment. It is hardly credible,' James continued gravely, 'that I would encourage the despoiling of an area of rare scenic beauty and I hope this settles the matter once and for all.'

James sat down with a flourish and the backbenchers settled in their seats, realising the drama was over, at least for the time being.

Now James was on another visit to the PM, the taxi making its way through the almost deserted streets. After his performance in the House, which he felt he had done well, he had returned home to nurse his cold, only to be roused from his bed by yet another summons to Number Ten.

As the taxi rounded the corner into Downing Street he wondered what ghastly cooked-up revelations were awaiting him this time. He knew in his heart he had acted honourably and had absolutely nothing to reproach himself with in his conduct – except, of course, the temporary lapse with Caroline, of which he was deeply ashamed, but surely no one could know of that?

Jenkins was looking extremely tired when James was ushered into his inner sanctum. He was alone.

'Good of you to come, Askew,' the Prime Minister said. His mouth managed a sort of rictus which might have been translated as a smile, though his blue eyes remained stony.

'I think a good strong drink might be a welcome idea.' Jenkins was known for his fine collection of malts. 'A malt? Or I have a very fine vodka here, given me by President Polkov on my last trip to Petersburg.' He held up a bottle of delicate amber. James somewhat cautiously opted for a Laphroaig.

'I've invited you here because I would like this Markham Court business settled.'

So it was the Markham Court business after all: James's heart sank.

'I hear you gave a very creditable performance this afternoon, Askew. As you know, my connections with Bertie Hampton go back a long way. And I would not like to see an old-established family

157

such as his being dragged through the mud. You were quite right to defend their interests in the way you did, and I have only admiration for the way you handled it. You have always proved yourself an honourable man!'

Despite your background, James could almost hear him think.

'I would simply like your confirmation that your dealings with Elliot – a rather dubious gentleman, let us be honest, though an extremely valuable asset to our Party funds,' the ghost of a smile, 'are totally above board.'

'Absolutely, one hundred per cent,' James said flatly.

'People like Elliot have their uses, but one must not become too entangled with them.'

'I assure you, Prime Minister, I have nothing to hide. I must tell you that my wife is engaged in painting his portrait, though that's purely a business arrangement, of course.'

'Humph. It was good to see your wife in the Gallery this afternoon. Wifely support when you're a minister is crucially important, especially when the Party seems to be hanging on by such a thin thread.'

'Indeed.'

'Yes, we certainly cannot afford to have any scandals about Members' private lives . . .'

James wondered where this conversation was leading. 'My wife has three children by her former marriage – she was widowed, you know. They take up a fair amount of her time,' he said, not quite sure why he had rushed to defend Helena.

'Quite so, quite so.' Jenkins was giving him a very shrewd look. 'Well, the reason I have called you in, Askew, at this late hour, is that as you may be aware, I am in the process of reshuffling the Cabinet. Poor Smythe will be out of action for the foreseeable future, I'm afraid.'

'Yes, sad news indeed,' James said unctuously, his heart beating.

'I'm therefore appointing Matthews as Foreign Secretary . . . And offering you his former post as Home Secretary. I think you are a man of immense ability and would be capable of handling the position. What say you?'

'It's immensely flattering. May I have a day to think about it?' James felt his spirits soaring.

'I hope you will accept. It would well and truly put a dampener on the press, whose gossip-mongering is not doing the Party any good. But, more importantly, the post requires a person of the utmost integrity and with a cool head, two attributes you have proved you have and I personally have the utmost confidence in you. Another?' He held out the bottle of malt.

James declined. His mind was racing with excitement.

Jenkins did not press him. After discussing details, and the possible successor to James's post at Environment, James finally left, braving the PM's infamously strong handshake. It was way past midnight.

On the way back to Richmond Terrace, James could not help thinking how gratified his mother would have felt had she managed to live just a few years longer. He remembered how tiny she was – like a little sparrow, her mousy hair, her kind eyes and careworn face. And he remembered the rows, the way his father used to try to bully her and how, small though she was, she always stood her corner. He recalled too how his father used to jibe at him. 'A wimp,' he had called James. 'Sitting on your arse, with your nose in a book, instead of earning an honest wage. How much longer are you going to be at that university? Pity there's no National Service. That would knock some sense into you.' Strange how after all these years James still remembered every poisonous remark. And when his father had died James had felt no pity, only relief for himself and his mother, that at last the tyrant was dead . . .

He made himself think of something else. Changes would have to be made to his life, *their* lives. Surely now Helena would feel that he had proved his worth.

So engrossed was he in his sense of achievement that until he got home he failed to wonder about any of the gentlemanly allusions the PM had made to the fact that things, as far as Helena was concerned, might not be entirely as they appeared.

It was not until two days later that James recalled the Prime Minister's words that afternoon and the reference to scandal. He had been much too excited by the thought of his promotion to concentrate on the allusions to irregularities at home. He was sitting in the front of the ministerial car on his way to a meeting when the word 'scandal' started to repeat itself in the back of his mind. It came slowly at first, just a small nagging thing, and then his stomach turned. Of course, how could he have been so blind? Helena was having an affair with Michael Elliot. He felt angry that he should have been so stupid. It was one thing to condone your wife's finding consolation outside a failing marriage, but to be the last person to know about it was a subtle wound to his pride, far more hurtful than the affair itself. He dialled home on the car phone. It was six o'clock. Helena answered.

'Helena,' he said abruptly, 'I am coming home between votes tonight. There is something I need to talk to you about.'

Later, as he put the key in the door, he knew exactly what he was going to say, convinced that there was no point in postponing the agony. Helena had got out some drinks on a silver tray, thin slices of lemon and ice indicated her intention of taking this seriously. She stood in the drawing room. She had had her hair done, or at least James thought there was something different about her. He seldom noticed these things but she had changed recently. There was a new sort of confidence and beauty about her , as if she knew how powerful her presence could be. No wonder Michael Elliot was attracted to her.

As James looked at his wife he felt a kind of terror, a terror that he might, by confronting the truth, force the issue, make her do something precipitate. He might lose her forever instead of just for a while . . . and she was too valuable to lose.

'Well, darling, what has happened that brings you home so suddenly?' Helena asked coolly.

He fumbled over the words. They were not at all as he had planned in his anger. 'You are not having an affair with Michael Elliot, are you?' he said, more as a statement than a question.

Her eyes did not even blink. She just stared at him over the rim of her glass. 'Of course I'm not. He has plenty of women without adding me to his list of conquests.' Her voice remained cool as she continued. 'You see, James, he has been a wonderful friend to me. In fact, he may well be the one thing which could save our marriage.'

James knew she was lying, but his relief that she had chosen to do so was intense.

'Is that the only reason you came home . . . to ask me that?' she asked.

'Yes,' he answered. 'You see, Helena, despite what you think, I do love you. I want to make love to you. I cannot bear the thought of another man touching you . . . but I feel unwelcome in your bed. I . . .' he stammered, 'I would like to take you out to dinner. I have put off my dinner at the House. Can I take you somewhere? We need to do things together more often.'

They went to Helena's favourite restaurant in Sloane Street and later Helena waited in the car as James rushed in for the ten o'clock vote. She had drunk rather more wine than was usual for her. When they got home he followed her upstairs. It was quite like old times, they made love . . . he had almost forgotten how pleasurable their lovemaking could be.

Chapter 22

James and Helena were at the breakfast table. Neither had slept well for days, worrying about the implications of James's news and Helena's affair. Helena realised what promotion would mean to James, but it also meant the chances of her continuing her affair with Michael were diminishing by the minute, especially now that James clearly suspected the truth. She'd had a brief call from Michael yesterday. He was in Plymouth. He said he'd had a break-in and masses of documents had been taken. He seemed in a state, quite unlike himself.

She'd mentioned James's possible promotion, but not their row, and Michael had gone very quiet, a bit remote.

She could see James was desperate to accept the Home Secretary-ship, and wondered why he seemed to be hesitating. Something was worrying him deeply, holding him back, but she could not work out what it was.

As usual James was riffling through the daily pile of newspapers. He picked up the *Guardian* and there, in the middle of the front page, was a huge headline:

TOXIC WASTE FOR DUKE'S ESTATE

'My God, listen to this,' James said. ' "The *Guardian* has obtained confidential information that the business tycoon Michael Elliot (46) who owns a conglomerate of companies under the group name of Western Environmental Services, and who has recently been imp-licated in the . . ." blah blah blah . . . "is planning to bury toxic waste on the site. A confidential source has sent documents to the *Guardian* offices revealing that Mr Elliot, through his company Gaia Impex, whose headquarters are in Liechtenstein, was planning to use the site for disposal of chlorinated residues of manufacturing, said to contain dioxin.

' "Our medical correspondent writes: 'Dioxin can cause chronic skin irritation, blindness and deformity in children, if released into the atmosphere'." '

Helena stood rigid and shocked.

'It does on: "The site was recently awarded a half-million-pound Government grant . . . We have written evidence that Gaia Impex was importing toxic chemicals for waste disposal . . . Labour spokesman for the Environment, Richard Baines, says that he will be calling for a public inquiry. Markham Court is situated within the constituency of Nunstead, where a by-election is to take place on Thursday."

'Where on earth would they have got their information from?' James said.

The break-in, though Helena, but could say nothing.

'Just as well I'm seeing Elliot today. I want to get to the bottom of this.'

Today! And he had told Helena he was staying in the West Country.

Five o'clock and James was still tussling with his conscience. The meeting with Elliot had not turned out as planned, not at all. Putting all thoughts of Elliot and Helena out of his mind, he had asked Elliot whether there was any truth in the *Guardian* article, and Elliot had replied with a shrug.

'Askew, we're adults, I'm a businessman. Don't tell me you aren't aware such things go on?'

'Under a public park?'

'Well under, I assure you. My scientists have told me that buried deep enough it can cause no possible danger to anyone.'

James was outraged, his anger compounded by his personal outrage. He told Michael Elliot he was a complete bastard, he'd reneged on their agreement, lied through his teeth – what he was planning was illegal! There would be no chance whatsoever of things going ahead. There would be no cover-up, and he would see that the second half of the subsidy was withdrawn immediately.

It was then that the bombshell dropped.

'There will be a cover-up,' Elliot said. 'What's more, you and the Cabinet will go along with me. Nor will you stop that subsidy.' Elliot seemed so sure of himself. 'I hear on the grapevine,' he went on, 'that you have been offered Home Secretary. I strongly advise you not to take it, not until you've seen this through.'

James stood his ground. 'I don't know where or how you obtained what is totally private information,' he immediately suspected Raymond, 'but since you know, you shall also know that I have every intention of taking it.'

'I don't think so. You see, the other day Simon and I had a very intimate chat. About his old university days. He's told me everything . . . everything. If you accept the Home Office, I might be obliged to whisper in Raymond's ear.'

Simon.

Now James sat in his office with his head in his hands, his heart pumping wildly.

When he had won his state scholarship from the grammar school in Wales and had got his place at Emmanuel College, Cambridge, he had felt a total outsider, and lonely. Utterly lonely. He was shy, gauche, and poor. Compared with all those bright, affluent, self-confident young men around him, he had felt hugely inferior. He was however extremely handsome, once he had controlled his diet and lost weight, in a Byronic sort of way, with his dark glossy hair and slim body. And it was almost against his will, beyond his belief, and certainly out of his control that he had suddenly found himself falling in love with the worldly-wise, sophisticated Swiss.

Simon was well dressed, well read, well travelled; he knew all about modern art and opera. He could ski; he had amazing connections in the banking world. He had a sports car. He was rich. He had all those things which James had never had. Simon had taught James so much and taken such pleasure in being his mentor. He had given James enormous confidence – though towards the end of their relationship James had begun to realise how spoilt and petulant Simon could be when he did not get his own way.

Sexually Simon had taken the lead. It was something that James had never come to terms with. He would have preferred to have had the relationship without the sex. He had always wanted it to be kept secret; sex had never been spoken of in his home. He had never even seen his father naked. Simon, on the other hand, in the atmosphere of Cambridge, would have been quite happy to have flaunted the affair, but James had always, always been deeply ashamed. He had told Simon it must be hidden, even from his other friends. It was

James who had brought it to an end, unable to sustain the guilt. It was a traumatic, desperately unhappy end, after which all communication between them had been severed. Simon had gone on to Harvard, though later, briefly, James had heard that Simon was back in Britain and had settled in Edinburgh. His parents had cut all connections with him when he had told them he was gay and was not interested in a career in banking. At the time James had heard this, he had been in the throes of his brief first marriage. The relationship, however, had haunted James throughout his adult life, knowing that inevitably one day it would come to light and his career in politics would be put on the line.

It was blackmail. There was no other word for it. He'd told Elliot he didn't give a damn about what he said to Raymond, but the time had come for a reckoning with his own past. He knew that, were it made public, his affair with Simon would wreck his political career.

There was another consideration too. The job of Home Secretary was a trap. It was a way of promoting him and shunting him off into the sidings at the same time. Every Home Secretary in the last hundred years had ended up reviled and unloved. It was a dead-end job. If he took it, his chances of the leadership were finished. He would have to turn down the PM's offer. Strange, he thought, that after his bout of realism about his homosexual past, his ambition still hungered after what had now become an almost impossible dream.

Chapter 23

'Mr Peter Bevington, New Left Imperative – 23; Mr Michael Harington, Monster Raving Loony Party – 1,401; Miss April Smith, Bats Need Friends – 4,192; Mr Roger Ogilvie-Bartlett – Conservative, 4,221; Mr Clive Brett, Liberal Democrat – 7,867; Mr Clint Westwood, Labour – 16,810.'

Helena was setting out the breakfast things, while James drummed his fingers impatiently on the table in front of the television, his face dour. The children were racing around upstairs.

'I hereby declare Mr Clint Westwood duly elected Member of Parliament for the constituency of Nunstead. Mr Peter Bevington and Mr Michael Harington lose their deposits.'

'Damn, damn, damn,' James said.

'It is quite amazing,' the TV reporter was saying, 'that this safe Tory seat which had a majority of some 7,000 at the last election, should have gone to Labour, leaving the Conservatives at Westminster with a precarious majority of one.'

James listened with growing despair, jabbing at his cornflakes with his spoon, as the debate moved to the studio and two political commentators.

'How do you regard the revelations about the Minister of the Environment and his connections with Western Environmental Services? Do you think they had an effect on the outcome?'

James stood up, shaking with rage, his face grim. He went to switch off the set.

Helena felt a stab of sympathy for him. And a feeling of alarm over Michael. What was his role in all this? He was a businessman, an entrepreneur. He could not be blamed for this fiasco, surely? But she said nothing to James. James had been reassured by the telephone calls he had had the previous evening, one from the PM and another, unbelievably, from old Smythe, who was making a good recovery and had wished him all the best. Jenkins had been quite magnanimous: we are backing you a hundred per cent, this will all blow over, you'll see.

Today James actually stooped down and pecked Helena on the cheek as he left. 'I doubt if I'll manage to be back before ten tonight. I expect a very heavy day. Just don't let any of those hounds outside get to you.'

From the window Helena watched him as he picked his way through the journalists on the pavement, seemingly unflustered by their importunate and often rude questions, and eased himself into his chauffeur-driven car. The car swung round the corner and out of Helena's sight.

She turned as Rollo came strutting into the room. 'Mum, Clovis found a white stick in a saucer on the floor near your dressing table. He's running about with it upstairs. I told him to drop it but he wouldn't,' he announced, pouring milk on his cornflakes with ample rations for the tablecloth.

'What . . . is he eating it?' Helena cried, jumping up from the breakfast table and turning scarlet.

'No, I told him not to,' Rollo replied.

Helena had forgotten about the saucer, probably because she felt so ill. She rushed upstairs to her bedroom, slowing her pace as she approached what she now suspected was inevitable. She simply had not dared to look. There was no sign of Clovis but the saucer was there, and nearby the little piece of stick, evidently not to Clovis's taste. It had gone blue. She was pregnant. She sat on her bed too shocked to move.

The telephone rang; one of the children picked it up downstairs.

'Mum . . . phone.' It was Rollo calling up the stairs.

'Who is it?' Helena called back.

'It's the one with the posh voice who looks like a man. You know, from Sussex,' Rollo lisped the word Sussex.

'Rollo!' Helena whispered round the banisters.

She dismally picked up the receiver.

'Helena, is that you?' Cynthia asked.

'Yes. How can I help?' She was resigned to one of Cynthia's diatribes.

'Can we have a talk about strategy?' Cynthia snorted the word.

'Certainly, but I have to do the school run now. Why don't you ring me in an hour?' Helena suggested.

'Fine.' With a click the line went dead. Cynthia had registered her displeasure.

Helena had fought through the journalists and returned from the school run. She made herself a cup of herb tea and ate a dry biscuit. The thought of coffee made her stomach heave. She went to her favourite chair in the kitchen and sat down.

The dry biscuit did the trick. The nausea gradually subsided and with it her inability to confront the latest twist in her life. She felt oddly happy, but this was her own very private happiness. She was going to keep this completely to herself. What action she should take partly depended on the action of others.

The phone rang.

'Now, are there going to be any interruptions? I really do need your undivided attention,' Cynthia said, much as a Head Teacher would speak to a difficult child.

'Yes, you have my complete attention, but not for long. I'm afraid as you can imagine, it's a pretty hectic day here, and I have my own work,' Helena said.

'Well, in case it had escaped your attention, it looks as if there might well be an election – sooner than we thought. The majority's dangerously low. And we need to do some forward planning.' Cynthia paused for a second. 'You will have to put in more of an appearance down here,' she announced.

'Oh yes, and what did you have in mind?' Helena asked, already irritated.

'Well, tours of all the old people's homes; more – and I mean *much* more – interest in all the women's groups; and a little fund-raising, bring and buy, that sort of thing,' Cynthia prattled on.

'Before we get too excited about all these jolly outings you're so kindly planning for me, do remember it is only the third week in June and we will have the whole recess to suck up to the constituents,' Helena replied.

There was a gasp from the other end of the line. It did not come from Cynthia. Someone else was listening.

'Well, that is obviously a matter of opinion, and I am not sure yours tallies with the sentiments of all those unfailingly loyal people who do so much work for the Party,' Cynthia replied nastily.

'Look, Cynthia, let's get one thing straight, shall we? The Party can look after itself, my family can't. Also, the Party is not going to pay my grocery bill or run my car. I don't want to have a row with you, Cynthia, but your tone is patronising and offensive.'

'Well!' Cynthia articulated in high dudgeon.

Helena could imagine Cynthia bridling behind her G-Plan desk in the constituency office, Beryl listening on the extension in the small adjacent room with the photocopier and the fax machine, donated by her husband. The room always smelt of boiled eggs and Helena felt sick as she imagined it.

'I think you've made yourself perfectly plain, Helena. I'll get Beryl to report back to all the ladies. She will have to scrub the itinerary she had so carefully prepared for you and try to reschedule things for the recess. James will be very disappointed. I told him I was going to plan it with you. There is one more thing, if you can spare the time. After all, it is only your husband's career we're talking about,' Cynthia said unpleasantly.

'Well, go on,' said Helena irritably.

'It's tights.'

'What do you mean, tights? Is Beryl's husband running out or something?' asked Helena.

'Really, Helena. No, it's about you and bare legs.'

'Bare legs?' Helena repeated incredulously.

'There were complaints last summer. In the hot weather you appeared several times in the constituency with bare legs. Some ladies didn't like it.'

'I bet the men didn't complain. Oh, there's my doorbell. Must go now, Cynthia. Goodbye, Beryl.'

There was a dual intake of breath at the other end of the line, as Helena rang off.

She didn't know whether to laugh or cry. She decided to laugh.

When she had pulled herself together, Helena tried to sort out her mixed emotions.

Yes. She wanted this baby she had so longed for.

Her longing for a baby had been one of the reasons for the estrangement between herself and James, why he had become so cold.

She was glad it was Michael's baby, not James's.

When she had so carelessly missed a few days on the pill a few months ago, life had been very different.

She added all these points together. There was no easy solution – just a terrible dilemma. One side of her thought: to hell with James. He was, she now believed, a calculating, cold fish, and she would leave him nonetheless. But of course the house in Richmond Terrace was hers. She couldn't just leave. And, more importantly, there was the stability of her children's lives to consider.

The more reasonable side of her said: what about Michael? She did not really know Michael all that well. Was he to be trusted? Would he marry her if she left James? Did he love her? Everything about him was exciting. He had feelings, and everything he had done for her had been caring, and yet . . . She remembered the newspaper report James had read out to her at breakfast about the toxic waste. An uglier side to her lover was emerging, one that she simply could not reconcile with the Michael she cared so much about, the Michael who was so protective of his extended family.

And what about his mistresses. What of Caroline Hampton, about whom he also refused to say anything?

Maybe she should have an abortion. No! The idea was unthinkable.

She would have the baby. But she would not tell James or Michael for the moment.

Chapter 24

Helena wandered into the kitchen to make herself a cup of tea, then decided against even that. She looked out of the window and saw a gaggle of reporters clustered on the pavement looking towards the house and wondered briefly why they were there yet again. She had not read the newspapers that morning or switched on the radio, having felt so nauseated. For the last few days she had hardly seen James, who left early and came home late; he had been grim and uncommunicative. She had also noticed he looked tired and stressed. She felt a twinge of distress for him, then rallied: after all, it was his political ambition that was causing him stress, that had driven her into the arms of another man. It was a sham of a marriage – the way he treated her house almost like a dosshouse or a waiting room. Worse still was the way he tried to use her like some sort of menial, always at his beck and call. Had he not been so appallingly ambitious they might once have had the chance of making the marriage work. Now it seemed too late.

That morning they had had a hurried meeting before he left. Helena had sat palely at the kitchen table, picking at some dry toast, fighting off her feeling of sickness. James apparently had noticed nothing different about her, but he had seemed very edgy as though he were holding something back. Perhaps there was another crisis brewing. He was very involved in the Markham Court issue, and there had been questions in the House where he had been heckled by the Labour benches. And there would definitely be an election this autumn now.

She sighed, wandered back out of the kitchen and into the studio and sat down. Not to paint, just to think. She simply could not go on drifting any longer.

She made up her mind: tonight she would have it out with James, however late he came home. She would tell him she was pregnant by

Michael, and that their marriage could be at an end. It had to be done. She thought about how the break-up of their marriage might affect James's political career. She did not willingly want to hurt him, or destroy him. But she did not want to destroy her own life either.

After she had told James about the baby, she would tell Michael, though she had not heard from him for days now – which also seemed odd. It wasn't as though they had quarrelled or anything. She thought how happy they had been the last time she had seen him. James, thankfully, had been down at the Constituency that weekend, a place where of late she had refused to go. Maria had looked after the children and Helena had spent the night with Michael. But then, after so much happiness . . . nothing but a brief phone call from him. Her newly found self-confidence foundered.

The phone suddenly started to ring. As she ran to answer it her spirits lifted.

'I have to talk to you. Can I come back at lunch time?'

Not Michael, but James. He sounded strained. She felt ill at ease. He had taken her unawares and she wasn't quite ready for what she had to say to him, but she knew whatever it was that he was coming back to Richmond Terrace for, she would have tell him now. It was no use procrastinating. She felt a new wave of nausea. What did he want? There was obviously something on his mind.

Helena was working on the portrait of David Banks's children when she heard the front door close. He came into the studio. He was just standing there, inside the door, looking over her shoulder at the canvas on the easel.

'What a beautiful painting. Whose children are they?'

Helena turned and looked him straight in the eye. 'Oh, they're Violet and David Banks's.'

'You've done a most wonderful job,' James commented. 'Absolutely brilliant.'

Helena felt herself going a deep scarlet, for she had deliberately gone ahead with the commission behind his back. She turned and carefully washed her brush in some turps, totally unable to believe what she was hearing. Was he being deeply sarcastic? She looked into his face again. No, he was quite sincere.

'Very, very good. When will you let them see it?'

'Oh, not yet,' Helena said. 'There's still work to do.'

'I have the lunch here,' he said, holding up a paper carrier. 'I think I need a drink. Would you like a glass of white wine?'

'How sweet of you, James, but I'm not drinking at the moment,' she apologised.

'Well, I think I'll have one anyway,' he said, walking out of the room.

It must be *now*, she thought. I must do it.

When she joined him in the kitchen Helena saw, to her amazement, that James had laid out the lunch, which was smoked salmon, on the table, even including some fresh brown bread.

She felt uncomfortable with his sudden domestication and thoughtfulness. She couldn't ever remember his coming into her studio, let alone complimenting her on her painting.

She sat down awkwardly. James stood by the table looking around the room as if seeing it for the first time, his expression halfway between hesitant and doleful.

'This is a lovely house. I regret I've had so little chance to appreciate it. You're a wonderful home-maker,' he said disconcertingly.

Helena thought: my God, what's going on here? How am I going to tell him now he's suddenly being so nice to me?

He sat down in his usual chair. Helena noticed he looked bedraggled – there was a thin snowstorm of dandruff on the shoulders of his suit; she guessed he hadn't washed his hair. His hands trembled slightly as he squeezed some lemon on to his smoked salmon and then absent-mindedly on to hers.

'James, what's the matter? You didn't come back here in the middle of the day to compliment me on my housekeeping or my painting,' Helena urged gently. For the first time in their relationship she thought he looked frail and damaged.

'I don't know how to tell you this,' he said, his voice catching alarmingly as he spoke. His hands began to tremble even more and then he angrily pushed the plate away from him and pinched the bridge of his nose with his thumb and forefinger.

Helena saw there were tears trickling through his fingers. She got up from her chair instantly and rounded the table. She put her arm about his shoulders; he didn't pull away.

He laid his head against the coarse linen of the smock she wore for painting. She smelt of oil paint and vanilla. His shoulders shook as he took a deep breath and composed himself.

'Oh God, it's all such a bloody mess,' his voice was thick with emotion.

Seeing James cry was deeply shocking. She had never seen a man cry before, and for it to be James of all people.

'What is it? Whatever's happened?' She felt herself turn pale.

'Sit down, Helena. I'll try to tell you. Anyway, you'll hear about it from some other source soon enough.'

He stared down at the tablecloth, unable to meet her intense stare.

'Years ago, when I was at Cambridge, I met someone and fell in love. We had a very emotional, painful affair. Then it ended.'

'And?'

'And . . . well, it never happened again. It was sort of a mistake really.'

'So what's all the fuss about then? If it was years ago.'

'Because it was,' James was still looking down at the table, 'a man.'

'A man? You mean you were in love with a man?' Helena was aghast. 'Who was it? This can't be true.'

'No one you need ever know about. It wouldn't help to tell you . . .'

'You mean,' Helena was still struggling with the reality, 'you're homosexual? I can't grasp the enormity of what you're saying to me.' She felt faint. She held her head in her hands and closed her eyes.

'No, Helena. It was a mistake. I'm not a homosexual. Well, that is to say, I occasionally do find other men attractive, but I find women attractive too. I've never . . . slept . . . with another man since. You'll have to believe me.'

Helena's voice faded to a whisper. 'Tell me, everything.'

'It wasn't so unusual in those days at Cambridge. I've never allowed myself to give way to those feelings again, Helena. It *is* important that you believe that. But I suppose it's why my first marriage failed. When I met you I thought I'd found everything I'd been looking for. I loved your completeness. You asked so little from me at the beginning. But then when you began asking for things . . . for babies . . . I felt inadequate, trapped, and I started to resent you.

Oh yes, I'm ashamed of the resentment I felt. I have not been fair to you, Helena.' He broke off and looked intently at her, then stared down, not daring to hold her gaze. 'Believe me, I never wanted you involved in something like this!'

'What do you mean, "something like this"?'

'This man with whom . . . I had the relationship, has wanted a favour from me, and well . . . through an intermediary he's been trying to blackmail me. I wouldn't compromise myself, and now, well, Mark Raymond has got to know about it . . . and there's a lot of gossip brewing all over Westminster. And you see there's the election coming up, in October and there may be a leadership challenge. There's been quite a bandwagon rolling and I was going to allow my name to be mentioned.'

So that was it, she though, suddenly angry. All this had been prompted by concern for his career, not for their marriage or her feelings.

'Look, Helena, you can imagine what the press will do with this if it gets to them. "Environment Secretary, a closet bisexual" let alone if I'm a front runner in the leadership contest. I'll never become PM if it gets into the press.'

'But, I mean, is that what you are, a bisexual?' Helena could barely absorb what he had said. 'When you used to make love to me, you had done it with a man as well? I can't bear it . . .'

'Don't be ridiculous, Helena. For heaven's sake, it was years ago. I was still in my teens. I was in a muddle about my feelings. Helena, I just need a little understanding. My career is on the brink of ruin if the tabloids get hold of this.'

'I don't see what I can do.'

'I just want you to stand by me, please, Helena, until this crisis is over.'

Helena, despite her shock, knew that her moment had come. It had to be said now.

'I'm pregnant,' she said.

James stared at her, his mind working overtime. Then: 'Pregnant!' he exclaimed. 'How pregnant?'

'It's not yours, if that's what you want to know,' she said.

'I did not think for a moment that it could be. It's Elliot's, I presume. There is a fine line, Helena, between suspecting and

177

knowing. I was glad when you denied it, I didn't want to know the truth. But now I can see I will have to face it.'

'Yes. I was never quite sure whether you knew about Michael and me, but I have always suspected you would not let emotion come between you and your career. Your self-control has always been your trump card . . . or perhaps, in this case, it has been our undoing. But I suppose that's why you've been so sanguine about it all. It obviously suited you.'

'Of course I knew about you and Michael, and no, it doesn't exactly suit me. Is he going to marry you?'

'I would rather not tell you any lies, James. I don't know. I haven't told him yet.'

'Do you love him? Would you want to marry him?'

'Yes, I'm in love with him, whatever that means, and your second question is more difficult to answer.'

'I assume you're going to keep the baby?'

'How could you even ask such a question? Of course I'm going to keep it,' Helena said.

'Well, I only asked, because I wondered how you envisaged bringing up another child on your own. I know Michael, Helena. I know the sort of man he is. He'll never marry you. Making you pregnant is all part of his ego trip. Think about it. You see when you tell him. See if he offers you his undying love. See if he says he'll look after you. Marry you? Be a father to all your other children? Take the rough with the smooth as I've had to . . . will he, Helena? Will he?'

James got up, seized Helena by the shoulder and shook her as she sat in the chair. He knew it was not rational to have such feelings, but he hated Elliot; hated him for the ease with which he played with love, with sex, with his wife, why even with the futures of his stepchildren. He had, James thought, tried his best with all of them. It wasn't his fault things had not turned out as well as he'd hoped when he married Helena. But what right had Elliot to force his way into James's territory and take it all away from him – his wife, and his reputation too?

Helena was ashen. 'No . . . no . . . I know he won't,' she cried, her face contorted with emotion. Her body stiffened, she had an over-whelming desire to allow herself to be comforted by James, but then she drew away. She knew the dangers of letting James through the private ring fence she had put up where he was concerned. She had been caught with her guard down too often . . . not now.

Helena turned and walked into her studio as if trying to get away from the scene of the drama. James followed, quickening his step to keep pace with her. They turned to face each other in front of the portrait of the Banks children.

'Helena, we can save each other. I can look after you and your child. I'll bring it up as my own, the child I never had,' he hesitated, 'the one I could not give you. We can start again, only do it right this time. Think of it, Helena. If I can ride this storm I'll get to Number Ten. I'll make it up to you. You'll be the most beautiful of First Ladies . . . Let's make a new start, Helena. You are so clever . . . so good. Let me, Helena.'

She had turned towards the garden. 'I don't know, James. It might be better if we parted altogether. I need time to think. This has all come as a great shock to me. Before I've had any time to work things out for myself, I know what you're saying, but it doesn't make the other thing go away. I don't know if I can live with that.'

'Do you have a choice, Helena? Michael won't come through for you. Where do you think he is now at this precise moment?'

'I don't want to hear!' Helena shrieked, blocking her ears. 'I suppose the bloody Whips' KGB know all about him as well, as if our Pandora's Box wasn't enough. I suppose they even know what time we go to the lavatory.'

'Sit down. Calm yourself . . . Think of your family . . .' James said. He was now completely in control. Helena's news had provided him with the perfect antidote to the latest scandal.

'I don't know how I can be calm,' Helena replied. 'What's going to happen, James? Have the press got hold of all this yet? Who would have told them? Someone's got it in for you, James.'

'I know it's Mark Raymond. He loathes Reggie Goodall and he's frightened of me. He realises I'm a threat to the Prime Minister and he doesn't want me in Number Ten. He'll stop at nothing. But, Helena, no one can prove anything, and somehow I don't think they'll press it further. Mark may get the pack on to it again but when we appear together as a family, and with your news, Helena, we can kill the whole thing stone dead. In fact, if they try anything, the public will be so disgusted I'll probably get a lot of sympathy.'

Helena stared at him. 'So what you're saying is, my baby can save your face and smooth your path to Number Ten?'

'If you must put it like that, there may be some truth in what you say, but from your point of view I'm no use to you or anybody else if I lose my seat and my reputation. And what about the family? If we can avoid all the horror of my name being on the front pages again, I think we owe it to the children, Helena, to do whatever we need to, to protect them.'

'I feel so ill, James. Do you mind leaving me alone for a while? I must be by myself . . .' Helena spoke quietly.

'Yes, of course. Let me give you dinner out tonight, Helena. We need to talk away from here. You seem to think I am some sort of robot without feelings of any sort. Has it ever occurred to you how many sleepless nights I have spent wondering how I could keep you, Helena? I am a simple man in many ways. You are a beautiful creature. I have failed you. I don't like failure. I'm deeply sorry. Won't you give me a chance to try and explain? It's not just my career – you are far more important than anything else. If I want success it is worthless without you at my side.'

James let himself out of the house quietly. Helena couldn't make sense of the things he had said. In a way James's sudden burst of emotion made things more complicated. She looked at the telephone.

She wondered where Michael was, but there was a bit of her which wanted to grasp at what James had offered her.

Where did all this leave her now? Was Michael going to pick up the tab, or did he just think of their relationship as another affair? Helena had an uneasy feeling that perhaps Michael was not, after all, a man of his word. Yes, she had been terribly in love with him. She would always be grateful to him for rescuing her from the role James had carved for her, of dull, dependent wife, happy with the crumbs from what he saw as his glittering table. Michael had given her back her zest, her own confidence. Thanks to him she would never let life engulf her, she would live it.

But after the initial excitement of her affair, she now had an urgent need for continuity, some calm to get on with her work, which she now looked forward to. And above all, she needed time for her children. She had let her house deteriorate, it was a mess. She simply hadn't had time to do the things she normally did . . . she wanted to cook, fill the deep freeze, make bread, make new curtains for the children's rooms. None of this was part of her life with Michael. As she wondered if it ever could be, she remembered some of James's words. And then she sat in the big wicker chair in the kitchen and thought of Anthony.

The house was silent, except for the faint trilling of a blackbird in the garden and the occasional noise of a plane coming into Heathrow. All she heard was the bird, and it reminded her of the big rectory kitchen in Suffolk. She closed her eyes and lowered her head to her folded arms on the kitchen table and cried. She imagined Anthony crossing the room and putting his strong arms about her. She cried for all the lost loving, for all the troubled years and months when she had tried to fill the emptiness she had felt inside. There had not been a single moment when she had not longed for him, for Anthony, who was both James and Michael and, in a sense, her father. He had been her universe, the very centre of her being. Without him, life had been a hard grey place. James had never been part of that happy time, her past . . . and when Michael came into her life he had at least brought passion into her empty heart.

As Helena cried she heard her own voice. 'Oh, Anthony, darling, why did you leave me?' And then it was as if she willed his voice to come into her subconscious. It seemed to be there, close to her, telling her to let go, to see that no man could ever replace that golden time in her life's journey. She must start to make her future and not try to recreate the past.

The telephone rang. She did not hurry to answer it. Whatever it was, the news must not affect her resolve to make her own future and build on the strength of the past, rather than trying to recreate it.

Chapter 25

Reggie looked gratefully at Hilda over the Frank Cooper Oxford marmalade. He had had a difficult time last night. James Askew had been round for a quiet confidential chat, to which Hilda had not been invited. Askew had been very ill at ease, and then had blurted out about some affair he had had at Cambridge – years ago – with Michael Elliot's half-brother, and then it transpired he'd only recently found out about Elliot monkeying around with his wife.

Reggie had told Hilda, of course – but only an edited version.

'You're a brick,' he observed, dabbing his overlarge lips with a paper napkin.

She looked modestly at her plate and buttered a piece of whole-meal toast.

'It's the least I can do. It's all part of the job, dear,' she replied.

'I know. But, all the same, it's not the sort of thing a woman like you can readily understand. I think you're very Christian wanting to help. I mean, the woman is totally . . . well, you know . . . not quite . . .' he searched for the word.

'Amoral,' suggested Hilda helpfully.

'Maybe. I wouldn't have put it quite like that, dear. Perhaps flighty would be more to the point,' Reggie said.

'I never liked her. Always thought she was far too arty and pleased with herself. I hope when she ends up at Number Ten we shall get some thanks for all the worry she has caused a lot of people,' Hilda said sourly.

'Now steady on, our man isn't there yet. We've a long way to go, and this business about that affair he had at Cambridge is going to be difficult if ever it comes out. We know chaps will be chaps and all that, but it's . . .' Reggie's voice faded as he stared over Hilda's grey permed hair and out of the window.

'I know what you're trying to say,' said Hilda. 'Poor James. What he's had to put up with while that silly woman was out at the opera every night. She's a Jezebel,' Hilda exclaimed.

Reggie noticed Hilda beginning to go red about the base of her neck. She took off her glasses and started to dab furiously at her face with the paper napkin. A bit stuck to her lip and wobbled up and down as she spoke; he noticed with horror it said 'Happy Christmas'. Well, that was Hilda for you, still using the Christmas serviettes from the Treasury parties. Yes, she was a wonderful woman, so very resourceful.

'Happy Christmas' was now wedged precariously on Hilda's top lip. It remained there for a second and then fluttered gracefully on to her toast.

'Hilda, I think I can smell drains again,' said Reggie, casting his eyes to the sink. 'It's ridiculous how we're expected to run this place out of our own pocket. Did you bend the Prime Minister's ear about the flowers?'

'Yes I did,' replied Hilda, 'but all he said was that it wasn't anything to do with him. It's the responsibility of the Department of Works and he is in a worse state than we are. He says his wife has to do all the cleaning in their flat at Number Ten. He didn't see why we should have more than two artificial flower arrangements a year anyway, when everyone was setting a good example with cutbacks and savings.'

'Well, Hilda, all this will have to be altered when we get our people in. That's the trouble, the Party is run by amateurs. Talking of which, when are you going to see Helena Askew?'

'In time for coffee. The wives' group is praying for me at eleven o'clock,' Hilda said.

'I fear it will take more than a few prayers to make Helena see sense and stand by her man,' Reggie said.

'Oh, I don't know so much,' Hilda said. 'The Establishment is very powerful. Helena should realise it doesn't do to fly in the face of the great and the good.'

'Don't be so damn stupid, woman,' Reggie bellowed, suddenly losing patience. Really, he did think Hilda went over the top some-times. So far over the top she couldn't see the wood for the trees.

'Helena *is* the Establishment,' he boomed. 'It's true she's only a woman,' Reggie added, 'but she is, make no mistake about it, one of the spoilt decadent upper classes. Her grandfather was off his trolley, you know, but the Establishment stepped in and helped him out time and again. That's how it works; they look after their own, Hilda, they look after their own.'

'Don't worry, Reggie,' Hilda said. 'I am more than a match for Helena.'

Reggie looked at her; he doubted it.

Chapter 26

Hilda didn't drive a car and one couldn't avail oneself of official cars for personal use, not that this was exactly personal. It was her duty. She got a bus to Pimlico Station and walked the short distance to Richmond Terrace.

She rang the doorbell imperiously. There was a disconcerting delay in the response and so she rang again, somewhat impatiently.

'OK, OK, I come,' said a foreign voice from inside the house. Rosaria threw open the door. 'I sorry,' she said cheerfully. 'Mrs Helena, she working. So no hear door. I tell her. She expecting you.'

Rosaria showed her into the drawing room and went to find Helena, who was in the studio with the door firmly closed.

'Is big woman for you,' said Rosaria, putting her head round the door. Helena groaned inwardly, got up, took off her painting smock and walked up the stairs to the drawing room.

Hilda stood over by the piano inspecting the vase of lilac and roses. Typical, she thought, the house full of extravagant flowers; all that stuff on the piano . . . and then as she might have expected, Helena appeared, her hair all over the place, wearing some sort of leggings and a ridiculous arty tunic. The thing was not done up, or so it seemed, because it flapped about and she could see flashes of gold chains against Helena's skin and she was certainly not wearing a brassiere. Hilda averted her gaze and looked towards the sofa.

'May I sit down? I can't stay long,' she said sharply.

'Of course. Would you like some coffee?' Helena asked.

'Yes, that would be nice,' Hilda replied, sitting down uneasily and putting her large black organiser bag on the floor beside her feet.

Helena called down the stairs to Rosaria, who soon appeared carrying a tray with coffee and herb tea. She smiled affectionately at Helena. 'I bring tea for you.' Turning to Hilda, she said, 'Mrs Helena,

187

she my special lady, I spoil her like I spoil Clovis. I feed him now for you, Mrs Helena.'

'Thank you, Rosaria, you're marvellous,' said Helena, smiling indulgently.

Hilda shifted in her seat. One thing she couldn't abide was familiarity with servants.

'Helena, my dear, do you think we could have the door closed? What I have to say to you is extremely private.'

'Don't worry, I've no secrets from Clovis,' Helena laughed.

'And how old is Clovis?' Hilda enquired politely, trying to take an interest in Helena's family arrangements.

Helena did a quick count on her fingers. 'Twenty-eight,' she announced triumphantly.

'Twenty-eight! But that's impossible!' cried Hilda in disbelief. 'You can't possibly have a child of twenty-eight.'

'Oh, I'm sorry, I thought you'd met. Clovis is my dog,' Helena said.

'Met? What do you mean? I obviously thought it was one of your children,' replied Hilda with barely disguised irritation.

'Oh, I can hear him coming now, talk of the devil.' The patter of four tiny feet and a good deal of snorting could be heard approaching up the stairs.

'Watch out; he'll jump up,' Helena warned as Clovis charged into the room and shot like a missile on to Hilda's lap.

'Get off. Oh do get off,' Hilda pleaded as Clovis transferred his attentions from something he had deposited in her ample lap to her face and neck. He snorted approvingly as he tasted her Yardley foundation cream.

'Oh, I am so sorry,' Helena cried, feigning concern. She picked Clovis up and put him firmly outside the door.

'He left something . . .' said Hilda with disgust, referring to a sodden object nestling cosily between her knees. It trembled on the easy-care fabric of her skirt. Her face froze in a mask of horror.

'What can it be?' Hilda wailed, as Helena swiftly removed the offending item.

'Oh, thank goodness, it's only Mrs Thatcher. I thought it was his lamb bone. At least it won't leave a mark on your nice skirt.'

Helena opened the door and casually threw the rubber chew into the hall. Clovis could be heard renewing his attempts to remove all extraneous parts from his favourite toy.

'Oh,' Hilda exclaimed in disgust, 'how could you? Margaret is a dear, personal friend. I admire her more than I can say.' She broke off as if the whole incident were too painful to contemplate. 'Disgraceful,' she muttered under her breath. She opened her handbag, produced a handkerchief and daintily dabbed her face.

'I have come here to talk to you about James and his future,' she began, her maquillage restored.

'Oh yes? How can I help?' Helena asked.

'Help is not quite what is required. Restraint is perhaps more what we had in mind,' Hilda replied.

'I'm not quite sure what you mean,' Helena said.

'Well, as you know my dear, the Whips' Office make it their business to be informed of anything untoward in the lives of high-ranking ministers and their families.'

'Yes.'

'Yes, dear, and this applies to all of us. In fact, even to the lower ranks of backbenchers.'

'Is there much of a difference?' Helena asked.

Hilda chose to ignore the question. 'It is for this reason we must be so very careful to behave in a most circumspect manner in all things,' Hilda said.

'Oh, so nobody has anything to hang their hat on?' Helena commented.

'Yes, if you wish to put it like that.'

'The thing is,' Helena said, 'I don't wish to put it at all and I don't know what you are trying to say. Why don't you come out with it and stop wasting time?'

'Very well. I know only too well what a lonely life it can be when we marry a politician, but we have to be long suffering and resist the temptation to find amusement and consolation elsewhere. This person whom you are friendly with . . . it has been noted, and James has enemies, people who want to stand in his way. They will make use of this.'

'Oh, you mean our dear friend Michael Elliot, whom you met in our house? I haven't heard from you since then, have I?' Helena added, referring to the absence of a thank you letter from Hilda. 'Oh yes, how priceless,' she continued, 'people do have the most awful minds, don't they? Are people implying that there is something going on between Michael and me? You know, it wouldn't surprise me, Hilda,' Helena confided.

'Yes, Helena,' said Hilda with less force than she had originally intended, 'and if we are to put James forward for the leadership, things must be absolutely ... well, absolutely ...'

'You mean one big happy family?' Helena smiled seraphically.

'Helena, I'm saying these things for your own good. One simply can't afford to take on the Establishment; women never win. One day all the pigeons come home to roost. James needs your absolute support. You owe it to him.'

'I do appreciate the trouble you've taken in coming here to see me,' Helena said. 'You know, of course, I'm painting Michael Elliot's portrait? I didn't really want the commission, especially when James and I were certain about my wonderful news. James is very pleased, you know, Hilda. It really is the answer to all our prayers,' Helena said with more than a ring of truth.

Hilda's face registered a complete blank; she simply didn't know what Helena was talking about.

'Oh, I'm hopeless,' Helena said. 'You probably don't know, do you? Why should you? I'm having another baby. I've been feeling rotten. Our friends, including Michael, have been very sympathetic. Why, he even included me in his family party to the opera. In fact, he's been so kind I think I may even consider doing his portrait for free. What do you think, Hilda? Would you if you were me?' Helena asked sweetly.

'That is a matter for you,' said Hilda, covered in confusion. She knew she was about to have one of her hot flushes. Perhaps a swift exit would be advisable. She thought quickly – and then it gradually dawned on her. This was excellent news. As Reggie would no doubt agree, the best possible way of keeping Helena out of trouble, and indeed getting James out of trouble, was a new arrival. Why, the more she thought about it, the better it was; perfect in fact.

'Oh my dear,' she said fulsomely, 'this is the best news I have heard in weeks. Are you going to make an announcement?'

'I think I should leave James to decide on that. After all, he is the man of the house,' Helena replied.

As Hilda walked to the bus stop she felt quite cheerful. Fate had a strange way of sorting things, she thought.

Only five minutes after Hilda had left, Michael phoned. And by twelve, with her painting materials as alibi, Helena was standing in his drawing room. She felt bewildered, but happy that she was with him at last.

'Where have you been?' she asked. 'You didn't phone and I needed you. Things have been awful. Someone is trying to do James down and the press have been hanging round outside the house. I thought you were in Plymouth but then James said you were here, in town.'

'Poor darling. After the break-in I was rushing round trying to pick up the pieces. I know I should have rung, but I'm here now.'

After they had warmly embraced, Michael said, 'I have a lovely bottle of cold Chardonnay here. Let's drink a toast to us! It feels an eternity since I've seen you.'

'No!' Helena saw immediately the dismay in Michael's eyes. 'No. What I mean to say is – no alcohol for me at the moment.'

'Helena, what's wrong?' Michael put his hands on her shoulders and looked straight down into her face, his own so tender and knowing. 'What is it?' he persisted. 'There's something. Is it me? Something I've done?'

He looked at her. She cast her eyes to the floor.

'There's something different about you. Tell me.'

'Michael. I'm pregnant.'

He turned away from her and stood by the window, looking out at the barges on the river.

Helena thought she had been foolish in trusting him enough to tell him when she was so ill-prepared for his reaction. She held her breath. She didn't want to ask anything; the asking would tarnish the giving, if it came.

The silence was immense. It opened a chasm between joy and anguish, and then he turned and came to her. He looked down at her again. His face had paled visibly as he digested Helena's news. He was stunned. Surely Helena, a mother of three, could not have let herself become pregnant accidentally. The thought that she had actually wanted his child occurred to him and the implications of that were enormous.

There were few occasions where Michael found himself at a loss for words, but this was one of them. He was in love with Helena. There was something about her. She had affected him in a way nobody else had, she had aroused feelings that were, in a sense, unwelcome, dangerous; they laid him open to rash promises which he could not fulfil. He needed more time to think, to take this in, to decide what best to do. Later, he could not exactly remember what he had said to evade the issue. Something about her brains and his beauty. She had not laughed. He remembered she had a rather unnerving expression on her face, one he had not seen before, challenging – or was it just icy calm? He didn't know.

Chapter 27

Mark Raymond was not entirely confident he could reassure the Prime Minister of James Askew's complete support in a cover-up of the Markham Court dumping. God forbid he ever knew the full extent to which James would be required to bluff his way through the next few days to avoid a scandal.

He had played his first card, and James had clearly got the point, turning down the Home Secretary post. The second could wait like a good vintage brandy, all the better for anticipation.

Of course it had been a case of being what one might call a little economical with the regulations where Michael Elliot's enormous business deals had been concerned. But no harm had been done, it was all pretty borderline stuff, and the Party was in no position to upset its benefactors, especially with an election campaign on the horizon.

He couldn't figure out who, exactly, had been responsible for the break-in at Michael's offices in Plymouth, but James was now well briefed and, Raymond had to admit, James was clever; if anyone could handle it he could. It was his legal training which gave him the cool analytical objective qualities which would combine to diffuse the ensuing rumpus.

As Mark Raymond looked at James's inscrutable face across his desk in the Whips' office, he felt a tiny seed of doubt begin to germinate somewhere in the back of his brain. James had seemed rather cool about the possible promotion which Mark had alluded to, and when he came to think of it James hadn't been very specific with his assurances of his connivance in a cover-up.

Mark thought for a moment and then, placing his hands in a position of prayer, he gazed at a spot somewhere just above James's head and decided to play his other card.

'Well, old boy,' he began, 'I am glad we understand each other. It is my duty to protect the PM. He knows very little about all the things we have to do to keep the ship afloat. But he is a fine man, a good Prime Minister.' He paused and lowered his eyes to James's as if for confirmation.

But James's expression remained impassive. He said nothing. James knew Raymond well enough to know he was getting round to something more substantial than seeking confirmation of James's admiration for the Prime Minister.

'We have great hopes for you, James. You should look forward to a brilliant political career, but as you know the Party asks a great deal of a Member, and indeed his family. There is a disturbing matter which I am obliged to mention to you.'

James was rattled.

'Indeed?'

'The matter concerns your wife. And strangely enough this brings me back to Michael Elliot. It appears they are frequently to be seen in each other's company. Not to put too fine a point on it, they are having an affair. It must end immediately or your chances of promotion are at considerable risk.' He flicked something from his Garrick Club tie and continued, 'Do I make myself clear? Get your marriage in order and bring your wife to heel.'

'For a man of your intelligence you surprise me,' said James flatly. 'Here you are giving me chapter and verse on Party loyalty and when my own wife goes well beyond the call of duty and devotes some of her time to chatting up one of your most valuable supporters, she is accused of having an affair.'

'Don't be ridiculous, Askew. At least two sources have informed the Whips' Office that she has been seen entering his house at lunch time on several occasions, and remaining there well into the afternoon.'

'Of course she has been there in the afternoon. She is painting the man's portrait,' James stared angrily at Mark Raymond. He had never seen him look rattled before. James continued, 'As a matter of fact it was my suggestion. I can't wait to tell Michael about this . . .' James feigned a chuckle, but his heart was pounding. He was angry. Mark Raymond was so bloody smug, the patronising tone in his voice as he spoke of yet another dysfunctional area in James's private life sickened him, and the ghastly thing was Raymond probably knew more about Helena's love life than James knew himself. He hoped his face gave no indication of his feelings. James just hoped that one day he would have something on Mark Raymond. He was a perfect example of power corrupting. James knew he would use the private sorrows of a man to manipulate him or put a stop on his career if it suited him, with no thought for the consequences.

Mark Raymond got up from his chair. James's reaction had been unexpected and suddenly Raymond wasn't sure of his ground. He would have to do a little more research into the Askews' private life. There was something in there which didn't quite add up.

'I'm sorry, old boy. I was just being devil's advocate. I look forward to seeing the portrait.'

The meeting was at an end. James went back to his office. He had work to do before the business of the House commenced at two thirty.

Environmental question time was in full swing, with James and his team of ministers dealing effectively with a wide range of questions on all aspects of local government, transport and housing matters.

The fifteen or so questions at the top of the list had been pulled out of a hat by the Clerks of the House, and as usual they split fifty-fifty between Government backbenchers and opposition MPs.

James had seen a helpful question from Dickie Sharpe, one of his environment backbench committee officers, asking the Secretary of State to make a statement on his proposals for dealing with landfill waste. James decided to use this as a means of dealing with the Markham Court problem.

The pressure upon him to turn a blind eye to Michael Elliot's blatant flouting of the regulations had reached its peak this morning when Mark Raymond had uttered barely concealed threats about his political future if he didn't find a way of legitimising the use of the gravel pits for the burial of toxic waste.

James had reacted impassively, but inwardly he had seethed with anger at once again being subjected to manipulation by the Chief Whip. He had been further provoked by the smug way Mark Raymond had conveyed his assumption that James would do as he was bidden. 'I know you will put the Party first,' were his exact words. James had said nothing. He had not revealed his intentions. He wanted them to come as a complete surprise. The Party was looking for an heir apparent but not too apparent. James would emerge slowly, giving the backbenchers time to think they were the kingmakers.

Determined to thwart the pressures, he had consulted with his Department and advisers and come up with the answer, which was to announce that the newly appointed Environmental Agency would be given increased powers to prevent unauthorised use of landfill sites for the disposal of potentially dangerous chemical waste products.

He knew he would be declaring war on the Chief Whip and the Prime Minister but he had the support of most of the backbenchers and many at the front.

There was a loud cheer from both sides of the House at the entrance of the party leaders for Prime Minister's Question Time.

As James moved down the bench to make room for the Prime Minister, Reggie Goodall leant forward and gave him a wink. This did not escape the attention of Jenkins, who crossed his legs irritably.

James rose to his feet and in the quiet studied voice he had perfected in his years at the Bar he delivered his remarks. The House gradually became silent.

As he resumed his front bench seat he glanced sideways at Raymond, who was in his usual Chief Whip's position in the corner of the Treasury bench, and saw his flashing look of barely disguised fury, a marked contrast to the encouraging smiles of support from all parts of the House.

At three thirty, the Prime Minister swept out of the Chamber followed by Mark Raymond, who stopped momentarily in front of James and hissed, 'What the hell do you think you're playing at?' The Prime Minister turned fleetingly and made a gesture to Raymond to follow, much as he would to one of his dogs who had stepped out of line.

There was a flurry in the press gallery, with journalists leaving to e-mail their editors.

Reggie caught up with James, patting him briefly on the back. 'Well done, old boy,' he whispered. 'I shouldn't be surprised if that bounder Raymond isn't looking for a job in civvy street tomorrow.'

The Chairman of the backbench 1922 Committee intercepted James at the door of the Chamber. 'I am off to a meeting at six tonight, Askew,' he said knowingly. 'Quite an unexpected turn of events, and not before time,' he muttered, as they went into the throng of MPs in the Lobby. Suddenly James appeared to be the man everyone wanted to talk to.

He heard someone calling his name. It was Helena. She had found her way into the Members' Lobby. He had been too preoccupied to look for her in the gallery, but now he saw her face through the throng. She looked happy, even radiant.

James felt better than he had felt for weeks. He had turned the tide of events. He was in control again and his wife was there supporting him for all to see, confounding the gossips. Mark Raymond could go to hell.

Chapter 28

Cornelia had slept badly. There'd been a severe thunderstorm and she'd had nightmares about Helena. She was glad when the morning came, albeit sluggish and grey.

Three pairs of canine eyes stared at Cornelia's cereal bowl, with which she had returned upstairs.

'No,' she said firmly. The heads drooped and the spaniels resigned themselves to abstinence until their mistress could get her act together and feed them. Yesterday they had enjoyed the leftovers from Hugh and Cornelia's shepherd's pie. Hunger and hope sprang eternal in the canine breasts. They dozed off fitfully on the eiderdown, keeping an eye on their mistress.

Cornelia liked this quiet time in her room with a breakfast tray in the mornings. It was only recently that her moments of solitude had become a luxury. She thought about what it might be like if Hugh and she were to live together. She had spent so long being mistress of her own plans, though she adored Hugh and couldn't imagine life without him. Their relationship had all been so romantic – no unwashed boxer shorts or ringed baths had sullied the freshness of their love affair.

What would it be like, for example, if Cornelia had to discuss the food bills with Hugh, ask him to take the car to be serviced? She had not been frank with him. Life on the side of a mountain in Tuscany or Umbria might be fine for a brief idyll in summer or spring, but she would soon be yearning for the reassuring feel of tarmac beneath her feet on her frequent raids on civilisation. She felt apprehensive; there was a look about Hugh. She knew things were about to change. He wanted more. She wanted things to stay as they were, with maybe a few additional frills.

'Oh well,' she said to the dogs, 'move over. It's half-past eight. I must get on with my day.' The nice thing about dogs, she thought,

199

was their unfailing good manners. They listened politely, even enraptured, and they never answered back.

The telephone rang; it was Helena. She sounded distraught, and said her mother must come to London at once. There were things she had to discuss with her . . . no, they couldn't be mentioned over the phone.

Cornelia suddenly felt terribly tired. 'Is it bad news?' she asked hesitantly.

'Not really, but it depends which way you look at it,' Helena replied unhelpfully.

'Can it wait until tomorrow?' asked Cornelia. 'I can just get the ten o'clock train from Tiverton if it can't.'

Of course it couldn't.

Helena met her mother off the morning train from Devon. Cornelia sat quietly on the journey back to Richmond Terrace. As they arrived at the house Rosaria was just about to leave. She greeted Cornelia warmly. She was very fond of her and they had a lot in common: both grandmothers, both women of the world.

Helena went upstairs for a moment, leaving the two women alone. Rosaria made Cornelia a cup of coffee and confided darkly her concerns over Helena's health.

This did not reassure Cornelia about the state of affairs in her daughter's household. The previous night there had been quite a row with Hugh. He had been checking up on Michael Elliot through some computer friend of his who worked on the *Telegraph*. Hugh had been trawling the Internet and come up with some alarming details of the sort of people Michael did business with. Cornelia had been so upset by it all that it had added to her restless night and she had decided to suggest to Helena that cooling the affair with Michael might be a cautionary step, especially as James had overnight turned into a Parliamentary hero.

Helena came downstairs to the kitchen looking very white, made herself a cup of her tea and sat down at the kitchen table with her mother.

'Darling, there is something I want to say to you,' Cornelia blurted out. She wanted to get in her concerns, the kind of thing Hugh had discovered about Michael.

Helena made a gesture as if to silence her. 'No, Mummy, you must listen. I'm pregnant.'

It took a moment or two for the news to sink in and then Cornelia decided congratulations must be in order. There had obviously been more of a compromise than she realised between Helena and James.

At a loss as quite how to put it she asked if Helena was pleased.

'Mummy, you don't understand. It's not James's baby, it's Michael's,' said Helena.

'Oh God, no, Helena! You can't be . . . How could you? I thought you were on the pill. What on earth are you going to do?' Cornelia could not keep the note of hysteria out of her voice. She didn't wait for Helena to answer all her questions. Instead she asked more: did James know? . . . Was she going to pass it off as James's or, more important still, did Michael know, and what was he going to do about it? She did not ask the question she knew would really alienate Helena, namely, had she thought of an abortion?

'Mummy, I am in love with Michael. I quite literally adore him. He has brought me back into the land of the living. I know more about him than you think. Of course he is what Daddy would have called a shit, but he is what I would call a delightful rogue. With the right woman he might well be a spectacular man and I hope I'm that woman. I don't know what he'll do but I want to be part of it.'

'But what will James do when he finds out?' Cornelia asked.

'James already knows,' Helena answered. 'I couldn't lie to him about something like this, but he needs me just at the moment and, who knows, maybe I need him? It depends on a lot of things.'

Cornelia decided not to say the things she had meant to about Michael. In a sense she was relieved that the responsibility had been taken off her shoulders for the time being. She thought Hugh was over-dramatising everything anyway, hence their row yesterday evening. But how was she going to tell him the latest? How would he take it? She didn't even know what to make of it herself.

'But there is something more,' said Helena.

'More? What else could be more than what you've just told me?' replied Cornelia, with more than a trace of alarm.

'Well, it's something about James. It happened a long time ago but it could cause a scandal if the media get to hear of it and I think you should know. Forewarned is forearmed.'

'Well, go on then, what is it?' asked Cornelia impatiently.

'James had an affair with a man when he was at Cambridge.

201

Apparently someone knows about it and could use it to harm him.'

Cornelia's face had frozen into a mask. She couldn't think of the right thing to say. Should she be shocked, disgusted, or just bewildered? She decided on the latter and fumbled with some appropriate words.

'The problem is James is now the media hero. I mean, have you been following all this stuff about waste tips and things? Well, James has been very brave and stood up to all those pompous prigs, and demanded a complete investigation . . . or something to that effect. It is the making of him, politically speaking, and if this thing gets put around he will just tough it out. I have thought about it a lot and I am right there with him.'

'But, darling, how does all this affect your future, your baby? Are you saying you are going to stay with James? I don't know how I would feel if I were you. It does seem a lot to take in.'

'Mummy, I can't help admiring James and everything he has worked for, but I don't see any long-term future for us.' Helena bit her lip, 'I will give up my share in his success, Mummy, for I have Michael and the baby, but I don't want James to go tumbling into obscurity. I feel we have all harmed each other enough already.'

At that precise moment they heard the front door bang and then footsteps were coming along the hall. It was James carrying an enormous bunch of yellow roses. When he saw Cornelia, James did a double take, in fact all three of them registered surprise in one way or another, Helena because James never usually came home in the middle of the day, and here he was again in the short space of a week; James because the last person he wanted to see was Cornelia, and Cornelia because the last person she wanted to see was James.

'Cornelia, what a nice surprise,' James lied.

He turned to Helena and handed her the roses. 'Darling, for you,' he said. 'I thought you looked a little tired this morning and as I was passing in the ministerial car I thought I'd pop in to cheer you up and remind you to have a rest this afternoon.' Both women looked at James with a mixture of amazement and disbelief.

'Oh, how very sweet of you. Would you like some coffee?' Sniffing the roses as she spoke, Helena turned to Cornelia. 'Mummy, do smell them. The second lot of yellow roses I've had from James.'

'Lovely, darling . . . Do you always give yellow roses?' Cornelia asked.

'Only when we have something to celebrate, and I expect you're here because you've been told that we do,' James confided.

Cornelia felt uncomfortable. What on earth were the two of them playing at? As she saw her daughter skilfully going along with the charade, she hoped she would also be able to perform her role, whatever it was.

'Well, I can't stop for coffee. Good to see you, Cornelia, catch up soon,' James breezed, and was gone. Cornelia watched him through the window as he got back into the car. She had to admit he was a good-looking man, and he had a most charming manner when it suited him, but Cornelia wasn't fooled.

'I wonder if I'm going mad, Helena,' Cornelia said.

'No, you're not mad and neither am I, and please take that expression off your face. I know exactly what I'm doing.'

'Well, you certainly have a room full of flowers,' Cornelia laughed. 'I hope you haven't any more lovers or husbands who're going to share in the celebration,' she said, 'because Hugh and I will be in Tuscany house-hunting for the first ten days in August. Jane is moving in to look after the dogs.'

Cornelia took a breath. She had to say something to Helena, something which would put some sort of genuine lovingness into the situation.

'Helena,' she said firmly, 'whatever happens, I still like Michael, even if he isn't husband material. I can't lose sight of the fact that he will be the father of my next grandchild. Whatever the future holds, I am there for all of you, Helena darling.'

Chapter 29

'Are you alone?' the voice asked. Helena turned up the sound on the mobile phone.

'Yes,' she answered Michael.

She was trying to be patient with him. He would have to take his time. The declaration of his commitment to her must be absolute; it must come slowly – the realisation that, at last, he must commit himself to sharing his future, all of his future not just little bits when and how it suited. But he was certainly taking his time.

'I must see you now. Can I pick you up, take you somewhere?'

Michael had not telephoned her for well over a week – ever since she had told him about the baby. She looked at her watch. It was one o'clock. The light was perfect. She had thrown herself into her work. She was in fact putting the finishing touches to the Bankses' portrait. Painting had become her only means of escaping all the demands of real life.

Yet she needed to see Michael.

'I can meet you in the park but not now – at three. I'll be taking Clovis for a walk, but I can't stay long. James and I have to be at Number Ten for dinner.'

She could feel the hesitation in his voice. She could upset him when she wanted to, and her patience with waiting was beginning to run out.

'All right,' he agreed reluctantly. 'Where exactly?'

'Opposite your house, by the Temple, in the middle of the Peace Mile, at three fifteen,' she said.

'I hope the venue suits the genre,' he said lightly.

Helena quickly put away her painting things and rushed upstairs. She threw off her clothes and ran a bath, her heart was pounding at the thought of seeing Michael.

She wanted to be beautiful, perfect, shining for him even for the few minutes they would be together . . . Suddenly she felt sick with anticipation. If he had come to a decision her future would be decided this afternoon. She washed her hair and lay for a second under the water as her hair floated behind her. Then out of the bath, she tossed her hair about in a token attempt to dry it, and stood naked for a moment in front of the long mirror on her cupboard. She chose a long cotton dress in shades of pink and yellow. The Indian fabric was soft and flimsy, and she wore nothing else except for the briefest of silk underwear. She dabbed some perfume about her neck and hair. The dress clung suggestively and her hair tumbled in massive shining disorder. She looked as he knew he expected her to look, calm and happy. She was neither, but she did not want Michael to know how worried she was. For a moment that morning she had even considered the possibility of abortion.

On the one hand, she was thrilled by her pregnancy, she had so wanted another baby, something tangible after the loss of Anthony. It would bring some joy into her life and her children's lives. A new baby would always be a matter of celebration for Helena . . . and her mother would be there for her. Even Hugh would come round in the end.

She had not intended to become pregnant. If she were not married it would be easier for her to read Michael's intentions. Women brought children up very well on their own. In a way this would be a better option, for it would not put quite so much pressure on Michael. Leaving the security of a marriage where a husband will give anything to maintain the status quo . . . this could frighten Michael. The pregnancy had come too soon.

And then there was James. If only she knew what he really thought about anything. She had a nasty feeling he didn't know himself. She would have to stop waiting for other people to come up with solutions.

Helena let Clovis out of the car. He ran yapping after a large Alsatian, who turned contemptuously and issued a scathing dog oath that sent Clovis's tail limp and feeble, a sign of surrender.

Michael was watching from the top of the Temple steps, and even from that distance, a few hundred yards, his heart missed a beat when he saw the breeze catch Helena's hair and the material of her dress cleave to her figure as she walked confidently along the grass under the chestnut trees.

Two children bent down to talk to Clovis and Helena answered them, smiling indulgently. He imagined her voice . . . he stood still, observing, and when she approached she didn't see him at first. She was calling the dog. He was aware of the symbolism of the scene, the woman approaching the man on the steps of the Temple. He knew he would never find another Helena.

And then Helena saw him. He saw in her face the joy she felt when their eyes met. He stood very still and she came up the steps towards him. She leant her body to him.

'Darling,' she said shakily.

He held her and put his face in her clean shining hair. It blew about him like a curtain.

She stayed still for a moment and then abruptly pulled away.

'Why did you take so long to call me?' she asked reproachfully.

'I'm sorry, darling. I can see you're furious with me.' He held her away in order to see her face.

She removed his hands from her shoulders. 'We're not talking about a lovers' tiff here, Michael,' she said. 'I have some dramatic decisions to make. After all, I'm still a married woman. I . . .' she hesitated, 'I have responsibilities and James has been in trouble. I . . . I've had to give him my support. I could do nothing less.'

She hesitated. 'Michael,' she continued, 'I must ask you to tell me the truth. What have you been trying to do at Markham Court? It's no use trying to fob me off, I'm not a fool. I know you bend the rules, but I thought the things you did were perfectly harmless. Now I'm beginning to wonder.'

Michael had long ago learned that the best line of defence was attack. 'I'll be frank with you,' he replied, looking earnestly at Helena. 'James could have resolved this in a trice, but instead he tightened up the whole shooting match and made it impossible for me. These things happen all the time. Putting waste under top soil is common practice. James knows this as well as anyone. I deal in landfill as well as many other things. I make a lot of money which I give to good causes. If I bend rules, and nobody is any the wiser, well, who's going to complain? Certainly not the benefactors, the many organisations who depend on the Elliot Foundation.'

Helena tried to interrupt. He silenced her.

'No, Helena, hear me out. Your husband is a pedantic, nit-picking prig. There was nothing wrong with the waste we planned to put in the ground at Markham Court. If we got bogged down in bureaucratic regulations we would go out of business. As it is, thanks to James Askew, my company cannot keep to an important contract and we are in considerable difficulty. I've had to withdraw my support from at least two of the charities which depend on us.'

Helena only half believed him. But looking at him, so strong, frank and compelling, she had to dismiss any doubts from her mind. She and he were bound. It was too late to start asking questions about the fine print of the man's business life. He could not be the sort of man who would be happy to pollute the planet, he cared too much about the people he loved. But just the same, there were so many things about the man which worried her. 'Michael – what about us?' She blinked back tears. 'Michael, when I told you I was carrying your child I . . . I was on cloud nine. I thought, in a mad way, you'd be there for me. You'd want to be with me; that we'd suddenly be together, committed to each other.'

He listened, knowing he must not interrupt.

'But you weren't there for me, Michael. I haven't seen you for days and I still don't know what it is you want.'

'What do you mean? Of course I was there for you. You knew I was going away and it would be difficult to get in touch.'

'I don't care what you say. I felt alone . . . and in addition James has had a near breakdown.'

'A breakdown? James isn't the sort to have a breakdown,' said Michael impatiently.

'He's needed me so much these last few days. I couldn't reject him. He told me things, things which explained everything . . . all the unhappiness, all the lack of loving me so that I ended up hating myself.'

'You couldn't hate yourself, Helena.'

'Yes, I've hated myself for some time, and then you changed that. You put me back in touch with my feelings, in touch with my deepest hidden desires, and now I'm having your child. I . . .' She sought the words, she couldn't find them. 'Let's walk by the river, or I'll lose the dog.'

He took her arm as they strode down the steps and along the path. The park shimmered in the heat of the afternoon. There was a smell of freshly cut grass, which clung to his shoes.

'So tell me . . .' He tightened his arm protectively about her shoulders. 'Shall I be forgiven for not offering what you could not accept? You have had to be there for James.'

'No, I suppose not . . . now . . . I can see I have no choice at the moment. I mean, things have moved so swiftly.'

James, in spite of the rumours, still hoped to be considered for the leadership, and a general election was looming, so he needed her support. She told him how she felt sorry for James, genuinely sorry . . . She spoke of her fears for her children, of the desperate need she had for continuity, how James understood.

'Understands what?' asked Michael, confused.

'What you mean to me.'

'And what do I mean to you?'

'He understands how I'm in love with you, but that you haven't committed yourself to me, Michael. I think he sees himself as doing something good and brave, offering me his support while knowing we're lovers. When our child is born who knows what will happen? Things may be different, but for the moment I'm not going to rock the boat, since you have not offered me an alternative.'

Michael stopped walking. He went to the river wall and, putting both hands on it, looked over the water to his house. So, he could keep silent no longer about their future together. He loved Helena, but he'd been in love before, and had fallen out of love too. And if he did not offer her a life with him now he risked losing her completely, for who knew what would happen if she went back to James? She might decide to stay with him for ever.

Helena came and stood beside him. She noticed his elegant hands, the dark hairs on the back of his wrist. She wanted to put her face to his skin, explore the smoothness of him. She followed his gaze to the house across the river. She knew what he was going to say.

'Helena, my own Helena. How could you have ever doubted I was there for you? There were things I had to do, you knew that . . . and I do have to keep my head together while all this is going on. I had to go to Liechtenstein, you knew it might be difficult to phone. I rang you the moment I got back. Come home with me now, Helena.

Let me make love to you. I can ring the staff and send them all home.'

'It's all so easy for you,' she said. 'You think I can remain in this stage of enchantment, but nothing would be solved today if I came home with you now. It's not just today I need. It's always.'

'How can you have so little faith in me?' he asked. 'Maybe for the first time in my life, I want more than just living for today.' He pulled her towards him roughly. 'With you I feel more intensely than I've ever done with a woman. Do you believe me?'

His voice had become rather loud. There were groups of mothers sitting on the grass watching their children playing and Helena thought his voice must have carried. One of the mothers put down her can of Coke and watched them, listening to their conversation. 'I'm phoning the house. You're coming home with me, Helena. You can't fight the inevitable. I know what you're doing and why you're doing it; I respect you for it. But don't let a misplaced conscience turn you from the path which I . . . I *know* is your future.' He wished he could explain to Helena how he had always circumnavigated problems in his life. He had learnt to do this as a child. He had never been able to look forward to conventional family happiness. His parents had lived apart and yet together but, compared to many of his friends, he had had an enviable childhood. He had never heard his parents quarrel. They had seldom talked of the future. All their joys had been immediate and yet life had been comfortable and relatively stress free. But Helena craved commitment, order, knowing exactly where she would be next Christmas. Yes, he wanted to be with her, but not because he was obliged to be so, only because anything else would be less than perfect.

He didn't touch her. He stood still as a statue just looking at her. Her resolve melted as she felt the power of Michael's body next to hers, but she could not risk all if she was not absolutely sure.

'Think, Michael, think about what sort of woman I am. What do I want? You've never mentioned the one thing which I think I should ask you for . . . and I'm never going to ask you for it, do you hear me? Never.'

The young mother was still watching them. Her eyes followed them as they walked slowly towards the car park, a little dog hopping along behind them. It looked as if the man spoke urgently to the dark-haired woman. The woman seemed to be in an agony of indecision and then she moved abruptly and got into the passenger seat of a large silver car. It moved slowly away into Chelsea Bridge Road.

Chapter 30

'The Duchess has just phoned,' Joanna said on the house intercom. 'She'll be fifteen minutes late. The traffic on the M4 has been very bad.'

'Thank you, Joanna. Will you warn Carla?' Michael said. Michael, for all his glamour and fast-lane living, was a creature of habit and he was irritated at these changes to the timetable he had arranged. Usually Caroline's visits coincided with an afternoon off for the staff. Eyebrows were not raised and comments were never, absolutely never, made. But today Michael had given Joanna a full afternoon's typing and told her not to be late back from lunch.

Michael didn't like shedding people and certainly never on a Friday, when they would have an entire weekend to think about it. But Caroline was busy every day, so Friday it had to be. She was to be guest of honour at a charity gala this evening and had pointedly told Michael she would have to be away by four o'clock for a hairdresser's appointment. In view of what he had decided to say to her, he suspected she would be away long before that.

'Hello, darling,' she crooned, as she swept into the drawing room at one fifteen, flinging the Hermès bag on the sofa and closing her eyes, with her lips in a kiss-receiving mode. She opened her eyes smartly when she felt Michael's peck on her cheek.

'Is anything the matter?' she asked sharply.

'Of course something's the matter,' Michael replied. 'Surely you've read the papers. James Askew, your *friend*—' the word friend was laced with innuendo – 'has cost me a fortune. In fact he may have broken one of my companies. You're a clever woman, Caroline. Did you put him up to it? How did he know so much about my plans at Markham Court? I suppose now you have your money you've conveniently forgotten your side of the bargain.'

Caroline shifted uneasily on the brocade sofa. She hadn't realised the lengths to which he'd had to go to get the scheme through. She knew his contributions to Party funds were enormous and she knew Central Office were in debt. Of course money was all it was about.

'Do you mean, Michael, that your power over Mark Raymond is such that he would have arranged a cover-up of your plans for our land? It isn't possible. Once they had the evidence you could not have quietly dumped that stuff in the dead of night. It could have brought down the Government if it was discovered the house had been misled.'

Caroline hoped Michael would not know how grateful she was to James Askew. She had never been happy about Michael's plans to dump the waste practically on their doorstep. She knew he'd been getting rid of stuff like this for years. She never asked questions, and when Michael came up with his plans for their estate, she had had no choice but to go along with it. It was her and Bertie's only chance to stave off bankruptcy. She had believed Michael when he told her how harmless the material was, but when she learnt the truth she realised just how ruthless he could be.

'I am sorry, Michael, truly sorry. I trusted you, I believed you when you said it was all perfectly safe. Why was it so important to get rid of this stuff on our land? I don't understand.'

Michael told her what the disposal contract was worth to him and how it would cost him getting on for half a million to dispose of the waste in another way.

'And the irony is,' he went on, 'that the entire episode has made James into a media hero who now has a much more realistic chance of becoming leader of the Party, and he may well end up as Prime Minister.'

With that Michael changed the subject. He guessed Caroline was secretly delighted at the way things had gone, for however hard up the Hamptons were, they couldn't want the waste in their own backyard, so to speak. He saw no point in prolonging the agony. He knew Caroline too well. If he said nothing, she would sense a difference.

'Let's go and have something to eat,' he said, looking at her gravely.

He told her he had fallen in love when she had consumed a large champagne cocktail.

214

'I came in on champagne, I might as well go out on it,' she said sarcastically.

Michael remained silent. He thought it better to let the situation sink in. Caroline would, no doubt, be probing further.

'So, you have fallen in love. Am I allowed to know who the lucky woman is?' she asked coldly.

'I'm afraid I can't tell you.'

'Is she married?'

'I can't discuss it. And it wouldn't help if I did. We both have our lives to lead. After all, you've a home, a husband and family, Caroline. I've never felt our relationship threatened those things. In fact I like to feel, in many ways, it strengthened them.' Michael paused and took the last mouthful of food from his plate. He hoped Caroline would do the same. He wanted to go back upstairs, have a cup of coffee and hand Caroline the envelope he had prepared for her.

Caroline had, so far, controlled her emotions, but suddenly she gave up the unequal struggle. She got up from the table, throwing her napkin on to the unfinished plate of food.

'You're a bastard,' she hissed, picking up her bag. 'You think you can buy everything. You're a Jew on the make. I would never have slept with you if it hadn't been for your money and, anyway, you're no fucking good at it.'

'Well, yes, I *am* a bastard, Caroline; my parents never did have a lovely wedding. I suppose you have just established your own job description,' Michael replied.

'You shit! You frightful shit!' Caroline wept. 'You're an authority on tarts. After all, your wife spread her legs like butter. She cuckolded you all over London.' She thrashed out at him, but he deftly caught her wrist just short of his face.

'Now that's more like it. You look even more magnificent when you're angry . . . but please, let's stay friends. We've shared a great deal, you and I, and I have something for you upstairs. Won't you come up to the drawing room and have some coffee and compose yourself? It isn't as if we shall never see each other again,' said Michael, pulling his silk handkerchief out of his breast pocket and offering it to her.

He placed a calming arm round her shoulder and they walked upstairs.

The envelope contained twenty thousand pounds worth of blue-chip shares in her name. Michael had arranged the transaction discreetly; it could not be traced to him and he suspected it would surprise her. He was fond of Caroline and he thought, after such a long affair, it was better to do more than less. He never liked to leave an open wound. He hoped she would come to see the inevitability of the situation and a little money would certainly pave the way.

Besides which, his company was still doing business with the Hamptons. Caroline might yet end up a rich woman.

She seemed calmer; getting out her powder compact, she repaired the damage to her make-up. She snapped her lipstick shut and looked at Michael as he approached with a cup of coffee.

'It's Helena Askew, isn't it?' she asked sharply.

Michael handed her the coffee. No trace of emotion showed on his face. 'Why should it be?' he asked.

'You were at the opera with her, *again*. Regine Ponson saw you.'

'Now, Caroline, I don't necessarily sleep with every woman I take to the opera,' Michael replied.

'Don't you?' Caroline sneered.

Michael lost his cool. 'The thing about you, Caroline, is one only has to scratch the veneer and out comes a fish wife. To be frank, it is part of your attraction . . . but your last remark struck a new low.'

Caroline shifted a little. She knew she had gone too far but she was seething with anger. How dare Michael bring their affair to an end so abruptly? But she had sensed something was wrong. The more she thought about it, the more certain she was that the other woman must be Helena. The chattering classes were rife with gossip and tucked into the ragged corners of the latest bulletins from the inter-locking circles of society the name of Helena Askew had begun to crop up rather too often.

'So if you won't tell me, I must draw my own conclusions,' she said, 'but whoever it is, I don't see why you feel it necessary to end our affair, unless you're going to get married or something and even then such propriety would seem out of character.'

'I think that is the second occasion on which, in the last few minutes, you've raised the subject of my married life. I recall you saying something offensive about my wife and I suppose you would imply I had the same lack of decorum. You've wrong. My first wife and I were not unfaithful to each other. The marriage came to an end because she wanted to have an international career and did not want children.'

'Oh, don't be so bloody pompous, Michael,' she shouted, picking a loose thread out of her Chanel jacket.

'Why don't you leave? The door is open,' Michael said.

'Look, I'm sorry I said those things.' Caroline's voice took on a conciliatory tone. She looked at Michael closely and felt more than a twinge of regret. Such was the perversity of her nature that now the man was slipping from her grasp she dearly wanted him. All those afternoons when she had used her acting skills to their limit now seemed like wasted opportunities . . . the man was gorgeous. She felt a strong and earthy desire to go with him to the bed she knew so well, take off her clothes and give herself to him in unrestrained rapture, to caress him, to carry the results of his lovemaking about with her for the rest of the day. Oh yes, now for some reason, it would actually be all the things she had made him believe it was. He would forget about Helena Askew . . .

Her pulse began to race. She moved closer to Michael; she could smell whatever it was he put on his hair. She leant back on the sofa and put her arms up behind her head . . . her jacket fell apart and she hoped he would see her nipples through the cream silk of her chemise. She moved her legs together, the silk of her tights made a slithery noise. 'Why don't we go upstairs?' she whispered. She looked seductive, soft, her eyes had a misty look he had never seen in them before. He moved towards her, his mouth coming to meet hers, then mastered himself. He withdrew.

'What is all this? You just told me I was a hopeless lover. Don't you think it's a little late to put the clock back?'

'Don't joke. I adore you, Michael . . . let's go up now,' she whispered urgently.

A therapist friend of his mother's had once said to him, 'There are no all-bad or all-good people, just people who are a bit bad and a bit good.' Michael looked at Caroline and knew she was the exception. She was more than half bad. Perhaps this had held them together for so long, but Helena was mostly good and very little bad. Her goodness was fragile, he knew how easily it could be damaged. If he went to bed with Caroline now – and he knew more of her acting abilities than she realised – perhaps for the first and last time she would give herself with the uninhibited abandoned passion which had so far eluded her. Once again the temptation was powerful, almost too much for his male vanity. After all, who would ever know? What harm could it possibly do?

Then he thought of Helena, trusting, good, funny Helena, and he knew she would know. She would know because she would feel it in the air and by doing it he would kill the most precious thing in his life.

'No, Caroline,' he said gently.

She rose quickly from the sofa. She knew it was the end. She would never have the chance now to give herself in unselfish, complete harmony to this man who had held her in his arms for so many years. But she didn't have it in her to leave the thing with dignity, she preferred to do it with rancour and bitterness; anger would disguise the hurt.

'Well, I didn't really want to. I always pretended, you know. I never really enjoyed it.'

'I am sorry,' Michael said. 'I often suspected as much. Shall I see you to your car?' He picked up the envelope and stuffed it into the Hermès bag.

As Caroline drove away she wondered if Michael knew who had broken into his office and found the evidence. As she drove along the Embankment she decided he hadn't the faintest idea. She smiled a little and turned on the car radio. The early evening news might just have something about James – he had been on TV earlier. Caroline peeked a look at herself in the driving mirror, reached for her car phone and dialled James's direct line at the Ministry. This was not the first time she had had cause to be grateful for the contacts she had made in the press during her early years as an actress. She made a mental note to send a case of whisky to her friend on the tabloid newspaper.

There would be no poison waste for Markham Court now, and Michael would never know it was she who had tipped off the press.

Chapter 31

The ministerial car picked James and Helena up at seven thirty. Helena thought James looked very handsome in his dinner jacket, and told him so. She wanted to be kind to him, especially as he had been very considerate since they struck their bargain. In fact, he was almost unrecognisable, he was everything she had hoped he would be in the early days of their marriage.

As for James, he didn't like Helena in black. He had often said as much, but she still continued to wear it. 'You look lovely as usual,' he said. 'But,' he added tentatively, 'I don't like black. Haven't you got anything else?'

'No, actually I haven't anything nicer than this,' she answered, touching the smooth black figure-hugging crepe dress she would not be able to wear for much longer. 'Is that better?' she asked draping a bright pink chiffon scarf about her neck.

'Yes, it makes all the difference. Now, come on, we must go.'

At Number Ten Helena was amused to see nearly all the women wearing black; she wondered if James had noticed. Before she could make a joke about it they bumped into Hilda on the doorstep.

'Oh, you do look nice,' Helena lied. 'I remember that dress when you dined with us in the spring,' referring to Hilda's electric-blue tailored frock with a pleated skirt, which made her look like a large sofa.

Hilda found Helena's comment mildly upsetting; she was not sure why, except she felt it was loaded in some way. But she put on a brave face and replied politely, 'Reggie's favourite colour,' glancing affectionately at her husband as she did so.

'Is someone talking about me?' asked Reggie, taking up the rear.

'Good evening, Reggie,' said James. 'Do you dine with the neighbours often?' He laughed.

'Good question, old chap. Couldn't afford it too often as one tends

219

to get sent a bill,' Reggie replied, referring to the recent occasions on which participants in working dinners at Number Ten had been asked to pay a share of the cost.

'Well, anyway, you didn't have far to come,' Helena laughed.

'Actually, we could have slipped in through the intercommunicating internal door but Hilda won't have it. She's a stickler for protocol, aren't you, dear?'

'Absolutely,' Hilda said. 'I dislike all this familiarity one has to put up with these days.'

The reception line had moved slowly up the stairs to the first-floor drawing rooms.

As they neared the top James hissed at Helena to be wary of the Prime Minister's infamous karate handshake. There had also been quite a few comments recently about the habit he had of flinging the offered hand past him, wrenching shoulders, a tactic for avoiding time-wasting small talk from Party greasers.

Just inside the door stood Jenkins and his wife Marion, and the French Prime Minister, Jean-Pierre de Rougement, and his wife, Christine.

On this occasion Jenkins's speedy dispatch of the reception line was curtailed unexpectedly. As Helena and James were shot towards the guests of honour, Christine de Rougement flung her arms around Helena and greeted her with an exclamation of delight. Their reunion was exhilarating. They chatted excitedly about old times at art school, and mutual friends while the line came to a halt.

The Prime Minister was clearly furious at the protracted greetings which held up the queue of guests. He glanced across at Mark Raymond standing by the window, who raised his eyebrows a fraction. The look they exchanged confirmed their joint displeasure that, as usual with James Askew, things were not going according to plan. This became evident again later on when, during dinner in the panelled dining room, Christine was clearly heard asking the Askews to stay with her in France.

To her surprise Helena was thoroughly enjoying the evening and later she found herself sitting next to Philippe Ponson, the French Ambassador, who was his usual entertaining self. Helena's affair with Michael had, in a strange way, made her more receptive to the male sex, and much more self-assured. She blushed a little as this handsome man let his eyes wander from her full breasts to her healthy skin, now complete with the bloom of pregnancy. Philippe was an expert on matters of this kind. 'I knew the moment she sat down, she was pregnant,' he was to say later to his wife as they travelled home in the ambassadorial car.

With difficulty he managed to disguise his curiosity about his 'belle Hélene' with a series of overt enquiries about mutual friends and love of music.

He subtly steered the conversation to opera. 'And how did you enjoy *The Magic Flute*? It was a nice surprise to see you there,' he said, admiring her marvellous hair, which seemed even more luscious than he remembered it at the fateful dinner party at Richmond Terrace.

'I loved it,' replied Helena enthusiastically. 'In fact it was the first opera my mother ever took me to see.'

'Your mother shows great discernment . . . I can think of no better introduction to the magic of opera.' Philippe paused and the skin around his eyes betrayed the faintest traces of amusement as he asked benignly, 'And does Michael Elliot share your passion for opera? I remember meeting him at the dinner party at your delightful house so I recognised him at the theatre.'

Helena flushed a little. The Ambassador found her remarkably attractive; she was so very teasable. He was enjoying himself, a little game of cat and mouse was a wonderful way of occupying a boring official evening.

Helena fixed her eyes on the tablecloth as she replied, 'He's a great friend of the family. It was very kind of him to give me such a nice evening.'

'Oh I see,' said the Ambassador with an inscrutable expression on his Gallic face. 'I do so admire the capacity the English have to make friends. Was it the first time you had met Monsieur Elliot, the dinner . . . at your house I mean?'

Helena said nothing, she knew the Ambassador would fill the silence. She was right, he probed a little further, and soon he knew just about all there was to know about Helena's love affair without her having told him a single thing. Eminently satisfied with his investigations and longing to tell his wife every detail, he made a definitive comment, looking towards James as he spoke: 'Oh I do love you English. You are such, how you say, dark horses . . .' He patted Helena lightly on her knee under the table. 'It has been a pleasure talking to you again. I have thought about you often. You look more beautiful than ever, and I suspect you have learnt the most unEnglish art of compromise in a marriage.' Helena caught Hilda glaring at her. 'I always remind myself of the analogy – ' the Ambassador went on – 'if you bring down a marriage it is like felling a tree. You bring down everything that lives in it, that depends on it: the ivy that clings to it, the birds that live in its shelter, and its branches can no longer give shade to those who need it. My wife and I . . . we have had our problems, you know, but we have found a way.' Helena looked at him. She felt very moved by what he said, the more so because it was so well meant and personal to her in the midst of this public occasion.

Philippe looked back at her. He knew he had touched a chord.

She glanced down, momentarily at a loss for words, and then she nodded. 'Thank you, Philippe. You're very sensitive. One is not used to it. At English social occasions nobody says what they think. We're afraid, you see . . .'

'Ah yes, fear,' Philippe said. 'Fear is the mother of unhappiness . . . but you, my dear, you have nothing to fear. You are in touch with your feelings. Do nothing dramatic . . . your life offers you enough drama, you do not need to go looking for it.'

Helena had tears in her eyes: she was not used to such fatherly, sympathetic dialogue. She was sorry Philippe must now turn to his neighbour. On an impulse she said to him, 'Can we talk again? I think I need a friend like you. You're so wise . . . I,' she continued, stammering a little, 'I would value some more advice very much.'

Philippe's eyes twinkled with pleasure. He felt a genuine affection for Helena. Yes, he thought, an avuncular role with this beauty would be a charming proposition.

'I would consider it an honour,' he said, getting out a pen and paper from his pocket and hastily scribbling a number on it. 'This goes straight to my desk. I will give you lunch and we can talk business. Bring some pictures of your work and maybe you could think about a portrait of my wife. She is *formidable*, is she not?' he said, glancing across the table at her. Helena nodded and put the

222

paper in her black velvet evening purse. Philippe turned to Mark Raymond's wife, on his left.

The momentary lapse in the conversation gave Helena the opportunity to look down the table towards James, sitting next to Hilda. He was clearly bored out of his mind; he had lapsed into one of his unnerving silences. He stared ahead impassively while Hilda rattled on in her indomitable way, blissfully unaware of anything except her own voice.

In the car going home, Helena turned to James, who was still moody, suffering the shock waves of an evening with Hilda. 'I really had a good time this evening.'

'I'm glad someone did,' James replied, staring out of the window at the traffic moving swiftly round Parliament Square.

'Oh, James, did your dinner companion subject you to one of her lectures?' Helena did not mention Hilda by name, aware that ministerial cars have ears.

'Yes, she certainly did, and not the abridged version.'

'I thought the Prime Minister gave a very good after-dinner speech. I didn't know he could speak French; it sounded very good, albeit two sentences. Why didn't he do the whole thing in French?'

'Because, Helena, he can't actually speak a word of it. Mark Raymond wrote it all out for him, and I happen to know he coached him for hours.' James was being unusually indiscreet. 'The two of them are like Mutt and Jeff, they work as a team.'

'I kept seeing them making faces at each other, especially when I was greeted by Christine. Were they cross about that?'

James put his finger to his mouth and then somewhat typically, Helena thought, he carried on boldly himself. 'Cross? Of course they were cross, Helena.' Suddenly his solemn features broke into a transforming smile and with uncharacteristic glee he continued, 'You're a dark horse, Helena.'

'Funny, that's exactly what Philippe said to me tonight,' Helena said, noticing the car was approaching Michael's house.

'I adored it when Christine flung her arms around you. You should have seen the look on Raymond's face and, by the way, Reggie asked me to tell you how pleased he is to see you getting on so well. You do seem to pull the rabbit out of the hat, don't you, Helena?' James turned to her as he spoke and noticed her gazing out of the window in the direction of Cheyne Walk.

'I just paid you a compliment,' he said.

'I know . . . Thank you, James . . . It wasn't hard work.'

There had been major roadworks along the Embankment and the car had to make a lengthy detour. Curiously, when they had passed Michael's house, the lights had been on in the first-floor drawing room. Helena had not asked him what his plans were for the evening. She imagined him there and felt more than a twinge of sadness. She remembered in detail the last time they had made love after the walk in the park. It had been poignant . . . something she would remember when she was old and could no longer imagine the thrill of that tempestuous love affair.

When they had parted there was something unspoken between them. She had cried as he drove her back to where she had left her car in the park. She didn't know why at the time, it was some kind of instinct which told her that nothing between her and Michael would ever be quite the same again. It was as if the news of the baby had hastened something which needed time to grow and develop, required a foundation. She had thought she knew every single bit of him, but she didn't. And she realised that if she had learned anything it was that a woman never knew a man completely, not in the way she knew her children or her mother. Even Anthony had slipped away from her secretly and finally.

She thought James was probably unaware of the drama which had been played out in the house as they turned the corner and made for home. But James was more aware than she knew. Just seeing the house, with its memories, was enough but the thought of Helena and Michael alone there sent a shiver down his spine.

He hadn't thought about Simon recently until he had been told that Sarida had been deported. He had contacted Simon and the relief in his voice had been surprising. Sarida had found a professorship in a good university and seemed rather happier than she had been in England. Her fears had been unfounded. It was all for the best, a weight off Simon's mind.

He dismissed thoughts of Simon and Elliot and reminded himself that a comforting calm had descended on his relationship with Helena . . . perhaps it was something to do with her pregnancy. He no longer felt challenged by her, she was now what he had often, oh so often wished she would be: a companion, a friend, a support. While she asked nothing from him, he didn't feel inadequate as he had done for so long. He felt strong: after all, he had helped her out of a jam. He was the one doing the caring, the protecting and, to be frank, it felt good. For the first time in a long while he was something approaching happy.

Chapter 32

'Fine,' James said. 'You go down to Maryzion and get the children settled in. I think the Prime Minister will call the election in October. I really am truly grateful that you can find some time to help me in Sussex. So you'll be there for the second week in August then?'

Helena reassured him. She had made it clear that from henceforward she had to have time for herself, though, but she was prepared to give the constituency a week now, a week later. It looked as though all the rumours had now been scotched. She hoped to feel better by then. The sickness was getting her down and the thought of long days canvassing was daunting. But she knew from experience, suddenly the day would dawn in about the twelfth week of her pregnancy when she would wake up and feel better. She was nearly there.

The lassitude she felt was terrible and packing for the children a nightmare. The long drive to Devon loomed. On departure day by nine thirty, the pile of luggage on the street had grown to enormous proportions: tennis rackets, Rollo's surf board, the rabbit in its hutch, Clovis's basket, Helena's painting things. Presents for Cornelia: twenty pairs of flesh-coloured tights from Peter Jones and lots of treats for the house, Cornelia's favourite liqueur, white wines . . . melon and proscuitto ham for that night's dinner and some special cheeses. With their practised skill the children set to work loading the car and miraculously by ten thirty they were ready to go.

Helena had told the children about the baby. She slipped it in casually one day, but none of them could take it in at first. Kirsty and Harriet went straight upstairs to discuss it, Rollo as usual listening at the door. They knew only too well the procedure that must have led to the prospect of a new half-sister or brother and the concept of James being its father was something that clouded the otherwise happy state that followed the ingestion. Of course they knew their mother had a special friendship with Michael Elliot and they couldn't help but make the connection between the arrival of Michael on the scene and Helena's improved state of mind. Except for their concern about their mother's health the mood was good, partly because they had been reprieved from the prospect of the school holidays at James's cottage in Sussex.

Helena was exhausted: she desperately needed a rest in Devon. She was looking forward to it so much, she had counted the days until they could get out of the unbearable heat and pollution of London. In high summer the streets baked and shimmered and the car felt like an oven when the family finally got in to start the four-hour drive.

'Oh, Mum, turn the air-conditioning on,' Rollo wailed, Clovis panting frantically down his neck. 'Clovis's breath smells of fish,' he complained, as the car pulled out of Richmond Terrace. Helena turned on the radio and told the children to put on their Walkmans. She wanted time to think.

Down at Maryzion preparations for the family's arrival were almost complete. Hugh had come up trumps, finding a firm in Plymouth who hired out an above-ground swimming pool complete with filter and cover. He was now in the process of filling it. Cornelia could see the top of his panama hat above the yew hedge which separated the formal garden from the kitchen area. He had sited the pool in the orchard away from the trees and near enough to the house to be able to run the hose from the tap by the greenhouse.

This domestic companionship was new to Cornelia. She was enjoying the sensation of sharing plans and Hugh was on terrific form. She hardly dared to stop and think how happy she actually was. Yesterday she had been to Exeter to get herself some last-minute shopping in preparation for the trip to Tuscany. She knew once the family arrived she would never have a chance to go shopping. Her new purchases lay enticingly on the chaise longue in her bedroom. Simple blue and white things from Marks and Spencer and a mass of new underwear. She could no longer hide her old underclothes behind a cushion on the bedroom chair. At least she didn't have to get a new nightdress. Hugh wouldn't let her wear one, so she invested in some crisp white cotton housecoats. They now hung on pink satin hangers on the back of the bathroom door with Hugh's battered but still elegant silk paisley dressing gown.

This morning Hugh had stated his intention of moving it to the dressing room before the arrival of the children. It was this announcement that had stopped her raising the subject of Helena's request the previous night on the telephone.

It was now eleven o'clock. She had prepared some iced coffee; she would take it out to the gazebo and bring the subject up.

'Hugh, darling . . . some iced coffee. Shall I take it on out?' she called from the kitchen window, which she had a job to open owing to the profusion of climbing roses now at their peak.

'Coming,' he answered. 'And be careful of the roses. I've been meaning to tie them back for you. I'll do it this afternoon,' he added happily.

He walked briskly across the lawn, having worked up quite a thirst, and plonked himself down on one of the new chairs, removed his hat, and wiped the perspiration from his brow with a large red and white spotted handkerchief. Cornelia's stomach did a little leap as she looked at him lying back in the chair with a contented smile on his face. She thought how this must be what life was meant to be like in a perfect world, but then she reminded herself that the world was not perfect, and the moment might not last more than the twinkling of an eye. For happiness, she told herself, is as fragile as glass; it can shatter when you least expect it to.

'Darling,' she said with an upturn in her voice, indicating the approach of a difficult question.

'Yes, what's coming now?' Hugh was enjoying the sound of a large honey bee working on the buddleia outside the gazebo.

'Michael wants to come and spend the weekend,' Cornelia said.

Hugh leapt from the basket chair, spilling some of his coffee on the stone floor. He stood facing Cornelia, blocking the morning sun. It spilled out around his silhouette and Cornelia had to shade her eyes to see his face.

He looked angry but perfectly in control.

'Cornelia, if he comes here, I will leave. I know exactly why he is trying to infiltrate your life, Cornelia. He is one of those men who slithers out of tight corners like a snake, and he likes to oil his way by trying to be liked by everybody, never mind that he may have buggered up a few lives on the way. For two pins he would even pop into bed with you if you would have him, just to secure his position when he gets bored with Helena and can see no advantage in his affair with her.' He bent down and picked up his panama hat from the floor beside his chair. He gave it a shake and bent the rim back into the right shape.

'Don't be absurd, Hugh. Why would he want to do that and why would that help if he ditched Helena now?' Cornelia asked.

'Because you would not be in a position to condemn him, and that man cares what people say about him, despite what you think,' answered Hugh flatly.

'Oh, I see,' Cornelia said awkwardly, dropping a piece of paper towelling on to the spilled coffee.

'I don't understand you . . . or Helena for that matter. I thought she had decided to stand by James for the moment. Pardon me if I'm on a different planet . . . I mean, God dammit, Cornelia.' Hugh shook the panama angrily. 'Nobody has ever called me a prude, but to allow your daughter to entertain her lover here, under the same roof as her children, when her husband is about to fight an election campaign – yes, her husband, Cornelia – is mind blowing. I won't be part of it, but the choice is yours.' He put the hat firmly on his head and stared at her.

Cornelia thought for a moment. Hearing such vehemence from Hugh made her think carefully. She knew if Hugh felt so strongly he was expressing the sentiments which were right and proper and about which he felt deeply. Yes, she decided, Hugh was right. He was being objective, something she found difficult in the troubled waters of her family's life at the moment, nor was it easy having a dominant man under her roof after all these years. But now Hugh's good kind face looked back at her and she didn't want to live life without it. There was perhaps something reassuring about not having to make all the decisions oneself.

'I hadn't seen it like that. You're quite right. I get things out of perspective. Helena always could twist me round her little finger and the main thing is the children. Poor things, they must be very confused,' she said thoughtfully.

'Not half as confused as I am. Children have a strange way of rationalising things. You know, darling, I stayed with Dorothy for the sake of the children but now I know they do not thank us for it. They think it would have been better to see us happy with another partner. It's not the parting they mind so much, it's the hating and uncertainty which creates the hurt. Helena is not behaving well, she should make up her mind between her husband and her lover now. It boils down to her wanting her cake and eating it.'

'No, it's nothing like that. I've tried to explain this to you . . .' Cornelia said defensively. 'Basically, she is being strong and circumspect and I'm glad to see it at last. She hasn't been like that since Anthony died. It's like the Helena I used to know. She can't take responsibility for removing yet another structure from her children's lives if she's not sure of a viable alternative. Michael has not said he'll marry her.'

'But you said you thought Helena and Michael would get married. Then what are the bloody man's intentions? The man's a shit, I tell you, a shit . . . If it were a hundred years ago he'd have been horse-whipped on the steps of the Carlton Club.'

'Oh come on, Hugh, that doesn't sound like you. Look, let's drop the subject. James is no angel. He's going along with all this because it suits him. Michael can take Helena away to a hotel for two days. It will do her good. There, does that satisfy you?' she said angrily. 'Maybe they will get themselves sorted out one way or another.'

'Not in this country, for God's sake, Cornelia. I suppose they could go away to France or somewhere. There are flights from Exeter, I think. They wouldn't be known there,' replied Hugh.

'Well, there you are then,' Cornelia said briskly.

Hugh leant down and kissed the top of her head. He gripped her shoulder lovingly. 'Well, all right,' he said grudgingly

Cornelia thought his response was rather annoying, but at least the matter had been resolved.

She got up from her chair. She had to go back into the kitchen now and get on with the lunch.

The two of them walked back towards the house rather more apart than they would have been an hour earlier.

Hugh was deep in thought. He was awaiting a phone call from London with more information which, he hoped, would confirm his suspicions about Michael Elliot. He didn't want to say anything to Cornelia until he had specific proof but all the indications were that, if she didn't know already, Helena was in for quite a shock.

Chapter 33

'I'm sorry, I don't quite know how to put this,' Helena said on the telephone to Michael the following morning. She lay in bed in her old room at Maryzion. The sun poured through the open window on to the flowery Laura Ashley covers of the bed where Clovis lay stretched on his back, his stomach exposed as if he were a fat middle-aged man in search of a tan; he snored loudly.

'What on earth is that noise? I can hear someone snoring,' Michael said.

'It's Clovis; he's on the bed.'

'Do you mean to say you're still in bed? It's ten o'clock.'

'I am actually. Mrs Finch brought me a tray of breakfast, my favourite boiled egg, tea and toast.'

'You deserve to be spoilt, darling. It won't be long before I can bring you breakfast. I'm in Plymouth. I can get to you by Friday tea time.'

The sun caught the silver egg cup and the small teapot kept for special breakfast-in-bed trays. With her finger she scooped up a blob of her mother's homemade marmalade which she had dropped on the white embroidered tray cloth. It tasted delicious.

'That's what I have to tell you. Mummy and Hugh think it would be better if we went to a lovely hotel for the weekend. They think it is too awkward with the children at the moment. They suggested France or the Channel Islands. Apparently there are flights from Exeter?'

'So it's Mummy and Hugh now, is it?' Michael said.

'Yes it is . . . and I'm so happy for them both.' She stopped abruptly, sensing an ominous silence on the other end of the telephone.

Michael felt extremely put out. He liked to be in control. The idea that his plans had been thwarted was alarming. He thought he had made a friend of Cornelia, he could twist her round his finger. She was a beautiful woman . . . she was part of what had attracted him to Helena. She would be integral to the scenario if things worked out with Helena in the way he might want. Part of the charm surrounding Helena and her family had been their vulnerability. It brought out the feelings of chivalry in him. He hadn't bargained on Hugh wading in and picking up the tab. In a mad way he had allowed himself to look forward to a few days at Maryzion playing the father figure, the masterful man missing for so long, and now his role had been usurped. He could not keep the coldness out of his voice.

'So you're one big happy family down there, are you?'

'It's about time, Michael. I haven't had much of that, and for the sake of my children I'll take it wherever I can get it,' Helena said pointedly. 'You shouldn't begrudge me that, you know.'

Michael assimilated Helena's comments and thought suddenly of his baby growing inside Helena as she lay happily in her childhood room at Maryzion with her family about her. He dismissed the jealousy he felt . . . it was better she be happy and secure at this time. Babies lived the hopes and fears of their mothers; even in the womb his child was all that mattered. Things would turn out all right if he kept cool and did not add pressure to a potentially disastrous situation. He felt a pang of alarm. What if Helena lost the baby? The very idea was too awful to think of.

'Darling, as long as you're getting some rest. I've been so worried about you. You must look after that baby. How are you feeling?' he ventured solicitously.

'Much better. The sickness is gradually getting better. This morning was the first time I have been able to keep down breakfast.'

'I meant to ask. What did the doctor say when you went to him on Tuesday?'

'He said everything was perfectly normal. The baby is due in February, the twenty-third to be exact. I have a picture of it,' said Helena. 'They did a scan, you can see its little hands and eyes. It looks like a little ET. I can show it to you on Friday,' she said hopefully.

The truth was the thought of a few days alone with Michael, away from everything, was a wonderful idea.

'Keep it safe for me. Now, while we've been talking I have thought of the very thing. There's a marvellous hotel in Guernsey – swimming pool, beach, five-star food. How about that?'

'Oh yes.'

'I'll phone them straight away. I'll ring you back when I've arranged it,' he said briskly. He was in control again. He felt better and the idea of not being allowed at Maryzion was not so bad. After all it would be better to have Helena on her own. He had to straighten a few things out.

After Helena had put the phone down, she could hear footsteps on the landing. Kirsty put her head round the door.

'When are you getting up, Mum? We're doing a barbecue in the orchard. It's fantastic fun. Hugh is a genius! It's great to have a man doing things.'

'I expect it's what Daddy would have done,' Harriet, who had now joined her, said wistfully.

'Come here. Let me give you both a kiss.'

Kirsty approached the bed first. She was wearing a thin blue and white cotton sundress. Her waist was so small Helena saw she could encompass it in her two hands. She had shabby white gym shoes on her thin feet and her hair was wet. She looked frail. She was on the cusp, neither child nor woman. Helena felt a lump in her throat . . .

'Your hair's all wet,' she said, feeling it.

'Of course it's wet. We've been in Hugh's pool, we told you.'

'Darling,' said Helena, 'we won't ever be alone again. Not like before.'

'You're a clever old stick, aren't you, Mum? Suddenly there seems to be lots of fathers about instead of none.' She stared at her mother knowingly.

Helena didn't ask what she meant, she just knew that, in a curious way, Kirsty was growing up.

Chapter 34

'Oh yes, Mrs Elliot. Your husband is out on the terrace. Shall I show you the way while we get your luggage taken to the suite?' The pretty girl at reception looked admiringly at Helena. Helena could tell Michael had aroused her curiosity – obviously she was not the only one to sense his attraction.

The girl took Helena out to the terrace and watched the way they greeted each other. It wasn't so much anything they said or did, just the silence and the look, and then off they went, up to the suite and just before lunch too . . . She was sure they weren't married; married people didn't look at each other like that.

'Why aren't you wearing a bikini?' asked Michael lazily from his reclining chair by the pool.

'In case you hadn't noticed, I have rather a telltale bulge already,' Helena said. She wore a bright fuchsia-pink one-piece bathing suit and her figure looked fantastic, as Michael had already remarked, having spent the last two hours exploring the new luscious Helena. 'Your breasts are lovely,' he had said.

Helena lay back soaking up the afternoon sun. They were the only people in the pool area. The other guests seemed to have made for the cool of their bedrooms or perhaps the private beach.

Michael watched Helena spreading sun oil over herself. He stretched out a tanned arm and laid it on her stomach. 'I adore you,' he said.

She covered his hand with her own and said tenderly, 'Darling, I'm so happy when we're together. Let's not spoil today by talking about things. Let's just enjoy it . . . I can't explain. I—'

'I know,' he said. 'I understand, but perhaps we could talk for a moment tomorrow.'

She squeezed his hand reassuringly.

Later they went upstairs and had a long leisurely bath. The hotel was under new management and had recently been redecorated. It had, Helena thought, been beautifully done. The room was much as you would expect to find in a smart country house: chintz bed hangings and curtains; good quality reproduction furniture; a lavish bathroom in peachy-coloured marble, and thick white carpets. There was a huge balcony which made the room light and airy. The room was obviously the master bedroom of the original house; it had superb views of the bay. They could see the bright fiery orb of the sun about to drop slowly into the sea which lay calm before them. They made love passionately and afterwards as voices carried up from the terrace below from people having their pre-dinner drinks he said, 'Let's have our drink up here before dinner. We can watch the sun falling into the sea. It's going to be a marvellous day tomorrow. Look how clear the sky is.'

The light from the sky bathed Michael in soft gold. The atmosphere was dreamlike, full of contentment and happiness. Helena's heart missed a beat when she looked at him. Surely he would ask her the fateful question, say something to help her make a decision about their long-term future instead of offering vague promises about being there. She looked at him wistfully. He was on the inhouse phone ordering drinks and the menu for dinner. 'Yes, the table in the window. That's right; pink roses and white carnations. Well done.' So good on the small ephemeral details but what about the rest of her life? Helena wondered. But still, if he cared enough to order special flowers for their dinner table and white lilies for the bedroom, he must have thought about the garden of their life.

He came back to where Helena stood looking out to the sea. 'Let's move the chairs on the balcony closer together; we want a good view.' He didn't wait for an answer. He set about moving the two wrought-iron chairs and changed the position of the small round table. 'We don't want a table to come between us,' he joked. 'Come on, my darling Helena. You take my breath away.'

Helena wore filmy harem trousers from her favourite Indian shop, embroidered in threads of gold and silver, and an almost transparent cream top. Underneath, for propriety's sake, she wore a white satin camisole.

238

'So tell me, when are you going to get on with my portrait?' Michael asked.

'I have started it,' Helena said, 'as you know. What do you think my alibi has been; but it's had to take a bit of a back seat. Getting the children down to Mummy for the holidays while I've been feeling so ghastly . . . then there's the election. I hardly dare think about it,' Helena said.

'When do you think the election will be?' Michael asked, walking towards the door to let in the waiter with the drinks.

Helena waited for him to sign the bill. When they were alone again she replied, 'It must be soon. James wants to be prepared, so I'm off down to Sussex in about a week's time, visiting old people's homes and generally showing the flag.'

She sat down and took the drink Michael handed her. 'What is it?' she asked. The glass looked pale and cool.

'A spritzer. It's very mild and refreshing. Try it. If you can't manage it I'll get you something else.'

Helena tasted it and nodded her approval.

'And are the children staying at Maryzion while you pound the streets in Sussex?'

'Hugh's taking Mummy to see some properties in Tuscany next week.'

'What do you think your mother has in mind? Do you think she plans to live with Hugh in Italy?' Michael asked tentatively.

'I'm sure not and I don't suppose they'll even bother to get married, even though Dorothy, Hugh's wife, is off any day to live in London and wants a divorce. I expect marriage would spoil it all. She likes her independence and she would never leave Maryzion.'

'Oh, why so? Is your mother against marriage for some reason?' Michael asked.

Helena guessed that her answer would be important. Michael would absorb it and mull it over, perhaps to assist him in whatever was going on in his mind at the moment.

'Of course she isn't,' she said. She broke off, looking into the distance. A ship moved slowly across the horizon and Michael watched it with her. 'It's just that she and Hugh don't have a family together and maybe my situation has a bearing on the matter. After all, it may well be that Mummy and I end up looking after four children. I think she feels it wouldn't be fair on Hugh.'

'Surely you're quite capable of bringing up your children without your mother's help?' Michael said in genuine bewilderment.

'It's not as simple as that. We've been through a lot together. The children have just got back into the swing of life at Maryzion, because James and I have found what at least is a temporary compromise. But I don't expect things can go on as they are, can they? And she feels she can't make any plans at the moment.'

Michael refused to respond to Helena's comments.

'Perhaps neither of you is ready to make dramatic decisions. After all, marriage is the biggest decision we ever make. Let's look at what matters at this moment and choose our dinner.'

He handed her the menu. They chose the same dishes, but only by chance – iced avocado soup and fillet of lamb. 'You have excellent taste,' Michael said, taking the menu from her and picking up the telephone to give the order.

'I usually get it right in the end,' said Helena, looking steadily at Michael. 'Whatever happens to both of us, I'll always be grateful to you for coming along when I had a crisis.' She hesitated, looking thoughtfully at the patterns the wine made on the rim of her glass as she cupped it between her hands. 'I've changed dramatically in the last few weeks. I have realised that whatever I have to be in my life I must be it on my own.'

'What do you mean, on your own?' Michael asked, putting down his glass and looking at her with what she thought to be a trace of alarm.

'I mean, I was brought up to think one's destiny lay in the gift of a man – husband, lover, father, whatever. Well, now I know different. We must both bring our individual gifts to the boardroom table, as it were. I am determined to make a success of my work. I hope to get to the stage where I can support my family on my own if necessary, and then whoever my husband or lover is, they will only be expected to add the frills, not provide the bread and butter.'

Michael listened to this with mixed feelings. On the one hand he should be pleased at the way Helena had become so self-reliant, but on the other perhaps he had done himself out of a job, been instrumental in the emergence of this strong confident woman. Michael had always known his head ruled his heart. He knew he would not have fallen in love with Helena if she had not had access to a way of life which would, whatever happened, enhance his image. He was wary lest she make some wrong moves. A public scandal might harm all the players on the board. He didn't want that, he never had rows, he had a clever way of avoiding confrontation.

He calculated how this change in Helena's pattern would influence his decisions as to where their relationship should go. He was weighing up the pros and cons as they spoke. He decided to observe one of his own rules – when in doubt, do nothing. With an election coming up a great drama would damage all of them. It would be better to wait till James had his life back in order then go to him, offer to do the right thing, perhaps discussing it with Cornelia first. At all costs he didn't want to make an enemy of Cornelia. She was a grand lady, one of the all-powerful great and good. Besides, he had in the back of his mind a picture of taking over Maryzion, restoring it to its former glory. If he set up house with Helena he would use all her credentials. Recently this idea had been gathering momentum, but he knew he must not mention it to Helena at this point. It must come when he was Michael, the hero on the white charger.

'Remember I'm here for you, darling,' he said. He recognised the banality of the remark, but it served the purpose for the moment, and at that moment he had never seen a woman more alive and beautiful than the woman who looked back at him.

Chapter 35

'Fucking Tory wanker,' yelled a youth with rings through his nose.

'Mum, what's a wanker?' Rollo shrieked excitedly, waving his 'Vote for Askew' flag.

'I can't explain . . .' Helena said.

The mood was definitely deteriorating. The crowd were belligerently staring up at James as he stood on an orange box in the market square. Askew supporters muttered their disapproval at the raucous element of 'layabouts' now shouting insults from all directions. A large Tory lady, wearing an outsize blue rosette, bore down on the ringleader. She came prepared for all eventualities: rain, headaches, hunger, lack of information, sore feet – and there were plenty of those. The youth noticed her out of the corner of his eye and leered contemptuously, uttering some unrepeatable suggestions as to where she should put her political beliefs. She slowly extended her umbrella. Helena watched fascinated. It looked as if she would hit the youth about the head. Instead she caught the collar of his leather bomber jacket with the crook of her umbrella and with terrifying strength, pulled his pock-marked face towards her. Eyeballing him she bellowed at him 'to stand up straight'. The crowd became silent. Even James broke off from his diatribe.

'When God put a tongue in your mouth he created the perfect arsehole,' she intoned slowly and clearly, with all the solemnity of a chairperson's address to the Women's Institute.

The crowd were delighted. A rousing cheer gathered momentum and the local paper bore down on the woman. Cameras snapped as the youth opened his mouth in terror, cringing as though the woman would hit him. Instead she made a handwashing gesture, folded her umbrella and ordered him from the square.

He slunk around the corner to his motor bike, nervously picking his nose.

243

Rollo jumped up and down. 'Mum, who's that woman?' he asked admiringly.

'You know who she is, it's Mrs Crawley-Baker. We went to a wine and cheese party in her garden the day before yesterday.'

The children had been allowed to stay off school for the last couple of days of campaigning. It would be half-term directly after the election was over.

'You mean the one where you had to talk to all the old women in funny dresses?' Rollo asked.

'They weren't funny, they were their best clothes,' Harriet said.

'I thought they all looked rather nice,' Kirsty said.

'I expect you didn't recognise Mrs Crawley-Baker because she wasn't wearing a hat,' Helena said.

The crowd gradually melted away and James alighted from his orange box handing his agent, Cynthia, his notes, which she officiously put into a black leather briefcase.

'Well done, James. Exactly right as usual,' she smarmed, straightening one of her executive shoulder pads which had clearly slipped. She took a whistle from her breast pocket and gave two single peeps.

A dozen rosetted canvassers appeared from various shops and assembled awaiting further orders.

Cynthia picked up James's loud hailer and addressed the group. She was in her element. 'We have an hour until the lunch break,' she announced.

Rollo groaned. 'Oh, Mum, my feet are hurting and my fingers are sore. Those letter boxes have brushes inside them and they bite me when I put the leaflets in. Do I have to?'

Helena entirely sympathised but she shushed Rollo as Cynthia continued.

'We can just do the streets to the south of the square. Your candidate will take the even numbers and Mrs Askew will take the odd ones. Supporters take up the rear and don't forget to replenish your literature,' she commanded.

'Oh Mum, please, do we have to?' continued Rollo. 'I'm famished.'

'Yes you do, Rollo. Stop whining. I expect Mum is a lot tireder than you are. Are you OK, Mum?' Kirsty sounded worried. She thought her mother looked terribly ill.

'I'm fine, darling, but I think we might have an afternoon off, unless you want to go round in the van with the loud hailer this afternoon.'

'Let's decide after lunch. Now, off we go, Rollo,' Kirsty said, giving Rollo a push from behind.

Rollo skipped up the street ahead of them and Helena found herself accompanied by Beryl.

'I must admit your children have been very helpful,' she said grudgingly, tidying up the bundle of leaflets she had ready to push through letter boxes.

To Helena's horror Rollo had burst into song just ahead of them. 'Wankers, wankers, who's a big fat wanker?'

'For heaven's sake, Rollo,' Kirsty hissed, putting her hand over his mouth to silence him and looking back anxiously at Helena.

'What did the child say?' Beryl asked in disbelief.

'Oh, nothing. Just something he heard at school,' Helena said.

'Why is it so bad? What is a wanker, Mum?' shrieked Rollo over his shoulder.

Helena quickened her pace. She caught up with him. Beryl had crossed the street and was saying something to James.

'A wanker is someone who plays with his willy all day,' she heard Harriet say to Rollo in a matter-of-fact tone of voice.

'That's enough,' Helena said. 'If you go on like this, Rollo, I shan't let you come to the count. Now there's an end to it.'

'I hope you don't mind me interrupting your little quarrel.' Cynthia had returned. 'You start at number one, Helena. I'll go on ahead and forewarn the houses on the right that their candidate will be coming shortly. And by the way, Helena, don't get involved in anything political. Just smile nicely and make notes of any questions for James.' She smiled patronisingly at Helena, swivelled on her black court shoes, and marched down the street.

Rollo marched forcefully up the short path of the first terraced house and rattled the brass letter box. A large red poster could be seen in the upstairs window, saying 'Vote for Frane'.

'Oh stop him!' Helena cried too late, as the mock-Tudor door of the tiny house flung open.

'Get off my land!' came a voice from the doorway.

'I'm here on behalf of the Conservative candidate. Can we depend on your vote on the day after tomorrow?' Rollo said importantly from the bottom step.

'Can't you bloody read?' demanded the man, pointing to the upstairs window.

A large Rottweiler dog appeared, dribbling ominously at the man's heels.

'Steady, Rambo,' the man growled, kicking the dog smartly in the hind quarters. It yelped and lay down trembling at his feet.

'What's going on? Can I help?' James walked briskly across the road. He extended his hand. 'I'm James Askew, your Conservative candidate. Is there anything you want to discuss?' he asked breezily with his immaculate campaign smile.

'I'm not going to shake your hand and you're not getting my vote and my dog wouldn't vote for you either. Now get lost, the lot of you.' The door slammed and the scooped net curtains on the double-glazed bay window twitched. The man's silhouette could be seen checking the departure of the canvassing team.

'Can I have a word?' James said, taking Helena by the arm and hustling her behind a telephone kiosk. 'What can you be thinking of? Beryl tells me your son is marching up and down chanting obscenities. And what is he doing knocking on doors? He's only supposed to stand beside you handing out leaflets. I've enough to cope with, Helena. Please get your family under control.'

Cynthia and Beryl were across the road smiling smugly. Helena didn't often feel hate, but she felt it now. She wished the Rottweiler would come rushing out and savage them both.

'Where are Harriet and Kirsty?' asked James, looking about him.

'They went into a house down there,' Rollo said.

'Will you please go and find out what they're doing?' James's mouth tightened as he looked at Helena.

'For heaven's sake, they are only trying to help. Where's your sense of humour?' Helena asked. 'I think I've had enough for one day. After lunch I'm going to take the children home. I'm very tired and my legs are aching and I've got a blister on my heel.'

'Oh dear, I'm sorry, but you wouldn't listen to Joan Crawley-Baker when she offered you the Dr Scholl plaster.'

'Well, we've knocked on twelve thousand doors and I've bleeding knuckles from stuffing things through those disgusting letter boxes with brushes inside. I've been insulted and pushed. Yesterday, when that woman shoved her horrid wrought-iron gate on to my ankle deliberately, you never said a word. I think that constituted an assault. I've had enough. I need a day off before election day. I'm taking the children to the sea for the day tomorrow.'

'Very well,' said James sourly. 'I'll have to notify Cynthia that you can't do the tour of old people's homes.'

'Oh dear, I must find the girls,' Helena said. She wanted to get away from James before she had a flaming row in front of all of them. She didn't want to give Cynthia and Beryl any more to talk about.

'Come on, Mum. I know which house they went into,' said Rollo unperturbed. He grabbed her hand and they hurried up the road.

Helena rang the bell and it pealed 'Edelweiss' through the shimmering corrugated glass of the partly glazed door. It opened and a little old lady in a floral apron smiled at them. 'Yes dear?' she said.

'I am Helena Askew, your Conservative candidate's wife. Are my daughters in there with you?' she asked. Sounds of a Hoover could be heard in the sitting room to the right of the hall.

'Yes, they are. Lovely girls,' the old lady said, beckoning her to follow her.

The neat front parlour smelt of fish and digestive biscuits. Harriet and Kirsty stood either side of the fireplace, Kirsty with a vacuum cleaner and Harriet with a duster and some Pledge. The room bore the signs of a recent spring clean – neatly fluffed cushions, gleaming furniture and Hoovered shagpile.

'There you are, Mum. We've cleaned this lady's room for her. She asked us to because she has a bad knee. Doesn't it look nice? She says she always votes for James so we knew he'd be pleased,' Kirsty smiled proudly.

'Well, you've made a wonderful job of it,' Helena said in amazement.

'Oh yes, you tell their dad he should be proud of them. James Frane's my favourite. Always comes round at Christmas. That other one – can't remember his name – typical Tory. Only see him when it's election time. Tories out, I say. But they're lovely girls. 'Bye, dearies. I expect your mum wants to get on.'

The girls' faces had fallen a mile. Helena took charge of the situation. Damage limitation was what was required. She bade the old lady goodbye and hurried the girls outside on to the pavement.

'Oh Mum,' wailed Harriet, 'how were we to know?'

'It doesn't matter,' Helena said. 'It was a nice thought and you meant well. I wouldn't tell James, though.'

With relief Helena heard three loud blasts of Cynthia's whistle; three meant the lunch break. 'Canvassers back in the bus,' she barked through the loud hailer.

By the time Helena and the children arrived at the bus, the large mini van with wooden seats borrowed from a local football club, it was filled with canvassers. James had gone on ahead to the lunch venue, The Horse's Arms, for a down-the-line radio interview.

Cynthia was in her element.

'Are we on the air?' she said the driver, Helena's friend Ray.

'Yes, Cyn,' he replied mischievously, handing her the microphone attached to the public address system on top of the van. 'Do you want the Austrian waltzes as a lead-in?' he said, fumbling with a pile of battered tapes.

'Please don't call me Cyn. I've asked you before,' Cynthia said curtly.

Ray pressed the button to start the tape and the van set off. A loud guttural Germanic voice bellowed from the PA system, followed by Austrian yodellers.

'I hardly think this is suitable music,' ventured the retired Colonel, in charge of navigation.

Heads turned in the market square. 'Nazis!' shrieked a man from a shop doorway.

'The Colonel's right, Cynthia. It's awful. It sounds like a Hitler youth rally. Where on earth did you get it, Ray?' Helena asked.

Ray hurriedly clicked off the tape and Cynthia tuned the PA system on to voice.

'Good morning, ladies and gentlemen of Honeywell Close. Your Conservative candidate, James Askew, who has been your Member of Parliament for ten years, will be with you this afternoon with his lovely wife, Helena, and their family. He would very much like to meet you. If you have time for him, he has time for you. At two o'clock we will be back. Just remember what it was like under

Labour. The dead left unburied, rubbish in the streets. Labour at Number Ten. Do we want that? No, we don't.'

'That woman's off her trolley,' hissed the Colonel to Helena. 'Yesterday, she got it wrong. She was telling them about the dead in the streets and the rubbish unburied. You must have a word with James. She's a disaster with a PA system. The voice is enough to start a revolution.'

Helena nodded resignedly. She agreed with the Colonel but she knew James wouldn't listen and, in any event, his majority was big enough to stand the odd protest vote.

'People like you are the backbone of the Party,' she answered inanely, as the van drew into the car park of The Horse's Arms where they were greeted by a group of Chinese protesters complaining about the Government's policy on immigration. 'Labour means liberty' their slogan said.

The awful thing was, Helena thought, she didn't really feel strongly about any of it.

Chapter 36

'Call it what you like, but the great British public is voting with its feet,' Hugh said from behind a tray of drinks.

'Do you think it's a protest vote?' Cornelia asked.

'Yes, of course it's a bloody protest vote. Too many banana skins, if you ask me.' Hugh let his half-glasses fall from his nose and hang from an old pair of shoe laces he had tied round his neck.

'Finchie, another sherry?' Hugh held up an empty glass towards Mrs Finch who sat next to her husband on the sofa.

The Finches were in their best clothes, she in the two-piece she had got from British Home Stores for her daughter's wedding the previous year, and he in his best dark blue suit.

This was the first time anyone in the room had watched an election which featured a member of the family. Perhaps they would see Miss Helena on the tele or even one of the children. Lady C. said they had all been working so hard down in Sussex.

'Fat lot of thanks they'll get for it,' she had said to Mr Finch last night over high tea.

'And, Jane, I know you'd love another.' Jane was working with Cornelia on plans for the stable conversions to holiday cottages and was to be found at Maryzion much of the time.

'Let's drink a toast to James and Helena,' Jane said.

An awkward silence descended on the room. 'Do we want our supper on our laps now, before things start hotting up?' Cornelia asked hastily.

It was agreed that supper should be eaten at once and the Finches were forbidden to move from the sofa. They were to be waited on for a change.

Hugh and Cornelia busied themselves bringing in coronation chicken and salad on a trolley, when the telephone could be heard ringing in the hall outside.

Mrs Finch, who always picked up the phone if she was at Maryzion, rushed to answer it, her voice echoed around the hall and staircase. 'Lady C., it's Miss Helena,' she called excitedly.

Cornelia seized the receiver. 'Darling, how's it going?'

'Not well.' Helena's voice sounded strained.

'It's a record poll. I can't work out if that's good or bad for the Government.'

'It's not good, but it looks as if James's majority will be safe.'

'Can you tell at this stage?' asked Cornelia.

'Yes, we can. The tellers are coming in with some results.'

'Has James had any feedback from anyone?'

'It's different across the whole country.'

'How's James bearing up?'

'You know him, he's very unemotional about everything.'

'Perhaps it's a good thing he is. There's nothing anyone can do now, but maybe it won't be as bad as you think. You must be on the edge of your seat.'

'A very good pun, Mummy. Anyway, I can't wait to get to Maryzion. I thought I'd come down quite soon, if you can do with me. Whatever happens, James will be inundated with press interviews and no one will notice if I'm there or not.'

'Poor darling, you sound exhausted. I should get here as soon as possible if I were you. And how are the children?'

'Rollo's in his element. He's indomitable. In fact, I think James had begun to quite like him. In the last few days we've had one or two bad moments, but on the whole the children have been a great asset to James. There's been a lot of TV coverage of the family working with him and stuff like that. The girls hate the whole thing, but they've been marvellous. I don't think I could have managed without them.'

'You must be proud of them.'

'I have to go now, the first ballot boxes are coming in. Can I call you later?'

'Yes, darling. We are all glued to the tele. The Finches are here, and Jane, of course. They all send their love.'

Cornelia replaced the receiver with a heavy heart.

The television election programmes were well under way. The commentator was explaining some computer graphics, his voice barely controlled at the excitement of the indications so far.

Hugh sat forward in his chair. 'There's nothing for it, we'll have to emigrate. There will be no place in the country for people like us by the time a Labour Government has had its way.'

Cornelia had made Mrs Finch promise to tell her husband to keep his political views to himself. The fact that he had voted Labour was something Mrs Finch found hard to accept. She had told Cornelia of his intention while they were bottling plums the previous day.

'I thought you were both ardent Conservatives,' Cornelia had replied.

'We are, but he says the country needs a change,' Mrs Finch had answered disapprovingly.

Hugh ranted for a while and Cornelia saw Mrs Finch dig her husband smartly in the ribs, and suddenly Jane let out an exclamation. There was Helena, talking animatedly to a blue-rosetted Party worker in the Town Hall and James, his hand on Rollo's shoulder, smiling down at him, as Rollo dragged Clovis to heel, a large blue rosette tied to his collar.

The news was bad for the Tories. David Banks was being interviewed at the count in his constituency, his expression bordering on triumph. Violet Banks had allowed herself to start thinking about how she was going to manage with three small girls at Number Ten. A programme presenter was asking her this very question as the first results started to come in.

By midnight it was a foregone conclusion: a tight victory for Labour. Mr and Mrs Finch had gone home and were already asleep. Mr Finch snored peacefully, content with the thought that Britain was now under Labour rule.

'I simply can't believe it,' Hugh said, pouring himself a large brandy. 'There's nothing for it but to drown one's sorrows with drink – for as long as one can afford it, that is.'

'Oh surely it won't be that disastrous,' Jane said from the depths of an armchair. She had fallen asleep some time ago and missed the latest results.

Hugh paced about the room irritably. 'It's goodbye to our plans for holiday apartments. Nobody will be able to afford one now. The middle classes will be the first to suffer,' he said.

'Don't be daft, Hugh, you're over-reacting,' Jane said.

'It's your sort of complacency which has led to this disaster,' Hugh looked fiercely at Jane.

'The country needs a change,' Jane continued bravely.

'You may call this a change, Jane, but it's more than that,' said Hugh.

'But we knew this might happen, Hugh.' Cornelia got up and turned off the television. 'Come on, let's go to bed. Things won't look so very different when we wake up tomorrow morning. The bantams will still have laid their eggs, the apples will still have ripened, so I want my beauty sleep.'

'You and Jane go to bed. I'm staying up to watch the rest of the results,' Hugh said rebelliously, determined to wallow in the awfulness of his predictions.

Chapter 37

James could not hear the sound of Helena's breathing. It was still dark, he guessed it must be about four o'clock. He stretched out a hand to the other side of the bed. It was cold. Helena must have moved to the guest room. During the election campaign they had shared a bed, as his secretary had stayed with them. She had left the previous day to set up the office again at Westminster. James had not touched Helena during those nights but he had wanted to feel the warmth of her body, experience the comforting feeling of being close to her. The last few nights he hadn't slept well, and not only because of the worry about his seat, wondering whether his majority would be halved or whether he might even lose it. It had been anyone's guess.

Now he could take a deep breath and forget about the constituency for a few days. He thought he might have got over the nagging concerns that pursued him for most of the night. But he had woken with a start and the word 'regret' repeated itself over and over again in the back of his brain. Regret about how he had so misunderstood Helena's needs, how he had not seen how important her work was to her. If he had just considered it, not put his own ambitions first, sidelining her road to self-esteem, she might not have been so desperate to have a baby. He realised now how cold he had been with Helena's children. He had failed to see how much they missed their father. He wished now he had thought of all these things, and saw how impossible it was to expect Helena, of all people, to become the hands-on do-gooding Parliamentary wife. She had an established life of her own – even Maryzion was part of it – and he had been intimidated by that, but in the end it was stronger than anything he had tried to inject into Helena's life. He knew if she stayed with him he would be able to walk side by side with her instead of thinking he should be a few steps ahead.

255

But with a feeling of abject sadness he knew that even if he were to go through the ritual of trying to explain, there was a certain remorseless inevitability about the future, for Helena's affair with Michael had gone too far. He lay there in the dark and thought of how it could be if she were to give him a chance. He knew he was not capable of the kind of erotic passion he was sure she had shared with her lover, but he loved her in a way he had never loved any other woman.

With these many imponderables in his mind he fell into a restless sleep.

James was at his desk in the cottage in Sussex when Helena came downstairs at nine o'clock. The room was cold and dingy despite the beauty of the autumn day. A sharp morning sun slanted through the last remaining russet-coloured leaves on the trees at the end of the orchard, but none found its way into James's study. Helena was struck by the absence of the red boxes. When James was at home they were as much part of him as the shoes on his feet, but the neatly stacked piles of paper were as large as ever. A wire basket on a small table beside his desk brimmed with House of Commons envelopes ready for posting.

James did not hear Helena as she crossed the hall and stood for a moment just outside the room quietly observing him. His fingers fluttered swiftly over the keys of his word processor and she noticed the fineness of his hands and the shape of his head. It was amazing, she thought, how he had the capacity to concentrate when his private life was poised on the edge of disaster. But then she wondered if that was how James saw it, or even if he had lost a single night's sleep wondering what their future held.

Helena knew she would have to tell James sooner or later that she had come to a decision, better sooner before he made any plans. The loss of the election and his ministerial job was very significant for him, but she was glad he had done so well personally. His majority had stayed the same. He had fought a brilliant campaign and even the children had felt involved. She had found that almost more disturbing than anything else. Helena was glad it was the half-term holiday next week and she had sent them swiftly down to her mother. Their presence here in the cottage would have confused the issue.

James had had his chance to make a family and missed it. And Michael was waiting to hear from her. He would be worried, desperately anxious about her. She resolved to go to Devon, spend a night and then get back to London with the children as soon as possible. If the worst came to the worst and it didn't work out with Michael and she had to start all over again on her own, at least the last few months had shown her one thing: she must be her own life's architect.

James looked up from his desk. Helena stood very still and their eyes met. Their gaze held. He thought she looked very beautiful. In the last few months she had put on a little weight. He had not really liked this more rounded, earthy Helena at first, it was not the woman he had married, the one around whom he had hung all his suspended hopes and ambitions. But he had begun to find it touching. He wanted to cross the room, take her in his arms, tell her how much he loved her. But he dared not; those sort of emotions were dangerous. They opened you to rejection and to all the unhappiness he had watched helplessly in his parents' sad unresolved lives. Helena turned and moved away. James looked at the pile of correspondence.

'I must finish this,' he called. 'Are you going to your mother's later today?' He feigned a lack of concern. He knew Helena wanted to talk, to sort things out, to be honest with each other, tell the truth. He would do anything for a second chance, but the truth sent a shudder through him. The thought of Michael Elliot was bad enough. Could he ever forget the image in his mind of the passion he knew Helena felt for Michael? The betrayal, Michael's smugness as he came into her life and bed, trawling his way through the intimacies of James's failures as a husband and lover. It was too painful. He bitterly regretted his brief loveless encounter with Caroline, but that was different. If Helena would stay with him such a thing would never happen again.

And what would Helena do when Michael let her down, as James knew he would? How would Helena deal with that? And James knew if he lied and said he would love the child as his own she would never believe him.

How typical, he thought, that in the last few days of the campaign there had even been a change in his relationship with the children. He had been genuinely surprised at how Rollo had suddenly become interested after the initial bad start of the campaign. A corner of the curtain of mutual animosity had lifted and there was a glimmer of something he could have built on, a subtle change in the dynamics. It was Kirsty who had been instrumental in that. A few days ago there had been no evening meeting and so Helena had prepared supper for them all and taken hers and Rollo's upstairs on a tray.

'I'll lay the table and dish it up,' Kirsty had said, bringing James a whisky and soda. The whisky had mollified him and the sight of Kirsty busy in the kitchen had touched him. He had hardly noticed her growing up and becoming a young woman. She had sat opposite him over Helena's delicious lasagne and salad and they had talked. James had never talked to a young person like that before. He told her things he rarely spoke of. Of the guilt he felt at the way he had grown away from his parents. How he had not even been there when his father was dying but arrived only for the funeral for which his mother had made all the arrangements. And Kirsty had talked about her mother and father, and about Rollo and why he behaved as he did.

'He needs a man to look up to, James,' she had said. They had not mentioned Michael but James knew she knew it all. The conversation had not resolved the future but in a strange way it healed the rawness of the past and when Kirsty went to bed he put his arm about her slight shoulders and said, 'Thank you for being my friend this evening.'

Helena's voice brought him back to the present.

'James, we must talk now, the letters can wait.'

He could tell by the flat tone that it was to be some sort of goodbye. He felt sick, as if he were in a bad dream and he hoped he would wake and all would be as it was when they first met.

Helena made coffee and they took it outside and sat on the garden bench in the crisp coolness of the autumn sun. She explained her confusion and talked of the happiness they had seen on the horizon when they first married and how it had all gone terribly wrong.

There was a tenderness between them that had been absent for a long time but it evaporated instantly when James let down his guard completely and said, 'I wish to God the baby was mine.'

Helena swung towards him, spilling her coffee.

'It could have been, James,' she said vehemently. 'But you didn't want it and whatever you say you can't pretend you want this one. It would always be a wedge between us.'

James stared at her. He knew the futility of pretence and decided to dwell on the practical issues.

'I have plans,' he stammered. 'I thought you should know. I shall not accept a position in the Shadow Cabinet.'

Helena was shocked. 'Why on earth not?'

'I've been offered Agriculture. I think that says it all, don't you?' he replied wryly.

'The bastards. Typical. I think the whole thing stinks,' Helena said, resisting the temptation to offer more of her views on the world of politics which he had heard frequently before. She asked him what he was going to do.

'I've decided to accept a big job I've been offered outside Parliament. I don't fancy being on the Opposition front bench and I'm going to recoup my finances. I might sell this cottage and get a nice house down here now I'll be able to afford it.'

He looked at Helena and wondered if she would pick up the bait. But Helena said nothing.

Her mind had moved away from James and his attempts to salvage their life together. But there remained a tiny part of her which explored the idea of life with a new James, one unshackled from the constraints of ministerial life. She knew James well enough to know that if he decided to make a success of a job in the city his lifestyle would be very different from that of an impoverished Government minister. And she knew that if it were not for the baby she would be listening more carefully to what James was saying. But a separation seemed to be the only answer. She needed to talk to Michael. Involuntarily she laid a protective hand on her stomach. It was getting cold. The day was already beginning to lose its beauty. The forecast was for storms later on and she didn't want to embark on the long drive to Devon in bad weather.

'There are storms coming, James. I must get on,' she said briskly.

And then she saw that James was weeping silently. His fine head was bent, cupped in his hands, and tears fell silently between his fingers.

'I am so sorry, darling,' she said quietly.

She hurried inside and when she drove away he remained on the seat under the darkening sky.

Helena decided to drive across country and pick up the M5 somewhere near Taunton. With the weather deteriorating it would take a good four hours. She said a quiet thank you to Michael for helping her to buy a new car. The long drives had been a nightmare. But on this occasion she was almost looking forward to some time alone with her thoughts. The last three weeks had been almost more than she could cope with. She wasn't feeling well, her ankles had begun to swell and she had a continual pain somewhere at the base of her spine. She knew she should rest, but how could she?

Helena knew she was going to have to deal with the logistics of her and James's separation. She had not been able to say the exact words to James but after living together for so long without the communication of happy chatter she had been used to with Anthony and again found with Michael, they had a certain way of understanding each other. She knew he understood she had gone too far with Michael. She had to give it a try to see if life with him would turn out to be all the things her marriage to James had not been. It might only be a separation, she simply didn't know, but she did know she needed to be alone for a while to see if Michael could commit, clear all the debris so there would be no excuses. James had been ruthless with her, when she had needed his understanding and love he had not given it. She must be ruthless with him. She owed it to herself. They had not even discussed where he would go if they were no longer to share the house in London. Moving out of the cottage in Sussex would be easy enough. She had put very few things in it. James had not wanted her to. She had secretly piled the boot full of her clothes the previous day and now, as she sped along, she finally allowed herself to confront the reality of what was happening.

At first she cried for all the lost opportunities. Her feelings about James varied, one minute she felt anger, the next a profound sadness. She could not forget the image of him alone on the garden bench, and the thought that soon he would probably go upstairs for a sweater and find her cupboards empty and realise how she had planned her leaving even before she had told him saddened her further.

The light was extraordinary. Heavy violet clouds hung low and at

260

one point trapped the rays from the fading afternoon sun beneath them and the intermittent squalls seemed to match Helena's mood. Banks of very dark clouds were building to the south-west and Helena knew the storm would break soon.

At one point she drove towards a perfect rainbow, always approaching it but never getting any nearer. She thought of Michael. Common sense told her that she was not really nearer to him than when they had first met. He had not tried to stop her when she had agreed to stay with James until the election was over. She even remembered him saying what a buzz it would give him to make love to the Prime Minister's wife. She had never really thought James would become Prime Minister but obviously Michael had considered it a real possibility. Could it be – and her heart sank – that Michael had even envisaged a scenario where he could influence the Prime Minister through his wife and his past? If that were the case she would be of no use to Michael now. She banished such thoughts from her mind. No, she and Michael had gone too far to go back now. He had restored her feeling of self-worth and purpose. Her work was flourishing and all would be fine. And there was the baby to consider.

But in the back of her mind were doubts about Michael's recent chilliness. Why hadn't he tried to get in touch with her? She hadn't heard from him for over a week. He had said he was going to America on business but when she had called his office Joanna had told her he was in Geneva. Why had he lied? Helena knew there were other women in his life even though he always refused to be drawn on the matter, but she thought they had been gradually sidelined as her affair with Michael had gathered momentum. But, realistically, she knew he would not have been living like a monk for the last weeks while she had been busy with James. But when Helena thought about the baby she felt reassured. This was her hold over Michael. This was the child he had never had. Everything would be fine when they were together and had a chance to talk.

Helena did not see the branch fall. The car hit it before she could avoid it. Then everything seemed to happen in slow motion. The car spun out of control as she wrenched the wheel, trying to correct the skid, and then it turned over as it careered down the bank at the side of the road.

261

She knew she was going to die. She had not expected it to be like this. She would not be able to tell her children how much she loved them, nor say goodbye. Helena went out of her body and saw a young woman in the midst of tangled blue metal. She felt no particular concern for the woman. It all had a feeling of calm, of inevitability. There was no pain, no fear, only regret.

Chapter 38

Michael was suffering from hurt pride. If he tried to reason with himself he had to admit Helena had been doing her best to keep all her options open and not pressure him, but seeing her on the television with James had been the last straw. He wasn't used to jealousy, and he didn't know how to cope with it, it just made him cross. No, he decided, whatever came out of all this she would have to learn he was not to be tamed, to come running and pleading to her. He must remain slightly unobtainable or the romance would quickly disappear. He thought he would call in at Maryzion on his way back from the offices in Plymouth, just before Helena was due to arrive. He would provide some disinformation, muddle Cornelia a little so she would see that Helena pulled out the stops and came to heel on his terms. He knew neither of them would like his immediate plan so a few seeds of doubt would be a good way of lowering expectations to the point where a compromise would be well received. He knew Helena would come round in the end but she must never, ever take him for granted. Anyway, he had things on his mind. He didn't want a great, momentous meeting with Helena until he had got over this next business hurdle. He lifted the phone. He didn't tell Cornelia exactly when he would be there, better to be vague. He didn't want to be accused of deliberately avoiding Helena. He would be cool but charming with Cornelia, and he made a mental note to buy a lovely plant for her conservatory. He would give it to her as he left, it would take the wind out of her sails a little. She was his greatest ally.

It had been one of the most awful mornings Cornelia could remember. Michael's car sped down the drive, away from Maryzion, as if he could not wait to get on to the next phase. Cornelia stood on the steps of the great porch stunned. It seemed so strange that he and Helena might even pass each other on the motorway. But whatever she had said he wouldn't stay. He had just dropped in on his way up from Plymouth and he had an appointment to keep in London.

At first she had misunderstood the meaning of his visit. She wished Hugh had been there; perhaps things would have gone differently. But when he heard of Michael's impending arrival he announced his intentions at once.

'I have nothing to say to the man and you should not receive him here. He's dangerous. I'll be out until lunch time.'

Michael had arrived with his usual aura of charm. It was nothing he actually said which alerted Cornelia, just the strange evasive remote way he talked. He wasn't sure about his plans. Some urgent business in New York was mentioned. He might even have to be away for some months, he had said casually.

'Does Helena know?' Cornelia asked.

'No, I haven't spoken to her for some time,' he answered. 'She's been impossible to get hold of. She did a great job for James, didn't she? He was one of the few who kept his majority steady. I hope to see her later this week,' he added, getting out an Psion organiser and making some sort of note in it.

Cornelia could hardly believe he was talking about Helena, as if she were a vague acquaintance. But his manner was so contained that she had not dared to come out with the things she wanted to say. But of course Rollo did. He came bounding into the drawing room full of questions but he had been rebuffed by a Michael Cornelia had not seen before.

He stayed for only an hour at the most, and shortly after he left the storms that had been forecast began to gather momentum.

Cornelia heard Hugh's old estate car come round the corner into the stable yard by the kitchen door, crunching on fallen twigs blown down by the wind. She went to meet him and as he let himself in a swirl of leaves scattered inside the door and came to rest under the kitchen table.

'I don't see his car. I suppose he's gone?' said Hugh, taking off his old tweed jacket, shaking it out and hanging it in front of the Aga. Turning to Cornelia he saw she looked very pale. 'So what did he have to say for himself?' asked Hugh.

Cornelia burst into tears. She couldn't help herself. 'Oh Hugh, I suddenly see it all,' she sobbed. Hugh handed her a piece of kitchen roll to blow her nose.

'He has no intention of marrying Helena. He's the sort of man who does this. He sweeps women off their feet, promises them things. He probably means it at the time . . .' She paused to wipe her eyes. 'But I am sure he still loves Helena. How could he not want to marry her? I don't understand. What am I going to tell her when she gets here, Hugh, and anyway, why did he come here when he knew she wouldn't be here? I don't understand any of it.'

'Cornelia darling, sit down. Let me explain something to you about men like Michael,' said Hugh gently.

Cornelia sat down at the kitchen table and Hugh pulled out a chair next to her.

'Michael Elliot is what he is, Cornelia. I've done some research on him as a matter of fact and, apart from his private life, his business affairs are, to say the least, shady. I have some information which I've been saving until the right moment. I think when you know the man may well be heading for quite a lot of trouble you may be glad he is not asking Helena to leave her husband and spend the rest of her life with him. Frankly she would be better off on her own.'

'On her own, Hugh? Don't be stupid. What about the child? Michael doesn't have any children . . . it must be so important to him.'

'That's just it, Cornelia,' Hugh paused. Should he tell Cornelia now, or later, as he had planned? He decided it should not wait. 'He has two children. One of them living in Switzerland – a boy, very clever, a brilliant violinist. He was adopted by Michael's sister when he was a baby. The mother was a married woman with whom Michael had had a long relationship and she didn't want the baby. But that's not all. He has a daughter in America, who is married with a child of her own. He lied to Helena. He has been married twice and he isn't even divorced from his second wife.'

Cornelia went ashen. After a few moments she went upstairs to recover herself while Hugh called the children and got the shepherd's pie out of the oven.

Just as they were finishing the telephone rang. Harriet answered it. 'It's for you, Granny,' she called from the hall.

The voice was calm and professional. 'Lady Douglas? This is

Sister Flemming from the Emergency Department at the Royal Devon and Exeter Hospital. Your daughter, Helena, has been brought in here. Now don't be alarmed, she's going to be all right. Her car went off the road. She was found very quickly.'

'Oh my God!' said Cornelia, alerting Hugh who now stood anxiously beside her. He saw her face going sheet white. 'Has she lost the baby?'

'Everything is fine at the moment but I do think you should come. We've been in touch with Mr Askew and I understand he is on his way here.'

At first it was too much for Cornelia to take in. There was no pretending with the children, they all wanted to get to the hospital as soon as possible. But Hugh waded in with his calm voice of authority. It was decided that Cornelia should go at once and take Kirsty with her and Hugh would stay at Maryzion with Harriet and Rollo.

'I'll get Finchie to prepare the spare room for James,' said Hugh.

Cornelia and Kirsty bundled into Hugh's car and set off for the hospital as fast as she safely could.

White, that is all Helena could see, and the light was very bright. She could hear a man's voice. It was soothing and gentle and the voice kept telling her it would all be all right. She couldn't make out who it was. Sometimes she thought it was her father, or Anthony and then it was James. It was never Michael's voice – why wasn't he there? Then she had a feeling something was wrong but she couldn't remember what. He had gone a long way away somewhere at the end of a long tunnel but she could still see him.

She didn't feel unhappy, just puzzled. In and out of the light she floated and then there was someone else, a child. It was Kirsty, her face was opposite the man's and they were clasping hands. And then the pain started. She knew that pain, she had had it before. More people came into the room. She wanted to get away from the pain. The child was gone now and there was just the man, James.

She held on to him. She felt his mouth on her forehead. 'Hold on,' he said. 'Hold on, darling. I'm here!' And then sleep, blessed sleep.

'I'm so very sorry we couldn't save the baby, but the main thing is she will be fine. She has recovered consciousness. Her husband has been wonderful. They are obviously very close . . . It's amazing how at times like this support does more than all the doctoring in the world.' The young doctor spoke gently to Cornelia. She had been outside in the corridor waiting. He hated people losing babies, but as he had said to the husband, Helena was lucky to be alive, let alone so slightly injured. 'It was the air bag which saved her, plus the build of the car.'

'When can she come home?' Cornelia asked.

'In a couple of days.' He put an encouraging hand on her arm. 'They'll have another baby, I'm sure. She's very strong and there is no lasting damage. She is one very lucky lady.' He walked off down the corridor, his white coat flapping behind him.

As she watched the door James came out. He did not see her at first, and he looked ashen. He was in his shirtsleeves and had removed his tie. His hair was ruffled in a way Cornelia had never seen and it made him look years younger. When he saw her his expression did not harden as it usually did. He slumped on the bench beside Cornelia and, leaning his elbows on his knees, he looked at the floor. 'I didn't want the poor little thing to die. She wanted it so much, I see that now.'

Cornelia put her hand gently on his shoulder. He did not pull away but looked up at her. 'I'll stay until she can come out and then I'll take us all home. I'll have to get those children back to school.'

'They need me, you know. We are a family,' he stammered. 'I see that now . . .' He looked distraught. 'She . . . they . . . It's what matters . . . I . . .' He looked up at Cornelia as at an old friend, something he had never done before.

'Do you think I can go in?' Cornelia asked. 'I won't stay long. Will you be OK?'

James took out a handkerchief and wiped his brow. He looked completely drained.

'Yes, I'll be fine. I'm spending the night here. I'm not going to leave her.' He stopped. He stood up, running his hands through his hair. 'You do know that, don't you?' he asked.

'Yes, I do,' said Cornelia quietly.

Chapter 39

'Yes, if you're passing,' Michael said ambivalently.

'Fine. I'll pop in on my way back down to Gloucestershire. I don't have to hurry,' Caroline said pointedly. 'I'm not expected back until late. There's a banking dinner, wives aren't expected and I have a whole evening free, which is rare for me these days.'

Michael knew exactly what Caroline had in mind.

Caroline arrived at ten past six. She wore a dark Armani suit with a scooped cutaway jacket which revealed a tight white ribbed jersey top – her cleavage much in evidence. When she sat down on the deep brocade sofa in the drawing room twirling her drink between her long fingernailed hands and crossed her legs provocatively, Michael couldn't help noticing she was wearing white satin suspenders. Her thighs were tanned and smooth at the tops of the stockings and not much was left to the imagination. He sat opposite her, not unreceptive to her body language.

'So, isn't it amazing about James Askew?' she said, examining her drink as she held it to the evening light from the window, bright and sharp from the reflection of the river now at high tide.

'I don't follow you,' Michael said warily.

'Well, talk about falling on your feet. Surely your friend Helena has told you?' she said, watching for his reaction.

'Helena hasn't told me everything,' he said, immediately regretting that he had unwittingly informed Caroline that his relationship with Helena was not going as smoothly as he had hoped.

'Well, I'm surprised she hasn't told you, but then maybe James hasn't told her . . .' Caroline paused and went on. 'Surely he would have told her, especially as they're so blissfully happy now. I'm told it's a joy to see. He's so thrilled about the baby. Apparently they'd almost given up hope.' Caroline was enjoying twisting the knife. She hadn't finished yet.

'James has landed an enormous job at Grunfeld's, a directorship, no less, with a huge salary, and what's so marvellous is that Grunfeld's is putting up another three hundred thou for our project at Markham Court.'

It took a moment or two for Michael to take the information in. He watched Caroline carefully and saw her look of pleasure. She had the face of someone who knows they have some good cards still to play.

'Oh, so within two days of the Government losing the election James has already feathered his nest,' he said.

'Yes he has. Of course Bertie and I have been in his confidence all along the way. It's a question of who you know as usual,' she laughed.

'I hear what you say,' Michael replied, 'but I'm surprised Mark Raymond didn't stop things in their tracks. His wife's family own the bank. He must be furious; he loathes James.'

'Oh, but that's just it. Mrs Raymond's family are selling out. There's about to be a huge takeover bid and James is very much part of it. We're thrilled. Bertie will at last get some recognition for all the years he's worked there.'

'As you seem to know everything, where does James stand in the Shadow Cabinet then?'

'Oh, hasn't Helena told you anything?' Caroline asked, thoroughly enjoying herself.

'Carry on,' said Michael in a resigned voice.

'He's out of the Shadow Cabinet.'

'No . . .' Michael was disbelieving.

'Good heavens, Michael, where've you been for the last few days?'

'But what about Mark Raymond, now he's lost his seat? Will he look for another one? I suppose you know that as well?'

'He's biding his time until he goes to the Lords. Obviously he will go up as part of the ex-Prime Minister's "thank you honours". I gather Mrs Raymond's thrilled to bits.'

Michael decided he might as well find out everything while he was at it.

'And when is the Party going to announce the leadership challenge?'

'Tomorrow I gather.'

Michael fell silent. So James was of little use to him now. Or, he brightened, he might be, now that he was at Grunfeld's.

Caroline had outflanked him, but as he looked at her he could see she still wanted him. The way she sat now, her thighs completely exposed, he would have no difficulty in taking her, if he wanted to, upstairs or even perhaps here on the floor with little or no ceremony.

Suddenly he felt angry – and aroused. He rose from the armchair, pulled her up from the sofa and pressed his mouth on to hers. Her yielding response was as never before. He pulled at her Armani suit, throwing the jacket on the floor. His hands found the zipper of her skirt, she wriggled, and it fell down her legs. She stood in her suspenders and top. He tugged off the top and then roughly fumbled with the bra, yanking it off. Her panties ripped as he pulled them down. He pushed her to the floor, unzipping his trousers as he did so. She lay open and inviting, her body responding to his violent, invasive passion. As they lay on the floor he reached an arm up to pull some cushions off the sofa. He pulled himself out of his trousers; she unbuttoned his shirt.

Caroline moaned as her body demanded him. The rough, terrifying strength of his lust excited her; she was out of control. He pulled a cushion under her thighs and raised her hips; his mouth sought the soft hair between the tops of the stockings. She could see his dark hair; as she looked down some of it fell on to the white satin of her suspender belt.

Caroline moaned and cried out for him. She pulled frantically at his head; she wanted him inside her. Slowly, tantalisingly, he raised himself, his face was level with her own. She could smell the musky sweetness of her own sex as his mouth came to hers. It tasted salty; he breathed into her lips as he spoke. 'You are a whore, a beautiful whore. You are wet with a whore's wetness . . . open yourself, you can't get away . . . I am going to fuck you until you beg for me to stop, you beautiful whore.'

She felt faint as if she were drugged. Her desire was consuming, she didn't know such pleasure existed. In a brief flash she began to understand all the things she had never known about men and women. He was inside her. She moaned she was his, his forever. She wanted him to do what he liked with her. She would never find this again. Now, at last, she understood and then her head fell back and she let out the cry of a trapped animal. She called to him from somewhere in her deepest being that she loved him, that he was her

271

master, she was his slave . . . and then he was up and getting dressed.

He didn't look at her. She lay there dreamily, her body still, soft and inviting, her eyes misty. He looked down at her, cold and dispassionate. He was doing up his clothes.

'Get dressed,' he said. 'That was just one for the road.'

When she had gone Michael sat down wearily on the sofa. He was ashamed of himself. He now regretted being so tough on Caroline, but she had provoked him. It was true the remarks about James and Bertie had got to him. The idea of them all cosily working together, riled him even though he took it all with a pinch of salt. James had obviously landed a good job at Grunfeld's, and to have Caroline prattling on about Helena playing mummies and daddies with James was more than he could take.

Michael was tired. The combination of post-coital depression plus jetlag from his various trips abroad rendered him uncharacteristically low. He could still smell Caroline's perfume and the room was in disorder, cushions all over the floor and dirty glasses on the coffee table. Normally he would have been clearing up at once, he had an obsession with order, but he needed to think for a moment or two.

Caroline had not, of course, known she was the third woman he had dispatched from his life in the last week. The trips to Geneva and New York had been gentler encounters. Michael liked to be generous. In neither case did the woman believe she would not see Michael again, but with Caroline, it was different. She had become an enemy and the fact that James now worked with Bertie almost made her an enemy within.

Michael had been so absorbed in sorting out his life, clearing the decks as it were, that he had forgotten to attend to the most important item of all, Helena. But then he had never doubted his women, for once they were on the team he knew they would be waiting for him. But he had a nagging worry. Helena had not really been unduly energetic in her attempts to get hold of him. Perhaps it had been her on the phone earlier. Caroline had answered it while he was getting the drinks. She said it was a woman who would ring back later and did not leave a message. 'My God,' he said out loud. What if it had been Helena? She would have recognised Caroline's voice, but then so would Caroline have known it was Helena. She would have made some remark, reacted in some way. He was going to ring Helena now, he had decided. It had been difficult for him, he had lived alone for so long, the mechanics had been the problem and then he had come up with the solution. He would set Helena up in a house in Chelsea, just a few minutes away, with a studio and plenty of room for staff. She could be his hostess 'en title' in the evenings. It would be a permanent arrangement, they would be an item. After the first shock of the news about the baby he had begun to like the idea. In fact it was the thought of the child which clinched it. He suddenly felt better. He would bath and relax and then ring Helena.

His reverie was interrupted by the telephone.

It was Cornelia. She told him about the baby. She did not spare him the details and when she had finished she more or less told him she knew he had been entertaining a mistress when she rang earlier.

Before she rang off, her last words were, 'Oh, by the way, I thought you might be interested to know it was a boy.'

Michael got up slowly from the sofa. He poured himself a whisky and then another. He was not accustomed to grief and he was angry. Why hadn't he been the first to know, why hadn't Helena rung him? Then he felt something akin to guilt.

The phone rang again. It was Gunter, he was on his way to London. Michael agreed a breakfast meeting at seven. 'Of course, it's difficult, but, yes, it can wait,' Michael replied to Gunter's, 'I'm sorry, Michael. I know you said you had urgent family business for the next two days.'

Michael tidied up the room and went swiftly to bed. He took half a sleeping pill. Tomorrow's business was crucial. If he didn't keep his head he could lose millions. Nothing, absolutely nothing, must blunt his wits for the next twenty-four hours.

Chapter 40

Helena picked up the mobile phone and dialled Michael's number.

Joanna answered. 'Yes, Mrs Askew, he is in London. He told me to tell you he would be in touch later today.'

Helena sank back on the pillows of her bed in Richmond Terrace. The room was full of flowers . . . everyone seemed to have heard about the loss of her baby. She could not understand how news travelled so quickly. For the moment she was alone, James had left for his first day at Grunfeld's; a large chauffeured car had picked him up at eight. He had dropped the children at school on the way.

The doctor had told her she must rest, but she couldn't bear to think of all the unattended things which called. She was just about to get up and run herself a bath when the phone rang. It was her friend Beth.

'Yes, I'm fine. I'm lucky to be alive. When something like that happens you look at your life quite differently,' she replied to Beth's concerned enquiries. She didn't have many secrets from her best friend. Beth deliberately didn't ask about Michael. She knew if Helena wanted to talk about him she would. She was more interested in what James thought of it all.

Helena told her how wonderful James had been. She didn't know he could be so caring. She told her how there had been a bit of a tiff between her mother and James at Maryzion, she had heard about it from Kirsty. Apparently Rollo had been very difficult and James had taken him in hand. Cornelia had interfered and James had, in Kirsty's words, 'seen Granny off.'

'Oh dear, your poor mother! A bit late in the day for James to come on the scene as the hands-on stepdad, isn't it?' Beth remarked.

'He genuinely seems to have thought about my children and how difficult it's been for them, not knowing where to look for their male support. I can't explain it, but losing the baby was so awful I don't think James had ever been confronted with real life like that before. He stayed with me throughout the whole thing.'

'Well, life has a funny way of not going the way you think it will,' said Beth. 'They do say people don't change but I think events change people.'

'He's being very tactful. He has more or less said he won't hurry me. He even offered to stay at his club. I know he wants us to start again.'

As Helena put the receiver down she heard footsteps on the stairs. 'It's me,' came James's voice. He put his head round the door. 'Oh, I'm glad you're still in bed. I thought I would pop in and see how you are. You were sleeping when I left. I took the children to school. They loved the ride in the chauffeured car.'

'I thought you were starting at Grunfeld's today,' said Helena.

'I have been in, but I have a meeting at the House. I am Chairman of the All Party Finance Committee. It wasn't far out of my way and there was something I wanted to drop in here on my way. Would you like a cup of coffee?' James asked.

Helena felt guilty. She never stayed in bed late in the mornings. Years of school runs and early morning wakings with her children had established a pattern. She made as if to get out of bed, pushing Clovis off the quilted cover onto the floor. The dog stood staring crossly at the bed. He snorted his disapproval and gave a loud yap, as if to say, I'm coming straight back up again.

'Please stay there, Helena, I would like to bring it up. The house is quiet, I thought we could talk for a minute, make some plans,' said James hesitantly, nervously fingering his collar as he spoke. He could see Helena was taken unaware by his sudden, unexpected return to the house. He hoped she didn't know he had overheard the last part of her telephone conversation as he came up the stairs. He was not used to hearing his domestic conduct praised in this way and this gave him some encouragement.

'Come on, Clovis, dinner,' he called quickly, taking advantage of the quizzical look on Helena's face. He made for the door, and to Helena's surprise Clovis followed, wagging his tail.

As James prepared a tray under the watchful eye of Rosaria, he looked around the kitchen. It was a happy room, warm and sunny, with many reminders of the busy life Helena led with her family.

While he waited for the kettle to boil he absentmindedly turned the pages of the kitchen diary which lay on a shelf beside the kettle. The previous evening he had looked at it for the first time. He had never bothered to open it before. Helena's perfectly formed italic writing covered the pages. Each hour of the day was crammed with detailed plans. At regular intervals there was a 'keep free for painting' area blanked off with a red pen, and there were copious domestic reminders – make marmalade, wash curtains, plant bulbs – and each evening she had written menus and usually added 'James out' in inverted commas.

He had felt a pang of guilt when he saw how often she had been alone, in fact most evenings . . . and then he noticed, in about May, the dinner menus stopped and the evenings remained a blank except for the words, 'Maria babysit'. This, more than anything, explained just how he had left the door wide open for Michael Elliot to sweep Helena off her feet.

Several things had struck him when he had assimilated this information. He hadn't realised how full her days were and how fragmented she was. She had to be very organised, yet she had always made her life seem so effortless. He had occasionally thought her day was full of idle visits to the hairdressers and shopping. He had, of course, taken her for granted. Last night he had sat in the kitchen long after Helena was asleep and assembled the mosaic of her life in his mind, and he began to admire her as he had not done before. He remembered the way she had clung to him when she had started to lose the baby, and how brave she had been. It was the first time in his life he had been confronted with the reality of the female thing he had found so repugnant. He had seen a beauty in the concept of birth, it had changed him. He had grieved at the loss of the child and then he had confronted his own sense of loss, for he knew his future with Helena hung in the balance.

He knew she would be getting in touch with Michael. God knows, he thought, what the man had said to her, but whatever it was James would put up a fight and for one very good reason.

James had fallen in love with his wife. He couldn't say when he had begun to realise, perhaps it was when he saw how determined she was to make her life work with or without a man, and this new strength in her had sharpened his own plans for his future. This, combined with his own change of direction, had opened up the dream of a happy future for them both. He no longer craved power in politics. He would concentrate on a career in business, take some of the financial burden from Helena, take her away. He had even talked to Hugh about buying a farm in Tuscany, somewhere near where Hugh and Cornelia were going. There, Helena could paint, the children would have a swimming pool . . . he could have a vineyard, something he had always dreamed of.

He had sat in the kitchen until he had fallen asleep in Helena's chair. When he awoke with a start, at about three o'clock, it occurred to him that he had never allowed himself to dream before. And as he scrolled the past few years he felt his life in politics had been a whisper on the lips of ambition, but all the time it was Helena who mattered. She was his rock . . . this was his home, this was his family. He would not let her go. He would make her happy, as Michael Elliot never would.

The kettle sang into life and brought him back to the present with a feeling of dread. Helena had moved on. She had overtaken him, she probably didn't care about him any more.

'Mr James.' It was Rosaria's voice. 'I done all your shirts. Mrs Helena, she usually do them but she no well. She say they must be special for you. She tidy all your things yesterday and she sew on many buttons. She wonderful wife. You lucky man.'

'Yes I am,' replied James.

He took the tray up to Helena. They didn't say much, just chatted with a friendly, unembarrassed ease. As he left he stroked her cheek. 'I've written you a note. It's in the studio,' he said, 'and if you like I'll bring dinner home tonight for all of us.'

She heard him go downstairs and the door shutting. The phone rang, it was her mother.

They talked about how Helena was, and then Cornelia asked her if she had heard from Michael.

'No,' replied Helena, her voice becoming shaky at the mention of his name. 'I have been trying to get hold of him. He'll be devastated about the baby.'

Cornelia could tell her daughter was about to get very upset. She agonised over whether or not she should tell her the truth. Hugh had told her she must stay out of it and his words still rang in her ears.

'Helena, he knows.' Cornelia decided to push ahead. 'I told him the day after it happened. I finally got hold of him after supper . . .' Her voice trailed off.

'Where was he?'

'At home.'

'What is it, Mummy?'

'Well, Joanna answered the phone. She sounded different.'

Helena's entire body stiffened. She felt no hurt, just anger, cold anger. The enormity of what her mother had told her solved everything. Suddenly her way ahead was clear. With the loss of the baby her ties with Michael were broken.

She said goodbye to her mother, bathed, dressed in jeans and a sweater and went down to her studio. The day was warm and sunlight filled the room. The house was beautifully clean, all in perfect order – Rosaria had been marvellous. It was so good to be home. There was a big bunch of red roses and a card on the table where she kept her paints. She looked at the room and a surge of unexpected pleasure engulfed her.

As she read James's card the phone rang again. It was Michael. His voice was as she remembered – rich, full of concern.

'Darling,' he said. 'I've just received your message. Can I ring you later and we can talk? I have people outside the door, a meeting with Gunter Strauss. There's trouble at the docks.'

While he spoke Helena had been reading James's card. 'Helena, are you there?' she heard Michael say.

'Yes, I'm here. I was just reading something,' said Helena.

'Well, you're obviously busy. I'll call you later.' Michael's voice had changed, a note of irritation creeping in.

Helena sat down slowly in the cane chair by her easel, the scent of the roses surrounding her. She looked at the card again and smiled.

'Don't bother,' she said and replaced the receiver.